Good w...

Robert A...

The Prince
and
the Poet

Robert Aitken

Aitken

Published by

MELROSE
BOOKS

An Imprint of Melrose Press Limited
St Thomas Place, Ely
Cambridgeshire
CB7 4GG, UK
www.melrosebooks.com

FIRST EDITION

Copyright © Robert Aitken 2011

The Author asserts his moral right to
be identified as the author of this work

Cover designed by Valerie Burton

ISBN 978 1 907732 36 2

Printed and bound in Great Britain by:
CPI Group (UK) Ltd, Croydon, CR0 4YY

FSC
www.fsc.org
MIX
Paper from
responsible sources
FSC® C013604

Chapter One

JOHN, TALL, LEAN, straight-backed with the loose gawkiness of a ten-year-old, stepped out from the dark cell onto the ramparts of Lancaster Castle. He stretched his arms high above his head, eased his tension and breathed deeply of the cool morning air. It was dawn. The pale pearly light was spreading out along the familiar estuary of the Lune. A cormorant caught his eye as it stood on a rock in the river drying its wings: black against the silver river. Far across the bay he could make out the grey smudged outlines of the Lakeland Hills and the rounded shapes of the Howgills.

He sighed deeply, remembering the agonies and joys of expeditions with Sir Ranulf into those very hills. The forced marches up from Kentmere, along the High Street among the ghosts of Roman centurions and sailing back down Ullswater. Making camp, grubbing for dry wood for the fire on which to cook the rabbit, birds or fish that had been snared en route. Or the fiercer routes enduring the biting winds of winter across Haystacks up to Red Pike and the awesome Striding Edge. And the last challenge set by Sir Ranulf in October, when he divided the group of six squires into three pairs, each of which were to make their own track across from Wastwater to Haweswater taking in Helvellyn. John and his companion, Richard Chandos, had arrived first having taken five and a half days over this, suffering a severe rainstorm on the second night but rejoicing in the bright warm sunlight as they descended down the High Street along Rough Crag to Haweswater.

Sir Ranulf had always stressed to them how important it was for a soldier to be able to rely on his own wits: to be able to assess a terrain and weigh up the possibilities, difficulties and advantages of routes across it. But also to be able to live off the land by finding water, sustenance and shelter – and this for weeks if not months at a time. He was a hard taskmaster who had forced John and his companions to practise and hone those skills in the Cumbrian hills. No soft options were allowed, particularly for this young prince or the sons of nobles who accompanied him.

John's reverie turned towards the room he had just left: the stone walls and flagged floor; rush wall torches with their aura of flickering yellow light; and the trestle cot on which Sir Ranulf lay. He had been brought here from the Crook O' Lune by boat with a broken leg, but then high fever and delirium had set in. Father Gervase, the monk who was skilled with healing herbs and served as physician at the castle, had been summoned. He had prepared draughts of hyssop, belladonna and lime blossom to combat the fever and applied poultices of camomile, cypress and elderflower to his chest and aconite and comfrey to the leg.

John had quickly joined him and had kept vigil throughout the last two days and nights. He had frequently raised up the old knight and held a beaker of one of the herbal draughts to his swollen, cracked lips. He had applied a cooling cloth to his hot brow and had sat on a leather stool beside the cot listening to his wracked breathing. At other times he had held Ranulf's hand and tried to follow his fevered mumbling.

Then towards dawn, the fever seemed to withdraw. Ranulf lay peacefully on his bolster and spoke softly to John.

"You've served your apprenticeship well, my Lord. Your father the King will be proud of you." John leaned forward to catch the quiet words, knowing that the valiant and loyal knight, who had been charged with his training, was near his end. "John, always remember the bond of chivalry into which you are born: service above self and loyalty above all to your lord. Never betray your oath. You are ready now to take your place at the high table… God walk with you, my Lord…"

At that, Sir Ranulf had suddenly sat fully upright with a rapturous face and fiercely shining eyes. He reached out with both arms as if to welcome the escort of angels which appeared before him, providing a bridge for his spirit to go forth.

John did not know how long he had stayed on his knees beside the cot after the knight's last breath. He had gently drawn down the lids over the staring eyes and had stayed, head bowed, holding the gnarled hand and gazing intently at the taut weathered face, etching on his mind the memory of this man who had been his mentor and father figure for so long. The man who taught him not only physical prowess in the field with lance and sword but also the courtesies and manners of courtly behaviour, including the duty owed to servants and tenants. Fealty was a two-way process: loyalty, service and obedience from below had to be matched with compassion, justice and protection from above.

John shook himself and came back to the scene beneath him with the river running its swift course towards the bay. He brushed the tears from his cheeks and sniffed back the mucus from his throat. At this a soft sound and flash of white along the terrace caught his attention. It was gone in an instant but his glimpse was enough to know from her golden tresses that it was Duke Henry's daughter, Blanche. How long had she been watching, he wondered? Had she seen his tears? Would she tell the tale for others to scoff at? Well, no matter. He was not ashamed of his emotion and love for his father's loyal retainer.

But her presence reminded him that the Lancaster household would be awakening to the day and, suddenly, he realised how hungry he was. When he found his way to the buffetry, which was alongside the great hall, he was met by Duke Henry himself, who greeted him with arms outstretched and a vigorous hug.

"Come, young sir, sit with me. You must be starved and in need of vittles. Sir Ranulf was a fine soldier and honourable knight who has our enduring love. He was honoured in turn by your vigil. Well done, John!"

John felt bolstered from his misery by these words. He had felt nervous and lost as he came down the ramparts, suddenly aware that he could no longer turn to Sir Ranulf for guidance and direction. The Duke's warmth was reassuring and, as if sensing John's uncertainty, he added: "We must return you to Court and take soundings of the King's wishes. No doubt he will now give you some commission or opportunity to prove yourself further on one of the royal expeditions. I hear that the Castilians are harrying the coasts in the south sporadically, and I expect my Lord will want to put down this impertinence opportunely. Perhaps this will provide your chance."

With a modest: "Yes, my Lord. I hope so and thank you," John fell to a full breakfast of oats, honey and cream with eggs and pork washed down with a flagon of ale. The needs of his stomach had put aside all thoughts of his future career. But he was soon to remember the Duke's words, although even then, he could not foresee the crucial role his uncle would play in his life in the future.

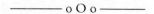

Six months later, John was standing next to his oldest brother, Prince Edward, on the foredeck of his father's flagship, the *Salle du Roi*. King Edward had assembled a fleet of three dozen ships from London and the south coast ports. They were anchored off the Sussex coast between Winchelsea and Rye, awaiting news of an armada of Castilian ships. Since his victorious battle of Sluys, King Edward had nothing to fear from the French but the wine fleets coming from Bordeaux, and the wool fleets passing between England and Flanders had suffered severely during the summer at the hands of the Castilians. The King had decided that it was time to act to protect his commerce and complete the work done at Sluys.

It was Sunday, the 10th August 1350. The ships were riding at anchor in a light swell. The King was seated on the foredeck surrounded by his senior captains. They stood around him talking quietly and listening to minstrels playing an air brought back from Germany by Sir John Chandos. John hummed with the music and was pleased to see the familiar figure of the Duke of Lancaster among the group of captains, with others he knew from Court and tales of their chivalrous feats: Hereford, Arundel, Holland, Beauchamp.

Suddenly a shout broke into the music from the lookout at the masthead: "Sail ahoy!" The whole Spanish fleet then began to appear on the horizon to the south-east. Forty sail were bearing down under a fresh northeaster on the English ships. The afternoon sun was striking on their canvas, lighting up the black and yellow Castilian arms. King Edward called for wine, which was quickly dispensed in goblets among the company by pageboys in the King's livery. Edward, the Black Prince, called a toast to his father: "King Edward and England!" which was shouted back by the captains before they drained their goblets in a single upturned flourish. These were quickly refilled for the King's pledge to his knights: "To clear the English sea for Englishmen to sail freely!" "Amen" shouted the chorus of captains as they drank to the toast.

With an: "Away to your ships. Through God's good grace we will prevail!" the King rose and moved aft with a sign to the ship's captain to begin preparations for weighing anchor.

The Black Prince strode quickly to the starboard where his pinnace was waiting, John keeping close behind him. Together they clambered over the side into the small boat and were soon rowed across to their ship where the crew eagerly handed them aboard. "Prepare to make sail," called the Prince and made his way to where his squire was ready with his armour. Quickly the Prince vested in his battle gear: a light, long-sleeved tunic of mail which reached to his knees, over which was strapped a padded metal breastplate, and then he pulled on heavy leather knee boots and gauntlets. His sword and dagger hung from the girdle round his waist. This done the squire stood by, holding in readiness the Prince's conical helmet and shield. Around him his retinue of knights were similarly attired, pacing restlessly to and fro like big cats with the whiff of a prey in their nostrils.

John, too, had been helped into his lightweight version of the man-at-arms gear. It felt familiar and comfortable and took him back to the many duels and tourneys with squires and knights which he had had at Court over the last six months. John had enjoyed these 'games' and was secretly rather proud of himself. He had fought well with sword, quick to parry and nimble with his feet to find openings with his long reach. It had taken him a while to master the use of the shield on his left arm but this had now become an integral part of his fighting.

But this was no tourney or game. This was for real, against real fighting men. John's stomach churned in tight knots. Would a Spaniard's skill and experience overwhelm him? How could his nimble footwork be of an advantage in the close quarters of a ship's deck?

Was he strong enough to parry the blows, let alone make a telling thrust at his foe? He grasped the hilt of his sword and found his grip slippery with sweat.

John's tension eased as he was caught up in the frenzied shouting and activity that broke out on deck. The large square sail was quickly hauled up and secured. The ship moved smoothly out to sea, gaining way as the wind filled the canvas. The helmsman, steering with his oar on the starboard side, shouted back the captain's orders as they settled to a course in the wake of the King's ship. Meanwhile, men hurried to their posts as the Black Prince despatched six archers to each of the castles fore and aft, deployed his knights around him amidships and men-at-arms on the port and starboard sides. John, standing at the foot of the mast, was soon encircled by broad meshed backs and silvered helmets.

As the fleet moved out to sea, it was clear that King Edward's tactic was to run along the coast into the wind so that he could then turn and bear down on the Castilians with the wind behind him. Seeing this, the Spanish ships also turned into the wind, seeking to trap the English on the shore. Quickly, Edward tacked and ran rapidly down on the other fleet. As they closed, there was a flurry of arrows from the English archers and agonised cries as some found their targets. Then the two fleets were at one another's throats in a melee of hacking and thrusting alongside an opposing ship. Grappling hooks and ropes flew; spears carved the air and were parried; swords flashed; guttural roars, shouts and screams mingled with the clashing and scraping of metal on metal.

But the Prince's ship was in trouble. She had been rammed on the port side as the fleets closed. Her clinker planks had been pierced and she began to list badly. This gave the advantage of a higher deck to the Spanish ship which had drawn alongside and the English knights were in danger of being forced back and their ship boarded.

John, still by the mast, was throbbing with energy, excited by the fury and din around him. He had deftly parried three spears with his shield. Dancing on his toes and with drawn sword, he was ready to step into the breach should one of the knights in front of him fall. Then he heard a furious cry from beyond the Spanish ship of, "Lancaster forward ahoy!" and could see the Duke's ship grappling their opponent and boarding from the other side. Caught on both sides, the Spaniards soon realised they were outnumbered and laid down their arms.

Like the sun coming out after a storm, quiet and peace descended. John could not calm down so readily. He felt flushed and paced restlessly with pent-up nervous energy. His brother flashed him a broad smile and with a slap on his shoulder and, "Good hunting, eh, John?" scrambled with his knights across to Duke Henry's boat. It was soon clear that the Spanish fleet had been defeated. Eighteen of their warships had been captured and would pay handsomely in ransom money. Three English ships had been boarded and, after fierce hand-to-hand fighting, had been rescued but with eight lying dead. Now the rest of the Spanish fleet could be seen making off south-westwards into the waning sun.

On Duke Henry's ship the babble and chatter among the knights, reliving their part in the battle, washed around John as he took off his fighting gear. His friend Richard Chandos, who had been with the Duke, joined him and they exchanged their own tales.

Later that evening at Winchester, refreshed after having bathed and dressed in clean hose with his favourite purple and red sashed tabard, John joined in the celebrations at Court. His father, the King, was in high good humour. Surrounded by lords and those of their Spanish counterparts who had been captured, he drank freely and smacked his lips as he munched at sweetmeats presented on silver salvers by royal pages. His mother, Queen Philippa, stood in a similar knot talking quietly with her ladies and gracefully nodding her head to the occasional bow from a passing knight.

John went to greet her, going down on one knee and bowing his head low in front of her. Her eyes lit up and she reached out to him with both hands outstretched. "John, my dear! Your first battle – and at sea at that! Tell me how it was."

"Oh, it was such a sight, my Lady! I was on Edward's ship and we all got tangled up with the Spaniards and they tried to fight their way onto our ship and the Duke of Lancaster got them from the other side. I had my sword ready in my hand but didn't use it before they stopped the fighting…" he gushed out excitedly. Philippa smiled warmly at his flushed face and rushed account. "Well, you were in the thick of it, John. You should be proud of that. Your father is pleased with you, and I am glad you are back here safe and sound. You must remember to be grateful to the Lord and remark that in your prayers."

The King moved to sit at the head of the festive table which was laid out with platters and goblets, wine and ale, crusty breads, some sweetmeats and grapes with dishes of scented water for use as finger bowls. Two heralds called the company to order with a brief fanfare. The Bishop of Winchester blessed the assembled company, gave thanks for the safe deliverance and for the food which was about to be provided. Hard on the 'Amens', royal pages and squires converged on the tables bearing high hot dishes piled with chicken, roasts of pork and beef, venison, pheasants and other game birds.

John joined the squires to stand behind the King and to carve meats for him and fill his platter with other fare as directed. This was a duty that was expected of him in his present station as a squire to the King, the correct manners of which he had learned in his last six months at Court. He carved swiftly and surely, using his favourite knife which he had whetted specially. He was aware of the sea of watching eyes around the table and was determined to perform faultlessly, not only for his own esteem but also in honour of his father. As he stepped back, his father turned in an aside to him: "John, you have done well this day. I see and hear that your work at Court with your fellows also goes well. I shall want you with me to campaign again when the occasion arises – so keep your sword and senses sharp!"

———— o O o ————

At the shout from the King's retinue ahead, John raised himself up and stood in his stirrups to catch his first sight of the skyline of Newcastle. He could just make out the silhouette of the castle rising above the smoke-laden haze, with the grey river below and the jumble of brown tenements along the quays. It was a pale December afternoon with the clear sky now streaked with a pale orange, promising a hard night's frost. John could feel the city shrinking into itself at this cold prospect. He imagined the hearths that were being stoked, the steaming broth pots hanging over the flames and the carcasses slowly turning on the spits.

For like his colleagues, John was hungry and saddle sore. They had left Hatfield, near York, soon after dawn that morning and had ridden through the day with only two short stops to change horses. The King had set a fair pace for he was anxious to review the army that he had ordered to muster there and the preparations that were being made for his Scottish campaign. A marauding band of Scots had taken Berwick on the 6th November, and the King was bent not simply on regaining the town but on striking hard right into Edinburgh to cow, with his sword and sacking, such impudence.

Edward's knights, including John as the newly created Earl of Richmond with his own retinue, were bristling for a fight. They had been deprived of combat on the expedition which the King had led into Picardy in October, because the French had retreated behind walled defensives which demanded siege warfare rather than open battle. Apart from ravaging the surrounding countryside, there was no gain for the English in this and the King had withdrawn to Calais, only to hear of the loss of Berwick. In some measure, the frustration in France gave an eager relish to meeting the Scots.

That evening, John relaxed in the warm company gathered at the castle. The fine high-beamed hall, with red-hot log fires roaring at each end, was brightly lit by wall braziers and candles in wrought-iron circular crowns suspended over the long rows of oak trestles which were set sumptuously for the banquet to celebrate the King's safe arrival. The King stood easing the saddle stiffness from his back in the heat of one of the blazing hearths. He was surrounded by a knot of his senior knights and the northern Lords Percy and Neville, also lately arrived in Newcastle with their retinues to serve the King's campaign. Mulled wine – hot, red and spicy – added an inner glow and sparkle to the gathering. Clustered round the other hearth, a group of junior knights, including John, were jostling and joking noisily like a litter of yearling puppies.

The hall was decked with colourful banners and tapestries, some of which emblazoned the coats of arms of the local lords and the King's retinue. These were echoed in the finery of the knights' peacock apparel. Their brightly coloured tunics displayed a variety of heraldic motifs, monograms, initials, floral patterns, often counterchanged and highlighted with gold thread and jewelled embroideries. These were set off with silver hip belts and brightly coloured silk hose. The bright silks – red, saffron, purple, blue, green – danced in the firelight, adding gaiety and vitality to match the vigour of the talking.

John, attired more soberly in a black velvet tunic, buttoned with pearls down the front and elbows to wrists of the tight-fitting sleeves, had his own insignia as Earl of Richmond embroidered on his left breast with the three royal leopards picked out in gold on the opposite side. Since he had knelt before his father in Picardy and had felt the sword of knighthood on his shoulder, John was aware of the change in his status. His heart had swelled with pride in swearing allegiance and undying duty and in knowing that he was fully one of the inner circle of the King's court. He stood now by the fire enjoying the companionship and respect of his fellows. He realised suddenly that he enjoyed Court life not so much for the majesty and ritual as the feeling of power and authority it gave him.

His reverie was broken by the shrill notes of the herald's trumpet and the King's move to table. John this time took his seat on the flank of his father's table and was attended by a squire from his own retinue – a thoroughly more enjoyable prospect than his own squiring at Winchester and further witness to his emerging status. As befitting a young knight, he straightaway addressed the solemn task of eating and drinking, letting the cares of the day, and of the morrow, fade away.

Next day, King Edward met with Lords Percy and Neville by the Town Moor, a large open space to the north of the city walls, to review the progress in assembling an army for his campaign against the Scots. Much of the supporting equipment and provisions had been assembled on the Thames and transported by sea to the Tyne. Cooking pots; ovens; kettles with hooks and tripods; dishes and ladles; shovels, axes, spades, hammers and scythes; spare weapons and tents; sides of meat – beef, mutton, bacon – and of fish; oats, peas, beans and salt had arrived and been carted from the Town Quay to the Moor where the army was quartered.

Men with a range of supporting skills had been drafted in from the whole of the north of England: bakers and physicians from York; smiths and carpenters from Newcastle; fletchers, grooms and heralds from Lancaster; labourers from the Tyne Valley and armourers from along the military road to Carlisle. Over 700 carts and wagons of various sizes and design were parked by Spital Tongues to the west of the Moor, ready for the assemblage of baggage to be loaded when word was given. Temporary stabling, with hay and fodder, had been set up on the Moor's northern edge so that there was space enough to exercise the horses. The whole Moor resounded with the bustle of activity, calls and curses, banter and bartering, under the blue haze from camp fires and forges.

All this the King, astride his horse, took in with an experienced eye.

"And what of the fighting men?" he asked Neville.

"Sire, we can count on fifteen hundred men-at-arms and three hundred armed knights to add to your own retinue."

"And archers, Neville? we must have archers."

"Lord Percy has his band of two hundred. I have brought three hundred and the Duke of Lancaster has sent a further five hundred."

"Mmhh," countered the King. "You know what a potent force our archers are and how they are feared. I cannot risk being short in that department. We may have to recruit further as we move north, although I doubt the Scots will match that strength."

At that Percy gave his appraisal. "We still have a problem with horses, sire. There are about four hundred on the Moor and double that number nearby. We will need as many again for the men and the wagon train with the baggage as we move north. The devil is, as you know, sire, that tenants are chary of letting their animals go in midwinter."

"Yes, yes, Percy," broke in the King. "You must requisition what you need and make secure arrangements for changes of horses on the stages north. This campaign is as much about protecting our people so that they can have a peaceful livelihood as it is about teaching the Scots a lesson. Make sure those who owe service know that. Use the time from now to have that done. See that the men feast well over Christmas. The baggage trains can leave straightaway afterwards. We will ride north on the first of the New Year."

John viewed this scene in awe. He had taken part in the recent campaign in France and knew something of the size of an army, but he had not seen before the full mustering of the support that was needed and the scale of the organisation that it entailed. He marvelled yet again at the assured manner of his father, the attention to detail and the loyal response he commanded.

The 20th January turned out to be a day to remember for John. He was riding with the King in his troop of ninety knights towards Kelso. The morning was bright and clear with the sun playing hide and seek behind scudding white clouds. There was a warm breeze from the south and the first early hint of spring in the air. John was feeling in good spirits; like his companions, he had put the disappointment of Berwick behind him. It had proved a tame affair. There had been no fight. No sooner had the vanguard of Edward's army been sighted than the Scottish border chiefs and their men galloped out of the town and melted into the hills. But that was a week ago and now there was this prospect of meeting and parleying with Edward Baliol.

King Edward had left the army at Coldstream to continue their progress north towards Edinburgh under the command of Lord Neville. A herald had brought him a request from Baliol for a meeting to discuss terms. Baliol, as a claimant to the Scottish throne, had influence and would be likely to know the temper of the Scots nobles. Edward had explained this to John and that a diversion to meet him might prove profitable. Or as he had put it: "A meal with Baliol will, I warrant, whet our appetite for greater feasting in Edinburgh!" for he had every intention of carrying forward the campaign into the heart of the capital and to stamp his authority on it.

As they drew near to Kelso, a group of six horsemen approached with two outriders holding aloft banners displaying the Baliol insignia. After greeting the King they wheeled and led the way into the town and through the castle keep to a cobbled courtyard where Edward and his close companions dismounted. Edward Baliol came forward, bowed low before the King and offered his welcome and greetings. As soon as his visitors were settled inside the hall of the castle, each warmed with a dram of whisky, Baliol addressed the King.

"Sire, you have been sorely and needlessly stressed in this unfortunate incident at Berwick. This was the doing of a rough element among the border clans which does not reflect the true mind of Scotland. Our two countries should not be at each other's throats. We need amity for people to prosper and trade between us to flourish—"

The King interrupted with an impatient and steely: "Yes, yes, my Lord! But how can that be? I had thought I taught that lesson on my last expedition on the bloody field of Neville's Cross – do you but remember? Thereafter, I had an armful of assurances, all sworn and signed over, but they have proved false, unchivalrous and count for nought. So how am I expected to proceed?"

"My Lord, I acknowledge the slight you have suffered and the power at your command. You will, if you must, lay waste our land. Yet I so much see the benefits of our two countries being together that I am prepared to lay down my claim to the royal throne of Scotland and to make this over in favour of you, so that, God willing, you may unite our two countries in your regal person."

At this, King Edward stepped back to consult with his counsellors and the close group of knights, including John who had joined him in the hall. "On the face of it, this is a gallant gesture but see you any treachery here?" he asked. He was assured on this although some voiced doubts as to whether Baliol's offer carried much credit with his peers and could therefore ever be cashed. John had kept quiet but wondered to himself what benefit there was for Baliol in this.

"Well, my good Lord," said King Edward, turning to Baliol. "This is a noble gesture which I gladly accept. If, indeed, this were to lead to a union into one kingdom, then I would pledge myself to serve the Scots as well as the English!"

Baliol knelt before King Edward and pledged his loyalty. Scribes were called and letters patent drawn up whereby Edward Baliol renounced his rights to the Scottish kingdom and the Baliol inheritance and made these over to the King of England. The document was sealed and signed by the principals and their senior companions. King Edward expressly called John forth to sign as a witness. John added his signature in a clear script as Earl of Richmond with a tremor of pride at this his first formal state document. Afterwards he reflected on the political aspects of the day and pondered on what he had heard about the hatred Baliol felt for David Bruce. Although he was a knight he knew he had a lot to learn about the political game.

On 30th January 1356, one month after leaving Newcastle, King Edward of England rode into the centre of Edinburgh. His army had met no real opposition on its march up from Coldstream, through Galashiels, where Edward and his retinue had rejoined them after the meeting with Baliol. There had been some skirmishes as the men-at-arms forayed into the countryside on the flanks of the main body but this was normal sporting plunder and did not count as fighting.

Edward was resplendent on his great black stallion, his armour glinting silver in the lowering afternoon sun set off by the silken sheen of his royal purple cape, which draped down from his shoulders over the horse's haunches. He was surrounded in tight formation by his personal corps of knights, who despite the docility of the populace were wary for any rash act of defiance. They too made a

magnificent spectacle: the gloss of their fine steeds shining brightly –
brown, black, grey and chestnut; lances aloft with banners streaming
in the light breeze; surcoats over their mail displaying their insignia
and arms; bright red cockades bobbing up and down on their horses'
heads. It was an impressive sight – and intended to be so. Opulence
and spectacle are the handmaidens of power.

Riding immediately behind his father, John sat as tall as he could
in his saddle, looking straight ahead with a serious face, conscious of
his place in the cavalcade and of the importance of this entry into the
historic capital city. He was aware of tall, stone-faced buildings with
high, sharply sloping roofs and glimpses, lower down, of a jumble of
shacks and yards wreathed in blue smoke from wood fires. He saw
groups of townspeople standing staring, no doubt wondering what all
this meant for them and their city. Some were well clad in stout woollen
jackets in plain brown or grey colours but these were set off by the
bright plaids of the many kilts on view. The women invariably were
less colourful and wrapped in cloaks or shawls. Some looked pinched,
ill-fed and cold with bare feet and with a child or two hanging onto
skirts. He saw wonder and worry in the faces but no delight.

Later that evening, having received the keys of the city from the
city officials and homage from a number of Scottish lairds, King
Edward's attention was drawn to a herald who had just arrived,
urgently seeking an audience. At a signal from the Chamberlain, he
approached the King and bowed deeply before addressing him.

"Sire. Thank you for receiving me. I bring urgent greetings and
salutations from my Lady, the Countess Douglas. She entreats that you
will receive her so that she may present to you certain gifts from the city
and petition to you the honest feelings of the people of Edinburgh."

Edward conferred briefly with his aides and then told the herald he
would be pleased to receive her Ladyship at ten o'clock in the morning.

Next day when he received the Countess Douglas, Edward,
wearing a gold coronet, was sitting in a brocaded chair, richly robed
in purple silk hose, with the fleur-de-lys and royal leopards embroidered in silver and gold thread on the breast of his black velvet tunic.
Her presence struck a sharply contrasting note. She was dressed in a

brown cape and hood with a plain grey gown loosely belted at her waist. She was small, dainty, with a fragile air. As she drew back her hood, her raven hair fell around her white face which seemed to be filled with dark, sad, brimming eyes as she looked up at the King.

"Sire, you have entered our city. Your knights are quartered with our burgesses and your men are camped on our inner leas and outside commons. We accept this, although it bears hard as our provisions in midwinter are low. Indeed you have our fair city at your mercy and it is to your mercy that I appeal. To sack our city in revenge for the rash folly of some of our lowland kinsmen at Berwick would surely be an act of injustice and alien to your royal person?"

King Edward hid a wry smile at such directness.

"It is true, fair lady, that I have no particular quarrel with Edinburgh or its people and it is becoming of you to represent their interests so sympathetically. Except that here is the seat of government and therefore also the seat of failure." And giving an edge to his voice: "Failure, that is, to control and punish those thieves who steal from me. How am I to act to protect myself other than to make my mark here?"

The Countess, unabashed, showed a dimpled smile and, looking directly at the King, replied: "I warrant your very presence here has made that mark, sire. And to forbear from further action will surely make a greater mark?"

At this the King laughed out loud and said: "Come, my Lady, walk with me. You shall have the keys to your city and there will be no sacking!"

John, who had been standing behind his father, had followed every word and facial expression. He was sure that although his father had no intention of despoiling the city, he had let it appear that he had been persuaded. But he also admired the way in which this spirited lady had reasoned with the King, and he wondered whether she always dressed so plainly or was this a subtle move.

He realised he had much to learn about the niceties of diplomacy and negotiation! Whatever, the occasion made a strong impression on John: one which was to come back to him thirty years later when he was again in Edinburgh.

Chapter Two

GEOFFREY CHAUCER, PERCHED on a high wooden stool, his feet curled round the legs and heels resting on a crossbar, sighed and lifted his eyes from the sloping wooden desk to look out of the window. It was a fresh spring day in May. He could see the young green leaves of a hornbeam dancing in the breeze and he sighed again. The others would be out in one of the alleys having a game of knucklebones or whipping tops. But he was more interested in the story about Greek gods that he was working on. He picked up his quill, recharged it from his inkhorn and started again on his translation.

He had been at school since eight o'clock that morning. Master Ravenstone, who kept the school, had heard Geoffrey and the eight other boys chanting lines 625 to 650 of the Doctrinale which he had set them to learn and the courtyard beside St Paul's had echoed with their thrice repeated '*audio, audis, audit, audimus, auditis, audient*' as he revised the present indicative tense of the fourth-conjugation Latin verb with them. Geoffrey had found this dull and mechanical and therefore difficult to keep his mind on, for which he had received his share of bony knuckles to the head to wake him up. But he had woken up with interest at the short lesson in comparatives. He realised that '*laetus, laetior, laetissimus*' and '*laete, laetius and laetissime*' sounded very much like Italian and, in any case, he could respond better to words for feelings like 'happy, happier, happiest and happily'! He was looking forward to showing off this new discovery at home and asking his friend Giovanni about similar words in Italian – like the ones he had to learn for 'miserable'. '*Miserimus*' sounded rather wonderful and just the sort of word for a lady who had lost her lover!

He had stayed on, after the others had gone at noon, to finish the task he had been given to translate – another section from the Roman poet Ovid's *Metamorphoses*. This was about Phaethon and how he had persuaded his father, Phoebus, to lend him his chariot and let him drive his winged horses across the sky for a day as proof that he was his son. His father had tried to dissuade him and warned him of all the pitfalls and 'the fierce spirits of the horses and the hard task to check their eager feet'. He had just come to the lines where the young Phaethon mounts the chariot, takes the reins and thanks his father: '*occupat iIIe levum iuvenale corpore currum statque super manisbusque datas contingere habenas gaudet et invito grates agit inde parenti*', when Master Ravenstone came into the schoolroom.

"What! Still here, Chaucer? Have you not finished?"

"I have just come to where you said I should stop, sir."

"Mmmmhh! Let me see."

The master read through what Chaucer had written, while Geoffrey gazed up into his face to see if he could judge the reaction. He saw frowns and stern peering looks, as well as flashes of amusement and what looked like surprise.

"Yes, well, you are coming along nicely, young sir, but there are words here you have not quite got the meaning of which I will write out for you tomorrow so that you can learn them. Well done, although you have a long way to go before we can call you a Latin Scholar! And your script is still hard to decipher."

"Yes, sir, and thank you! What happens? Does Phaethon ride the heavens and manage the horses?"

Master Ravenstone chuckled at this: "Goodness, no! Like many a youngster, he was in too great a hurry and caused havoc by losing his path and burning parts of the earth so that Libya became a desert, the Nile fled in terror into Africa and the men of Ethiopia became black-skinned with the searing heat from his wrong-coursed chariot! It is a marvellous tale and allegory."

And then the master greatly surprised Geoffrey. He moved over to the far wall which was lined with shelves on which were stacked his books and manuscripts – strictly forbidden territory to the pupils – but at which Geoffrey had cast many an inquisitive glance. Master Ravenstone took down two slim volumes and inspected them. Then he turned to Geoffrey and offered one of them to him.

"Here, take this home and read the rest of the story tonight.

I have translated it and had it copied out in English. Mind you take good care of it: no scribbling or creasing the pages. And you must bring it back to me in the morning. Now, off you go home!"

Geoffrey flushed with excitement, his eyes brimmed brightly and he could only manage a mumbled, "Thank you. Yes… yes, I will."

He gathered up his quills, knife, inkhorn and the rough book where he kept his reminders and experiments with words and stories and rushed out into the welcome freshness of the afternoon.

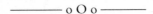

Geoffrey was soon home. He had skipped out of St Paul's churchyard and jogged down an alleyway to Thames Street where he stopped to watch as two draymen, cursing and red-faced, sweated to recover a barrel that had fallen from their cart. He didn't recognise the men but he hoped it was not his father's wine that was being so mishandled. Further along he walked quickly past La Riole, the mansion owned by Queen Philippa, keeping his eyes down on the street as he went by. He always felt this shyness on passing her house, maybe because of that time when he had been chastised for racing in the street, kicking a bladder with his mates, and had been threatened that the Queen's men would beat them. Near home, he looked up to see if his friend John was about at the Philipots' house but there was no sign of him. Then, still clutching his leather bag closely to him and the precious book, he rushed in to find his mother. Agnes Chaucer was sitting quietly sewing a chemise before a log fire in the hall. She looked up and smiled indulgently as her son swept in with the force of a March gale.

"My, my, Geoffrey? What is this excitement? You quite take my breath away!"

"Mother, mother," gasped Geoffrey. "Master Ravenstone has lent me one of his books. It is in English so that I can read the tale without having to work it out from Latin."

"And what tale is that, dear?"

"Oh! It is about Phaethon who borrowed his father's chariot and rode across the sky and could not manage the horses and made a mess of things because he was in too much of a hurry – or so Master says."

His mother threw back her head and laughed out loud at this: "Well, who else is in a great hurry! I am sure it is a great honour for the master to lend you this book – so mind you look after it! Now go and wash away those ink stains and change your tunic and hose. Remember, your father is due back from Southampton tonight."

Dusk was gathering when John Chaucer arrived back in Thames Street. His groom had been waiting for him and had taken his horse off to the stables behind the Wallbrook. He strode into the hall exuding energy, much like his son had done earlier. Agnes, amused at this likeness, rose to greet him. They embraced and looked affection-ately into each other's faces, searching for affirmation and reading current moods after five days' separation. John immediately called for some ale.

"Ah, that's better!" he exclaimed as he half-drained his tankard. "It's a dry road from Southampton at this time of year but at least I'll not be going again."

"The business went well then?" asked Agnes, knowing well her husband's need to unwind.

"Yes, well enough," replied John. "I've quit the post of Deputy to the King's Butler in Southampton, as I told you to expect. It means losing the annual fee from the Exchequer but I'll not have to pay my agent Baldry to manage that, and I've made a good contract with some Italians to supply wine from Tuscany. That should make up for it and more."

"But does this mean you will no longer be accepted at the Royal Household, John?"

"Well. Not really, Agnes. The appointment could have been stopped at any time. You know how whimsical this is. It depends muchly on the state of the King's finances. When the King gets the grant of further customs and excise duties from Parliament, he will be looking to raise money by selling the collection of these off to City merchants, like our neighbours Brembre and Ricard, and they'll want help with this. I've no doubt we stand in enough good stead to benefit – if not directly from another royal appointment, then from our connections and strengths in the wine trade."

At this, John turned to his son who was sitting quietly by the fire, listening to the news but knowing it was his place to wait until he was spoken to.

"Well, Geoffrey, what have you been up to? Have you been attending to your duties?"

"Oh Father!" cried Geoffrey eagerly. "Just today Master Ravenstone sent me home with a book of his own to read – and it is a translation he has made into English. I stayed on after school to finish taking from a Latin text and he said I could finish reading the story about Phaethon and the Greek gods in this book and—"

"Whoa! young sir! Hold your horses!" his father interrupted with a laugh. "All in good time. I am sure Master Ravenstone would not wish you to gabble like that. Now, you say he has lent you one of his books?"

"Yes, Father, here it is," His father took the book from Geoffrey, turned it over in his hand, stroked the leather binding and opened it to look at the fine manuscript pages inside. He screwed up his eyes and began reading slowly to himself while Geoffrey stood solemnly by his side.

"I shall look forward to hearing you read some of this to me before you go to bed. Now go and tell the kitchen we are ready to eat and bring a flagon of the red wine for your mother and me."

When Geoffrey departed, John said to his wife: "Master Ravenstone would not have done this unless he was impressed with the boy. I've thought for some time that his liveliness with words is remarkable. We must support him in whatever way we can but we mustn't crow too much about it – especially to him!"

John and Agnes Chaucer then turned and went to the table where they were joined by Geoffrey bearing the wine which he then poured into the silver goblets for his parents. Soon they were tearing the pheasant apart and licking their lips at the juiciness of it.

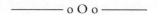

Some days later, Geoffrey was hurrying along Thames Street in the direction of London Bridge. He crossed over the small culvert where the Wallbrook flowed into the Thames and then turned right between two tall houses which were owned by Hanseatic merchants from Germany. As he came out of the dark, cool alley between the houses he had to shade his eyes from the glint of the sun bouncing off the river. He stood scanning the wharves and the bustling scene before him. The riverside was lined with a variety of seagoing, broad-bellied vessels with tall masts and furled sails and a mixture of local lighters which had brought the cargoes from larger vessels anchored downstream beyond London Bridge.

This scene never ceased to fascinate the young Chaucer. He was excited by the bustle and tension as gangs of men winched and wrestled with casks and bales to lift them from the holds of the ships onto the quayside where they were stacked or loaded direct onto drays and handcarts. They shouted directions, and resounding cries mingled with other oaths and the clatter and stamping of hooves on the cobbled quays. For Geoffrey the scene also brought the alluring whiff of foreign places: the romance of France brought with the red Burgundy wines from Bordeaux; the sweet-smelling timber from the cold Baltic; and the rich cloths and pungent spices brought from Italy and the faraway sun-baked Mediterranean.

Then Geoffrey espied Tom Castle, his father's foreman, and remembered the errand he was on. He made his way along the wharf, his clogs ringing on the stones, and dodged his way between a line of carts to the ship where Tom was supervising the unloading of a cargo of wines.

"Good morning, Mister Tom!" Geoffrey called.

"Master Geoffrey, what brings you here on this fine day?" asked Tom Castle.

"I've a message from my father. He wants you to send twenty of the special Burgundy directly to Sir Henry Picard's house please."

"Oh ho! Yes. I expect he's having one of his fine dinner parties again with half the City aldermen present!" grinned Tom, who enjoyed being brushed by the glamour of such occasions.

"And Father said to remind you to be sure that the casks come from the batch marked with three red crosses."

"Oh yes, to be sure. I've got most of those off already. There they are, standing on the quay. I'll get them carted right away and you can tell the master, job's done."

Geoffrey left him calling loudly: "Bill, Harry! Get down here, lads! We've a special order for the Picard household. They want twenty of these taken up there directly," pointing to the stack of barrels. "Look lively now," he shouted to his workmen. "I expect there'll be a quaff of ale up there and some pence in it for you!"

Geoffrey wandered along the quay and up the alley back to Thames Street. On the corner by London Bridge he saw a knot of his friends gathered in some arm-waving debate. Geoffrey smiled. He could guess the subject and the drift of things. The group included the sons of several of the foreign merchants who lived around Thames Street in the Vintry ward.

As Geoffrey drew near, he could see three of his Italian friends, Giovanni, Luigi and Roberto, with Armand and Michel from France and his local friends Richard Chandos and Henry Witherspoon. Although, except for Henry, they were mostly older than Geoffrey he always liked meeting with the group to enjoy the mix of language and topics and the never-ending debate over which were the best wines. The rivalry between Italy and France especially, and, on occasions, the Germans, who were absent today, was always passionately engaged.

This time, however, the debate had taken a delightful turn: the argument was all Italian between Giovanni Gregoletto and Roberto Bava. Henry rushed up to Geoffrey and explained excitedly.

"Roberto has claimed that the best of fine wines are like the sound of a delicate musical instrument, and the greatest pleasure is when the two are brought together – the question is which instruments go with which wine!"

As they joined the group, Giovanni was saying: "Well, I agree with you in favouring the *viola da braccio* with its so clear, smooth and laughing tones. Surely, that fits *musica perfecto* to the magnificent vintages of *prosecco* we produce in the hills above Venice at Corregliano?"

"You describe the qualities of the viola so well, Giovanni," replied Roberto. "But the musical embrace you describe intertwines so exactly with the light airs of my wines from the Asti region that anyone would count your *prosecco* as an inferior experience – and especially if you remember the *spumante!*"

Michel decided, at this, to widen the debate. "Yes, my friends, but surely we should consider also the qualities of other musical instruments. I wonder, for example, what would be the best drink to go with the sound of the sackbut!"

The group exploded into laughter at the incongruity, which was renewed when Richard said, "And there is always of course the bagpipes, or for your benefit, Luigi," on seeing his puzzled look, "*la zampogna* or what they call *cornemuse* in France! What drink would go with that embrace?"

Geoffrey produced more laughter when he added: "The skirl of the pipes would be well matched by the swirl of a good whisky!"

Geoffrey was clapped on the back as the group broke up and drifted off home. And, his imagination fired, he continued to conjure up appropriate connections between the sounds of music and various types of drinks, but he could not better what his Italian friends had said.

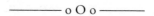

Nearly a year later, Geoffrey was preparing to lead a debate himself but this was a more formal and serious affair. Each year the schools attached to the religious foundations in the City celebrated a saint's day with a festival of maypole dancing, games, verse and quiz competitions, ending with the highlight which was a debate between the leading schools. This year, St Paul's Day was chosen for the celebrations and Geoffrey's school were the hosts. Geoffrey had been chosen as the principal speaker for St Paul's. His role was to oppose the proposition by the philosopher Aristotle that: 'In evil counsel, women conquer men.'

Geoffrey had risen early that morning. He had dressed carefully in clean grey hose and the brown tunic with embroidered school badge which his mother had put out for him. He had pulled on his new leather shoes and had hurried down Thames Street to school. He was greeted by an excited bunch of his schoolmates who were decorating the courtyard outside St Paul's with flags and streamers.

He helped them to set up the maypole and fix the coloured ribbons which the dancers would use to weave their patterns. Then he went into the schoolroom to look over his notes and rehearse the quotations he had prepared to support his arguments. He was repeating these out loud to himself when Master William Ravenstone came in.

"Ah, Chaucer, warming up I hear! Have you found and learned all those references we talked about?"

"Yes, sir. I have several from the Holy Book, including Solomon, and some others from Seneca, Tullius and Cato."

"Good. You will do well, I am sure. Mind you command your audience with a strong voice and fix them with that clear eye of yours. Remember: fine words butter no parsnips without good delivery!" and he went off chortling at his own witticism.

Soon, teams of boys from the other schools began to file into the courtyard which echoed with the low babble of voices, pierced by the occasional high-pitched laughter. In the distance a fife and drums could be heard making their way to join the scene to lend their beat later to the maypole dancing. Gradually the trestle seats, which had been taken from the schoolroom and placed around the yard, began to fill as City ladies arrived in twos and threes and sat down, talking quietly together, flashing an occasional smile at a neighbour or bowing a gracious head to acknowledge a City alderman or his wife. Behind the seated women stood the menfolk, splendidly arrayed in scarlet or azure or brown hose and richly embroidered tunics.

Quietly watching from his schoolroom doorway, Geoffrey took in the rich scene. His eyes searched the seated rows for sight of his mother. Then he spied her sitting at one corner. She was looking resplendent in her new green velvet gown with gold embroidery at the hem and black buttoned sleeves beneath a brown sleeveless over-cloak which was edged all round with fur. She was sitting with their neighbour, Mistress Witherspoon, his friend Henry's mother, who added to the colourful scene with her long saffron silk gown and coquettish feathered hat. The lavish spectacle excited Geoffrey. He felt like an actor waiting to go onto the boards. His heart throbbed with the commotion and he felt thrilled at the thought of perform-ing before such an audience.

And then the fifes and drums began their catchy rhythms and the team of dancers trotted out to their places, took up their ribbons and began to twirl away around the maypole. Geoffrey stood for a while watching the patterns made by the ribbons folding and unfolding and then slipped away behind the throng and into the street. He knew it would be another hour at least before the debate started and he felt the need for less intoxicating air.

So, he made his way down to the quayside and the slower gliding rhythm of the river. There were the usual busy sounds of boats being loaded and unloaded, but Geoffrey blocked these noises out and listened instead to the lapping of the waves against the timbers of the wharves. The gentle 'tap-tap' of the brown-grey river water soothed him.

When he returned to the festivities, the last two quizzes were finishing and the winners were celebrating their rewards amidst laughter and applause. Geoffrey felt a mild lurch of anticipation in his stomach and knew that he would soon be listening to the opening arguments of the opposing team in the debate in support of Aristotle's claim about the evil wiles of women.

At last the time for the debate had come. The Chaplain of St Paul's stood in the centre of the courtyard and raised his arms. A hush fell over the crowd. The two lecterns which would be used by the principal speakers in the debate were brought out as he addressed the gathering: "Good people. Welcome to our festivities on this Holy Day. The verbal joust today is on the text of Aristotle: 'In evil counsel, women conquer men'. William Buckler from the Trinity School will set out to prove this and Geoffrey Chaucer of St Paul's will seek to gainsay it. You may think this a stiff task for such young men, and we shall see how well they shape up to it. So, let the debate begin!"

As William Buckler began his address, Geoffrey stood still, reading the faces of the audience and listening intently, noting the tales, allusions and parodies and laughing with the crowd at his mocking mimicry of low women. Solomon had said: "It would be better to live in a desert than dwell with a riotous woman." It was rumbustious stuff. Surely women's heads were turned too much by gossip and self-awareness to be listened to in the affairs of men? Rather, men should be masters in their own house and rely on friends for advice since as Solomon said: "The counsel of true friends giveth sweetness to the soul."

There was clapping and murmurs of approval, even from some of the ladies, as William finished. Then the crowd subsided as Chaucer stepped up to his lectern.

"My Lords, Ladies, friends. You are, I judge, well persuaded by the clever talk of my friend: if so, I am undone! But tarry a while and consider: Are all women so shallow? Are all men so wise? It is true that friends can be the best counsel but are all friends true? Remember the warning of Tullius: 'Amongst all the pestilences that there have been in friendship, the greatest is flattery.' Albeit that many a woman's counsel is self-seeking and worthless, yet men have found many a good woman who was discreet and wise. Remember the wisdom Rebecca gave Jacob; how Abigail saved her husband from King David; how Judith saved her city and Hester her people.

"And consider too: Jesus was not only born of woman but also, on rising from death, he appeared to a woman rather than his apostles. And Our Lord decided after creating Adam that it was not good for man to be alone; so he created woman as the helpmeet of man – rather than, as was put before you, a confusion of man! Surely, the fault lies not in women but in a man who, having free choice, knows not where to seek good counsel and, out of manly arrogance and pride, denies the virtue of women? I put it to you that Aristotle's philosophy this time is false!"

As Geoffrey stepped back and bowed, he was pleased to see his father had joined the crowd and was standing behind his mother. The clapping and cries of appreciation seemed more fulsome and prolonged than they had been for William, and indeed, when the Chaplain took a hand count of the audience it was clear that Geoffrey had won the day. He flushed with pleasure at the Chaplain's kind words and the generous handclasp of William. Then, somewhat flustered, he made his way through the backslapping of his school-mates to the warm embrace of his mother and the gruff but smiling congratulations of his father.

Some weeks after Geoffrey's debating triumph, John and Agnes Chaucer were invited to dinner at the house of Sir Henry Ricard who was a leading merchant in the vintner trade and a senior figure in the Corporation of London. Indeed, the dinner was to celebrate his nomi-nation as Deputy Lord Mayor of London which meant that he would be installed as Lord Mayor for the next year, 1356–7. John was rightly pleased with this invitation. Although he had helped Sir Henry on several occasions to obtain some special wines, John was in a small way of business compared with his host who had connections with royalty and with most of the great merchants and financial figures in the City. John was honoured and pleased by the invitation and the recognition it awarded but it had flustered the normally placid Agnes so much that John had had to promise her a new dress for the occasion!

But now he took great pleasure at how radiant she looked in the fashionable black sleeveless surcoat and cream damask gown with its low neckline, close-fitting bodice and full skirt flowing from the embroidered hip girdle. He felt his own attire in blue velvet tunic with gold embroidery and green hose was somewhat drab compared with Sir Henry's richly jewelled and quartered purple tunic with his monogram appliquéd in silver and his parti-coloured hose in scarlet and black. John noted the long pointed toes of his host's shoes – the new fashion at Court – and, with a wry smile, imagined the hoots he would receive if he went wearing such to the wharves!

John and Agnes were pleased to see familiar faces among the guests who were gathered in the spacious hall around the red-embered sea coal fire sipping a musky Madeira wine.

Agnes was soon comparing notes with Jane Witherspoon and Mary Philipot who had introduced her to the Flemish dressmaker who had made her new gown. John meanwhile stood with a group listening to Sir Henry explaining an obscure point about the new liquor tax on spirits. His eye roved over the fine furnishings, especially the tapestries hanging along two of the walls and the carved oak chests on which stood pewter bowls of fruit, including oranges and grapes which must have been brought as a special favour for an esteemed patron on one of the newly arrived barques from Portugal. The silver dishes, gilt cups, knives and spoons, which were set out on the long wooden table, danced in the light from the circles of candles overhead.

Talk flowed freely round the table as they enjoyed a well-provisioned meal: pheasant, quail, roast beef and pork, well whetted with ales and fine red wine. The state of trade – in wine, of course, but also fish, wool and cloths, spices and weaponry – was the prime topic. But then talk turned to politics and the perennial rivalry with France. There were rumours that Charles, the King of Navarre, was at odds with King John of France; that Henry, Duke of Lancaster, had made a pact with Charles and was even now assembling a fleet in the Thames to sail to Cherbourg in his support.

"Well, if this be true," said James Witherspoon, "it will be a great advantage to use the port of Cherbourg with its sea crossing much shorter than Bordeaux."

"Ah yes, but meanwhile our ships may be taken over for the fighting and our trade disrupted," interposed Richard Philipot… "Charles of Navarre is not a bargain I relish. He is not known for his chivalry or honouring his word and in some quarters is known as Charles the Bad!"

After they had used their finger bowls and pages had brought the fruit and a cleansing white wine to table, Sir Henry switched the conversation by turning to John Chaucer: "I hear your son Geoffrey showed a nimble mind – and tongue! – at the Holy Day debate last month. How old is he now?"

"Why he's thirteen coming up to fourteen, Sir Henry."

"Mmmmhh! High time he was out in the world. With his gift of the gab he could make a great priest or lawyer. Or do you intend him to follow you in the business?"

John glanced quickly at Agnes, knowing her views on that score.

"It is good of you to ask, Sir Henry, and, yes, Geoffrey has a talent with words but not just in speech. He has an imaginative and original use of language, in French and Italian as well as English. His ideas range far and wide and too freely, I fear, to be constrained by metaphysical or legal rhetoric. And though he figures well, I do not see him satisfied by trading as a vintner."

"Just so; he has both French and Italian, you say. Well now, it seems to me he could well earn a place at Court. There is a greater need for such skills now with the King's forceful involvement in Europe from Flanders to the Pyrenees and beyond. I have contacts at Court, as you know. But first I will talk with my good friend, Sir Paon de Roet, who is Guyenne King of Arms to Queen Philippa. Let me see what I can do."

Just before the Whitsuntide Festival, Geoffrey was surprised when he got home from school to find his father there talking with a tall lean stranger. He was further surprised when he noticed Queen Philippa's coat of arms on the breast of his tunic. What could this mean? Surely he had not come to bargain over barrels with his father for he had too refined an air for that. He was about to seek out his mother for an explanation when his father called to him.

"Geoffrey, I want you to meet Sir Paon de Roet, who is at the court of the Queen and is one of her close advisers and countrymen."

Geoffrey came forward and bowed before his father's guest and responded with the polite greeting: "Your servant, sire."

"Your father tells me you will soon leave school, and I have been hearing good reports of you, Geoffrey – especially of your flair with languages. The royal court today has – how do you say it? – fingers in many foreign pies! I am myself from Hainault like the Queen, where we keep many ties, but also we have much to do with the other courts of Europe. We need trusted servants who can carry messages and negotiate an answer where necessary. I think you could give good service at Court and perhaps, in time, if you prove yourself, you might be an ambassador like this for the King."

Geoffrey listened attentively at this, his blue eyes widening in wonder.

"I think this invaluable advice, Geoffrey," his father added. "Better for you than being a priest or a lawyer as Master Ravenstone has suggested, don't you think?"

"Oh! Yes, sir!" Geoffrey almost shouted. He certainly did not want to be a priest nor a dry-as-dust pernickety lawyer.

Turning to his guest, his father said with a bow: "Thank you, Sir Paon, for your courtesy. We are truly honoured."

"Well, well, yes," answered Sir Paon. "We must now see if my judgement meets with approval and where there might be a place for him. It may be that a start could be made in the household of one of the King's sons: perhaps Prince Lionel, who has need of a larger retinue following his marriage to the Countess of Ulster, or with Prince John of Gaunt, although I think him too young yet to have much of a retinue."

At a signal from his father, Geoffrey withdrew and rushed to find his mother to tell her the news. She was in the kitchen supervising the preparation of the evening meal with Fanny the cook. As usual, Geoffrey entered in a flurry, talking as he approached her.

"Mother, I might be going to Court. There is this man from Queen Philippa who thinks I should, and I might be sent to Prince Lionel's court in Ulster. Where is that?"

With a chuckle, Agnes Chaucer caught hold of Geoffrey's arm and said: "Come and sit by me. You can be shelling these peas as a

31

help to Fanny. Now, the idea of your getting a place at Court is an excellent one and I am as excited as you are about it, but we must wait until your father is ready to explain what he has agreed. And I don't think Prince Lionel lives in Ulster, which is in Ireland; he is married to the Countess of Ulster but I believe they are mostly in England and move around quite a lot between their estates and following the royal calendar."

"Does it mean that, if I joined his court, I would have to move about like that as well?" asked Geoffrey.

"Well, yes, I am sure that would be so."

"And so this would not be my home anymore?"

Agnes could see that this was something Geoffrey had not taken in and he needed time to think about it. "Well, of course, silly, this would always be your home and when you were not needed at Court I would expect you to be here with me."

Agnes gave Geoffrey a quick kiss on the forehead and said, "Let's wait and discuss it further with your father when he has more to tell us."

Some days later, Geoffrey's father called him into the room where he kept his records and books and where he wrote up his accounts. When he was young, Geoffrey had been forbidden ever to enter this room – which, of course, gave it an air of mystery and foreboding. Now he was older, he had on occasions sat with his father and had helped him copy out some of his tradings into one of the big ledgers. He enjoyed this rare closeness with his father who had explained that such careful records were needed to satisfy the tax collectors. Sometimes, especially around Michaelmas, they would suddenly arrive and demand to see the records of all the wine he had imported during the last year and check to see that the correct duties had been paid. Just as St Paul's Cathedral had a hushed air of grace and holiness imbued with the smell of incense, so too this room breathed for Geoffrey the weight of serious business and leather-backed volumes.

But there were no ledgers open on the desk this time. His father wanted to talk to Geoffrey about his future.

"I have seen Sir Paon de Roet again and had a long talk with him. Apparently, Prince Lionel has no need of another page in his household at this time. But, there is a place for you in the household of his wife, the Countess Elizabeth of Ulster. Sir Paon tells me it is quite usual for a prince of the realm and his wife to keep their own personal retinues and, of course, the two retinues would often be together. So, this is a real feather in our caps, Geoffrey! You will be close to the Court and at the centre of the nation. After all, Prince Lionel is King Edward's son and second only in rank to his older brother, Edward the Black Prince."

Geoffrey had been expecting this ever since the meeting with Sir Paon. He still was not sure of his own feelings. He was churned up with a mixture of excitement and dread. Watching his father, he caught some of the excitement he felt, but his own dread at leaving home and taking on strange duties in a strange household lingered.

"What will I have to do, Father?" he asked.

"I expect you will have a mixture of duties. You will be given these by the steward of the house or by an esquire who acts as tutor to the pages. There will be tasks such as serving at table; you know, like you have done here when we have had guests – carving the meats, serving the wine and portions of food. You may have chamber duties too – such as laying out the bed or clothes to wear and you will probably be called upon to read to the Countess and her ladies and to recite poems and ballads – maybe even some of your own contriving!

"And there will be outdoor activities to take part in – maybe some hunting or hawking and you will do quite a lot of riding, if only when the household is travelling between estates."

"Will I have to empty chamber pots and make fires and do scullion work in the kitchens?" asked Geoffrey, projecting his fears and wrinkling his nose in distaste.

"Oh, I doubt it: there'll be servants enough for that," replied his father with a dismissive but not totally convincing laugh. "But, look you," he continued with a sharper and more urgent edge to his voice. "This is an honourable chance for us all. My life is in the City and its affairs. I am likely soon to be an Alderman and I may one day even be Lord Mayor like Brembre or Walworth. But that is nothing compared with a place at Court with its power and authority. The King has domains in France and is vying with kings and dukes in Spain, Portugal and Bavaria as well as links with Italy and His Holiness the Pope in Rome. You will be part of that and you will be a royal servant; and, I am sure, if you attend to your duties well, eventually an ambassador – just as Sir Paon hinted."

Geoffrey heard the gruffness in his father's words and knew better than to question them.

"When will I have to go, Father?" he asked.

"As soon as we can fit you out. You will need a horse, sword and other vestments. I will see to those. You gather together things you will want to take with you. No doubt you'll want some of your beloved books – and something to scribble on!" he added more warmly. "Sir Paon tells me the Countess is travelling to Windsor and will be there for another week. You will join them there!"

"Yes, Father. And thank you. Will there be anyone there that I know?"

"I've not heard of anyone. John Chandos is in Prince Edward's retinue. You will be able to see him at Windsor, and Sir Paon tells me that his daughter Philippa is in the Countess' household. She is about the same age as you so no doubt you will get to know her. Now, I must see your mother and tell her the news."

Later, Geoffrey joined his mother by the fire in the hall. Her eyes were shining brightly as she welcomed him with open arms and clasped him to her.

"Oh Geoffrey, I am so happy for you. Your father has done well by you. It is an honour for us all."

"Yes. I know, Mother, and I am grateful but will I be able to live up to it? And will I have time and space to read and do my writings? You know how much I need to do that!"

"Why, yes, you will. In fact you will be expected to continue your studies. Being a page at Court is an education and training. You will be able to develop your Latin and French – and, Italian. I've no doubt, too, they will be raptured by your versifying! But you will also, my dear, learn all the courtesies of manners and behaviour. You won't be able to flounce into a room as you do here! – and you will have to curb your noisiness – and no belching or farting!" she added with a twinkle.

Geoffrey was taken aback at his mother's bold words but smiled because he knew the truth of them.

"But will I have to fight and joust? You know I'm not a dashing fellow, and I don't like that sort of roughness."

"Oh, I doubt there will be much of that, Geoffrey," she replied quickly. "Not with the Countess' household." But Geoffrey noticed she lowered her eyes and a shadow crossed her face as she spoke and he wondered how this would turn out.

Chapter Three

EARLY ON A bright spring morning in April 1357, Geoffrey Chaucer emerged from a side door of the Queen's mansion in Thames Street, went out of the iron gates and turned left down towards the family house where he was born. He sniffed the air appreciatively. The street was cleaner than he remembered. Freshened by recent showers, it lacked the familiar stench of rancid rubbish. A cool breeze was blowing up from the Thames. He caught its salty tang and knew that the tide must be up. He could see in his mind's eye the busy scene at the riverside with the lighters and wherries moored alongside and all the bustle of loading and unloading. He wondered if his father might be down there. He took a deep breath of pure pleasure. It was good to be home.

The houses in the street were all so familiar with their solid wooden frames, plasterwork, studded doors and here and there an overhanging solar room. There was the Philipot house with the coat of arms above the door and, nearby, the Witherspoons'. He half expected to see his friend Henry run out to greet him. And yet how strange it was to be staying at the Queen's house: the very place where, as a boy, he used to scuttle by in fear of the guards! He hurried on with a spring in his step, anxious to be home to meet his parents. He had not seen them since that day over a year ago when he had left for Windsor to join Countess Elizabeth's retinue. So much had happened; he had so much to tell them.

He let himself in through the main door off the street and announced his arrival by calling a courteous, "Hallo! It's Geoffrey." This brought Fanny, his mother's helpmeet, bustling to the entrance.

"Why! Master Geoffrey! It is good to see you." Geoffrey grinned and squeezed her in a warm hug. "Your father went out early and your mother is dressing but will be soon down. Come into the kitchen while I call to her. She will be that pleased!"

Geoffrey went into the kitchen with its yeasty smell of warm bread, scrubbed table top and familiar array of pots and pans. He spied some oatcakes by the oven and took one. He had just finished this sample when he heard his mother calling: "Geoffrey, where are you?" Then she was framed in the doorway with arms outstretched and face brimming. They hugged happily. Then she drew back and studied his face with a long look.

"My! You look well. Such a ruddy complexion. And you've grown, I swear – including in girth," she added with a playful pat of his stomach. "Come," she said, leading him by the hand. "Let us sit in the parlour. I am agog to hear all you have been doing."

"Well," she said, as soon as they were seated. "How is it? What are your duties? What is the Countess like and do you see Prince Lionel? Have you made any friends and what about your writing? Are you doing any?"

Geoffrey smiled, remembering how his mother used to say he rushed in like a March wind. He knew now where that trait came from.

"The duties are much as Father explained to me. Preparing and serving at table and learning about all the different foods and what goes with what, because they have a richer table than here at home, with the benefits from hunting in the royal forests, except sometimes when we are travelling and lodging at a more lowly house. Those duties aren't very difficult, although I am still not the best carver of meats. The Steward says I don't carve, I hack! But he says I know my wines and often asks me to do the cellaring, which means choosing for the table. Of course, I have had to learn some new ones because they have wines sometimes from Greece and places beyond Bohemia that I did not know of."

"You must remember to tell your father about that. I am sure he will be eager to hear of it, especially if you can tell of its taste and usage as well as its origin. What is the Countess like?"

"She is a fine and gentle lady. She has almost black hair, thick and waving, which I have heard her complain about because she says it is so unruly. She has creamy white skin and blue eyes and is quiet and demure, especially when the Prince has company and is roistering. He is tall and straight and handsome, full of energy and often away hawking or hunting. John Chandos is in his retinue and I see him sometimes. He has put me wise on courtly ways at times."

Agnes Chaucer smiled at this, guessing that some of Geoffrey's mocking wit had chafed authority somehow. Almost as if sensing her insight, Geoffrey went on: "The thing I like least, Mother, is having to share sleeping quarters with another page and sometimes with two or three others. There are virtues in comradeship: learning to share and value others and to receive their support and appreciation. There's value too in competition: it puts an edge to your strengths and finds your weaknesses. But personal habits – sometimes gross in nature – I can tell you – they can grate in the close quarters of the bedchamber and deny friendship."

His mother saw the strength of his feeling and sought soothing words but found none. Instead, she asked: "Isn't Sir Paon de Roet's daughter, Philippa, a member of the Countess' household? Do you see her? What is she like?"

"Oh yes! Philippa. She is one of the little maids to the Countess. She is still quite young, not much more than twelve, I reckon, and serious with it. She doesn't favour Sir Paon in looks, though, for she is small with brown hair, has a plain oval face and a plump figure. She has a lively wit at times and, sometimes, a sharp tongue. Her eyes are her best feature: blue as forget-me-nots – and blue as ice when she is teased!"

His mother laughed, guessing that Geoffrey, having discovered this, teased her the more. But by the sound of things, she could fashion her own barbs.

"Well, I'll want to know more – where you have been and what you have seen – but your father will want to know too, so let us wait on him for further talk. What are your plans? Are you able to stay a while?"

"The Prince and Countess are attending the festivities at Court and in the City to celebrate Prince Edward's victory at Poitiers and his capture of John, King of France. This is a feat of arms which has caused a flurry at Court. The King is mightily proud and the whole family is bent on celebration but in a manner to honour their royal guest. This will be at Westminster and the Savoy, and there will be a feast at the Guildhall given by the City. I am not directly involved so I can stay while the celebrations last."

"Splendid! Your father will be pleased. Your room is there and already aired, if I know Fanny, so why not settle yourself in and we will wait on your father."

London was in festive mood, excited by the capture of the French King. The city felt he belonged to them as their hostage as much as to the Black Prince. They had amassed ships and money and men in support of the campaign in France and now took ownership of the celebrations. Around the Tower, at Charing Cross and in Fleet Street crowds were gathering in holiday high spirits. Jugglers and jesters, fiddlers and pipers, dancers and acrobats, marionettes and mummers amused the throng. There were cheers and clapping to greet any coach which moved through on its way to Westminster and "Hurrahs" and shouts of "Long Live the King" and "God bless Prince Edward", whosoever was in the coach. In their joy, the populace poured out their warmth to the royal court and embraced any liveried connections.

John Chaucer was at the wharf supervising a shipment from Portugal when he heard that Prince Lionel and his Countess had arrived to join the royal festivities. He guessed that Geoffrey was with them, so he told Tom, his right-hand man, how to finish the business and hurried home.

Geoffrey was standing outside the house, fascinated by the rag, tag and bobtail of the motley crowd who were wending their way slowly towards London Bridge. His father spotted him, his face lit up and he cried out, "Geoffrey," as he quickened his pace towards him. They embraced and went inside linked together arm in arm.

"Well, this is good cheer. I'd heard the Prince was here and hoped we would see you. You look well, Geoffrey: filled out, more of a man. I take it, you have seen your mother?"

"Why, yes, Father. She was very welcoming. My heart is filled to see you both; I've a lot to tell."

"Aye, well. We will have a banquet tonight: kill the fatted calf. Not that you're a prodigal – or are you?" his father joked.

"No, nothing like that… yet!" Geoffrey riposted with a mischievous grin.

He had been warmed by his father's blessing when he had left home and felt anew the growing companionship between them.

That evening, over a sumptuous meal and afterwards with Benedictine liqueurs by the fire, Geoffrey, prompted by their questions, regaled his parents with his exploits as a page. He told them, with much joking against himself, of his mock fights with the sword and his attempts at jousting. He swore that his arms were shorter than any of his peers and that he would be of no use mounted in battle because he spent more time on the ground than in the saddle!

Recovering from her laughter, his mother said: "Well, that is encouraging because I don't want you going off to fight. They are not likely to choose you if you perform like that!" And his father added: "And now with this victory we have more chance of peace."

Typically, his father, ever the cautious merchant, wanted to glean other insights into the aftermath of the capture of the King of France.

"The French will have to pay a hefty ransom, I'll warrant, and that will fill King Edward's coffers. Maybe we can expect a lighter levy on our imports?" his father mused. "And less taxes as there'll be no need to keep a standing army, the French are so cowed."

"I've no hint of any of this, Father," replied Geoffrey. "Prince Lionel is not much involved with affairs of state at Court and did not join his brother at Poitiers. But I have heard that our King is intent on proving that life at the English court is as rich and magnificent as in Paris or anywhere in Europe. There will be recitals and dancing in the French style and actors and musicians to engage. And we are to have new livery to wear on court occasions."

"Ah, yes. I see," said his father. "But that spending comes from the privy purse, not taxes."

Mention of entertainments at Court prompted Agnes Chaucer to ask: "Will this French focus favour your writing, Geoffrey?"

Geoffrey shifted in his seat and sat forward, looking at her with the intensity of a cat poised to spring: "I don't know, Mother. But the Countess has a full library and I'm able to use it. I've found a copy of the wonderful French ballad 'Roman de la Rose' by Guillaume de Lorris. It is inspiring.

"I am learning so much from it. I love the way he writes in ten-syllable couplets. I am beginning to translate it into our own language so there may be a chance to use some of this because it is well known in France and, I fancy, hearing it in English will both be a new experience and an honour to their culture."

"Oh! Have you it with you? I would love to hear you read a verse or two."

"Yes, I did bring some of the early verses which I have translated as I had thought to show you them. I will fetch them."

When Geoffrey had left the room, his father said: "You've lost your boy, Agnes: he's fast growing to be a man of the world and one with a shrewd head on his shoulders. I vouch that it will not be long ere he is sent on a mission, maybe to France, as Sir Paon forecast!"

"And can't you feel the excitement he has for his writing, John? I rejoice so much at that. Let's hear what you have for us, Geoffrey," she added as he rejoined them.

"De Lorris tells his story in the form of a dream which he says he had when he was aged twenty. It starts like this:

"Within my twenty year of age,
When that Love takes his tollage
Of young folk, I went soon
To bed as I was wont to done
And fast I slept; and in sleeping
Me met such a dreaming
That pleased me wondrous well

But in that dream is never tell
That does not afterward befalle
Just as this dream will tell us all.

"Now this dreme will I rhyme aright
To make your hearts gay and light
For Love it prayeth, and also
Commandeth me that it be so.
And if there are any ask me,
Whether that it be he or she,
How this book, which is here,
Shall be called that I advise you to hear
It is the Romance of the Rose
In which all the art of Love I close."

"Oh! Lovely!" said his mother, clapping her hands. "Do go on."

"I am not yet much further on in translation, Mother, but I can tell you that de Lorris goes on to portray characters like Felony, Villainy, Avarice, Envy and Sorrow and he does it so wondrously well, with such lusty words, that you can see people who are like that! Such as Felony who was:

"Like an old woman afraied,
Wrinkled foule was her visage
And grimacing for spiteful rage
with her nose snorted up for trouble!

"Or Sorrow who:

"Well was seyn in hir colour
That she had lived in languor
Her semed to have the jaundice
That made her ful yellow and nothing bright."

His father smiled at this and said: "So that was why you were study-ing the crowd when I arrived, to see if you could find any of these characters!"

Geoffrey laughed: "Well, not exactly, Father, but I do find people interesting. You can learn a lot about them from their looks and the way they hold themselves. And, you see, that's what I like about de Lorris: he is so keen in his portraits."

"And have you been able to recite any of this to the Countess?" asked his mother.

"Not my translations, yet. But I have on some evenings recited a number of French lyrics and I've read some of the story of the 'Romance of the Rose' in French and told some more of the story. I'm not sure enough yet of my verses to air them."

"Well, I'm sure it will not be long before you get your chance, Geoffrey," put in his father. "Just you keep it up. We need to hear these things in our language, not just in French or Latin, and that goes for the Church as well as the Court, in my view!"

Agnes Chaucer put her hands to her cheeks in mock surprise at such blasphemy but she knew well enough her husband's Lollard tendencies.

"I think it is time we retired to bed," she said tactfully, before he expounded further. "Thank you, Geoffrey. I really enjoyed that. Sleep well!" and taking her husband's arm, drew him to the stairs.

Geoffrey sat half-dozing in the warmth of the kitchen with the large black and white mouser draped across his knees, his legs throbbing in tune with her loud purring. He had arrived at Hatfield House three days ago on a snowy December afternoon with Prince Lionel's steward and a small party to get the house ready for the arrival of the Prince and Countess. They were to spend Christmas here and already there was a lightness of mood in the air at the prospect. The rooms had been aired and allocated, and now Geoffrey was taking a well-earned break in one of his favourite places: the snugness of the kitchen!

He was glad to have come to rest. It seemed as if he had been sitting on a horse since he had left his parents in London in June. The Countess and her retinue had been on the move ever since – like sheep on the moors always seeking fresh pastures – never staying in one place for more than a night or two. And then, in November, following the death of the King's mother, Queen Isabella, he had been sent to Castle Rising to help settle up the tallies and draw up the exchequer accounts for her household.

The castle, where she had been kept for so long since her downfall with Mortimer, was set on a bleak shore by the flat seas of the Wash, near where King John was said to have lost his treasure in some treacherous swamp in 1215. Geoffrey had thought it a wonder that the Queen had lived for so long in such a place. But for the big skies, the rich wildlife, the calls of the curlews and dunlin and, on some evenings, the spreading russet of the westering sun, the two weeks he had spent there would have blighted his soul. And the whipping wind from the North Sea and the cold stone of the place would have frozen his heart had buxom Mary, the cook's wench, not warmed his bed at night. Forward and coarse she may have been, but her lusty joy had taught him more than all the courtly phrases of love and romance. He could not have come to manhood with a better or more willing partner.

He roused himself from these memories at the sound of the Steward's call and went out to join him in the passage outside.

"Chaucer," he called. "We will have to make more dispositions. A herald has arrived to say that Prince John, Earl of Richmond, is to be expected next week and will be staying with us over Christmas. Fortunately, he is younger than Prince Lionel and not married so he does not yet keep a large retinue."

Geoffrey followed him out and across the cobbled yard towards the south wing of the house, where they began to inspect and make arrangements for the rooms. He mused on the news. He knew that Prince John was the one commonly called John of Gaunt because he had been born in Ghent when King Edward and his Queen were there making friendly overtures to the Flemings in 1340. He had often wondered why Lionel was not called 'Lionel of Antwerp' since that was his birthplace. Odd that the place of birth stuck to the one and not the other. And, since he was but a year older than himself, it would be a chance to take stock of this younger Prince.

John sat astride Sorrel, his black stallion, moving easily in his high saddle to the horse's swaying rhythm and listening to the sound of the clopping hooves in the puddles. He had left the Bishop's Palace in Lincoln with his retinue that morning and had stopped off at the Old Hall, Gainsborough, on the banks of the Trent, to visit one of his tenants, Sir George Purvis, and to gather some fresh fish for the forthcoming Yuletide Festival. Now they had left the River Torme behind them and were riding up on the moors above Hatfield Woodhouse.

It was a sullen, sodden day with low cloud and clinging soft rain. It had been an unhurried, easy journey but John was eager now to get to his brother's house at Hatfield and the warm welcome that no doubt awaited them. As they moved along towards the village, his mind went back to that other Christmas when he had descended down to Newcastle with his father to meet his army on the way to teach the Scots a lesson. He smiled to himself at the thought of how proud he had been to be in the King's close circle and how callow and earnest he was then. Now with his own retinue and household, his tenancies to administer and his regular place at Court, he felt more assured.

And he knew that Lionel, with his young wife, kept a good table and would likely have a lively house at Christmastide: less formal than at the court at Windsor with fewer eyes to pry and tongues to wag. It should be fun. He urged his horse to a gentle canter and took the lead down the last slope and into the approach to Hatfield House.

Geoffrey was together with Philippa, helping her to fold some linen sheets, when they first saw John. She had asked him to help her pull the sheets tight and to smooth them so as to straighten out the creases before putting them away in the linen cupboard, which backed onto the kitchen and caught the warmth from the ovens to air the linen. Geoffrey was glad to help.

He liked Philippa. She was a sturdy, no-nonsense girl who, despite being his junior, upbraided him at times for dreaming and not paying attention when he should have been listening to the Countess or one of her ladies. Philippa had a stern eye for manners and proper behaviour and seemed to have to taken it upon herself to keep him up to scratch. He imagined that if he had had a sister she would have been rather like that and he would have felt a similar fondness and protective instinct.

They heard the sound of hooves on the cobbles in the yard outside. As they looked out they saw this straight-backed, tall, lean figure swing easily from the saddle and hand the reins to Joshua, the groom, who had run out from the stables opposite.

"Give him a brisk rub down and some warm mash. He'll be chilled else, after this steady wetting," they heard him tell Joshua. Then he thwacked the horse's neck with the flat of his hand, pulled his ear and turned towards the front of the house.

"And the others too, mind," he called over his shoulder before he disappeared round the corner.

"Well. So that's Prince John, is it?" said Philippa. "He's not so much like his brother Lionel, is he?"

"There's a fair resemblance of face and they've a similar way of walking but this one is taller, thinner and, somehow, he's sterner, don't you think?" replied Geoffrey.

"Yes, Lionel has a better figure and he smiles a lot and has an open face. His brother's legs may be longer but they are much thinner."

Geoffrey smiled at this womanly observation. "John's face is longer too and he has the King's pointed chin. Perhaps that is why he seems to have a serious air. But he has come to the right place. Lionel will soon jolly him up if need be!"

It was Christmas Eve. The whole household was gathered in the great hall. The royal brothers and the Countess sat at one end on a raised dais behind an oak refectory table, flanked by their two senior knights and three of the ladies from Countess Elizabeth's household, including Marie de Saint Hilaire who was seated next to Prince John. They made a fine sight: the ladies with their soft silks and satins embroidered with gold and silver thread and gem-studded hip girdles; the princes in their richly coloured tunics, both with their chests quartered with the royal leopards besides their own insignias; the knights displaying their lord's arms under velvet fur-edged capes and with parti-coloured hose in rich red and blue hues.

Geoffrey remembered such fanciful dressing that he had seen among his father's guests from the City of London. He could see now how the fads and fashions at Court were caught up and copied by aspiring merchants and gentry. And, with the French King in their midst, there was a lively rivalry between English and Continental styles. But Geoffrey was not grumbling, nor envious. He, like the rest of the household, had this Christmas been given, according to status, the makings of new clothes – some velvets and finely woven plaids for the men and satins and linen and, for some, ribbons and buttons, for the women. His allotment was fairly homespun, brown and plain, which suited him. He was no peacock.

Philippa caught his eye. He knew she thought he was dreaming when he had these detached moments of watching. He smiled, shrugged and renewed his attack on the chicken leg on his platter. They were sitting among the rest of the household on forms at trestle tables arranged around the sides of the hall which left a space in the middle for dancers and entertainers to perform. The hall was filled with the bubble of excited talk and laughter mingled with the soft strains coming from the viols in the minstrel gallery.

When the food was finished and the platters and baskets of leavings had been cleared away, the hall hushed as, at a signal from the Countess, two of her ladies came forward into the central space. After a dimpled curtsey to the Princes, they began a roundelay, singing in unison at first and then in a delicate counterpoint, their sweet sound carrying through the hall like spring water tinkling over stones. As they finished, with a bob to the top table, a page left the Countess' side and came towards Chaucer.

"Geoffrey, the Countess bids you come forward and present some of your stories from the 'Romance' and your new verses in English."

Geoffrey was not surprised. The Countess had hinted at this

when he had last read some verses to her. He stood and walked slowly up to the top table and bowed low with a flourish of his arm before the Princes and the Countess and then stepped back and to one side so that he could address the whole company.

"My Lords, my Lady, friends," he began in a clear and practised voice. "Let me tell you briefly the story of the 'Romance of the Rose' and then I will read some of the verses I have translated. It is a love poem which is well known in France. It was written over one hundred years ago by Guillaume de Lorris as a gift to the lady of his heart."

There were smiles as Geoffrey put his hand over his heart and sighed with upturned eyes. They knew he tended to act the part when he was reciting.

"He dreams that on a lovely morning in May he comes to the Garden of Love where he meets the God of Love who causes him to fall in love with a Rosebud by shooting an arrow into his heart. He is eaten up with yearning and the pangs of love. But others in the garden are jealous. They build a fortress and imprison Rosebud. He is shut out and so loses her and is left with sleepless nights to wander away in sadness."

To which Geoffrey added, while looking fiercely at the women around the hall, "*And that is what happens when cruel damsels reject their lovers!*"

The audience answered with cries of "Ooohh!" in mock surprise.

"The God of Love was also called Mirth," Geoffrey continued, "and Guillaume describes him as:

> *"Ful fair was Mirth, ful long and high;*
> *A fairer man I nevere sigh*
> *As round as apple was his face*
> *Ful ruddy and whit in every place…*
> *His shouldres of a large bredth*
> *And smallish was he in his girth*
> *He seemed like a portraiture*
> *So noble was he of stature.*

48

"Dame Gladness who was his wife
That syngeth so well with glad courage
That from when she was twelve year of age
She of her love grant him made.
Sir Mirth her by the finger had
Dancing and she him also…
Great love was atwixt these two."

As he recited this, Chaucer twirled round in a few light steps with his arm held high and his fingers extended.

"Thanne when I into the garden went
The savour of the roses sweet
Me smot right to the herte-rote
Among the rosebuds I chose one
For it so well illumined
With colour red and as well fined
As nature could it make fair
And it hath leves well four pair.

"The God of Love when he saw how that
I had chosen so eagerly
The rosebud…
He took an arrow full sharply whet
And in his bow when it was set
He straight up to his ear drawth
The strong bow that was so tough
And shot at me so wondir smarte
That through mine eye into mine heart
The arrow smote and deep it wente.

"When I was hurt thus, in a swoond
I fell down flat unto the ground."

Geoffrey, miming to the verse, had been reeling around holding his hand to his eye and now fell full length to the ground. His audience roared, banged the table and whistled their enjoyment. At the top table John turned to his brother.

"Who is this fellow?" asked John. Lionel chuckled.

"His name is Geoffrey Chaucer. Elizabeth took him in as a page in her household. She dotes on him for his verses. He's a young man of many parts, though I've not seen him in such comic vein before. He promises well as he can render in both French and English and he has some knowledge of Italian too, I believe."

"His father is a City vintner," added Marie de Saint Hilaire in a whisper in John's ear, "and trades with Burgundy and Genoa. He has a house in Thames Street nearby your royal mother's mansion. He was put forward to the Countess by my countryman, Sir Paon de Roet, the same as is Herald to the Queen."

As they were talking, Chaucer told the next part of the story: how the poet had learnt the finer points of love from Sir Mirth; how Venus had taken pity on him and helped him win a kiss of his Rosebud; but then how Wicked Tongue, Shame and Jealousy took over the garden and built a castle round it so that:

> "…*no gluttons*
> *Shudde stele his roses or boutons*
> *The roses weren assured all*
> *Defenced with the stronge wall.*
> *But I – alas – now mourne shall*
> *Because I was without the wall.*
>
> "*It is of Love, as of Fortune.*
> *That changeth ofte, and nyl continue*
> *Now frend now foe shalt her feel*
> *For in a twynklyng turneth her wheel.*
> *She can writhe her head away*
> *That is the concours of her play.*
> *A fool is he that would her trust!*

"And when the night is come, anoon
A thousand angers shall come upon
For when thou wenest for to sleep
So full of pain shalt thou crepe,
Start in thy bed about full wide
And turn ful oft on every side,
Now downward groft, anow upright
And walowe in woo the long night.
Thine arms shalt thou spreade a-bed
As man in werre were defeated
Then shall thee come a resemblance
Of hir shape and her semblance
Naked between thine arms there
All sothfastness as though it were,
The which, in soth, nys but fable.

"For it ne shall no while last
Then shalt thou sigh and wepe fast
And say 'Dear God, what thing is this?
My drem is turned all amys.'"

Geoffrey got up from the floor, where he had been writhing with the torments of a sleepless lover, turned towards the top table and bowed deeply. There were shouts of "Bravo" and clapping. The Countess beamed at Geoffrey, nodded her head and called after him, "Thank you!" as he walked away to his seat and the fulsome back-slapping of his fellows.

He caught sight of Philippa's brimming face and thought he saw a slight puzzle in her eyes. Afterwards she told him she thought the verses were beautiful but asked why he had acted the fool so.

"But it is Christmas and I thought some clowning would fit the occasion otherwise the words alone would sound precious."

"Yes! Well, it was good fun but you should beware being dubbed as a court jester, Geoffrey. Your verses are much more worthy than that."

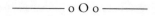

Chaucer was down in the stone-flagged cellar helping Jacob the cellarman make some order out of the chaos caused by the heavy raids on stocks over the Christmas festivities. They had neatly stacked all the empty beer barrels under the trap ready for them to be hoisted when the draymen arrived. Alongside, they had arranged the smaller wine casks and empty flagons.

Jacob paused to ease his back and brush his brow with his forearm, for it was warm work even in the cool of the cellar. He grinned at Geoffrey, "My, by the looks of this lot, there'll have been sore heads this Yuletide, I shouldn't wonder!"

"Aye," agreed Geoffrey, "Prince Lionel keeps a generous household at times like this and you are right, Jacob. There's been some frolicking these three days. But it is back to normal now. We've to sort out the wine for the Prince's table tonight and tomorrow, and we might as well make some handy for next week too."

As they moved towards the rows of casks at the back of the cellar, the door above them was thrown open and, with a call of "Hullo there!", Prince John came nimbly down the steps, screwing up his face to adjust his eyes to the gloom.

"Ah, Geoffrey Chaucer," he called, "I was told you'd be down here."

"My Lord, this is a rare visit," replied Geoffrey, as he looked up at the Prince who stood before him, slim, erect and nearly a head taller. "I am helping Jacob, our cellarman, tidy things up after the festivities."

"Just so," acknowledged John and, with a nod to Jacob, went on: "I hear you have inherited a nose for a good wine, Geoffrey. I've a request to make. It is Marie de Saint Hilaire's birthday tomorrow and I would like some out-of-the-ordinary wine at table to toast the occasion in her honour." And, smiling easily into Geoffrey's face, asked, "What can you suggest?"

Geoffrey paused, looked at Jacob and rubbed his chin for a moment.

"Well, my Lord, if you want something not often found on an English table, we do have two small casks of a wine from Castile called Rioja. Jacob, do you get a goblet. We will draw some for the Prince to taste."

Turning to John, he went on: "It is a deep red with a fuller body than a Bordeaux and lingers on the tongue marvellously well."

Jacob handed a half-full goblet to the Prince who raised it to his nose and sniffed deeply over the rim. "My, it has a strong bouquet," he exclaimed and then, taking a sip, rolled it round his mouth. "I can taste the whole grape: skin, pips as well as the flesh of the fruit. It has a distinctly earthy quality. This is perfect."

"We will decant some flagons directly and let them settle upstairs in time for the table tomorrow evening, my Lord."

"I am well suited," replied John, before asking: "Does your father maintain my brother's cellar?"

"No, my Lord," replied Geoffrey. "Except that he does send special lines on occasion when he has them, like the Rioja you have just tasted."

"Ah! I thought so. Then, I must join this club!" replied John with a laugh. "I will send my steward to see him. His business is in Thames Street near the Queen's house, is it not?"

"Yes, my Lord – and I am sure he will be most pleased by your custom."

John made to go, but paused and turned round to face Geoffrey. Catching hold of his arm and looking directly at him, he said earnestly: "I enjoyed your recitation. You must continue your writing in English. It is paramount that we distinguish ourselves from the French if we are to flourish as a nation, and you are an ambassador to that cause in your writing. Keep at it – and send me copies, if you will."

As he bounded up the steps and out of the cellar, Geoffrey for once was left speechless.

Jacob, who had been watching, chuckled, and then asked: "And who is this lady that has taken his fancy?"

"Oh," said Geoffrey, "she's taken his fancy alright and has been sharing his bed these past few nights. She comes from Hainault, the same country as the Queen, and is one of the Countess' guests. Probably, Prince Lionel had her invited to keep John amused."

"It sounds a bit more than amusement to me. Wouldn't be surprised at a wedding not long off," said Jacob.

It was Geoffrey's turn to chuckle. "Goodness no, Jacob. That's not the way of things. King Edward will expect to arrange a marriage for John which will make an alliance to England's advantage. I have heard that the daughter of the Count of Flanders is a possible bride for John and that would be important for our interests in the wool trading. This Marie is but a plaything!"

"But what if she falls for child?"

"Oh, she and the child would be provided for. That also is the way of things! Prince John has a lot of his father in him. He is ambitious and shows signs of being hard-headed. He will follow his father in making a match which adds to his power, you wait and see. But he holds to the code of chivalry."

"Aye, I can see that. But you seem to have caught his favour, Master Geoffrey, and a friend at Court is worth a lot, isn't it?" asked Jacob, unaware of his surprising play on words.

Geoffrey smiled. He was fond of the older man who, although unschooled, was shrewder than many of his betters. He was broad and deep-chested like the barrels he wrestled with and his brown eyes twinkled out in merriment from his shining apple-cheeked face. He put his arm round his shoulder and said: "Yes, maybe, Jacob, but it's not wise to put too much trust in the word of princes."

Little did he know how soon the word of that friend would be honoured.

Chapter Four

KING EDWARD WAS seated at a walnut table in his privy chamber at Westminster. He had returned to London just yesterday, having spent the festive season feasting and hunting at Windsor. Now there was a backlog of state affairs to attend to. He seemed to have been receiving petitions, signing and putting his seal to documents all day and he was weary of it. He skimmed the last of them, as was his wont, for although he had the gist spelt out for him and some clauses read to him, he never passed a document without this last personal check. As he dipped his quill and scratched his authority on the parchment, his chamberlain approached.

"Sire, the Pope's envoy has arrived from Rome and beseeches an audience."

Edward, grateful for the interruption, nevertheless said: "Inform his Grace I am engrossed in urgent business with state papers and ask him to be so good as to wait. Sweeten his wait with wine and canapés – and summon the Duke of Lancaster to join me forthwith."

Henry, Duke of Lancaster, soon joined him for he had not long left the royal presence after discussing affairs in France. He bowed his head briefly as he approached.

"Ah, Henry. There's news from Rome. Maybe at last we will have some word of support from His Holiness on our claim to the French throne. I want you to join me when I give him audience and to mark his words. You know how silver-tongued these clerical diplomats are!"

"At your pleasure, sire," replied the Duke, as the King called the Chamberlain to usher in the papal envoy.

After kissing the royal hand and expressing fulsome greetings, the nuncio began his peroration about the sanctity of blood ties and the undoubted strength of King Edward's claim stemming from his royal mother's lineage as a princess of France. And since King John of

France was presently Edward's 'guest', His Holiness saw opportunity for John to be persuaded to name Edward as his legitimate successor.

At this, Edward turned in his chair towards Duke Henry who, quickly sensing the impatience behind the gesture, asked the nuncio: "And if that were so, would it be that King Edward's inheritance would have the blessed support of the Pope?"

"Surely so: since His Holiness has made the suggestion," replied the nuncio with well-practised unction. "And, sire," addressing the King directly, "as further proof of His Holiness' bounteous regard, I have brought his dispensation of the consanguinity of your royal son John and the Duke's daughter Blanche. There is no bar to their marriage."

After further felicitous expressions and bowings, the papal envoy withdrew.

"Ha, the cheek of it!" exploded the King with a laugh and a slap of his thigh.

"He sweetens an empty pill with your fair Blanche! But there's cleverness in it. If King John will see it my way, his weight surely tilts the scales in my favour! But we might yet have to take arms to France to prove it."

He strode over to the table and took off the gold circlet crown he had put on to receive the papal nuncio.

"But enough of that, good cousin. We have a wedding to arrange! Let's make it a right royal occasion!"

John stood inside the arched stone doorway of the Savoy Palace, took off his riding gloves, undid the gold neck clasp to his heavy cloak and handed them to a young page.

He had been before to the Savoy, the magnificent white stone palace on the Thames founded by the brother of Edward I, the first Duke of Lancaster, and lately rebuilt by his uncle Henry, the present Duke. He had attended banquets and feasts, sometimes accompanying his father, for Duke Henry was a lavish host who devoted some of his spoils from his campaigns abroad to celebrations at home.

John remembered the first such occasion well – when he had attended with his father the grand banquet to mark the capture of the King of France by the army led by the Black Prince and Duke Henry.

But on this occasion he felt ill at ease, tense and nervous. For he was to meet his cousin Blanche alone, face to face for the first time since the papal approval of their marriage. The scene on the battlements of Lancaster Castle came to him when she had surprised him in his grief at the death of Sir Ranulf. He smiled at the memory. Would she remember? It was nine years ago – half a lifetime! He had seen her only a few times since, though never alone. Yet he had a strong sense of her presence for she had grown to be tall and graceful, with flowing golden hair, but with an alluring richness of form and full measure of womanly beauty and with a serenity which affected those around her. He wondered how she felt at this prospect of marriage to him.

For himself, John knew that royal marriages were made in the market place of politics and commerce. It was commonplace in Europe for kings and dukes to strengthen their position and power through dynastic alliances abroad or at home. Had he himself not been paired with the daughter of the Count of Flanders until the match fell through over the details of the settlement, to the chagrin of the City merchants and the wool trade? John could see the shrewd-ness of his father's choice. The Duke of Lancaster was the greatest feudal baron in the kingdom. Yet he had no male heirs. Blanche's older sister, Matilda, was already married to the Duke of Zealand. If Blanche were matched with another foreign prince, the wealth and power of her inheritance would be strapped to foreign loyalties. Better to tie it in with a royal knot.

His nervousness increased. Surely her father would have told her the rules of this game? But she was still a pawn. What if her heart was given elsewhere and she bitterly resented him? Cool logic could outweigh hot emotion. Romps with a willing maid were one thing: a cold marriage bed would be no comfort.

The inner door opened and the Duke strode in, hand outstretched and eyes ablaze in welcome. "John. Welcome! Blanche is with her mother and awaits you. Go to her with our blessing!"

He led John down a passageway and pointed to a heavy oak door at the end. Approaching the threshold, John drew himself up, took a deep breath, knocked firmly twice and then slowly pushed the door open. As he entered, he saw Blanche standing by the fireplace facing her mother, the Duchess, Lady Isabel. They drew apart as he entered.

The Duchess moved quickly towards him with arms open and, with a broad smile, said: "My Lord, this is indeed a happy day. You are truly welcome. Come, Blanche awaits you. I will withdraw," and with a brief curtsey she left the room.

John moved forward, his eyes searching Blanche's face. She came towards him and bobbed in a deep curtsey. John was dismayed.

"No, no!" he cried. "Please, no bowing and scraping between us," and he moved forward to take her hands in his. Looking fully into her face, he was transfixed. The deep clear blue of her eyes fringed with dark lashes held him so that when he began to speak he lost his words and faltered. "I…"

Seeing his confusion, Blanche bowed her head and took the lead, saying softly as she held tightly to his hands: "My dear Lord John. I really am greatly blessed. I, Blanche, do plight thee my troth, as God is my witness."

John drew her closer to him, lifted her chin and, looking into her eyes, said: "Nay, the blessing is mine. And I, John, do plight thee, Blanche, my troth as God is my witness." Then he leaned forward and threaded onto the third finger of her left hand a large ruby ring and added: "There, 'tis done: proof of this compact for all to see!"

She, likewise, drew forward his left hand and slipped on a diamond encrusted ring. As she looked up at him, John leaned forward and they kissed lightly before stepping apart, both somewhat flustered by the happening.

Five months later, on Sunday, 29th May 1359, John was standing with his brother Lionel before the altar rail in Queen Philippa's Chapel at Reading, waiting for his bride, Blanche of Lancaster, to arrive and process down the aisle to his side. He was richly attired in a purple silk tunic with sleeves slashed and embroidered with silver thread, the three royal leopards worked in gold on his right breast counterpointed on the opposite breast by his own arms as Earl of Richmond. He wore a black leather hip belt which sparkled with jewels woven into the leather and a short black cape edged with white fur which hung loosely over his shoulders. This was set off handsomely by his long slim legs in parti-coloured red and blue silk hose and matching dyed leather shoes with fashionable tapering toes.

John was standing erect, relaxed with feet apart, following with his eyes the tracery of the arched ceiling above. He felt the blood running powerfully through his veins. He was alive, eager and excited. He had met Blanche several times since they had exchanged betrothal vows. They had walked together in the garden of the Savoy and on three occasions had contested together indoors at chess. He had laughed with her at shared items of gossip which always seemed to buzz like a cloud of gnats around the Court. She had surprised him with her knowledge of Europe and of the codes and proprieties of chivalry. They had talked of music and poetry and recited verses together, including some by Chaucer whom Blanche said she was eager to meet. He had been undone by her fierce concentration at chess and determination to find solutions to his bold moves so that on each occasion he was vanquished.

But most of all, John realised, as he gazed upwards, that he was gaining a partner who was shrewd in judgement, a natural peacemaker, wondrously loyal and giving. No wonder that he felt eager: he rejoiced in the destiny that gave him a consort he could so admire and one, he already knew, he could love.

He was startled out of his reverie by the piercing notes of a fanfare, which announced the arrival of the bridal party. He stole a glance around to see Blanche, on the arm of her father, beginning the slow procession down the aisle. She looked radiant in an ivory silk satin gown with full skirt and train embroidered with pearls into shapes of peacocks' feathers.

The low-cut, close-fitting bodice revealed the fulsome swell of her breasts and the inward curve of her slim waist. An ermine-lined mantle in dark green velvet, which was edged with red silk with the Lancastrian emblem of a large red rose crocheted in the centre, trailed from her shoulders.

A second double fanfare rasped rawly round the Chapel, echoing back from the stone walls like sea spray off rocks. With it, King Edward and Queen Philippa entered and, in the hush, followed the bride and her father down the aisle. John could hear the rustle of silk as she neared and the faint waft of her sweet perfume. Then she was standing by him. Their awareness of each other was drawn away by a cough as Thomas de Chynham, the priest, moved forward and began the marriage ceremony.

"Dearly Beloved, we are gathered here in the sight of God Almighty to join together in holy matrimony this man, John, Prince of this realm and son of our beloved Sovereign and this woman, Blanche, cherished daughter of our noble Seneschal of England, Henry, Duke of Lancaster, Earl of Derby, Lincoln and Leicester…"

John's focus on the words wavered until he felt a sharp nudge from his brother Lionel and he recovered in time to pledge himself with a stout, "I do!" Then he watched with tenderness as Blanche followed intently the words of the priest and quietly replied with her own, "I do".

De Chynham's ringing announcement that they were now man and wife released John. He clasped Blanche to him and kissed her fulsomely, only drawing back when he felt the wetness of her tears on his face.

"Oh my Lord, 'tis but overjoy that's got to my eyes!" she said.

With that, they turned and followed the priest, knelt before him and received the bread and wine of communion and his blessing before turning again to face the congregation to be engulfed in their joyous blessing too.

The next morning, after a night of intimate and urgent coupling, the fires of passion still glowing in their faces, John and Blanche lay in the marriage bed lazily reviewing the array of wedding gifts which had been presented to them.

"Look, John, at this beautiful girdle from your father. I swear it is too fine for me to wear. I shall be afraid the jewels will fall out," said Blanche as she handed the belt to him.

John inspected the rubies, emeralds and pearls woven into the belt.

"It is indeed richly garnished and a fair expression of the King's regard for you, Blanche. He will expect you to wear it but you need not fear shoddy workmanship. This is the finest craftsmanship from Tuscany."

Blanche continued to rummage in the pile of presents, as a kitten with a new toy.

"And look, John: a pair of silver buckles… and, see here, this tripod with silver cup!"

"Yes," replied John. "And this set of chased gold goblets from my brother Prince Edward. They will grace our table splendidly."

They were interrupted by a soft knock at the chamber door. Rosalind, Blanche's close maid, entered with lowered eyes and a quick bob.

"Beg pardon, my Lady, but you asked me to rouse you in time for the journey to London in preparation for your father's celebrations at the Savoy tomorrow eve."

"Yes, Rose. Thank you," and turning to her husband began, "my Lord…" but John quickly seized the moment: "And we must be prompt for that for we are the principal guests, even in the presence of my father!" and moving lithely from the bed said: "I will withdraw, my Lady, and make my separate preparations."

Taking hold of Blanche's hand, he bowed his head, brushed his lips across it and left the room, calling for James, his page.

At the Savoy there was feverish activity and excitement. The Duke of Lancaster was bent on a lavish celebration of his daughter's wedding. Yeomen, foresters and falconers from his estates had been carrying out his detailed orders to plenish his tables. They had brought in: hogs, deer, prime beef; pheasants, partridge, plovers; eels, trout and lampreys. His cooks had made pastries, pies and sweet confections. His cellarman had scoured the vintners for especial wines and vintages, not just lusty reds from Bordeaux but also rare varieties from Italy and Spain and hocks from Bavaria.

All was now in place. The warm and dry early summer had encouraged Duke Henry into making it an *alfresco* feast in the palace gardens. Sides of pork, beef and venison were turning slowly on wrought iron spits over glowing wood fires with game hanging alongside. Trestle tables were set out on the lawn edges laden with fruits, pastries and sweetmeats, pallets and goblets and sweet-watered hand bowls. The tables were garlanded with May-time flowers and scented herbs. Torches fixed on the walls and in iron stakes around the garden were ready to light when dusk crept in.

Away from the fires, a raised dais provided secluded space for the royal party: King Edward and Queen Philippa, with John and his bride, the royal brothers – Princes Edward, Lionel and Edmund with their wives – and Duke Henry and Lady Isabel. At the farther end opposite, a platform had been built with scaffolding to act as a gallery for the Duke's minstrels, for, with the Duchess, he had arranged entertainments with singing, dancing, juggling as well as music and – especially to please Blanche – some recitation by Geoffrey Chaucer.

The crews of men and servants who had created this sumptuous arena had withdrawn to the kitchen yard where they were now tucking into the food and ale which was reward for their honest labours. Their place had been taken by squires, pages and maids all dressed in the Lancaster livery, who were standing in their allotted places awaiting the arrival of the guests. The Duke's chamberlain, eagle-eyed and sharp-tongued if need be, filled the main doorway, ready to search out any hint of disorder.

As the first guests arrived he signalled to the minstrels who began to play some traditional airs with a lute taking up the melody backed by harp and fiddle. For later, the minstrel master had prepared a programme of ballads and rondeaux using a variety of voices and instruments in the French style, but for now, this light music was enough and wafted like a scented breeze round the assembling company.

Soon, John and Blanche were engulfed in a melee of welcome and well-wishing as more guests arrived. The manner of greeting varied. Initially some of the lords and ladies were deferential and formal, but with the arrival of John's three brothers, gaiety and laughter abounded as each in turn claimed Blanche in a brotherly embrace and kiss. On the notes of a short fanfare, everyone hushed and turned to the doorway. The King and Queen, escorted by the Duke and Duchess, entered. There was a swish of silk as the whole company curtseyed and bowed. Then King Edward blessed Blanche with his own embrace and the excited chatter resumed.

Pages moved among the groups, offering wine and canapés from silver trays. The Queen, radiant in a deep red gown, stayed talking with Blanche and her mother while the King was in discussion with the Lord Mayor of London and Sir Charles Chandos.

The Mayor, Sheriffs and Aldermen had proclaimed a tournament to celebrate the royal wedding. Twenty-four knights wearing the City arms would enter the lists and undertake on behalf of the City to hold the field against all challengers. The King was eager to know the arrangements and was pleased to hear that the tournament would last for three days and be held at Spitalfields. He thanked the Lord Mayor for this token of loyalty and support and said he would attend personally. The Lord Mayor bowed, said that the citizens would be delighted by the royal presence and withdrew.

The King immediately summoned his son Edward, the Black Prince, to him.

"Edward! You've heard of this tournament that the City have proclaimed?"

"Yes, sire. It is a handsome gesture."

"Well, I reckon we can make capital on this and prove our might. How would it be if the King and his sons took the field for the City – incognito, of course?"

"What a bold stroke, sire!" exclaimed the Prince. "My arm itches already at the challenge," and then with a grin added, "but are you sure you can prise John away from his bride?"

The King chuckled and then nodded decisively: "We'll do it. You tell the others and I will get Chandos to make the arrangements privily."

The Duke, who had been watching, moved forward and asked leave for the food to be served. The King, now in high spirits and suddenly hungry, clapped him on the back and took his place on the dais where he directed his squire in his choice of meats and other refreshments to be brought to him.

While the guests moved around filling their platters with whatever they fancied from the spread, there was opportunity aplenty for mingling and talking. Pages and squires moved between them filling drinking vessels and replenishing finger bowls as they were used. The Chamberlain maintained his watchful stance. He had already had the torches lit and these spread a warm yellow light which was reflected back from the white stone of the Palace. Now, after a word with the Duke, he signalled for the tables to be cleared and chairs to be set in a semi-circle for the entertainments.

Suddenly a team of acrobats and tumblers bounced into the arena with whoops and yells and thrilled the audience with a seamless whirl of jumps, falls, leaps, wheels, turns, tableaux and pyramids. As they withdrew, six jugglers took their place, each seemingly vying with the others in the dexterity of the loops and heights they could achieve, before forming a circle to juggle daringly with flaming torches, each with their partner opposite.

While the acrobats and jugglers were performing, the minstrels were taking a breather. Geoffrey Chaucer, who had walked from his parents' house in Thames Street, stood talking with the minstrel master, Andrew Destrer from Bruges.

"Yes, *monsieur*, I have included some new pieces that I learnt at the last annual school in Brussels where I was attending with many of the most famous minstrel masters. I am pleased to have some pieces by Machaut. Perhaps you will be interested in that?"

"But of course!" replied Geoffrey. "Guillaume de Machaut from Rheims is one of the most inspiring poets and musicians of our times. Was he there? Did you meet him?" he asked eagerly.

"Oh no. He does not travel now, but there were some who had worked with him and so were able to translate his ideas to us."

"What of his will you be playing?" asked Chaucer.

"I have chosen a ballade called 'De toutes fleurs' which has a single tenor voice accompanied by three instruments, one pitched above and two below the voice. And then I have a very clever piece – a rondeau, called 'Ma fin est mon commencement'."

"Ah! I have heard of that," said Chaucer. "Isn't that one of his amusing puzzles which read exactly the same from either end?"

"Indeed so," smiled Destrer.

"Then play well, my friend. I am sure everyone will enjoy this as much as I will."

And indeed, the minstrels' performance was well received. As many as eight voices at times combined with a full range of instruments including a psaltery, citole and, in one of the more doleful pieces, a rebec, as well as lutes, harps, flute and fiddles. The Machaut pieces, delicately performed with the tenor voice counterpointing with the three instruments as a finale, were rapturously acclaimed – not least by the King and Queen Philippa.

Then Duke Henry, flushed with pleasure at this success, called upon Chaucer to present some of his writings. Geoffrey came forward into the circle and bowed low before the royal party. Then he stepped back and quietly looked round the audience, gathering himself and their attention before beginning with two poems about the raptures and ravages of enduring love, which he had translated from the French. Then after a dramatic pause he announced: "And this I have written to celebrate the qualities of my Lady, Countess Blanche, and in tribute to my Lord, Prince John:

"Among all the ladies everyone
Sooth to say I saw one
That was like none other
That as the summer's sun bright
Is fairer, clearer and hath more light
Than any other planet in heaven
The moon or the stars seven
For all the world has she
Surmounted them all of beauty.

"I've seen her dance so comily
Carol and sing sweetly
Laugh and play so womanly
And look so debonairly
So goodly speak and friendly
That certain I know that evermore
I'll not see so blissful a treasure.

"And good fair White she's called
That is my Lady's name alright."

Chaucer finished with a deep bow to the King and Queen and then moved a step towards John and Blanche, bowed deeply again to them before standing up, turning round and raising a hand to the clapping audience. He would then have retreated to rejoin the minstrel master but Duke Henry took him by the arm and led him to where Blanche was beaming widely. He bowed again before her as she said: "Master Chaucer, I am so pleased to meet you and to thank you for your so sweetly wrought words. May it be that you could copy me the verses so that I have them to read myself?"

"Why surely, my Lady. Take this copy I have already made for you."

Chaucer nodded his head as Prince John stepped forward and said: "You have honoured us well, Geoffrey. Again, our thanks!"

For over a week, there had been much activity at Spitalfields, the wide open space just outside the eastern entry into London at Aldgate. Under the direction of the City's Clerk of Works, Hugh Gresham, carpenters, smiths and labourers had been marking out and setting up the arena for the Grand Tournament proclaimed by the City. First they had chosen the site for the tilting – a good level space topped with firm dry turf. Then Gresham had measured a line of three chains' length, making sure the orientation was from north-west to south-east so that the sun would not dazzle either contestant. Then he had set in along the line stout posts four feet high, six feet apart and joined these together with a railing along the whole sixty-six feet length.

The Clerk of Works checked each post and rail personally. His reputation was in these stakes. They must be able to keep the jousters separate – one each side of the railings – as they rode at each other and be secure enough to withstand any buffeting from the horses. Then he marked out a clear space of a further forty yards at each end where the horses would gather and begin their charge. Around this would be gathered armourers, saddlers and smiths, who would be needed to service the contestants. On one side, six sets of steps were erected where the armour-suited riders would mount and dismount their horses – unless they had been unhorsed in the joust!

Satisfied that they had established the focal point for the tournament, Gresham turned his attention to where the tiers of seating would be built. He made sure that the prime central position, from where royalty and City dignitaries would be watching, was correctly aligned with their backs to the sun and with the seats higher than the rail tops – near enough for a clear view but distanced enough to avoid any debris flying from the fray. He had ordered canvas in red and gold stripes to provide cover for the royal pavilion and plain canvas for the lesser nobles and merchants. Tough wooden tiers without cover would be put up for the populace on the opposite side.

Two flagpoles had been erected in front of the royal seating – one for the royal standard when the King or Queen were present – the other for the City coat of arms. At each side there was a yardarm which would display for each joust the insignia of the contestants. On the eve of the tournament, the final touch would be added with brightly coloured flags and bunting adorning the pavilions and tiers of seating.

Content with his preparations, Hugh Gresham paid off his workers but kept a select group with him to camp overnight as surety against any gangs of ruffians.

Next morning, Hugh Gresham watched the sun rise, spreading a golden flush across a cloudless sky. He walked the length of the arena, testing again the posts and rails.

"This dew has greased the grass," he said to one of his men. "Will it rob the horses of a foothold, I wonder?"

"Nay, Master, 'twill burn off with the sun, sure enough, long before they're ready, God willing."

"Yes, I'm sure you are right, Amos. I'm worrying overmuch! But we had better have some straw on hand for later in the day, in case the turf gets churned." And then added, as he turned round: "But come! Let's break our fast before the crowds arrive."

By midmorning, many of the seats in the open stands were filled. A regular procession of people had been streaming in through Aldgate, bringing bundles of food and drink with them, for they were in festive mood and bent on a full day's entertainment. Apart from the jousting, which would not begin until noon, there was plenty to enjoy. Jugglers and musicians, clowns, puppets, stilt-walkers and itinerants with performing pets had swarmed to the spot like bees to nectar. Soon appetites were whetted with the smells from braziers over which pies were warming and chicken, rabbit, hare and other meats were sizzling. Thirsts were quenched with ale from barrels set up behind the stands. Gossip flowed and speculation as to which nobles would defend the City's honour and where would the challengers be from. Rumour held that renowned knights from as far as Bavaria and Bohemia had come to match their skills against the English.

There would be the fun of watching the lords and ladies as they took their places in the stands opposite. There were fine clothes and fashions to wonder at. What new designs and extravagances, what new combinations of colours, what array of jewels would be seen? And then, above all, who would be there? Rumour had it that not only would the King and Queen be present but also the royal princes and their consorts. And there was the bride of John of Gaunt to appraise. But who else? Which ladies-in-waiting would accompany them – and which mistresses? Would Alice Perrers, known to be the King's mistress, be on view? The self-appointed cognoscenti in the crowd fed the speculation and kept the tongues wagging.

As noon approached there was an increase in the hustle and bustle in the two saddling enclosures at opposite ends of the arena. The deep-chested, thick-legged and well-haunched jousting horses – white, grey, black, brown – were being walked round or harnessed and girthed up with the solid high-backed saddles needed for support to steady the rider in deflecting blows from his opponent's lance. The sounds of smiths' hammering rang out as a shoe was shaped on an anvil or a dented piece of armour was mended.

The canvassed stands with their gilded guests were nearly full. Necks craned to see who was present and then, heralded by a strident fanfare, the royal standard was hoist and King Edward with his Queen, and with the newly-weds John and Blanche, appeared under their awning. A great volume of cheers, whistles, hurrahs and clapping greeted them. The citizens of London were bent on sharing the glory that their sovereign and his family brought to the nation, a feeling they had been indulging since the victory at Poitiers and the capture of the King of France. But Edward, the Black Prince, the victor at Poitiers, was not with them; nor were the other Princes, Lionel and Edmund. Maybe the day was reserved for John of Gaunt and Blanche of Lancaster.

There was no more time for puzzling over this. The tournament was to begin! Heralds with their tabards richly embroidered in gold and blue appeared from the ends of the arena leading out the first two contestants. They wheeled as they approached the centre and stopped in front of the King's pavilion.

The heralds raised their trumpets, blew a brief fanfare and then addressed the assembled company: "Your Highnesses, my Lords, Ladies, knights and people: be it known that His Worship the Lord Mayor of London with the Aldermen and Sheriffs have appointed twenty-four knights to uphold the honour of the City against any and all who come to make challenge in a chivalrous tourney.

"Each pair of knights will contest against each other in three courses. The winner will be decided by loss of horse or helmet or otherwise by the greater number of hits to the body."

And then, with the flourish of another fanfare, declared: "With the Grace of God's blessing: Let the tournament begin!"

The first two knights wheeled their horses and cantered away to opposite ends of the course where they wheeled again and stood ready to begin the charge at their opponent. The heralds' flags were held aloft. The knights closed their visors and straightened their lances out beyond their horse's head. The crowd hushed, waiting.

The flags flashed downwards. Rowels dug into flanks. The horses leapt forward, muscles rippling across their deep chests. The crowd roared. Hooves thundered. The tips of lances raced through the air ahead of the galloping horses. Then as they came abreast, there was a clash of metal, sparks flew as the lances struck shields and were fended off. The contestants raced past each other, then slowed to a trot with no advantage to either side this time. The excited shouts of the crowd subsided into a groan.

The knights slowly turned their horses, letting them recover their breath. Then they checked their lances and shields and gathered themselves for another tilt. The flags came down again and the mighty horses surged forward. The roar of the crowd grew as the horses bore down on one another and then descended into groans as the challenges were again shrugged off.

As the knights regrouped for their last tilt, there were shouts of advice mingled with some ribald ridicule: "Come on, London is waiting!" "Get your poke up his nose." "Ride him down, Master." "Hey, is this the best you can do? Let me show you the way!" "I could do better with my pig!"

As the knights renewed their charge, the crowd began to roar again, eager for a tilt.

"Come on, London. Unhorse him!" And this time, the lance of the City's knight struck home onto the shoulder of the challenger, rocking him back like a rag doll. The crowd shouted, expectant of a fall. But he managed to stay in his saddle and was able to turn towards the royal pavilion and acknowledge that he had been bested. The City had withstood its first challenge.

By the time of the eighth and last contest of the day many in the crowd had either lost their voices through shouting or their wits through too much ale. But there was a quickening interest among the rest. The challenge had been well delivered, for the tally stood at four to the City and three against. This last contest would decide whether the honours of the day would be shared. A shout went up when the challenger was proclaimed as Guy de Roquet, a renowned French knight and champion of many tournaments in Europe. Speculation ran through the crowd. Who would represent the City? Then out from the City enclosure rode their knight, resplendent in shining silver armour with a blue and yellow crest on his helmet and mounted on a huge black stallion.

Murmurs ran round the crowd like wildfire. "It's Edward, the Black Prince!" "No. That cannot be; he wears black armour." "Who, then?" "Well, it can't be Gaunt, for look... he's still with the King." "Maybe it's the Duke of Lancaster." "No, he's in the royal pavilion too." "I know! It must be Prince Lionel. He's not been in the party all day!"

But there was no time for further speculation.

The horses were lined up at the end of the course. The black stallion was pawing the ground. The herald's flags came down and released the great beasts into a huge forward surge. The drumming of their hooves was matched only by the swelling cheers of the crowd. Lances were levelled as the two knights rushed towards each other. Then there was a mighty clash. The French knight's lance broke into splinters as it was parried by his opponent's shield and he was hit squarely in the chest. He arched violently backwards, cartwheeled out of his saddle and thudded onto the ground. A jubilant roar split the air as the crowd danced and shouted with glee. The City had won the day!

The third day of the tournament dawned with the promise of another fine day. The early haze would soon clear and the sky was flecked only by some light, high cirrus cloud. Hugh Gresham had already walked the course, arranged for a rail to be replaced and for two rough patches of ground, which had been badly scuffed by the horses, to be raked even and firmed down. The open stands had been cleared of rubbish and he was now inspecting the royal pavilion.

"We need to rehang the canvas, Amos," he said to his assistant, "for it has sagged in this corner. And see that the walkways round about are besomed."

"Aye, Master. Do y' know if the King is to be present again today?"

"Oh yes, surely. Although there may be a surprise in store for I've had word to screen off part of the City's saddling enclosure. There's rumour that the Black Prince may enter the lists, but keep that to yourself."

"That would be something to see!" cried Amos. "I will be as dumb as a church door," he promised, although Hugh knew he would pass on this titbit to the gossips at the first opportunity.

Soon, there was a regular procession of people coming from the City to stake out their claim to seats on the terraced stands. The crowd were accompanied by the usual flock of hawkers, pedlars and entertainers. A press of people in holiday mood was always fair game for the glib-tongued and light-fingered who were ever ready to prise pennies from their purses. They had had two thrilling days of jousting. Their lust for drama had been met when no less than five knights had been unhorsed and left flailing in their armour on the grass.

They had been hauled upright by the squires who had run to them, bruised and shaken but with no one badly wounded. The outcome of the tournament was still in the balance with eight bouts to the City and six to the challengers and two with no result. Today's eight bouts would be decisive.

By midmorning the senior worthies of the City with their ladies were also taking their seats in the tented stands. A fanfare announced the arrival of Queen Philippa who was escorted by Prince Lionel and her daughters-in-law, Blanche and Elizabeth, wife of Prince Lionel. The crowd watched, openly enjoying the spectacle and knowingly ticking off who was who and noting that the King and his other sons had not joined them.

The knights in the first joust were so evenly matched that neither could gain an advantage. The City's knight in the second joust had easily unseated his opponent and the crowd had roared their delight at the tangled spectacle of the floored knight. But the next two jousts had gone against the City. The score stood at nine for the City and eight against. The crowd knew that the honour of the City rested on the four final jousts.

A growing tension crept round the field. The next two knights squared up to face each other. Both had big powerful horses. The City's knight sat tall in the saddle, his armour gleaming in the sun, visor down, tensed ready to ride at his opponent.

Blanche was sitting next to the Queen, who noticed how she was wringing her hands in her lap. She leaned over and stilled them under her own hand and said: "Don't worry, child. John is a fearless jouster. He will come to no harm and yet honour the City, you'll see."

"Praise be to God that you are right, madam," replied Blanche.

Her hands flew to her mouth as the horses spurred towards each other. Then she was on her feet laughing and crying at the same time. In the moment of clashing, John of Gaunt had vanquished his opponent who was sprawled on the ground while a squire ran to catch and calm his horse. The crowd whooped with joy. The tally now stood in favour of the City with two jousts yet to come. The discerning among them had seen Blanche's unrestrained joy and concluded rightly that the Duke of Richmond was in the saddle. Did this mean that royal knights would fight the last two jousts?

Rumour spread and turned to cheering as the next knight lined up. His big black stallion stood at the end of the course with ears eagerly pointed. His armour matched the horse... black and shining. They were sure this was the Black Prince and chanted his name: "Edward! Edward!" His opponent had been named as Ferdinand de Rouse, a well-tried knight from Bavaria. Blanche looked at the Queen and caught her eye. A faint flush of excitement had spread at her neck but she smiled sweetly and, with an uplift of her eyebrows, turned her gaze back to the contest.

The riders passed on the first course without registering a hit. For the second tilt, the black knight had urged his horse to a faster gallop. His lance smote the Bavarian squarely in the chest with such force that he was catapulted out of his saddle. He bounced off the hind quarters of his horse and fell, arms and legs flailing, to the ground. The crowd went wild with a roar that filled the air. The black knight wheeled in front of the royal seating and doffed his lance low before the Queen who, smiling broadly, waved in acknowledgement.

Blanche leaned towards the Queen: "That was magnificent, my Lady!"

"Yes!" replied the Queen with a light laugh. "And now we must hope for a repeat performance!"

Blanche was impressed with her composure and confidence. She doubted that she would ever be so calm. Her heart had been in her mouth when John was jousting and she felt that it would be ever so. And now, unbeknown to his opponent and to the groundlings, the King himself was to tilt at the final joust. He was still strong and straight-backed with a fierce will, the strength of which awed his opponents as much as his physical prowess. But his opponent, leading the challenge to the City, was Maurice de Bartres, a renowned knight from the French court who had overcome Sir Thomas Percy, one of the premier knights from King Edward's court, at their last meeting at a tourney outside Calais.

As King Edward rode out to take his place at the head of the course, the sun bounced off his metalled sheet and helmet sending blinding shafts of light into the eyes of those nearby. His armour superbly polished, light and flexible had been specially made for him by the finest metalworkers in Italy. Sitting erect on his grey stallion, holding the reins in his left hand with his lance pointing skywards, his whole bearing breathed the spirit of the tournament as a chivalrous feat of arms.

The heralds' fanfare rang out around the field. The crowd hushed. Queen Philippa sat upright in her chair, her gaze riveted on her husband. Lances were lowered. The horses began their charge, eating up the gap between them. At the moment of impact the French knight deftly knocked the King's lance aside and scored a hit to the body. A low groan ran round the crowd and then there was a stunned silence as they watched the horses regroup and begin their second charge. The crowd roared encouragement and burst into a mighty cheer when King Edward replied with a hit to his opponent.

Blanche and the Queen exchanged glances. Emboldened, Blanche said: "He is the veriest true Garter Knight, my Lady, and head of the Round Table."

"Yes, my dear, and God willing he will prevail," replied Philippa.

As the third charge began, the crowd erupted. The horses' heads bobbed in rhythm with their flashing hooves. The lances cleaved the air. As they met in a climax of furious energy, the King with an unerring eye and strong twist of the wrist flicked his opponent's helmet and it sailed high into the air. The crowd was a forest of waving arms, and hats sailed as high into the air as the helmet.

Maurice de Bartres turned his horse and, grinning broadly, doffed his lance as he joined the King in loyal gesture to the Queen. The King removed his helmet and the whole arena chanted happily, "Long live King Edward!" This was renewed when the other knights, unhelmeted, rode out from their enclosures to line up in front of the royal pavilion and among them, for all to see, were the King's four sons – Edward, Lionel, John and Edmund – who had fought for the City and upheld their challenge. The crowd roared and danced, glorying in this unique occasion which would be the talk of the taverns and a tale to tell for years to come.

Chaucer was sitting with his mother in the kitchen at Thames Street with a pot of ale at his elbow. She was preparing some vegetables for the evening meal. He was looking glum with his head propped on his hand.

Agnes looked over at him and said: "Geoffrey, don't take on so. You've always known that you might be called to arms and, after all, it is the King's campaign you will be joining. Just think what a triumph it will be if he succeeds and is crowned King of France at Rheims. You will be able to tell your grandchildren you were there!"

"Oh yes, I know, Mother," said Chaucer and then added testily: "I'll warrant there is no one more loyal than me. It's just that I know I can give more honest service than prancing about on a horse, waving a lance and looking falsely fierce. I'm better with a pen than a sword, you know that!"

"Yes, I do and so does Prince Lionel. But hush! I hear your father. Don't let him catch this mood. He is so proud of you."

They went together to join John Chaucer in the hall.

"Ah, Geoffrey!" beamed his father. "I have just been bargaining for a horse for you: a sound, deep-chested animal. It will be brought to the stables directly for us to view. And Tom Castle has found a Flemish metalworker who will fit you out in armour. What do you think you will need?"

"Nothing too heavy, Father: some chain mail and just a light chest plate, I reckon. And of course I'll need a helmet with a hinged visor."

"And underneath that? Will you want anything made specially?"

"A thick leather habergeon with padded sleeves would be good, both for protection and warmth. And I can wear one of mother's knitted hoods under the helmet."

"What about gauntlets? Do you want the smith to fashion you some iron ones?"

"I'd rather have leather, Father," said Geoffrey. "They give a better grip and are more flexible."

"Very well… and what about weapons?"

"I still have the long pointed knife you gave me, and I'll be fitted out with a sword or, maybe, a lance when I join Prince Lionel's unit."

"Good, good," said his father, pacing restlessly up and down.

"I've been told I will be attached as a squire to serve with Sir Richard Sturry. Do you know him, Father?"

"No," replied his father, "I've not met him, but I know that he is a veteran of campaigns in Spain and Italy and he was with the Black Prince at Poitiers when they routed the French and captured King John. Keep by him, Geoffrey. He is well experienced."

King Edward had gathered together the largest army that had ever left England: men aged between 20 and 60 who owed service to their lords and through them to the King. The King's sons, who had so recently jousted alongside him, were all present including John of Gaunt who had over 100 men from his estate and Lionel with his contingent of 70 men, Geoffrey Chaucer among them. The great host, comprising hundreds of knights, squires, archers and foot soldiers had crossed to Calais in September 1359, carried by swarms of little ships. Horses, carts, field ovens and provisions of all sorts had also been ferried across. Calais was so swollen the overflow spread into fields around.

When the army moved out from Calais, it made a splendid sight: long columns of gleaming armour, rich banners fluttering, trotting horses and marching men. In the vanguard rode 500 armed knights and 1,000 archers, led by the Duke of Lancaster. Then came the King's division of 3,000 men-at-arms and 5,000 archers followed by the baggage train of 6,000 lumbering carts.

After that came the Black Prince's division, also with knights, squires and archers all mounted and in good order to protect the valuable provisions and the rear.

As the army moved slowly through northern France it became clear that the French had learnt from their defeat at Poitiers. They would not engage in open battle, where the English archers were so potent, but had fortified the towns and withdrawn within their walls. This was frustrating: there were few Frenchmen to fight or capture for ransom and little among the peasantry to ransack or pillage. The wages of war were denied to the English fighting man. This discontent became common talk among Geoffrey's colleagues and around the campfires.

By early December, the English army was camped outside Rheims, laying siege to the city where Edward hoped to be crowned as King of the French. By now Geoffrey knew his colleagues well and had gauged their manners. He was closest to Jack Steadman, a forester from Prince Lionel's estates in Hereford, who reminded him of Amos the cellarman at Hatfield.

Jack was short in stature but not in temper, broad, deep-chested and with a close-cropped head that shone like a hazel nut. Cheerful, with a countryman's economy of words, he wore a coat and hood of green with a silver St Christopher medal hanging at his breast. An archer, he showed Geoffrey how he dressed his peacock-feathered arrows so that they did not droop and how he kept them neatly sheathed. He wore a leather brace on his left arm to guard it from the twang of the string from his longbow. He was a quiet, solid companion who read well the lie of the land – both among the fields and woods, and between his fellow men.

The cook and storeman in their group were more like a pair of starlings: noisy, quarrelsome, greedy, coarse and dishonest. Alfred, the cook, rarely for his trade, looked ill-fed for he was thin and angular – all elbows and knees. He made a good thick broth spiced well with garlic and onions and baked a tasty pie, but he liked his ale and rough red wine. When he was drunk, he picked a fight if he could and jabbered lewd tales. The storeman was his drinking partner: a great stout fellow of sixteen stone or so, big in brawn and bone. He had narrow eyes, a fox-red beard and was hot and lecherous, full of oaths and crude innuendos. On the march, he wore a short sword and buckler. With his strength and temper, hurling oaths from his mighty mouth like a furnace door, he put many foes to the sword or flight. Moreover he played the bagpipes, the skirl of which was as frightening. In camp, he played dice and backgammon with the cook and together they rejoiced in cheating others who were fool enough to join them.

For Chaucer, the saving grace of his life as a soldier was his knight, Sir Richard Sturry. As his squire he had divers duties in serving him: seeing that his weapons and armour were well kept and ready; his horse fed, stabled and well shod; his food prepared, hot and to his taste. But Chaucer liked best the times when they went foraging or hunting together, sometimes joining a foray led by Prince Lionel.

A stern taskmaster, Sir Richard had shown Geoffrey how to use a shield and wield his sword to better effect in open fighting and his lance at full gallop. He had a true understanding of horses and had taught Geoffrey how to get the best from his steed and adjust his saddle and riding posture to suit the conditions. Sir Richard, himself, sat bolt upright in his saddle, alert black eyes shining like wet pebbles from his leathery face. His bearing told of the man: purposeful, direct, without frills. He wore a plain fustian tunic, smudged with dark stains from the weight of his armour. Modest and never boorish but fierce in the face of injustice, he was to Geoffrey a true, noble and chivalrous knight.

Sitting by the fireside after a long day's ride, Geoffrey enjoyed listening to Richard's tales of his campaigns and battles abroad in Christian and heathen places. He had been at the fall of Alexandria, had fought in Russia and Morocco and had battled with the Saracens in the south of Spain at Granada and Algeciras. He had, too, a good grasp of military tactics. He held the whole unit spellbound when he told how the Black Prince had deployed his forces at the battle of Poitiers. With the aid of a stick he drew the battle plan in the sandy soil.

"Prince Edward skilfully positioned his men along a length of road outside Poitiers. It was protected by hedges on either side – here and here," as he drew a double line in the sand. "He placed his best archers to line the hedges and more archers and men at the end in a harrow formation, like this…" as he marked the end of the gulley, "…and he kept a battalion of mounted men and archers with him to one side. The French attacked by riding three hundred of their best knights directly up the road intending to overwhelm and disperse the archers. But the archers shot murderously from both flanks. The terrified horses refused to go on, swerved or turned back or fell beneath their riders who could neither use their weapons nor get up again. Our men at the end of the road advanced while the Prince galloped his mounted men round behind the French. Then there was fierce and bloody hand-to-hand fighting until the French King was captured and they fell back and surrendered. We took more prisoners for ransom that day than we ever had in our army!"

And now, as he sat with Geoffrey round the dying embers on a cold December night outside Rheims, Sir Richard aired his doubts about the present campaign.

"I fear that the King's hopes will be dashed. Rheims is too well walled and guarded to fall to our siege. The winter too is our enemy and on their side. Our foodstuffs are short and stale and there is little to be poached from the farms hereabouts. It will not surprise me if the King abandons the siege."

"But what will happen then? Won't that be a defeat?" asked Geoffrey.

"Oh, the King won't go away without plundering in Burgundy and probably towards Paris. But his main purpose has been frustrated and he has not been able to draw the French into an open and decisive battle. This Charles, who is regent for King John, has been clever, or more probably Bertrand du Guescilin who is advising him. I would call it more of a stalemate than a defeat. A lot will depend on how they parley at the end and what sort of treaty comes out of it."

With that he stretched and stood up: "But come, 'tis time we were abed. Tomorrow we will reconnoitre out beyond the camp and maybe test their mettle. We have not finished with Rheims yet!"

Geoffrey was to ponder many times on the prophetic but fortuitous force of those remarks in the weeks to come.

Next day, Geoffrey rose before dawn and, with the help of the groom, had the horses saddled and ready when Sir Richard emerged from his tent. He was in full armour accompanied by his page, Thomas of Chester. Geoffrey too had put on his light armour and now made sure that his dagger and sword were secure in his belt. Together with Thomas, who carried a lance, he helped Sir Richard mount his horse and swung himself up onto Janus, the chestnut horse that his father had given him. Sir Richard led the way out of the camp into a wet and pearly mist.

"We will patrol out towards the eastern gate of the city," said Sir Richard. "I fancy the French may use this mist to slip a wagon of supplies into the town. Look sharp about you and keep close to me."

The three horsemen advanced in an arrowhead formation, senses pricked as sharply as their horses' ears. After a while, Richard stopped with his arms raised. Geoffrey too had heard the jangle of harness. There it was again over to the left. Richard waved them forward at a walking pace towards the sounds. A cart pulled by a donkey and laden with vegetables and a sack of corn emerged from the mist. Sir Richard spurred his horse forward, his sword held high, and shouted at the peasant who was leading the donkey: "Halt! There will be no supplies to the city this day!"

The startled peasant stopped and fell to his knees with cries of, "Mercy, my Lord."

"We will take this fellow and his cart to our camp," said Sir Richard. "These provisions will supplement our rations nicely!"

But as Sir Richard wheeled his horse, six mounted soldiers galloped up from behind the cart and quickly surrounded them. Geoffrey urged his horse alongside Richard. His heart had leapt at the sight of the soldiers and his blood rushed as he leaned forward and pointed his sword at them. This was his first fight for real. He felt keyed up and ready to slash and twist his weapon alongside Sir Richard.

"Hold hard, Geoffrey!" called Sir Richard. "I fear we are outnumbered."

"That is wise, Englishman," called out the leader of the French troop. "Do you submit to ransom then?"

"Yes, we do," replied Richard and then said quietly to Geoffrey, "I should have foreseen this. But there is no need to fear. I have been ransomed before. We will be fairly treated and I could not have the harm that might have been done to the boy on my conscience."

Geoffrey slumped back into his saddle but said nothing. His head was in a whirl as his heart stopped racing. All at once, he was relieved, deflated, angry, frustrated and ashamed. And then he caught the humour of it, as in his mind's eye he saw the scene and his puny show of defiance. He relaxed as they were led into the city and grinned to himself. Maybe there is some honour in being ransomed? And then his grin faded as he thought: but who will raise the money to pay for his release?

The truth of Sir Richard's words was proved when they entered the city. He and his two young colleagues had been taken to a house near the cathedral where they were given wine, a bowl of hot broth and some freshly baked crusty bread, served by a grey-haired widow who, if she eyed them suspiciously, nonetheless made them comfortable. They were finishing the food, when in from the street swept a French knight who immediately filled the room with energy and radiance as he came forward and embraced Sir Richard.

"*Alors, mon ami!* I heard rumour that you had been brought here, but I could not believe it! You, the comrade who saved my life at Algeciras – taken by a motley patrol! *Tiens!* It is like an oak felled by a dormouse!"

"Giles! It is good to see you," said Sir Richard, grinning broadly with obvious pleasure, and turning, he said: "These are the colleagues I so misled: Geoffrey Chaucer, who as well as being a faithful and brave squire is a courtly poet… Thomas of Chester, my page."

Giles de Duroc looked quizzically with a practised eye at the two young men as they came forward and bowed to him.

"Aha! Now I understand how you put discretion before valour!"

And then, with a slight bow to Chaucer, asked: "So, young sir. Do you know the works of our renowned poet Guillaume de Machaut?"

"Indeed I do, sir. I much admire him and have learned a lot from his verses and songs."

"Ah yes. He is a fine musician too. He is a canon in residence at our cathedral here. Did you know that?"

Then, turning to Sir Richard, he asked: "Maybe, if you would allow it, we could arrange for your young poet to meet Machaut?"

Sir Richard had no hesitation. The eager look on Geoffrey's face told him all, and he replied with another bow to the Frenchman: "That would be very welcome and very gracious of you, my friend."

Three days passed without any further word about a meeting with Machaut and Geoffrey began to fear that the French knight had spoken empty words. But then, on the morning of the fourth day a thin, sallow-faced young man, dressed in a grey habit, came to the house to take Geoffrey to the cathedral.

They went along a narrow cobbled street, picking their way between carts and dogs and knots of people crowded round a stall armed with baskets or talking at doorways with neighbours. At the far end of the street a stone archway led into the cathedral precinct. As they went through it, suddenly the noise and bustle of the street and the cloying closeness of the houses fell away. A pool of peace and calm opened up and there before them stood the cathedral. Geoffrey paused for a moment to wonder and marvel at the sight of the massive stone structure with its high windows and walls elegantly broken by tall lancet arches and niches holding carved biblical figures. Then he was ushered through a small side door into the cathedral itself.

At first Geoffrey could hardly see; the contrast between the morning brightness outside and the dim, barely lit interior was too great. As his eyes adjusted, he saw a white-haired figure in a brown habit approaching, carefully shielding a lighted candle. He moved forward eagerly and bowed before him.

"My son… welcome. I am Jean de Machaut. Like my brother, I am a canon of this cathedral. I will take you shortly to where he is working beside a small altar by the choir screen where there is more light."

"*Merci, monsieur.* I am most grateful," replied Geoffrey.

"Is it true that you are a poet writing in the English tongue at the court of King Edward?" asked the canon as they walked down the stone-flagged nave.

"Oh, that is overstated, *monsieur*. It is true that I have recited before the King but I am not at his court. I have written a few short verses in English. But I have translated many more from your French poets and I have much to learn from them."

Jean de Machaut smiled. Modesty was an engaging virtue, especially in the young.

As they approached the choir screen, they could hear the faint humming of a voice echoing round the vaulted walls. Then Geoffrey saw the 60-year-old Guillaume de Machaut for the first time. He was sitting on a stool at a high desk with a sloping top which reminded Geoffrey of his school days at St Paul's. He was poring over a manuscript sheet of music and sounding some of the notes to himself as he studied the score. Hearing their tread, he turned and looked straight at Geoffrey with his twinkling, blue forget-me-not eyes. Geoffrey was spellbound: the vital life force which shone forth from Machaut's kindly wrinkled face was overwhelming.

As Jean withdrew with a slight bow and swish of his habit, Guillaume moved aside and motioned for Geoffrey to sit with him on a nearby bench.

"You know, my son, we have heard of Geoffrey Chaucer who is writing in English. So it is a great pleasure for me to meet you, although I could have wished it had not been occasioned by war. Why not tell me about yourself and what you have been doing?" he said kindly to Geoffrey.

Geoffrey fumbled with his words at first, saying that he was not at the English court but was a squire in the household of Countess Elizabeth, Prince Lionel's wife, who had let him use her library where he had found a copy of the 'Romance of the Rose', which he had translated into English and parts of which he had recited before the Princess and her guests.

Guillaume smiled as nervousness left the young man, enthusiasm took over and the words began to tumble out. Then he asked: "The

'Romance of the Rose' is in the traditional French style of ten lines of eight-syllable rhyming couplets. Did you not find the stresses and rhymes difficult to match in English?"

"At times, yes," replied Chaucer. "Syllable stress is more definite in English and I had to juggle the order of words a little at times. But I enjoyed making the rhymes. And although it is allegorical, I especially enjoyed the descriptions of Envy, Mirth and Sorrow. They were acutely observed – just like pictures of real people!"

"Ah yes, I remember," said Machaut. "And sadly true of the world too! But where else can a poet get his inspiration but from the world around him – and from his spiritual insight of course."

"But I am not sure," said Chaucer, "that I always want to write in the eight-syllable form. I am interested in the ten-syllable line with five stresses. I fancy that may better suit our English tongue."

"It is good to experiment. I have always enjoyed playing with words and different forms and sometimes making up games. It is an idle pastime of mine which I seem to indulge more often now and this sometimes earns a rebuke from my more serious brother!" confessed Machaut.

"Is that how you came to write your rondeau 'My End is My Beginning', which I heard sung at Prince John's wedding just before we left England?"

"Why, yes, exactly; I am honoured that you should have heard it!"

And then after a reflective pause, he went on: "I think it was the ancient rubric which served as a kind of altar at which the early Christians prayed that gave me these ideas. Do you know it?"

Seeing Chaucer shake his head, Machaut pulled a sheet of parchment to him and a quill and began to explain, "There are five Latin words arranged so:"

ROTAS
OPERA
TENET
AREPO
SATOR

"Which as you can see, make the same words whichever way you read them! The meaning of the words are important. But these same letters also make the ancient Christian cross:"

```
                    P
                    A
                    T
                    E
                    R
      P A T E R N O S T E R
                    O
                    S
                    T
                    E
                    R
```

"Except that, if you notice, there are two letters left over: A and O, which stand for the Greek Alpha and Omega which is the Greek biblical description of God."

Machaut stood back smiling as Geoffrey leaned over the desk and studied the words. "So you see, Geoffrey, we are not so clever. Our forefathers have often been there before us!"

"May I copy these?' asked Geoffrey.

"Oh, please take this script. And come again on Saturday at noon. The choir will be here because we are trying out a religious work of mine, 'The Mass to Our Lady', which I was revising when you arrived. It is rooted in the liturgy of the church and dedicated to the Virgin Mary and, although not yet finished, will be, I think, one of my best works."

They walked together down the aisle to the door and, after bowing his thanks to Machaut, Geoffrey made his way back to his lodgings, light in step and eager to tell Sir Richard and Thomas of his meeting with Machaut and the things they had discussed. Maybe he would even try the paternoster rubric on them!

On Saturday Geoffrey made his own way to the cathedral and once inside went down the nave to the chapel by the choir screen. Guillaume de Machaut was sitting at the same desk talking to a tall man with a pointed black beard, sharp aquiline features and bright brown eyes. As soon as he saw Chaucer, he beckoned him over. "Geoffrey, *bon jour*! This is Philip de Grosse, our choirmaster," and turning to him, said: "And this is Geoffrey Chaucer, the young English poet I was telling you about."

Philip turned and shook Geoffrey's hand warmly. "*Mon plaisir, monsieur.* You are very welcome."

"We will be joined by a small four-part choir shortly," explained Machaut. "We are going to rehearse some of the Mass I told you about. It has six movements, the usual five of the Ordinary of the Mass – Kyrie, Gloria, Credo, Sanctus, Agnus Dei – plus a closing Ite, Missa Est. Today we are going to try out the last three because these are in a new freer contrapuntal style which means the voices and rhythms will have to be highly organised. But" – turning to Philip – "we have expert singers, do we not? It will be exceptional, you will see!"

Soon the singers arrived, eight of them, including two boys who sat on the bench playing a game of cat's cradle while the others talked and joked quietly together. Then de Grosse called them together, gave out the parts and explained what was wanted. They arranged themselves in a semi-circle, the boys standing in the middle, the choirmaster facing them. He raised his arms, counted four beats and then brought them in to the beginning of the Sanctus.

Chaucer was full of wonder at the running rhythms and the way the sounds seemed to hang in the air, suspended like silver cobwebs trailing into the darkness of the high vaulted canopy. It was fascinating, mysterious and flowed with a strange beauty. He did not think he had heard anything so beautiful in his whole life, even in St Paul's.

After the choir had departed, he sat quietly on the bench by himself in a reverie with the sounds still running round his head. Machaut returned after speaking with the choirmaster and joined him.

Geoffrey looked up at the kindly, wrinkled face which seemed to shine with an angelic light and said: "Maestro, that was magnificent and so beautiful. I am profoundly honoured and grateful."

"The honour is mine, my son," said Machaut. "And let me urge you forward in your writings, for you have a talent which your countrymen will be proud of."

"But I shall never compose music like that, for I am no musician," replied Chaucer.

"Maybe not. I am privileged to have this cathedral and its brilliant choir to inspire me! But there is music too in the cadences of words and in the ways you use them."

They walked together to the west door where they embraced in a mutual gesture of pleasure at their fortuitous meeting. Geoffrey turned, as he crossed the precinct, and raised an arm in salute as Guillaume stood in the doorway. As he made his way through the archway into the street, he brushed the tears away that had welled up at his last sight of the great man.

John of Gaunt was with his brother, Lionel, when the news came of the capture of Sir Richard and Geoffrey Chaucer and the claim for ransom. Both expressed surprise, for Sturry was a well-known campaigner with much experience.

"The King will readily agree a payment, won't he?" asked John.

"Oh! I've no doubt about that. Certainly in the case of Sir Richard. I'm not so sure about the others. There's a page involved as well, I believe. It is not the war that Father reckoned on and nothing like as profitable as Poitiers. But then, we have caught a few Frenchmen in our skirmishes, so maybe the spoils will come out even?"

"I will come with you to see him," said John. "I am anxious to secure Chaucer's release for he promises to be a fine poet and writer in English. We cannot afford to lose him."

Lionel laughed. "Well, you persuade him or I will end up paying his ransom as he is in my service!"

John gave his brother a sharp look and was about to offer to pay from his own estates but thought it better to wait and see what happened. When they saw him, King Edward readily agreed. He knew Sir Richard, who had fought with him in Scotland, and, looking at John, said: "Was this the Chaucer who presented that pretty poem to Blanche at your wedding?"

"Yes, sire," replied John with a bow.

At that, King Edward beckoned his chamberlain forward.

"Arrange for these ransoms to be paid, and don't quibble about the amounts. They are valued by our person and should be restored to us forthwith. And arrange for the page too, at the usual amount."

It was several days before Sir Richard, Geoffrey and Thomas regained the English camp, for King Edward had lifted the siege of Rheims and moved on into Burgundy. It was several weeks later that Geoffrey learned that the King had paid £50 for the knight's release, £16 for his own and £1. 6s. 4d. for Thomas.

His father would be impressed!

But such material values seemed far away from the priceless meeting with Guillaume de Machaut and his sublime music in the cathedral at Rheims.

Chapter Five

GEOFFREY JUMPED FROM the deck of the barque onto the familiar wharf on the Thames. One of the crew threw his two bags down to him. He settled them at his feet and looked around him. Not much had changed in the ten years since he had come down here as a schoolboy with messages from his father for Tom Castle, his foreman. No sooner did the thought arise than he espied him further along the quay, checking off some newly arrived barrels. Geoffrey picked up his bags and moved down towards him.

"Tom. Tom Castle!" he called.

"Why, Master Geoffrey," exclaimed Tom as his lean weathered face lit up with the broadest of smiles. "This is a pleasure, and that's the truth. What brings you here?" and looking back at the ship, "You are not taking up foreign trading, like your father, are you?"

"It is mighty good to see you, Tom! No, I'm no merchant like Father was. In a manner of speaking, I suppose I have been trading abroad, Tom, but in words not wine! I've been to France and Italy on the King's business. I was lucky to get passage back in this ship from Bordeaux right up into the Thames. And how about you? You are still in the wine trade, I see. Who are you working for now?"

"Well, after your father died, his trade was passed on to Nicholas Brembre, and he was kind enough to want me to carry on managing the shipments and storage. So here I am, still at it!

"And how is your lady wife… and the baby?" asked Tom.

"Oh!" laughed Geoffrey. "They were fine when I left them in July. Praise be to God that they still are." And then he added with a twinkle in his eye, "We've named the boy Thomas, you know, so I'm sure he will do well!"

"Oh, I do hope so," cried Tom. "And your mother… how is she?"

"Well, I believe. You know she married Bartholomew atte Chapel after Father died. So we have the house in Thames Street to ourselves.

I must get up there, Tom. They don't know I'm here. Call in and see us when you are by!"

Geoffrey hoisted one of the bags onto his shoulder, sailor fashion, picked up the other and began the climb up the steps to the street, eager now to get home and see Philippa and the baby.

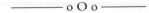

As Geoffrey pushed open the door of his house in Thames Street, he was greeted by the sound of Thomas crying. He smiled to himself at this welcome, for it was a lusty normal cry which told him all was well with the child. The sound was coming from the small parlour by the kitchen. He dumped his bags inside the door and made his way in that direction, calling out a loud, "Hullo! It's Geoffrey!" so as not to alarm whoever was in. The door to the parlour was ajar and, as he got to it, Alice, the nursery maid, came out with Thomas in her arms. When she saw Geoffrey she cried out in surprise: "Why, sir! How you did startle me! The mistress said you wouldn't be back until next month."

"I know, Alice. I couldn't stay away any longer! This young one has a good pair of lungs. How is he?" pulling back the shawl from his face and gently stroking his cheek with his forefinger.

Alice beamed. "Why, he's a little darling and no trouble really. He's growing bigger and stronger by the day. He's such a wriggler too! He'll be crawling soon, I reckon."

Thomas meanwhile was busy sucking noisily at his knuckles and gazing wide-eyed at this half-remembered newcomer with a deep voice.

"The mistress is attending on the Queen, Master. But she will be home before nightfall," explained Alice. "Shall I send someone down to Westminster to tell you are here?"

"No, Alice. Let it be a surprise to her." And then Fanny came out from the kitchen.

"Master Geoffrey! It is you!" she exclaimed. "I thought my ears were deceiving me!"

Geoffrey's face softened as he turned to greet Fanny. She was older, slower, more ample with greying hair and fewer teeth than he remembered from when he used to sit in her kitchen as a boy. But he was very glad that she had stayed with them and not been needed by his mother in her new home. He embraced her fondly.

"Fanny!" he cried. "I thought I would surprise you all! And have you anything special you can prepare for dinner tonight? I'm famished for some proper food!… and some fine wine?"

"I do have a salmon and I could make some oatcakes and mushrooms with an onion and light mustard sauce to go with it. But you had best go to the cellar yourself and choose the wine. There's plenty there still which your father put down."

"That will do splendidly, Fanny. Thank you. Now I will unpack my bags and wash the dust and salt of the journey away."

Geoffrey was in the upstairs chamber when Philippa got home. He heard her calling urgently for Fanny as she entered, so he gathered up the few presents he had brought back with him – some olives, dates and a silver amulet – and went down to meet her. He stood stock still on the steps, arrested by a fearful anguished cry from the kitchen. Whatever could have happened? He hurried down and saw through the kitchen doorway Fanny holding Philippa's hands and peering into her face with an anguished look. He hurried forward.

"What is it? What has happened?" he asked.

Philippa turned and flung herself into his arms, sobbing: "Oh Geoffrey! Thank God you are here. Oh, my love, I've dreadful news. Duchess Blanche is dead." And as she saw his stricken face, she went on quietly: "She died just two hours ago at the Savoy – of the dreaded plague – like her father," and then wringing her hands and stamping her foot, "Why, oh why, such cruelty and waste?"

Geoffrey sank onto a bench at the table, his face drained of colour, his lips and legs trembling. He looked up at Philippa.

"She was so brimming with life and so joyous in her children…

And the Duke... how is he? Was he with her?"

"He's escaped the infection, praise be to God. He has been away in the north settling tenants' claims. But he is expected from Kenilworth tonight."

"He will be distraught." He sat looking down at his hands and after a while added: "I will go to the Savoy tomorrow, light a candle in the chapel and offer our sympathy and support as far as we can. Happenstance, I will see the Duke too."

And then, after a pause: "I wrote something for their wedding, which she received very kindly. Do you remember? I feel I would like to capture her in a remembrance which may also offer some solace to John."

Philippa put her arm round her husband's shoulders and gave him a hug.

"I am sure that would be welcome and much cherished by him," she said.

The next day Geoffrey Chaucer made his way to the Savoy, the great white palace on the Thames. To passers-by he had an abstracted air, looking neither to right nor left. He was consumed by the contrast between the gaiety of the marriage feast nine years ago and the stark reality of the present. Immersed in courtly society with its romantic ideas of love and lyrical tales, Blanche had been Geoffrey's ideal heroine and inspiration. Now she was no more. He felt a personal loss; almost a betrayal.

As he entered the dark space of the small family chapel, silence and stillness settled round him. He moved forward, crossed himself and bowed towards the cross at the altar. He collected a candle and walked towards the bier on which Blanche was laid out. He lit his candle, stood it carefully among an already bright flickering forest and moved to stand at the side of the coffin.

Blanche was dressed all in white, her hands clasped across her chest. Her pale face and delicate colouring, skin as smooth as marble, her golden hair, full lips and long eyelashes, etched themselves in his memory. After several minutes, he sighed, bowed and turned away. Then he saw the figure of John of Gaunt standing in the shadow of a pillar nearby, his face white and drawn. As their eyes met, the searing pain leapt out at Geoffrey. For a moment he was transfixed. Then he bowed in acknowledgement and quietly withdrew with no word spoken or needed. As he reached the door, he heard a priest begin chanting a mass to ease the passage of the departed soul.

John meanwhile maintained his vigil. He had been at the chapel all night, ever since they had brought her down and placed her on the bier. He felt he had to stay with Blanche, to keep to himself the last vestiges of her presence. He had hardly noticed the respectful comings and goings of her household. He knew he should have felt their loss and gained some solace from their compassion but he was numb, beyond feeling, as if he had been poleaxed in battle and cast down, alone, lost in a wilderness. In his grief he felt a caustic bitterness over their fawning politeness. What did they know of his loss in their courtly comfort? But he had seen in Chaucer's eyes a true recognition and even a shared agony.

Two days later, Blanche's coffin was escorted from the Savoy to St Paul's by twelve senior knights of the Duke's Lancaster retinue. Behind the coffin walked John, a lone, bareheaded figure dressed entirely in black. The coffin was carried aloft into the great cathedral by six of the knights and placed on trestles beside the principal altar while blessings and Mass were chanted. Then it was slowly lowered into a space prepared in the marble floor nearby. Soon, as arranged by John, a tomb of alabaster would be raised over it with a painted effigy of the Duchess so that her form and features should not be forgotten. Thereafter, each day two priests would chant masses for her soul at a small altar built beside the tomb.

After the ceremony, at her urging, John went with his mother, Queen Philippa, by barge to the Palace of Westminster where they withdrew to the Queen's privy chamber. After settling herself in a brocaded gilt chair, she looked at her son and said quietly: "John, my dear, it was plain for us all to see that yours was a love match. I feel the pain of your grief and I share it, for Blanche was a true and gentle daughter to me. But she has given you four children which she cherished and cared for and you must look to their needs now.

Philippa has only eight years and, although she has a full character, she cannot manage Elizabeth and young Henry – let alone the new baby, Edward."

"My Lady! It is hard for me to think beyond her just now," and leaving his chair, he paced the room restlessly, stroking his brow. "But, yes, you are right to spur me on this."

"Well, I have an idea. One of my ladies-in-waiting is Philippa Chaucer. She has a younger sister, Katherine, married a year ago to one of your knights, Sir Hugh Swynford."

"Swynford! Why, he's a coarse sort of fellow! I couldn't have his rough manners near my nursery."

"No, no, of course not, John! He will be away managing his manor outside Lincoln or campaigning abroad with you. She is gentleness itself and worthy of my patronage as the daughter of my Herald from Hainault. She is devout and refined, for she spent ten years at the nunnery on the Isle of Sheppey. Furthermore she has a son of the age of Edward and can well supervise his nursing."

John relaxed, resumed his seat and looked at his mother.

"Well, Chaucer seems to be well catered for. If the sister is as you say and does as well for the children – so be it," and then added, prophetically, "we will be blessed."

Back in the house in Thames Street, Chaucer was in his father's old room. The ledgers, tallies and bills of the vintner's wine trade had gone. Now, the room was full of Chaucer's books: Latin texts including his beloved Ovid, Catullus, Virgil, Cato's Distichs, the Eclogue of Theodulus, Maximian's Elegies, Claudius' 'Rape of Proserpine'; Greek translations from Homer and Diogenes and excerpts from Socrates, Plato and Aristotle; French romances including the 'Roman de la Rose' and works by Guillaume de Machaut; and a treasured collection of writings in English with romances and stories, mostly in tail rhyme, some of which he had read with his father when he was a young boy.

Sitting among this treasury of literature were works on astronomy and mathematics, including Leonardo Fibonacci's *Liber Abaci* which was based on the decimal system. Beside the shelves of books, stood a desk with a sloping top, not unlike the one he had seen used by Machaut in Rheims, and a sturdy wooden stool with a shiny well-worn seat. Parchments of various sizes covered the desk top with an inkhorn and quills, for this was where Chaucer did his writing and copying of manuscripts.

But, now, he was sitting in a leather padded chair by the window so as to catch the light. He was studying a poem by an Italian, Guido Cavalcanti, about love and emotional suffering, which he had bought in Milan on his recent visit to Italy. He was pleased with his modest purchase. Cavalcanti had been a friend of Dante, and Chaucer had heard enthusiastic talk of their writings and also those of the newer writers, Petrarch and Boccaccio from Florence. He was keen to learn from them and, although his reading from the Italian manuscript was slow and painstaking, he already felt that some of the rhythm and sentiment matched the mood he wanted to create in his elegy of Duchess Blanche.

He had also been rereading some of Machaut's poems, which he had obtained in Rheims. In 'The Judgement of the King of Bohemia', the poet overhears a lady and a knight lamenting: she because her true-love has died; he because his beloved proved faithless. They argue over which has the greater cause for sorrow. The King's verdict is that infidelity rather than bereavement merits the greater grief. But in another poem, 'The Judgement of the King of Navarre', the King rules in favour of the woman. Geoffrey wondered whether he could use a form like this for his elegy.

Geoffrey got up from his chair, moved to the desk and searched among the manuscripts. He had already drafted a poem based on the sorrowful tale from Greek mythology of King Ceyx who was drowned and lost in a shipwreck at sea and how Morpheus, the God of Sleep, had allowed him to take leave of his grieving wife, Alcione, in a dream while she slept. Perhaps this lament would provide an apt beginning to set the mood? As he sat down again to reread this, he heard Philippa calling his name as she arrived home.

"Geoffrey! I've such news! The Queen has persuaded the Duke to take Katherine into his household to look after his children! She's to go to Hertford directly."

Geoffrey looked fondly at his wife in her excitement. He knew how fiercely loyal she was and how much she had always hoped that her sister would get a place in one of the royal households. She had been bitterly disappointed over her marriage to Hugh Swynford. She felt Katherine had been lured into it because he was a knight and lord of a manor. She had probably petitioned the Queen on her behalf in the past. But he was surprised at this outcome. Katherine was young and scarcely out of childbirth herself. She was kind and willing but somewhat demure.

He doubted that she had will enough to cope with Blanche's spirited children, especially Elizabeth and young Henry. Philippa noticed his hesitation.

"Why are you frowning? Are you not pleased?"

"Yes, I am, for I know how much this means to you. I am only anxious for Katherine. Can she manage this, do you think? She's a young baby of her own and, from what I hear, the four-year-old Elizabeth is wilful and naughty."

"Oh fie!" said Philippa impatiently. "You are too cautious at times, Geoffrey. She will be fine, you'll see. She will have the two girls eating out of her hand – and Henry too, I shouldn't wonder."

Geoffrey smiled. He was used to his wife's bossiness. "But she should have help with the babies, don't you think?"

"There will be a wet nurse for Edward and, yes, she should have help in the nursery. It would be a good place for a young girl. I shall speak to Katherine about it. Maybe she already knows of someone."

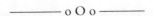

Katherine Swynford arrived at Hertford Castle on a brown pony escorted by Giles, a squire from the Lancaster retinue. Thomas, her young child, was securely swaddled in front of her. Her belongings were strapped in panniers on a mule which trotted dutifully behind Giles. She was wearing a long brown surcote with a hood pulled up over her head so that her face was framed by its grey fur trimming. Her plain green gown was only set off by an embroidered hip girdle. Her leather shoes, brown also, lacked the fashionable long pointed toes and were laced up round her ankles.

Giles called out a loud, "Hallo there!" A groom came out to hold her pony while Giles helped her dismount. Holding Thomas tightly to her, she went through the arched stone porch and entered into the household of John of Gaunt, Duke of Lancaster. Inside she was welcomed by Lady Marion Villiers, a lady-in-waiting who had until recently served Duchess Blanche. Lady Marion explained the layout and the routine of the castle, that the Duke would be coming on the morrow and would expect to see her then. Meanwhile, a maid would show her to her room, which was in the nursery wing, and help her with her unpacking. Then, Lady Marion would take her to meet the children.

When they had finished unpacking and Grace, the maid, had left her, Katherine stood and took stock of her surroundings. The room was dark with wood panelling, low oak beams and wooden floor and only one small recessed window. There was a table and chair with a bowl, pitcher and candlestick by the side of a hearth which had not seen a fire for some time. The single bed, opposite the hearth, was soft and inviting enough, judging by the now sleeping figure of Thomas. Katherine sat on the bed next to him, then jumped off and twirled round with her arms above her head.

This dark room could not daunt her spirits! She was excited at being here and, she admitted guiltily, glad to be away from damp Lincolnshire and her husband. To be in the Duke's service and to have charge of his children was a wonderful prospect! She knew she would enjoy it! Oh, she knew too there were things she would have to learn and to be careful about. Her sister Philippa had filled her head with instructions, especially on how to behave with the other staff and to be respectful to those senior to her. She just hoped the Duke would accept her, for, so it was said, he could be gruff and impatient. The secret could lie with the children. If they liked her and they could have fun together, then she was sure all would be well. She was glad she would be able to meet them before the Duke arrived.

There was a tap at the door and Lady Marion entered. She appraised Katherine in her plain green gown.

"Ah," she said. "We have all been given cloth for mourning clothes. The Duke is quite strict about it so we must arrange this for you too."

"Oh dear," exclaimed Katherine, "and you said I am to meet him tomorrow." And then, wringing her hands, for she truly wanted to do well, she looked beseechingly into Marion's eyes: "I surely can't have a new gown ready by then, can I?"

Lady Marion saw the anxiety and her face softened; the girl wants to please, she thought, and that is a good attribute.

"I will call for the seamstress and she can tell us if she can fit you out. She is very quick but if it cannot be done so soon, I will tell the Duke. I am sure he will be understanding. Now let us go to meet the children."

As they walked along a passage, Lady Marion explained: "Philippa, the oldest, is eight. Elizabeth is four. There was a boy, John, between them but he only lived a few short weeks. Then there is Henry who is nearly three. Here we are," as she opened the door to the nursery. Three pairs of eyes turned towards them as they entered and Katherine felt them fastened on her.

"Children, this is the lady I told you about: Lady Katherine Swynford. She has come from Lincoln at your father's behest to look after and help you in your learning – and to report to him, when he requires it, on your progress. So I hope you will be attentive to her."

Katherine looked back at them. Philippa had blonde hair with a creamy skin and blue eyes which looked steadily and solemnly at her. Elizabeth's hair was not as fair as her sister's. She had darker skin and brown hazel-flecked eyes which looked away and back again uncertainly and carried a hint of resentment. Henry had brown hair and clear blue eyes which gazed at her watchfully.

"Hullo," said Katherine, leaning forward towards them. "I am truly glad to be here."

She was surprised when Philippa stood up and said with quiet composure, "And we are pleased to welcome you, Lady Katherine. I am Philippa. This is my sister Elizabeth and my brother Henry. Edward is with Mary, the nurse." She finished this introduction with a simple curtsey which brought a giggle from Elizabeth.

Before Katherine could reply to this, there was a tap at the door and a quick bird-like woman with greying hair came in and said to Lady Marion: "You sent for me, my Lady?"

"Yes, Mildred. This is Lady Katherine Swynford who has just arrived. She needs to be fitted out immediately in the same cloth as we all have."

Mildred looked at Katherine, cocking her head to one side, taking in her size and shape with a well-practised eye. "If you would come with me, my Lady…" she began, moving towards the door.

But Katherine stopped her: "Why not take the measurements here? I am sure Philippa and Elizabeth will help, and they will also be able to tell me what is seemly."

So Katherine began her involvement with the Lancaster children.

The next afternoon, Katherine was sitting on a low chair in the children's day room. An autumn sun shone through a window, casting a pool of light on the floor beside her. Elizabeth was standing at her knee while she showed her some simple stitches on a plain piece of linen. Philippa was sitting alongside, sewing some bright threads in an embroidery she had already started. Henry was sitting on the floor, building a castle and walls with some wooden blocks.

Suddenly the door swept open and in came the tall lean figure of John of Gaunt. Fresh from the hunt, his face flushed and tanned from the sun and wind, he brought with him a smell of leather and horses. His presence radiated a vitality which filled the tranquil room, like waves from a stone thrown into still waters. Startled, Katherine looked up, straight into blue eyes which matched those of young Henry.

"Oh! My Lord!" exclaimed Katherine as she hurried to stand and curtsey to him. "We did not expect you so soon."

John had taken in the calm scene, the children absorbed in their tasks and the attentive figure in the green gown and flaxen hair. He did not notice at that moment the clash with the household in mourning, for he had also registered, with surprise, the serenity of her face and the luminous grey of her eyes. He had not expected such poise in one so young.

"Well – you seem to have settled in," he said rather gruffly. "I hope you have all you need?"

Henry ran to his father and curled himself round his leg. Elizabeth could contain herself no longer and burst out: "Katherine has been showing me how to do stitches... look!" holding up her piece of linen for him to see.

"Yes, that is good, but you should address her as Lady Katherine..." and then he caught Katherine's eye as she took a step forward.

"That is my doing, sire. I have said that they do not need to use my title when we are together in the day room like this. I fear that it puts a barrier between us, my Lord."

"I see. So be it. But," he added more weightily, "they must know their manners and behave at all times in accord with royal custom, so do not let the familiarity of the nursery spoil that."

"Yes, my Lord," replied Katherine.

Holding Henry's hand as she disengaged him from his father's knee, she curtseyed to him as he turned and left the room.

Chaucer was perched on the stool at his desk, a quill poised in his hand as he developed his ideas on the structure of his elegy to Duchess Blanche. He had decided to use his poem about Ceyx and Alcione for the opening. It was a harrowing tale of loss and hurt that would indirectly show an empathy for the grieving Duke and serve to set the scene. Now he was working on the main theme. He would present himself as a poet who, in a dream after reading the story of Alcione and Ceyx, joins a king's hunting foray into the forest. Deep in the forest, he meets a distraught Man in Black lamenting his sorrows. He questions the knight about his grief and is told the story of his beloved – of her beauty and gentle character – but that she has died. This would give him scope to portray Blanche as the lost love and to show and share his own grief with the Duke, who would be represented by the Man in Black.

He had described the King's hunting party and how the poet had met the knight:

> *…down in the wood*
> *I was 'ware of a Man in Black*
> *That sat and had turned his back*
> *To an oak, an huge tree.*
> *"Lord" thought I "Who may that be?*
> *What aileth him to sitten here?"*
>
> *For why he hung his head adown*
> *And with a deadly sorrowful sound*
> *He made of rhyme ten verse or twelve*
> *Of complaining to himself:*
> *"I have of sorrow so great a store*
> *That joy get I never more.*
> *Alas, death, what aileth thee*
> *That thou hadest not taken me!"*

Chaucer took up his quill, charged it from the inkhorn, and continued, in the manner of Machaut, with the poet questioning the knight about his sorrow:

"Ah, good sir," quod I, "Say not so!
Have some pity on your nature.
And tell me of your sorrows smart
Perhaps it may ease your hurt."

"Alas! and I will tell thee why
My song is turned to complaining
And all my laughter to weeping,

"My health is turned to sickness
To dark is turned all my light
My wit is folly, my day is night,
My love is hate, my sleep is waking."

"Good sir, tell me wholly
In what ways, how, why and wherefore
That ye have thus your bliss lost."

"It happed that I came on a day
Into a place where I saw
Truly the fairest company
Of ladies that ever man with eye
Had seen together in one place.
Among these ladies I saw one
That was like none of the rest.

"I have no wit that can suffice
To comprehend her beauty.
But this much dare I say, that she
Was White, ruddy, fresh and lively hewed
And every day her beauty renewed.
For every hair on her head,
True to say, it was not red,
Nor either yellow nor brown
Me thought most like gold it was.

"Right fair shoulders and body long
She had, and arms, every limb
Rounded, shapely, not great therewith;
Right white hands and nails red,
Round breasts and good broad
Her hips were; a straight flat back,
I knew her nothing lack.

"For certain Nature had such will
To make it clear that truly she
Was her chief patron of beauty
And chief example of all her work."

Chaucer laid down his quill, stretched his arms above his head and eased himself from the stool. That was enough writing for today. In any case he would need to think on how to conclude the elegy. Eulogising the beauty of the departed loved one and describing the agony of the stranded lover was not too difficult – especially as he had such noble examples to portray. But death was a harsh reaper and the stark emptiness of the stubbled field had to be faced. He would read again some of Machaut's poems, especially the 'Judgements' of the Kings of Bohemia and Navarre. And he was thirsty, so he went in search of a pot of ale.

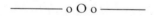

When he was satisfied with the ending that he had drafted for his elegy, Geoffrey went over what he had written. He had read passages of it to Philippa who had, in her usual forthright way, enthused and encouraged him overall but had also said what she disliked. For the most part he agreed with her comments and, accordingly, he had scratched out and replaced words and phrases here and there. Then he had made a fair manuscript copy. Advised by Philippa, he took this down to the Savoy where he sought audience with John, Duke of Lancaster. After waiting some time in an anteroom, he was shown to the Duke's privy chamber. John of Gaunt, still dressed in black and looking sombre, brightened as Chaucer approached and bowed to him.

"Geoffrey! I am pleased to see you!"

"The honour is mine, sire. I am truly sorry at your grievous loss, as we all are."

And then, taking a step forward, he took the manuscript out from under his cloak and offered it to the Duke.

"Out of love for the gentle Duchess and respect for you, my Lord, I humbly present this elegy which I have written. May I hope that it will burnish her memory and assuage your pain?"

John took the proffered manuscript and glanced over the early verses.

"This is most gracious and welcome," he said rather hoarsely, with a nod of acknowledgement towards Geoffrey. "I shall study this at my leisure."

And then, remembering those other times when he had heard Chaucer reciting his own works, he turned towards him: "But, better than that: let us arrange for you to present your book and narrate it before a small gathering here. Let us say, in two days' time, after we have dined. I am sure Queen Philippa will wish to be present and that your wife will be able to accompany her."

"I am greatly honoured, my Lord. Thank you."

And, bowing to the Duke, he withdrew and hurried home to give Philippa the news.

Geoffrey Chaucer had joined the small number of guests and members of the Duke of Lancaster's household who gathered, two days later, in the small hall at the Savoy for dinner. He had been especially pleased to be presented to Queen Philippa, the gracious consort of King Edward III, whose hair was now greying and her face lined, but whose eyes still danced with a lively spirit. She was accompanied by two of her ladies-in-waiting, one of which was his own Philippa. Among the guests he noted two of John of Gaunt's close friends, Sir John Chandos and Sir Robert Knolles, and their ladies; senior members of the Duke's retinue – Sir John Dypre, Chief of the Council; Sir Robert Swylyngton, Chamberlain, and Sir William Goyser, Steward; four ladies who had served Duchess Blanche, including Lady Marion Villiers; and the Duke's chaplain, John de Turnstal. All had been close to Duchess Blanche and knew her well.

Although the food was ample and richly presented, Geoffrey had been careful not to eat or drink too much. His mind was on his 'Book of the Duchess' and how he would present it. The occasion was too serious for play-acting and, in any case, the audience was too sophisticated to need his foolery to keep their interest. Nonetheless, he felt that too grave and serious a delivery was not suitable and could be boring. He would need to modulate his voice between the woefulness of the knight at his loss and the joy of his remembrance of his love's beauty.

Later, when he was well into his recitation, he felt he had succeeded in keeping a balance between the heavy weight of sorrow and the lightness of pleasures remembered. The ancient tragedy of Ceyx and Alcione had been well received as a fate that could be shared. The audience had stilled and held its breath at the complaining of the Man in Black. Now, as he took up the tale again of the Man in Black and came to the finale, he drew a deep breath and continued:

> *"'But wherefore that I tell my tale?*
> *For certain she was that sweet wife,*
> *My suffisuance, my lust, my life,*
> *My fortune, my Health and all my bliss,*
> *My world's welfare and my goddess,*
> *And I wholly hers in everything.*
> *Our hearts were so even a pair*
> *That never was one contrary*
> *To that other; all was us one.'*

"'Sir' quod I 'where is she now?'
'Now?' quod he and started to swoon
Therewith he wax as dead as stone.
'Thou knowest full little what thou meanest
I have lost more than thou kenest.
God wot, alas! Right that was she!'

"'Alas, Sir, How? What may that be?'
'She is Dead!' 'Nay.' 'Yes, by my truth!'
'Is that your loss? By God it is sore heavy grief.'

"And with that word right anon
The hunting horn called: all was done.
With that methought this king
Gan homeward for to ride
Unto a place was there beside –
A long castle with walls white
By Saint John on a rich hill.

"As I dreamed, thus it befell.
That in the castle there was a bell
As it had smitten hours twelve
Therewith I awoke myself
And found myself lying in bed.

"Thought I: 'This is so quaint a dream
That I will by process of time
Find to put this dream in rhyme
As I can best and that anon.
This was my dream: now it is done.'"

As Geoffrey bowed low to the Queen and the Duke, there was silence in a shared memory and then a quiet clapping from the other diners. Geoffrey moved forward and presented his 'Book of the Duchess' to the Duke. John stood up, leaned forward over the table to receive it, and said: "I shall treasure this. Thank you," and then, looking directly into Geoffrey's face, said in a quiet voice: "And thank you for your understanding. I know you share my loss."

John could not bring himself to say more. His feelings were too raw. Chaucer's words had evoked memories of Blanche – her beauty and tenderness – and of their companionship.

"All was us one."

Abidingly, that was how he would remember her.

Chapter Six

"**W**HAT DO YOU mean, crisis?" demanded King Edward. He was seated at a gilt table in his chancery, leaning forward aggressively, his jaw thrust out as he stared severely at Lord Latimer, his chamberlain. "Explain yourself."

Latimer bowed slightly before him. "Sire. The problem is twofold. The borders of Acquitaine are shrinking as some nobles transfer their allegiance to France, and others are wavering – even in Gascony – and we hear that King Charles is sending the Duke of Anjou to Toulouse and the Duke of Berri to Limousin…"

"Pharrghh!" exploded the King. "They are no match for Prince Edward. He will soon deal with them!"

"Of course, no doubt, my Lord. But you know that the Prince is weakened by the wasting sickness he caught in Spain after his great victory at Najero and," with a hasty glance at the King, "resentment at the hearth tax he has imposed is fomenting discontent."

"Yes, yes. Taxes are never popular, don't we know! But he is popular and will soon rally them. What is the second problem?" asked the King impatiently.

"King Charles has used the nine years of peace to build up his army and to train the levies from the communes, including in archery. And he has developed his navy. Ships are being built at Clos des Galées, and from Harfleur to Rouen the Seine is full of shipping. Ready, we think, to cross the Channel and attack our southern ports."

At this the King rose from his desk and paced round the chamber, stroking his chin.

"Mmmmhh. So, Charles, who has never stood and fought a battle in his life, has turned tactician, has he? Harass us in the north while Berri and Anjou attack in the south. We must counter this, Latimer. Call the herald and tell him to summon Prince John to join us forthwith."

John of Gaunt was at the Savoy when the royal herald was shown into his presence and gave him the summons from the King. He had been receiving reports from his steward, Sir William Croyser, on the management of his castles in the north and from Sir Walter Ursewych on the state of the forests in Blackburnshire where there had been persistent poaching.

"Gentlemen. I must leave you to go to the King. Please continue what we have started and, Sir William, let me know who you think should take over as Constable of our castle at Knaresborough. It is a castle vital to our interests and the slackness there cannot be allowed to continue."

The two knights bowed as John withdrew, calling to his page to tell Anthony, his bargeman, to make ready for the trip to Westminster.

Soon, he was standing in the stern of the barge, alongside Anthony at the tiller, as the eight oarsmen deftly propelled the craft upstream. John nodded to Anthony as he watched the rhythm of the oars, their golden-tipped blades dipping and skimming the water in perfect unison as the sun caught the braiding of the Lancaster crest on their red tunics.

"Your crew do well, Anthony. You shall have a tun of wine between you when we return to the Savoy."

"Thank you, my Lord. 'Tis much appreciated," replied Anthony. The men hoisted their oars to the vertical and he brought the barge neatly to rest at the stone wharf.

"Careful of the steps, my Lord. Tide is low and they be slippery."

John stepped lightly ashore, climbed the dozen steps and disappeared through a stout oak door into the Palace.

As he approached the chancery, he met the Earls of Cambridge and Pembroke waiting in the passage outside. They bowed in acknowledgement to him as he knocked and went in to join his father.

"Ah, John! Welcome. Come, join us," called King Edward as John bowed before him. "You know that the King of France has broken his word and is now reclaiming sovereignty over Acquitaine."

"Yes, sire," replied John, "and that, rightly so, you have reasserted your inherited claim to the throne of France!"

"Yes, so be it," said the King. "But now he is threatening Acquitaine. I have no doubt that Prince Edward will deal with this but you were with him in Spain at Najero and afterwards when he caught this flux. How fit is your brother?"

John paused, looked at his father, noted his serious demeanour, and considered his reply carefully. "The disease weakened him, my Lord, and at times his vigour is sapped. His temper too can be short. But when I left, he was recovering and, with the Princess Joan and the little Princes around him, I am sure he has progressed further."

"Good. It is as I thought. And now, call in the others, Latimer," he added.

The King resumed his seat at his desk as the four stood in a semi-circle before him.

"I've been considering the situation in France with Lord Latimer here. As you know, King Charles has never honoured the Treaty of Bretigny and indeed has been using the nine years of peace since then to build up his army and navy. Now he has devised a cunning tactic to threaten our principality of Acquitaine while marshalling ships along the Seine to launch against our channel ports."

John, remembering the campaign led by his father nine years ago, when the same French King had refused to engage in battle, scoffed: "But, sire, this adversary is not a worthy or wise prince: he is but a lawyer, a paper tiger!"

King Edward roared with laughter and slapped his thigh. "Oh, well said, my son. How apt…!" as he continued to chuckle. "But be that as it may, I fear we must counter his tactics. "Prince John, I want you to lead an expedition into northern France from Calais to see if you can draw the teeth of this tiger, if he has any, and if possible to despoil his shipping which is amassed around Harfleur."

And addressing Cambridge and Pembroke, he continued in an acid tone: "My Lords, there are some nobles in Acquitaine who begin to think their bread would be better buttered by serving the French King than under our sovereignty. This has encouraged King Charles to assume, such are his paper tactics, that the principality is his for the taking and he has sent the Duke of Anjou to Toulouse and the Duke of Berri to Limousin to encircle the province to this end. We are confident that Prince Edward will counter this threat, but a diversionary expedition from La Rochelle to link up with the Prince would warn him off. I want you, my Lords, to lead this expedition."

As was customary on receiving such a commission, John and the earls knelt before the King and swore their allegiance and loyalty in accepting and carrying out his command.

"I will sign the ordinances for these expeditions as soon as they are prepared. This will enable you each to draw on the Exchequer, requisition the ships and muster the men you need beyond your own retinues."

When the news of John of Gaunt's expedition reached Hertford Castle, there was a stir of excitement and activity. Although there was no garrison there of men-at-arms who would be going to France, everyone knew that, as throughout the Lancastrian estates, they would be expected to contribute to the preparations. And there was plenty for them to do: beef and pork to salt down in barrels; tuns of wine and casks of ale to be stacked; field kitchens to be packed; banners, tunics and undershirts to be washed and sewn and items of chain mail to be checked and repaired; horses and wagons to be assembled and loaded. It was a familiar routine and the house, courtyard and barns were soon throbbing with busyness.

It was a warm May morning and Katherine was in the garden of the castle when she heard the news. She immediately wondered what this would mean. Her husband, Sir Hugh, served in the Duke's retinue and would surely go with him. Would she see him before they left? And would the Duke want to see his children? She called them to her and told them the news. Philippa, the oldest, gave her a straight and solemn look, but Elizabeth and young Henry were excited and bouncing with questions.

"Will we see Father? And will he take his big black horse?" asked Elizabeth.

"And I want to see him on his horse and his shiny armour and big feather in his helmet," said Henry.

"Well, I don't know if he will have time to see you. We will have to wait and see."

"Oh fie!" said Elizabeth, stamping her foot. "It's always wait and see!"

Katherine laughed and gave her a little hug. "I am sure my Lord will send a message to you even if he cannot come himself."

It was a week into June before a message came. Then, at noon, a herald with the Lancaster arms blazoned on his chest, clattered into the cobbled yard with sealed messages for Lady Marion and the steward, William Baker, and one for Lady Swynford. When it was brought to her, Katherine broke the seal with a twinge of excitement and read that:

> *Prince John, Duke of Lancaster, Earl of Derby, Lincoln and Leicester, Seneschal of England, hereby requires Lady Swynford to attend on him at the Savoy Palace forthwith and to bring his children Philippa, Elizabeth and Henry to him. She is to make arrangements in her absence for the safe care of infant Edward.*

The document was signed by the Duke and impressed with his signet.

This was the first formal message she had received and it left her suddenly nervous. She had enjoyed being at Hertford with the children. Over the last nine months, she had learnt the customs and manners of the household under Lady Marion's guidance. She it was who had complimented her on the smooth running of the nursery and had said what a happy place it was. London and the Savoy were a daunting prospect: big, and bustling with so many people. It would be difficult for her to know who was who and what was what and how she should act. She felt she would be lost in the great palace. If only she could stay with her sister Philippa at the Queen's residence.

But her worries were soon forgotten as she was caught up in the children's excitement and the flurry of preparations for the journey. She was to ride for the first time in one of the Duke's covered coaches with the three children. But first she gave clear instructions to Grace, her maid, and Mary, the nurse, that the routine of the nursery was to continue and that the strictest of care was to be taken of the baby, Edward. They were to ensure that her own son, Thomas, did not upset the baby and caused no nuisance.

Soon they were on their way, following the old Roman Ermine Street down through Hoddesdon and Cheshunt. The coach made a fine sight, pulled by two well-matched white horses whose red cockades bobbed up and down as Alfred, the coachman, drove them forward at a smart pace. They were escorted by four mounted lancers, two on each side, from the Duke's retinue. Holding their lances aloft, their presence ensured a clear thoroughfare and drew glances from those curious to know who was travelling in such style. There was an occasional cheer as the red rose of Lancaster embossed on the doors of the coach was recognised.

The horses slackened to a walking pace as they approached Shoreditch. There were more houses and a greater press of people in the street. The noise of their cries woke Elizabeth, who had nodded off with the motion of the coach, her head resting on Katherine's lap.

"Are we nearly there, Katherine?" she asked as she sat up, peered out and saw the houses and people on both sides.

"Yes, I believe so," replied Katherine. At that moment they trundled through the stone archway at Moorgate, through the City walls and into London.

John of Gaunt was busy with his two captains, Sir Walter Manny and Sir Henry Percy, discussing the best way of getting his contingent of 600 men-at-arms and 1,500 archers across the Channel to Calais, when a page brought the news that Katherine and the children had arrived from Hertford. He gave him instructions to check that the nursery had been prepared in the east wing and that a message be delivered to Lady Swynford that he would visit the children this evening. He then turned back to his colleagues.

"Sir Henry is keen that we use the shortest way, my Lord, certainly for the troops, and I agree," said Sir Walter. "That means using Dover and the other Cinque Ports. But they do not have enough quay space to embark the baggage and horses as well."

"So we need cargo space assembled in the Thames and, we suggest, Portsmouth," added Sir Henry.

"Do we need to requisition more shipping for this?"

"Yes. I think we do," replied Sir Walter, "at least another hundred. Portsmouth can draw some from Portland and Lyme so the need is mainly in the Thames."

"I can muster a small squadron from the Humber," offered Sir Henry, "so we need to requisition ships from the merchants on the Anglican coast down from Lynn to the Blackwater."

"Very well; so be it. Make plain the terms of recompense for this and mark that I want to be away within ten days, say by 19th June, God willing with favourable winds."

Henry was already in bed when John got to the nursery. Lady Swynford explained this as she welcomed the Duke with a curtsey.

"Is he asleep?" he asked.

"I doubt it, my Lord, unless his excitement has overcome him. But in any case he made me promise I would wake him," she smiled.

"Then I'll go to him straightaway."

Katherine led the way along the wooden panelled passage and stood aside for John to enter into Henry's room first. The boy immediately sat up and said brightly: "But you haven't got your armour on!" John laughed and sat on the bed beside his son.

"Oh, I don't wear it until there is a battle to be fought, and first we have to go to France," and then, seeing the disappointment in his son's eyes, he added, "I'll tell you what, you shall inspect it with me in the morning. How is that?"

"And Elizabeth wants to see your horse too," burst out Henry.

"Well, we will see," said John, smiling and standing up.

"And now I think you should settle down to sleep, Henry," said Katherine, tucking up the bedclothes.

After John had seen Philippa and Elizabeth and promised that they could join the tour of inspection in the morning, he drew Katherine aside and asked after baby Edward.

Katherine turned a serious face to him: "He is still chesty and catches his breath at times, my Lord," she replied. "Nurse rubs his chest with liniment and gives him honey and the herbs made up by the apothecary. I have taken him into the garden when the weather suits to air his lungs. He is getting stronger but still needs care."

John watched her face as she was speaking and was again struck by her poise and the direct honest look of her dark-lashed grey eyes.

"Well, thank you. I trust you in your care of him." And then, as he turned to go, he paused: "Queen Philippa has been asking after the children. I will arrange an audience for you to take them to her."

Seeing Katherine's quick look of surprise and excitement, he added in a softer voice: "And no doubt you will be able to confer with your sister."

"You are very kind, my Lord. And in the morning...?" she prompted.

"Ah, yes. My promise to Henry! Bring him and Elizabeth down to the courtyard at eight o'clock, and Philippa if she wishes to come..." he added over his shoulder as he left the room.

Three days later, Katherine and the children left the Savoy in the Duke's coach to go to the Queen's house in Thames Street for the visit to their grandmother. As she stepped down from the carriage in front of the house, Katherine looked up eagerly but could not see her sister. Philippa helped Elizabeth and Henry to climb down and then joined Katherine as the younger pair ran ahead to where a page was standing in the open doorway. He bowed as Katherine approached and led the way along a stone-flagged passageway to a small garden where Queen Philippa was sitting on a bench in the shade of a lilac tree with Katherine' s sister and one of her other ladies-in-waiting.

The page approached, bowed and announced: "My Lady, Prince Henry and the Princesses Philippa and Elizabeth have arrived with Lady Swynford."

The Queen clapped her hands together and exclaimed, "Oh, what joy!" and held her arms out wide as Elizabeth rushed towards her. Henry was soon engulfed too but Philippa with more mature dignity came forward with a beautiful curtsey.

The Queen responded with a regal bow of her head and then reached forward to take her oldest granddaughter's hand, "My dear, whenever I see you I realise your dear mother is still with us. You have her grace and fair, slender form."

"Thank you, my Lady." Then she stepped closer and took a small embroidered kerchief from a pocket in her gown and presented it to the Queen. "I hope you will accept this small token which I have made for you."

"Why, this is beautiful. I did not know that you had such skill as a seamstress."

"'Tis Lady Katherine who has helped me with it," explained Philippa.

"Yes, of course!" and seeing Katherine standing by, she called to her, "Lady Swynford, do please come forward."

Katherine moved in front of the Queen and dropped a deep curtsey. The Queen smiled and her eyes twinkled.

"So, you are the other daughter of my good Hainault country-man and Herald, Sir Ralph. And I see a family likeness although you are taller than your sister. Welcome! Come sit with me and tell me about the children and especially about baby Edward."

While her sister played with the children in the garden, Katherine sat with the Queen, answering her questions about how she managed the nursery. Soon, under the Queen's prompting, she was telling her about ways she kept the children amused and of the games they played. The Queen laughed out loud at some of the antics of Elizabeth, who she thought was a born actress. Then the Queen asked in a serious tone about Edward. She explained, as she had done with the Duke, about his frail chest and the remedies they were using as directed by Father Julian, the Duke's physician.

"Edward is precious to Prince John," explained the Queen. "Duchess Blanche gave him another son called John between Philippa and Elizabeth but, sadly, he did not live very long. He fears the same might happen to Edward, and if so, since Blanche herself has died, he cannot get another son. So, you see how important it is to care for him."

And then she patted Katherine's hand, stood up and said brightly, "But you are caring for him very well."

Later, while the children enjoyed cakes and cherries with their grandmother, Katherine talked with her sister Philippa. As usual, Philippa played the older sister and wanted to know if she was minding her manners with Lady Marion and in the household. She warned Katherine against being too familiar with the children or with the Duke and to guard against gossips whose spite often stemmed from jealousy. Katherine turned the conversation by asking after Geoffrey.

"Oh, he is busy as usual with his nose in his books," she said, somewhat tartly, "and he will be going with the Duke to Calais, not as a soldier like the last time, but as an envoy on the King's business." And then she asked, "Sir Hugh, being in the Duke's retinue, will be going as well, will he not?"

"Yes, I am sure so, although I have not had that from him, for he is away mustering at Kenilworth," replied Katherine.

The children had finished their eating and the carriage had come for them to return to the Savoy. The Queen kissed them all and bade them attend to Lady Swynford. Katherine embraced her sister and, after thanking Queen Philippa and curtseying to her, mounted the step of the coach which, with the children waving, wheeled away down the street past the Chaucers' house on their way along the Thames back to the Duke's London home.

Katherine hurried out of the nursery after the children who were scampering along, eager to get into the courtyard to see their father, Prince John, who was assembling with his senior captains, ready to ride down to the Tower where they were to embark for France. For once the children's boisterous excitement had flustered her. This was partly because of Sir Hugh's sudden arrival from Kenilworth late last evening. She could still feel the crush of her husband's first embrace and his weight on her as they had lain briefly together before he went into a deep sleep, noisy from the quantity of ale he had supped.

He had left early to join his men but not before she had given him a bright green garland to wear on his helmet and called with him for God's blessing to protect him.

Now, she stood with the children admiring the horses with their shining coats, plaited manes and gilded harnesses as they were led around in a circle by the grooms. Sir Henry Percy stood opposite bantering with a small group of keyed-up knights. Then the Duke himself came out, resplendent in a black velvet tunic with, on his chest, the royal leopards halved with the Lancaster insignia. Henry tugged at Katherine's hand to run to him but she held him back for fear of the horses' hooves until the Duke saw them and started towards them.

He bent, hoisted young Henry to him and said to Katherine: "Well, my Lady, take good care of them. And," looking down at Elizabeth and Philippa, "you tend to Lady Katherine."

Then with a mischievous look at Katherine he asked, "What, have you no favour for me, my Lady?"

Sensing his humour, Katherine replied brightly, "Would it could be so, my Lord, but my token is already on Sir Hugh's helmet." She noticed a quick shadow flit across his face and quickly added, "But Philippa has a ribbon for you."

"Yes, Father, please wear this, for all of us, and come back safely."

"Why, yes, my Princess. Indeed I shall," as he took the garland, kissed his two daughters and set Henry down on his feet. "Now let us be away. Mount up!" he shouted as he turned and moved towards his great black charger.

Katherine watched with the children as the cavalcade filed through the archway in pairs on their way along the Thames to the wharf at the Tower. The courtyard was suddenly silent and empty: only the brooding stone faces of the walls stared down. Katherine felt a little shiver run down her spine and was suddenly filled with foreboding. Then she shrugged and shepherded the children back up to the nursery.

——— o O o ———

Geoffrey Chaucer arrived at The Swan Inn in Canterbury just as dusk was falling. He had had a long day and was looking forward to a hot meal, some fine wine and, later, a comfortable bed. But first he must see his horse attended to. He dismounted stiffly and called the stable boy. He gave instructions for the horse to be well rubbed down and to have some mash and clean straw in his stall. He pressed a silver coin into the boy's palm to spice his work.

Geoffrey had sailed from Calais on the early tide and had ridden up from Dover. He was on his way to London with a sealed despatch from the Duke of Lancaster to King Edward. Geoffrey knew the contents and was to elaborate if the King wanted further intelligence. Geoffrey had smiled wryly when the Duke had told him this and he did not relish the thought. The King's temper could well be roused when he heard that the French had refused again to fight and had suddenly decamped during the night, despite having much the larger army.

Soon he was sitting quietly in an alcove downstairs, supping a pint of ale. He was beginning to relax when the landlord brought him a steaming bowl of fish broth.

"Here we are, Master Chaucer. This will go down well, I'm sure, after your long journey. And we've a good ham shank stew with peas and parsnips to follow."

"That will do splendidly," replied Geoffrey. "And bring me a good Bordeaux."

"'Tis sad news of the Queen, isn't it?" continued his host.

"Oh! What is that?" asked Chaucer, pausing as he raised a spoonful of soup.

"Why, did you not know? She died just two days ago. 'Tis said it was the plague come again…" he faltered as he saw the effect this had had on his guest. Geoffrey was sitting stiffly and staring at him with a stricken look, the soup spilling from his spoon.

"No. I did not know…" He paused and then added quietly, as he put down his spoon, "This is a blow. The King will miss her sorely – and so will we all."

Geoffrey went back to his meal and slowly digested this news as he sipped his broth. Indeed, he thought, she will be missed. She had, he knew, counselled her husband wisely over the years and restrained his choleric temper and more impetuous acts. The time when she had pleaded on her knees before him to save the lives of the burghers when the siege of Calais was raised was now a legend. She was a supreme example of queenly virtue, of compassion and justice and duty, as well as beauty. Chaucer wondered who now would place a restraining hand on the King's shoulder, and what would the future hold for his own Philippa who had served the Queen for the past nine years. She would, he knew, be greatly distraught.

The landlord returned with the ham and vegetables and a draught of red wine. Geoffrey had been watching the large group seated across the low-beamed room round a large refectory table.

"You've a lively group of guests there, landlord. Are they pilgrims come to do penance at St Thomas a Becket's tomb?" he asked.

"Why, yes, Master Chaucer. They arrived this forenoon from Southwark. They'd been four days on the way and are pleased now to be out of the saddle and easing their bones, I can tell you! As you see, there's some merry characters among them," and then, leaning forward confidentially, he added with a chuckle, "but some sober sides too!"

Chaucer looked with relish at the steaming ham and pea stew, for he had eaten little since he left Calais and settled down to satisfy his hunger. As he did so, his gaze kept running over the group of pilgrims and this set him musing on their backgrounds, for they were indeed, as the landlord had hinted, a mixed bunch, not only in manners but also in dress and deportment.

He smiled as he watched the friar who was at the centre of the table and of the gaiety. Fat and merry, well dressed in a fine habit of double worsted, he was full of amusing tales. And, Chaucer thought, he was no doubt a very persuasive beggar when it came to granting pardons and raising money, even from poor folk, for his order – and, no doubt, for his own comfort – by selling relics and receiving gifts as a penance.

Sitting opposite him was a nun, probably a prioress, Chaucer decided, as she had two nuns in attendance. She too was finely dressed in a well-made cloak and stiff wimple that framed her face which was round with a broad forehead, small red mouth and grey eyes which twinkled at the friar's tales. While the friar was very expansive, she was dainty and coy, very precise and proper in her eating. She had two small dogs at her feet to which, Geoffrey noticed, she quietly slipped morsels from her platter.

Next to the prioress was an impressive deep-chested figure with a shining red face and a cropped beard as white as a daisy. He beamed at the company from his ruddy face, clearly mainly intent on his food. Geoffrey sensed that an ample table was commonplace to him and he probably had a well-stocked fish pond on his estate and hunting rights in the forest. He had all the airs of a feudal landlord and could well be a Sheriff or Member of Parliament for his shire.

At the end of the table nearest to Geoffrey sat four wiry, more serious men who talked mainly among themselves and who wore the livery of a guild. Geoffrey guessed they were craftsmen, but prosperous ones, with a richly embroidered coat of arms on their tunics and silver daggers at their belts. The colour and fine workmanship of their tunics suggested they were dyers, weavers or tapestry makers and fit to be burgesses, who had the wherewithal and grace to be leaders, or aldermen at their guildhall. And, no doubt, Geoffrey thought, remembering social occasions at his father's house, their wives would enjoy this status and take on airs and graces and expect to be addressed as 'madam' whenever they could!

At the furthest end of the long table were four individuals that Chaucer had difficulty in placing. One was so ugly that it was, perhaps, not surprising that he sat away from the merriment. He had a fiery red, diseased face, all pimpled, with swollen eyes and knobs sitting on his cheeks and brows. He had drunk well of strong red wine and declaimed in Latin about the 'Archdeacon's curse', '*Questis quid juris*', absolution and imprisonment, from which Chaucer deduced that he was an officer of the Church – probably one who issued summons for immoral behaviour from a religious court.

Sitting with him was a bird of a similar feather, for he wore the badge of St Veronica with an imprint of Christ's face on his cap, which showed that he had been on a pilgrimage to Rome. His hair was long and yellow and hung in streaks down to his shoulders. His eyes bulged and glared like a hare's. His voice was thin and reed-like and he wore no beard – nor was he likely to, thought Chaucer with a smile. He had a bulging bag by his side which Chaucer guessed was brimful with relics, supposedly brought back from Rome, and with which illiterate innocents could be persuaded to purchase a pardon for their sins.

Alongside were the two quietest men at the table. One was clearly more at home with books than people, for he had a book beside him and spoke no more than he needed and then in short formal ways. He was as thin as a rake, sober and saturnine. He wore a short threadbare coat. He reminded Chaucer of some scholars he had seen in Oxford, and he wondered if he was an unplaced clerk without a parish benefice.

The other quiet man wore a plain but neat smock. He was respectful, polite and pious, for he was foremost in prayers for blessing and giving thanks for the meal. It was then that Geoffrey noticed his big hands with red knuckles and gnarled fingers. He had a weather-beaten open face with brown eyes used, judging by the crow's feet, to scanning distances. He was broad in the shoulder, straight in the back with a muscular frame. Chaucer decided that he looked like a person skilled in country crafts, such as ploughing. His skills would be much in demand since the Black Death had taken so many. He was probably increasing his land holding and status in his community, which was how he was able to come on this pilgrimage. He was, Geoffrey concluded, the truest pilgrim of them all.

Chaucer arrived at Westminster soon after midday, having left Canterbury at daybreak. He had not long to wait before he was called into the King's presence. As he entered he saw the King seated at his table, silhouetted against the light streaming over his shoulder from the large leaded window behind him. Lord Latimer was standing at his side. Chaucer approached and bowed formally before offering the despatches he had brought from John of Gaunt. Lord Latimer leaned forward, took them and handed them to King Edward who broke the seal and began reading.

"God's teeth, Latimer!" he exploded. "Charles has done it again: withdrawn his army, decamped in the middle of the night, like some skulking fox. Is there no end to this man's cowardice?"

He stood up, threw the despatch on the table and stomped impatiently round the room. Then, remembering the messenger, barked out: "You were there, Chaucer. How was it?"

Chaucer was not surprised. Messengers were often the first to be blamed for the tidings they carried. He had prepared himself on his ride from Canterbury and chose his words carefully.

"Sire, we had found the French army north of Abbeville at a place called Tournehem. Prince John had deployed his archers and men in strong positions facing the enemy, who were more than three times our number. We could see their campfires, and all of us were as taut as bowstrings for battle the next day. Then at dawn, as the first foray advanced, we saw that the foe had fled – melted away like mist before a rising sun. It was gut-wrenching, sire, for Prince John – and all of us."

The King slapped his thigh in natural sympathy and cried out "What's to be done, Latimer?"

Picking up the despatch from the table, Latimer said: "Prince John has added, my Lord, that he will advance to the Seine and despoil as much shipping as he can around Harfleur."

The King nodded. "Yes, that is all he can do. But send word to him to return when that is done. Pursuing a foe who will not fight is a useless waste of energy." And then he added as an aside almost to himself, "Maybe that is what this lawyer King intends."

At this Chaucer stepped forward and bowed. "Sire, may I say how much my wife and I share your burden of grief and offer our prayers for Queen Philippa."

King Edward stopped his pacing, blinked and frowned at Chaucer, as though forcing his mind back to the present, before replying, "We are grateful, Master Chaucer, and especially for your wife's service to the Queen."

Chaucer bowed deeply and, stepping backwards, withdrew to go home to his wife.

All was quiet at the house in Thames Street when Chaucer arrived home. He found his wife sitting alone before an empty hearth. He went to her, knelt down and held her in an embrace as she began to sob. Then she drew back and looked through her tears into his face.

"She was so gentle and kind, Geoffrey. She made me feel part of her family since we both came from Hainault. She used to talk to me sometimes about her life there. We all loved her."

"Yes, I know, my dear, and the King made a particular point of thanking you for your service to the Queen when I offered our sorrow and prayers."

Philippa's eyes brightened at this, and she brushed the tears from her cheeks with the back of her hand. Geoffrey looked at the sad round face and then sat beside her.

"But I am loth to say that I have other dark news, my love. Sir Hugh Swynford, Katherine's husband, is dead."

"Oh," cried Philippa, "that is dreadful. Was he killed in battle?"

"No. Although I am sure he would have preferred it that way, for he was a ferocious and valiant soldier. The flux that he first suffered in Spain returned and this time defeated him. They took him into Calais but by the time he got there he was in a pitiful state. He was a blunt, plain character and he certainly lacked courtly virtues, as you know, but he was a loyal and much valued knight in John of Gaunt's retinue."

"Yes, I suppose so," said Philippa, who had never approved of him. "Has Katherine had this news?"

"No," replied Geoffrey, "I must go to Hertford and break it to her. And I have a despatch from Prince John for her which will give her some comfort as he will provide protection in her widowhood."

"Well, as Hugh was in his service, that is only proper," replied Philippa, rallying on behalf of her sister and then, ever the practical one, added: "She will need his support until she finds another husband."

Her face softened as she remembered playing with the children in the Queen's garden and that it was the Queen, on her prompting, who had persuaded John to take Katherine as governess of his children. "And I think she is valued for herself, for she takes good care of his children."

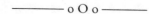

Katherine was pleased to see Geoffrey. She sprang up from her chair and with a little skip towards him cried: "Why, Geoffrey, this is a pleasant surprise," and then she faltered and the excitement left her face as she saw how grave and worried he looked. Chaucer took both her hands in his and led her to the settle.

"Katherine, my dear, I am sorry to be the bearer of such news, but Sir Hugh died in Calais a week ago yesterday."

"Oh," cried Katherine, covering her mouth with her hands and looking startled. "So that was it! I had a premonition when they left that something dreadful was going to happen, but I thought…" her voice trailed off.

"You thought what?" prompted Geoffrey, glad that Katherine was talking and had not collapsed into a weeping heap. She looked up at him.

"I thought… it was about Prince John," she said looking flustered. "But tell me about Hugh."

"He developed the flux again and became very weak, not being able to keep anything inside him. The Prince sent Father Gervase, his physician, to him, but to no avail…" He paused and went on, in a soft voice, "Look, I have brought a despatch for you from the Duke."

Katherine took the sealed manuscript, looked up at him, broke the seal and began reading. Chaucer studied her as she did this. She was taller and slimmer than her sister and fairer with lovely flaxen hair. He was struck again by her composure and almost serene presence. She looked up at him when she had finished reading and searched his face with troubled grey eyes.

"Geoffrey, the Duke is arranging for his steward at Lincoln to visit Kettlethorpe and," she read from the letter, "'make all good and true arrangements for the management and security of the manor'. And, Geoffrey," she hurried on, as though to hide her discomfort in words, "I know I should be more sorrowful… and I am! Hugh was a good man at heart despite his rough ways and, praise be to God, he has given me a fine son in Thomas, hasn't he? I was a dutiful wife but, I fear, I did not love him." She turned a stricken face to Geoffrey and cried out, "Is that sinful?"

"Why, no, sister. I think not, and you should not chide yourself over it. It is a rare marriage that is a love match. Duty rather than love is more often the touchstone of marriage. At best it settles down to tolerant affection."

Katherine looked at him. She guessed that this was probably the way of his marriage to Philippa, which reminded her: "But, Geoffrey, the Queen! How is Philippa taking it?"

"She is much upset, for she truly loved the Queen, who was gentle and kind and almost like a mother to her. She will be missed, not least by King Edward, although," he added almost to himself, "I doubt that he realises how good she was for him."

"Will you take a letter for my sister? I must see her or, perhaps, she could come here for a while. I am sure Lady Marion would approve. What do you think?"

Geoffrey smiled. Katherine was still covering her feelings with a gush of words. But she meant well and it would be good for Philippa to have Katherine and the children to think about. He would see if he could persuade her.

"I will gladly take a letter to your sister. Be persuasive for her to come here as I think it will be helpful to you both."

Katherine straightaway went to her table, found a parchment and quill and wrote briefly to her sister, asking her to come to Hertford. She smiled as she gave it to Geoffrey: "I do not have a grand signet to seal this with: a thumbprint will have to do!" as she pressed down on the folded letter. "Please add your persuasions, Geoffrey."

"Rest assured I will, my dear. Now I must leave you."

He stood in front of her, put his hands on her shoulders and said directly: "Promise you will call me if need be?" leaned forward and brushed her cheek with a kiss.

"Yes, dear Geoffrey, I will." Tears welled up in her eyes as he withdrew.

Philippa stayed a fortnight at Hertford, helping with the Duke's children and Katherine's own son Thomas. She did not have her sister's gentle manner and her tendency to bossiness led to some sulks from the younger children and direct naughtiness from the high-spirited Elizabeth. But it was a pleasant and comforting interlude for both sisters.

They talked about the Duke. Katherine confessed her admiration of him and her intense desire to please him. Philippa sensed there might be something more than this and warned Katherine sternly against any dreams or fantasies. John of Gaunt was a royal prince and, like his father, demanded obedience and service as a right and could be cold and unforgiving over indiscretions or trespass into familiarity.

They talked too of Geoffrey. Typically, Philippa expressed some impatience with her husband. With his facility with words and languages he was useful to the King as an envoy and was often sent to France or Italy, but nothing more. His writings were a distraction to getting a proper post in the Chancery or Exchequer. Katherine smiled and tactfully said that she liked him and found him kind and amusing, especially when he was putting on a dramatic voice or mimicking some pompous official. Philippa softened and agreed that he was kind and generous and better than many husbands. But he was too easy-going!

Katherine admired her sister and knew that Philippa's protectiveness and ambition were born of a fierce family pride and loyalty. Was their father not Herald and Knight of the Court of Hainault? Was he not a close adviser to Queen Philippa and thus the equal of any knight at King Edward's court? Philippa saw her own service to the Queen as a continuation of a family tradition. Her distress at the Queen's death had been partly because that link had been broken.

The sisters shared a common friend in Lady Marion, who had also at some time been a lady-in-waiting to the Queen. Katherine encouraged Philippa to talk with Lady Marion. They shared a practical wisdom, and Marion encouraged Philippa to think, with her record of service, that she would soon be called to serve in another royal household. Philippa was quite certain, however, that she would never serve Alice Perrers, the King's mistress, who it was said was now strutting like the leading lady at Court.

Philippa was pleased therefore, and hopeful, when a royal summons came for her to go back to London to assist with the settlement of Queen Philippa's household.

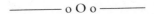

John of Gaunt returned from his campaign in France in late September, feeling frustrated but satisfied that he had done as well as he could against a shy foe. He wished that he could have done more damage among the shipping outside Harfleur but he had too few resources to cross the river and there were early signs of fever among the troops brought on by the damp of autumn mists. He had related all this and more to the King, who was keen to relive the campaign through John's eyes and vent his anger and disgust at the unchivalrous conduct of the French King.

John had also been kept engaged on the business of discharging the army, paying off the shipping and settling debts arising from the campaign. With his chamberlain and steward, he scrutinised closely the payments received from the royal exchequer to ensure they were correct and in full measure and so that he could reckon what needed to be raised from his own resources. He set the level of the scutage tax to be paid at the Michaelmas accounting by those tenants who had not rendered military service. He had discussed with Sir Henry Percy and his other commanders which knights and men had given distinguished service and how they should be rewarded.

He thought again of the loss of Sir Hugh Swynford. He had been a godsend in battle with his ferocious fighting, although a coarse man overall. His marriage to the poised and gentle Katherine was an odd match. He wondered how grieved she was. He remembered that he must see her and the children and decided that they should come to the Savoy since the demands of attendance on the King and the business of the Lancastrian estates meant he could not leave London. He brightened at the thought and summoned his clerk to prepare a message.

It was therefore nearly two full weeks after his return from France that Lady Katherine and the children arrived at the white palace on the banks of the Thames. Soon after their arrival a page delivered a message for Katherine to join the Duke in his chancery. He was sitting alone at a table, reading and signing documents, when she entered the room. John stood and came towards her as she curtseyed before him. He welcomed her with a slight bow and, gesturing with his hand, said: "Come, join me by the fireside."

As she sat down, he studied her to gauge her mood. She was perhaps a little pale but not pinched and overwrought or red-eyed from weeping as he had seen in some newly widowed women. She seemed as calm and composed as ever. As she joined her hands across her lap, she looked up at him and he was struck again by the beauty of her large grey eyes and her direct open gaze.

"Katherine," he said, "Sir Hugh was one of my truest soldiers, a lusty fighter who served me in many campaigns in France and Spain. The same allegiance he gave to me I now owe to you and you shall have my protection."

Katherine dropped her eyes and flushed with pleasure at his words.

"My Lord, I am indeed blessed." And then she looked directly at him and said with a fierce intensity: "And for my part, I shall be honoured, my Lord, to serve you just as faithfully as did my husband."

John nodded in acknowledgement and turned to more immediate matters.

"My steward at Lincoln reports that part of the roof at Kettlethorpe has fallen in. I have ordered that sixty oaks be felled so that the roof may be restored and the manor be made good. Also he will oversee the bailiff who served Sir Hugh. So you need have no concern about the management of your manor."

The manor at Kettlethorpe had been much on Katherine's mind since Geoffrey had told her of Sir Hugh's death. She knew that it was not in good condition and that Sir Hugh had been absent for long periods. She did not fully trust the bailiff for she thought him lazy and too fond of ale. She felt it was her duty to look after the Swynford inheritance, especially for the sake of her son Thomas, who would one day inherit the title.

"But should I not go there, my Lord?" she asked.

John smiled at her earnestness and protested: "But who then would rule my nursery? No, Kettlethorpe will be well looked after, I assure you. And I need you here. And," he added lightly, "what would my son Henry do without the devotion of his playmate Thomas?"

"Very well, my Lord," replied Katherine, with a dimpled smile, her eyes shining brightly. "And, thank you."

John nodded and added: "And, Katherine, I want you to join me at my table for dinner tomorrow evening."

"Yes, my Lord," Katherine replied with eyes wide with surprise as she stood and curtseyed to him.

As she left the room and returned to the nursery, her head was spinning with relief from the fear that she would have to go away to Lincolnshire and her heart sang with joy.

At the Duke's insistence, except when her duties kept her in the nursery, Katherine regularly sat at his table for the evening meal. She was at first shy and diffident, especially when engaged in conversation by whichever guests were sitting by her. She found the lords and knights easier to talk with than their ladies. Their easy banter and unaffected romancing amused her. She had even had love poems recited to her, including one by Chaucer!

Through this she absorbed something of the manners of the Court and had been surprised at the free flow of gossip about people and events at Court, especially tales about Alice Perrers.

At one such evening in mid-November, her maid, Grace, appeared at the side door and nervously made her way to Katherine.

"Grace, whatever is it?" asked Katherine.

"'Tis baby Edward, my Lady. He is choking badly for his breath. Nurse said I was to fetch you," replied Grace, wringing her hands and looking about with big round eyes in her nervousness.

"I will come at once," said Katherine.

She stood up and made her way to the Duke's place at the centre of the table, curtseyed and whispered to him as he turned towards her.

"My Lord, please may I be excused? I am needed in the nursery. Prince Edward has had a coughing fit."

"How bad is it?" asked John.

"Bad enough for me to be called, my Lord, but we will see…"

"Yes. You go… and summon me if need be. Otherwise I will join you directly."

"Thank you, my Lord," replied Katherine and, lifting her skirts, hurried after Grace to the nursery, filled with a fearful foreboding.

Along the way they met Father Gervase, the Duke's physician, in his monk's habit, who had also been sent for by Mary, the nurse. They entered the nursery together. Mary was kneeling beside the cot with her arm under the baby to help ease his breathing. Katherine gasped at the sight of him. His face was purple, his arms flailing weakly with his little fists clenched as he fought for breath. Father Gervase bent over him, took a phial from his purse and spread a few drops of oil on the baby's chest. He looked up at Katherine and explained.

"This is a mixture of camomile, pine and camphor. It should soothe the walls of his chest both inside and out as he takes in its airs – but I fear he is too weakened to gain much from it."

"You mean…" started Katherine, but stopped in horror as she saw a small froth of blood appear at the corner of Edward's mouth. "Quickly," she cried, "we must send for the Prince."

"I agree," said the monk, "but hurry."

When John of Gaunt arrived, his son was fighting for his last breath. He made a gurgling sound as a further dribble of blood ran from his mouth and then lay limp and still. John paled, a knot working at his jaw as he clenched his teeth. He bowed his head, clasped his hands together, knelt by the cot and asked the monk to administer the sacrament. In a quiet voice, with John, Katherine and Mary kneeling round the cot, Father Gervase blessed the child with the sign of the cross and prayed for Edward's departing soul on its path to heaven. When he had finished, John nodded, stood and said quietly: "Thank you, Father. Please make due arrangements for the lying-in in the chapel," and turning to Mary, who was sobbing quietly with her apron to her face: "Thank you for the love and care you have given to my son. I shall not forget."

Then he turned towards the door, said brusquely, "Come, Lady Katherine," and departed with Katherine hurrying after him.

Once outside, John stopped and leant against the wall with his head bowed and his face in his hands. After a while he straightened, took a deep breath, sighed and said to Katherine: "I could not bear to stay longer. Two sons have I lost, both weaklings from birth. I begin to wonder that there's some fault in me."

Katherine moved towards him, tears running down her face.

"No, my Lord, not you. The fault lies with me and my lack of care. I have betrayed you. I should have…" she faltered at his look, searching, she felt, into her very soul.

Suddenly he pulled her towards him and held her tightly against his chest. Their tensions thawed like snow in the sun from the warmth of their embrace. He drew back, looked into her face, sought her mouth and kissed her hungrily. Katherine responded as readily. Then he raised her into his arms, carried her upstairs and laid her on the bed in his chamber.

As they came together on the bed, the cup of their desire, inwardly known to each of them but pent up over the past months, overflowed as the volcano of their passion erupted, sending a flood of hot lava through their veins.

Spent, they slept: to awake to a new dawn as lovers.

Chapter Seven

CHAUCER PAUSED IN the seemingly endless task of unpacking his books and went over to stand at one of the leaded windows, where he could look down at the human traffic moving through Aldgate beneath him. The dwelling was above one of the six gates in the City wall and had been leased to him, rent free, by the aldermen of the City through the good offices of the Mayor, Adam de Burgh, who had been a friend of his father.

Chaucer's wife, Philippa, had not liked the idea of his moving to this eastern gate in London. Why shut himself away up here when he could live at his father's old house in Thames Street? He knew how shrewd she was and reminded her that it was rent free for life and this had appealed to her practical sense. He also reminded her that, as she was lady-in-waiting to John of Gaunt's Spanish wife, Constance, who was claimant to the throne of Castile, and was responsible for the running of her household, she was not likely to be staying at Aldgate very often. But when he told her that the daily bustle of people below fascinated him and was a throbbing pulse from which you could read the humour of the City, she scoffed and told him, again, that he spent too much time people watching. He smiled at the thought. "Guilty," he said aloud. Yes, he was continually trying to fathom people from their looks and how they behaved, their language, postures, groupings. He liked to read the temper of crowds, just as he had on his travels in Italy last year. And this was a fine crow's nest from which to do just that!

But Philippa was thrilled with his new appointment as Controller of the Wool Custom and the Petty Custom at the Port of London. The King, she said, had rightly, though tardily, rewarded his worth. Secret missions abroad on the King's business were all very well but of little import at home. This post gave him a status and a title he deserved. And, Geoffrey thought, this house was well positioned.

Aldgate was less than half a mile from the Customs House at Billingsgate on Lower Thames Street. There were several ways he could walk: down Jewry Street to Seething Lane or Fenchurch Street to Mincing Lane and St Dunstan's Hill. He felt at home here with memories of his father's business, the busy quays and the noise and hustle of cargoes being unloaded. And he knew many of the leading merchants he would be dealing with – including William Walworth and John Philipot who were Collectors of the Customs.

Geoffrey turned back to his books. He had already had some timber shelving fitted around the walls of the room he had chosen as his study. The window faced eastwards, out towards the Essex countryside, which is where he had placed his desk and manuscripts. It had a fireplace which backed on to the one in the larger room which he intended to keep for receiving guests. There was a pantry and small kitchen next to the study and above, up a stone stairway, two bedrooms. Geoffrey already felt at home. The place had a solid air and would give him the space and peace he needed for his writing.

As he sorted his books and manuscripts, he reflected on this. Solitude fed his soul. It gave him freedom to study the classical poets and writers as well as tracts on science and astrology. He could let his mind wander and experiment with imaginings, try out rhymings and metres and work through the difficulties presented by the different intonations and stresses in English and French words. But the company of friends would be a joy too. The large room, which stretched the width of the building with windows overlooking both sides of the gate, would provide an ideal space for debate and gossip! Ralph Strode had recently taken up a similar residence over nearby Aldersgate and had no doubt already unpacked his lawyer's books and philosophies! He must seek him out soon: and Gower too, who, for all his insistence on versifying in Latin, was a lively wordsmith. They were both good value and he looked forward to entertaining them in his new lodging and the stimulation of social discourse.

After a while, Chaucer went to the window and decided, from the position of the sun, that it was time for him to go to the Customs

House where he was to meet Tom Castle, his father's old foreman. As he came into the street, a woman approached him.

"Master Chaucer. You will be wanting help with your laundry and cooking, no doubt? And I could fulfil that duty for you, if you please, sir," she said with a brief curtsey.

Chaucer looked at her. She was a motherly sort, with round cheeks, bright eyes and ample figure. She seemed amiable and clean with no stench about her. She touched Chaucer's instinct favourably.

"What is your name?" he asked.

"Margaret Martin, but mostly I am Maggie," she replied.

"Well… mostly Maggie," said Geoffrey, his eyes twinkling, "We could have a trial to see if we suit. Come tomorrow morning with the makings of breakfast."

"Oh! Thank you kindly, sir. That I surely will."

Chaucer turned left into Jewry Street, which was cobbled and gloomy because of the closeness of the houses, the narrow street and the overhanging solar rooms. He walked on through Crutched Friars Street into Seething Lane where he bought a hot pie for a farthing from a street vendor who had a stall outside a bakery. He crossed Lower Thames Street and entered the tall stone Customs House which stood on the north bank of the Thames near the Tower and beside Billingsgate Market.

He climbed the worn stone steps to the main room on the first floor, which was the Controller's Office. A wide window on the river-side gave a commanding view of the wharves and jetties and of the comings and goings of ships and all the busyness of loading and unloading of cargoes. A door led onto a balcony for use as a convenient way of hailing ships' captains and workmen below. A wide sloping table was set in front of the window with rows of pigeon holes around the walls. There were five large oblongs of slate on the rear wall on which the times of high tides were chalked with columns on which the ships' arrivals and departures, type of cargo and duty paid could be entered. Underneath were quills, an inkhorn and a large leather-bound ledger in which the details were meticulously recorded.

Geoffrey appraised all this with a keen eye. He could see the simple logic and the mark of the Exchequer in the painstaking method laid out before him. No wonder that the efficiency of the English accounting system was the envy of Continental courts! He knew that his maintenance of this would be tested when he attended at the Exchequer for the Michaelmas reckoning.

He heard voices and footsteps approaching on the stairs and Tom Castle, thinner and greyer but still with the same cheery grin, appeared, accompanied by a fresh-faced, rangy youth who, a chip off the same block, could only be his son. Chaucer's face lit up as he moved towards them with hand outstretched.

"Tom! It warms my heart to see you!"

"Aye, and you too, Master Geoffrey, praise be to God! And as you see, I have brought Harry along as you asked."

Harry was standing politely a pace behind his father and now bowed with a polite, "At your service, sire."

Geoffrey smiled at him and then began to explain.

"As you know, I am newly appointed as the King's officer to act as Controller of the Customs here in the Port. That means keeping exact records of all the bales of wool being shipped to Flanders and Calais and other parts, even as far as Italy and Morocco. And also of shipments coming in, such as wine from France and Spain. I have to keep records in my own hand in this big ledger here, and, as you see," pointing to the slates on the wall, "this is where we make our daily records. And this, Tom, is where I will need some help: keeping the tallies with all the ships' names, times and loadings; and toing and froing, as need be, down to the quays. What d'you think, Tom? Would this suit Harry?"

Tom had quickly taken in the layout of the room and what the entries on the slates meant. It was akin to the reckonings he had kept for Geoffrey's father for his wine imports.

"Well, Master Geoffrey, it is right pleasing of you to think of him. He has a good head for figures and he can write enough. And he's lively and willing. He has helped me at times, so he's familiar with the life of the quays, as you used to be at his age when you came on errands for your father."

Geoffrey turned to Harry: "How about it, Harry? Does it take your fancy?"

Harry reddened slightly, swallowed and looking directly at Geoffrey with a steady gaze, which mirrored his father, replied: "Why, yes, if you please, Master Chaucer. I would like the chance and I would serve you well."

"So be it then," said Chaucer. "We will shake on it all," offering his hand to Harry and then to Tom. "And let's seal it with a draught of ale!"

Two weeks later, Chaucer was sitting in his parlour with his friends Ralph Strode and John Gower. They had dined well on rabbit stew laced with mushrooms, onions, peas and herbs, prepared by Maggie Martin – an asset already – and were relaxing with a fine malmsey.

"Geoffrey, have you seen Gaunt since he came back from France?" asked Strode.

"No. I hear he is at Hertford – resting no doubt after such a long campaign," replied Geoffrey.

"Hiding, you should rather say!" snapped Strode. "It was a disastrous campaign with nothing to show for it: no battles, no booty, few hostages – only eight thousand men-at-arms lost and an empty treasury."

"True, but surely not all his fault," countered Gower.

"King Edward saddled him with an impossible task. He was expecting another Crecy or Poitiers. He should have known, from his own last campaign when he withdrew from Rheims, that King Charles would not let the French risk open warfare and the murderous fire of our archers. Instead he adopted the tactic of luring Gaunt on and melting away into the fortified towns to draw him into siege warfare."

"That was certainly his tactic in 1369 when Gaunt led that short expedition out from Calais to Harfleur," put in Chaucer.

"But the Black Prince raised the siege at Limoges well enough," Strode protested.

"It was Gaunt who managed that, if you recall," put in Gower, "since the Black Prince was weak with the flux and had to be carried on a litter. And it was a slow, costly, bloody and far from glorious affair. Perhaps that memory deterred Gaunt."

"Well, however it be," said Strode, "Gaunt is widely held as a failure and blamed for this heavy burden of taxes. There are rumblings of corruption and diversion of funds for private ends. And, I hear tell, there was some pelting of stones at the Savoy yesterday by a gang of apprentices. No wonder he stays at Hertford!"

The friends were used to Strode's choleric humour, and Gower tactfully turned the conversation by asking what news there was of Edward, the Black Prince.

"He still has this wasting disease," replied Chaucer, "not helped, I gather, by the leeches trying to bleed him. He is at Kennington with Princess Joan, who is much troubled but unfailing in her devotion to him."

"It is a cruel fate," said Gower. "A prince of his valour and decisiveness struck down like that. It is a tragedy, not just for himself but also for the nation. The government needs his leadership. It is suffering a sickness too with the King's judgement awry because he is obsessed with that mistress of his, Alice Perrers."

"A Parliament should be summoned," said Strode. "The Members should steer the government and appoint a strong Council of Peers and Commoners."

"I don't disagree," said Chaucer, "but there is no sign of that."

"More's the pity," said Strode. "The longer we go on without a Parliament the worse it will get, and I fear there will be turbulent scenes at the end of it."

Gower stood. "Come, Ralph, time we were away before the City gates are shut. Geoffrey, much thanks. I venture you are well blessed in this snug lodging! We'll meet again soon, God willing."

As the two friends departed, Geoffrey mused on their talk. Indeed, he thought, these were troubled times with factions in the

Church as well as honour slipping at Court, too far away from the chivalrous code of King Edward's prime. How much Queen Philippa was missed.

Chaucer was not far wrong in supposing John of Gaunt to be at Hertford for he had spent most of his time there since his return from Bordeaux. He had first been to Tutbury to stay with his young wife, Constance, rightful but usurped Queen of Castile whom he had married at the urging of his father in September 1371 after the great victory at Najero. But he found the ritual of the Queen's court, the stilted formality of her Spanish noblemen and the continual need for him to maintain a position of King of Castile, wearisome. He needed the exhilaration and physical zest of hunting like at Hatfield Forest. And he needed the peace of Hertford and Katherine Swynford's sweetness and lovemaking as a solace to his wounded pride.

He felt deeply the failure and futility of the campaign he had led in France. He agonised over his tactics and whether, faced with the shyness of the French to engage in open battle, he should have made a direct assault on Paris rather than push south to consolidate King Edward's possession of Acquitaine. But that was the plan his father had wanted: because he was angered by the defections and loss of territory there and he wanted the authority achieved by the Black Prince to be restored. Acquitaine was the bastion from which Castile could be rescued from French influence and the menace of Castilian ships attacking English merchants in the Channel could be stopped. But his army had been wasted with sickness and hunger on the winter crags of the Auvergne – broken like crumbling masonry.

Now, however, he was in Lincoln. He had been moved by the welcome he received at his castle from his Constable, Sir William Scott, and some of his long-standing tenants and liege men, including Sir Ralf de Radcliffe and William Bagote who had been with him in France. He had spent the evening of his arrival feasting with them, major tenants and his retinue of armed knights, listening to the local gossip. Tongues wagged well with the ale and wine. He had learned how useful this was. Winnowing the tales like a careful corn harvester, he was able to judge the mood of the people and the state of the county. This intelligence would help him on the morrow when he held court to hear petitions and appeals against the decisions made by his stewards or the Manor Courts.

Next morning John dressed carefully. The flashy fashions of Court were not appropriate here. He chose a favourite close-fitting black silk tunic, with the royal leopards embroidered in silver, halved with the gold and red arms of Castile. The tunic and sleeves were buttoned with pearls and finished with tippets and a metal hip girdle. He wore plain grey hose and black leather shoes with silver buckles.

In the great hall of the castle, a table and three chairs had been set out. John took his place in the centre, flanked by Sir Robert Swylyngton, his chamberlain, who had accompanied him from Hertford, and Sir William Scott. Two armed knights in the Lancaster livery stood at the door and another behind the Duke's chair.

John of Gaunt asked the Constable to open the Court and present the first petitions. Sir William stood and bowed.

"My Lord, the first two are petitions from widows of your last campaign, appealing against the decisions of your steward, in one case, and, on the other, of the Manor Court."

"Are the appellants here and able to present their case?" asked Sir Robert.

"Yes, sire. And the first is the widow of Sir Stephen Framlington."

"Ah, yes," said John, "a loyal and worthy knight but a plain man. Show his lady in then."

The door was opened and Lady Mary Framlington was ushered in. John did not know her and watched carefully as she approached the table and curtseyed with her head bowed low. She was fair haired, thin and bird-like with a sharp face and bright blue eyes. Her gown was cleverly embroidered but her velvet cloak was faded in parts. John of Gaunt leaned forward.

"Lady Mary, your husband, Sir Stephen, was a valiant and honoured servant. It was a sad and great loss to us when he fell in a sudden skirmish when crossing the Seine near Harfleur. How can I help you?"

Lady Mary took a hesitant step forward, clasped her hands together and addressed him.

"My Lord, your kind words console me but I humbly beseech you on two counts: First that I be allowed to marry free of charge with John Sturges, a distant cousin and a freeman with an estate near Sleaford. And second that my late husband's estate be not farmed out as proposed by your steward but held by me for my son until he comes of age."

Sir Robert, who had listened carefully to her words, asked: "Are you sure you can manage well enough to pay your rent and other dues? You fell into arrears during Sir Stephen's absence."

Mary blinked, looked down at her clasped hands and then raised her eyes to look directly at the Duke.

"My Lord. It was our misfortune to suffer murrain in one flock of sheep, and I fear we lost some animals too from thieves. But with the steady hand of John Sturges, I pledge that we will fulfil our duties to you."

John smiled at her spirited showing and looked over at Sir Robert, who gave a slight nod, and then said:

"Lady Mary, I regret your troubles. We are happy to bless your wedding and remit the marriage dues. I am content too to return your estate for you to hold for your son and trust that you will prosper. How old is your son?"

"He will have ten years next Michaelmas, my Lord." Turning to Sir William, he asked: "Can you take the boy under your wing, Sir William?"

"Why surely, my Lord."

"Lady Mary. If you so wish, and in honour of the service your husband rendered to me, I will take your son under my patronage and place him for two years with the Constable here. He will do the duties of a page, which means that he will be trained in courtly manners and in the chivalrous arts of jousting, archery, hunting and swordplay."

Lady Mary beamed: "Oh yes, my Lord, I am indeed honoured and grateful. May God bless you!" Then she curtseyed and withdrew.

John turned to the Constable: "See what you can make of him. If he has his father's bulk and enough of his mother's spirit, he could do well. Who is next?"

"We have a petition from Agnes Snell, the widow of Thomas Snell, but also one from her brother-in-law Amos Snell. The brothers were archers on your campaign. The older one, Thomas, died of the fever at Troyes, at which Amos absented himself and made his way home. The Steward has granted Agnes tenancy of her house but not the same rights that her husband enjoyed of forest grazing, culling wood from undergrowth and the taking of small game as licensed by the forester. And he has demanded repayment of half her husband's wages since he was paid in advance for the campaign. She is appealing against these constraints."

"How is the other brother tied in with this?" asked Sir Robert.

"Amos claims that he lost contact with the army because he stayed with his brother when he was ill and that he was worried about what Agnes would do because she had five children to look after – three of her own and two of his. He is in custody here in the castle. He is pleading for amnesty in the light of events and of his previous good service."

"And what is his record of service?" asked Sir Robert.

"Both brothers served with you on earlier campaigns, my Lord: in Bordeaux in 1370 and at the siege of Limoges. By all accounts they were staunch archers, although Amos also claims he helped with mining the walls at Limoges and was one of those who followed when you broke through."

"Mmmhh! Not a time I care to remember," said John. "The town had betrayed us by going over to the French. Prince Edward was furious and insisted that the burghers paid for it with their blood. It was like an abattoir, and I only just managed to save the Bishop of Limoges from my brother's fury." And turning to Sir Robert, said: "So what's to be done here?"

"Clearly the brothers responded loyally to your calls to arms and were excellent archers. This could perhaps be recognised in treating with the widow? But absence without leave is a serious misdemeanour. Maybe you should see what this Amos has to say so that you can better judge how to deal with him?"

"Yes, I agree. But first I will see the woman, show her in."

Agnes Snell was ushered into the chamber, curtseyed before the Duke, then clasped her hands together and looked up at him with anxious pale grey eyes. She wore a plain brown fustian gown with a rounded neckline which was loose fitting but showed ample breasts. As she looked at the Duke, he noticed the dark smudged bags beneath her eyes.

"I am sorry we lost your husband in my last campaign," he told her. "He was a fine archer and served me loyally. You and his children have good reason to be proud of him. In recognition of that I will confirm your tenancy and forego repayment of his wages."

Agnes curtseyed and a dimple appeared in her cheek. "Why, thank you and bless you, my Lord."

"But I cannot restore the grazing and other rights to a lone woman," he said. "How is it that you have the burden of Amos' children?"

Agnes, emboldened by the Duke's sympathetic manner, put her hand on her hip and said in a neighbourly manner: "Well, you see, my Lord, Amos' wife died in childbirth two years back, and when the men were called to follow you to France I took in his two bairns to look after them with my three. I mean, what else could I do? But they all need a father, which is why Amos and I have talked about getting wed because we are well suited and he is a good father, only we can't see our way to it with him locked up in the castle and in such trouble."

"Well, maybe that would be a sensible solution," said the Duke, smiling to himself, "but first I have to see Amos and deal with this serious matter of his desertion. You may go now and no doubt you will hear about it soon enough."

With a, "Thank you, my Lord," Agnes curtseyed again, and withdrew.

"Well… have him brought in," said the Duke.

Amos entered and shuffled towards the table, for his hands were bound and his ankles hobbled. He was unkempt, dirty and reeked, having been kept in the castle dungeon for three weeks. He kneeled before the table.

"My Lord, I beg your forgiveness. Have mercy upon me."

"Why did you break your oath to serve the Duke and flee home? Is it that you are a coward?" demanded Sir Robert.

"Nay, my Lord! I swear not," answered Amos, his eyes blazing. "I have served honourably in my Lord's campaigns but I could not leave my brother when he went down with the fever. And then when he died I had to bury him and make what sacrament I could for him. By then the army had been gone for three weeks. My brother and I were close. I was distressed and confused and worried about how Agnes and the children were going to cope."

"If you could get back to England from outside Troyes, surely you could have followed the track of the army?" asked Sir Robert.

"Yes, sire. That is what I should have done."

John of Gaunt had been studying the man and, despite his unkempt appearance, recognised him as a staunch fighter at Limoges.

"I am told you were with me at Limoges," he said.

"Yes, my Lord, and when you set the siege and began mining under the walls, my brother and I joined the sappers as we were idle as archers. And then there was that fearful charge into the city when some of our pikemen were so worked up they were merciless," replied Amos.

The Duke looked sternly at him and delivered his judgement.

"I cannot condone your desertion, Snell, although I recognise your otherwise good service. Your record shows you are not a lily-livered man. But once desertion starts in an army it can be as infectious as a fever. You must renew your oath of allegiance to me. You will serve one day a week for the next year in the garrison at the castle here under the Constable to help with the training of young archers and such other duties as he may determine. You will forfeit your tenancy, quit your house and pay a fine of ten marks."

"Yes, my Lord," and, kneeling forward at the feet of John of Gaunt, Amos Snell proclaimed: "I swear by the Holy Sacrament that I give my solemn oath of allegiance to serve and protect with my life your person and good name in all things, so help me God."

"You are concerned about your brother's widow, are you not?" asked John.

"Yes, my Lord – she is fazed by his death and 'tis hard for her with the children, including two of mine and the loss of the privileges he had."

"Indeed. When I saw her she hinted at the prospect of marriage with you. Are you of that mind?" asked the Duke.

"Why, yes, my Lord," he said brightly. "We would make a fine and loyal family, but not until I have made my atonement to you and received your grace for such a union."

"Well… so be it. But you must pay the proper marriage dues and then I will restore the rights your brother enjoyed," and, turning to the Constable, said: "Release him."

As Amos Snell shuffled from the chamber, he said, "I warrant he's learnt his lesson and will be a most loyal tenant." Then he turned to Sir William and asked: "How are matters at the Swynford Manor at Kettlethorpe? Is the new bailiff satisfactory?"

"Yes, my Lord. He comes here to me once a month and gives a detailed report on the buildings and the farm work and presents his accounts, although I have not been over there myself since you were here last."

"I am going hunting now so I will call at the manor on my way. And, Sir Robert, will you finish hearing the other petitions and see that Snell gets a good dousing to cure his stink before his release!"

"Indeed, my Lord," replied Sir Robert, smiling as John strode across the chamber with the spring and assurance of one of the prize bucks he was about to chase.

———— o O o ————

Chaucer left the Customs House early and was hurrying home along Seething Lane, his cloak flapping round his legs in the March wind. His wife Philippa was coming home and he wanted to be there to greet her (and to make sure everything was in order). He had not seen her for six months, for she had been with the Duchess of Lancaster in Flanders where the Duke was negotiating a truce with France on behalf of his father King Edward III.

As was often the way in their marriage, however, Chaucer was wrong-footed. Philippa arrived before him and already had Maggie scurrying round. Geoffrey nonetheless strode in beaming tenderly and hugged his wife tightly to him.

"Why, Wife, it is good to see you!" he cried and, looking into the familiar blue eyes, kissed her generously. Pleased by the warmth of his welcome but flustered by his rough maleness and the expectations it signalled, Philippa retreated into fussing and busying herself with the house and scolding Maggie for the untidiness. Maggie hurried in with a bucket of coals to mend the fire and left with a quick bob and a quiet, "'Scuse me, my Lady," eyes lowered to avoid Geoffrey's amused gaze. His eyes twinkled, for he could read the cunning in Maggie whose deference was in self-defence. She was playing dumb to give Philippa space as the mistress and no cause for her to think Maggie had been acting above her station with the master.

Later, warmed by the glowing fire, fine wine and ample dinner of pheasant, trout, apple pudding and cheese, Geoffrey listened contentedly to his wife as she related the happenings in Flanders, at Bruges and Ghent.

"It was a great occasion for ceremony and feasts and festivities," she said. "And oh! You should have seen the splendour of the ladies' dresses – the silks and satins and bright colours – the elegance of the lords – and dancing and some wonderful music by that Frenchman you met in Rheims."

"Guillaume de Machaut," said Chaucer. "That was sixteen years ago. I hear he is frail now, although he must be well over his three-score and ten years."

Philippa hurried on: "The French envoys, the Dukes of Anjou and Berri, vied with each other in their extravagance to see who could put on the most lavish banquet and entertainment. And, of course, Duke John, as the King's envoy, had to respond. He insisted on using his title as King of Castile and even sent home to the Clerk of his Great Wardrobe for his collar and circle of gold to emphasise his royal dignity."

"Oh ho!" chuckled Geoffrey. "And how was that received, since Castile is an ally of France?"

"Politely of course," said Philippa sharply, for she did not share her husband's wit, "but I was told they would not agree to his royal title being used in the official documents for the truce."

"Well, at least let us praise God and be thankful for this respite from war," said Geoffrey. "The King has emptied his treasury and the Black Prince is on his sick bed. Duke John has done well on this but I wish he would give up this fanciful claim to the throne of Castile."

"Oh Geoffrey, how can you say that? The claim is not fanciful. My Lady, Constance, is the rightful Queen as the daughter of Pedro I who was murdered and usurped by his own brother, that dreadful Enrique."

"Yes, I know, my dear," said Geoffrey gently, acknowledging and admiring his wife's fierce loyalty. "It is only fanciful in the sense of being unrealistic because it would take a huge feat of arms to succeed in wresting the throne away from Enrique and France."

"Oh… you and your words!" said Philippa, but with a smile, as Geoffrey put his arm round her and took her to bed.

Back in London at his Savoy Palace on the Thames, John of Gaunt resolved that he must visit his brother Edward, the Black Prince. He had been in the habit of seeing him regularly since his return from Acquitaine but because of his negotiations in Bruges it was more than six months since his last visit. John was not relishing the prospect. His brother was shrunken in body, though undimmed in spirit, fierce in his opinions and a stickler for the royal courtesies and etiquette he demanded. John was afraid he would find the Prince yet weaker, more dogmatic and irascible. He summoned his barge and set off up the Thames, past Westminster and along to the south bank at Kennington.

He was welcomed by Joan of Kent, Prince Edward's wife, from whose strained looks John immediately read the omens. He clasped her hands and kissed her cheek.

"No better then?" he asked.

"No," she replied. "But he is buoyed by your coming and impatient to know everything."

John smiled: "He hasn't changed in that then."

They went into the chamber where the Black Prince was lying on a gold and red brocaded couch. John immediately went to his side, knelt, kissed his hand, bowed his head in homage and said: "God's blessing on you, sire, and greetings from our royal father."

"God's teeth, John, where have you been? I've been fretting to know about this truce and what you are doing about Acquitaine."

John explained the terms of the truce he had concluded with the French at Bruges, which, he carefully emphasised, their father had endorsed. These would stop the attacks on our shipping in the Channel and the sporadic raiding on the borders of Acquitaine and relieve pressure on Calais.

"So, we can use this truce to assemble forces to push out from Acquitaine and from Brittany and finish the job you failed in last time! Because you can't think that that lily-livered French King won't be using the time to strengthen his forces. That's what truces are for, aren't they?" rasped the Black Prince.

John winced. He had felt before the lash of his brother's tongue over his last campaign.

"But, sire, we've walked this ground before," he said patiently. "Charles won't fight your type of war and, here, the King's Exchequer is empty."

"Well, he must summon Parliament to grant the necessary levies," barked Edward.

"I agree, sire, and soon. But Parliament will not be easily managed as it has not met for three years, and there are grumbles about the King's close advisers and the management of monies voted before."

"You ever were careful with your words, John! I swear you're a better diplomat than general! Why don't you say what you mean? Alice Perrers is a comfort to the King just as the Swynford girl is to you. Who would deny this to him in his old age?"

"Edward, the problem is not just Alice Perrers. She is greedy and flounces her opinions too readily; we know that. But the real concern is that the administration of the Royal Household is too lax and this allows funds to be misused."

"How so?" demanded Edward.

"I have no proof," replied John, "but rumour has it that even Latimer looks to his own advantage and others feather their own nest."

"Ha! The jealous will always tell tales!" proclaimed Edward. "The King is above all this. Don't the Commons know that? It is their duty to meet his needs. I should like to give them a piece of my mind, but at present you will have to see that the royal prerogative is honoured."

"I agree, sire, and I will," said John. "But I fear trouble ahead and our royal father is not as vigorous as he was."

In this, John was correctly reading the way the wind was blowing up for a storm, but he could not see how damaging that storm would be.

Soon afterwards, in April 1376, writs in the King's name were sent to the sheriffs and mayors throughout England and Wales, requiring them 'to secure the appointment of representatives to sit in the Commons in a Parliament to be held at Westminster'. Lords and bishops were also summoned to the second chamber. Soon small cavalcades of burgesses and yeomen, knights and retainers were making their way to London, using the traditional inns and hostelries en route as way stations to refresh themselves and their horses.

Proceedings began on Monday, 28th April in the Painted Chamber, a large lofty hall with a barrel roof, high windows and stone walls decorated with fine tapestries. Wooden tiers of seats which had been erected on one side were packed by the Commons' representatives, chattering and fidgeting like a flock of excited starlings. Opposite sat the Lords, some talking quietly together but most were silent, solemn, watchful, their silken hose, embroidered tunics and glinting jewels contrasting with the more sombre hues of the brown and black tunics and woollen cloaks of the Commons. On the floor, sprigs of rosemary and lavender had been strewn to sweeten the air against the press of unwashed bodies.

The Chancellor, Sir John Knyvett, sitting in a high-backed brocaded chair between the rows of Commons and Lords, addressed the assembled Parliament and explained the summons and their purpose.

"Our Sovereign Lord, King Edward, is desirous of your counsel and help to provide for the good government of the realm, the defence of the King's dominions and the prosecution of the war; to which end, you are asked to pass a liberal vote of funds."

Immediately there were cries from some on the Commons' benches of: "No." "Not so fast." "Not without redress of wrongs." "Where has the last subsidy gone?" But gradually wiser and more experienced voices were heard. A Speaker, Sir Peter de la Mare, was chosen and order was restored as he took the chair next to the Chancellor. Sir Peter was an experienced Knight of the Shire for the County of Hereford and Steward of the Earl of March. Fifty, balding and greying, thickset, solid in presence and in purpose, he was well chosen to guide and represent the Commons.

Choosing his words carefully so as to avoid direct criticism of the King, he said: "We have been asked to vote more supplies. This, I am sure, we will readily do: provided we can see these means turned into ends which advantage the country. It is three years since Parliament met when the last subsidy was voted. It is not clear how those monies were spent or what advantages accrued. We have lost ground in France and the military operations were not successful. There is suspicion that the King is kept poor by greedy and corrupt ministers. It is imperative that a close scrutiny be made of the public accounts and, I suggest, this be done as in 1373, jointly with representatives of the Lords."

The Commons applauded and the Lords readily agreed to appoint twelve peers, including four bishops, to a joint committee to scrutinise the accounts. John of Gaunt had been watching, outwardly calm, but inwardly irked by the implied challenge to the King's prerogative in choosing his ministers. He stepped forward and, seeking to smooth things over, acknowledged the sacrifices made by the country. He invited the Commons to declare their grievances and offered to mediate by using his influence to secure redress.

But John of Gaunt had misjudged the temper of the Commons and of the country. It was widely known that, since the death of Queen Philippa, the King had declined into self-indulgence which included favouring and following those close to him at Court. There was not the same clear purpose or control in the government of affairs at home or abroad. Gone were the days when the French were defeated in open battle and their King captured, the Spanish ships chased from the Channel, the Scots defeated and rich profits made from the booty and ransoms won in these campaigns. The country was frustrated, disillusioned and the Commons were determined to express this.

This soon became clear in the following days when the Committee appointed to scrutinise the accounts met. They insisted that Lord William Latimer, Chamberlain to the King, had embezzled public money and had kept for himself fines inflicted on Sir Robert Knowles and the City of Bristol. Richard Lyons, a prominent London merchant, had lent money to the King, charged fifty per cent interest and had made a 'corner' in imported goods, charging exorbitant prices. Both, the Committee decided, should be impeached. The Committee also insisted that Alice Perrers, the royal mistress, should be banished from the Court and her property confiscated, since she had abused the influence she had over the King, interfering with the course of justice, making her own nominations for appointments and enriching herself.

John of Gaunt kept in close touch with the proceedings of the Committee through his friend Sir Henry Percy, a member of the Committee and who, in turn, was kept aware of what John thought about the Committee!

"Henry! Do these petty Commoners not know their place?" Gaunt demanded. "Their fealty is a bounden duty of loyalty to the King. It is not their remit to question his decisions or to say who he can appoint to carry them out. Such impertinence is close to treason!"

"It is a fine balance, my Lord," replied Percy tactfully. "It is proved that Latimer and Lyons have themselves been disloyal by abusing the King's trust. And Alice Perrers…"

"Yes, yes!" burst out Gaunt. "We all know about her greedy and domineering ways. But I will not tell my father he has to get rid of her because the Commons say so!"

Lord Percy had felt the force of the Plantagenet temper before and in this could see the likeness with the King and his older brother.

"My Lord," he ventured, "must it be so? Why not persuade Alice herself to leave the Court for a time. She could still be with the King privately at Sheen away from the Court and, maybe, she would allow you to 'administer her property'?"

John rubbed his chin and studied Percy's face thoughtfully. "And the others?" he asked. "Do I go with that too?"

Lord Percy nodded.

"So be it," said John, slapping his thigh, but then added, with a sharp look: "for the time being."

And so Latimer was arrested and dismissed from office. Lyons suffered forfeiture and imprisonment. Alice Perrers left the Court but not the King's bed.

———— o O o ————

But before the business of Parliament could be finished, the country and John of Gaunt were thrown into a new crisis. On Sunday, 8th June 1376, Edward, Prince of Wales, died leaving his only surviving son, Richard, a boy of nine, as heir to the throne. This increased the tension at Westminster and the doubts about the leadership of the country. Even during the lying in state, the solemn rites and dignity of the funeral and mourning, rumour was rife.

With the Black Prince gone – an heroic figure to so many, with his thrilling victories at Crécy, Poitiers and Najera – and with the King old and ailing, fears and imaginings festered and ill-founded gossip became fact. As the eldest surviving son of the King and the pre-eminent power after the King, John, Duke of Lancaster, claimant to the throne of Castile and senior uncle to the young Richard, was inevitably at the centre of this suspicion and the target of much venom, especially from the clerical chroniclers.

Chaucer, too, almost felt himself caught in this whirlpool. He knew Richard Lyons. His father had traded with him and, through his own position at the Customs House, he knew him as an ambitious merchant with a reputation for driving a hard bargain. Chaucer was also close enough to the Court, through his occasional readings of his poetry and through his wife, to have some insight into the state of the administration and the doings of Alice Perrers. So it was that Ralph Strode, John Gower, John Clanvowe and others were often in debate at Chaucer's house or in a local alehouse.

Chaucer was sitting with John Gower in his parlour. Mostly Maggie had just fetched in two pots of ale. "God's blessing on you, John," he said, raising his tankard.

"Aye, and on you!" responded Gower and then went on: "Geoffrey, what is this young Prince Richard like? Has he the makings of kingship?"

"I have only met him once, last Yuletide, when I was summoned to Kennington by Princess Joan to present and recite that poem of mine, 'The House of Fame', that we discussed."

"Oh yes! I remember," said Gower. "The one in which you poke fun at yourself: *'dumb as any stone, thou sittest at another book, till fully dazed is thy look, and livest thus as an hermit!'* Fie on you, Geoffrey!"

Chaucer smiled and went on: "Richard is a good scholar, well grounded in French and Latin but favours English at Court, praise be! He's tall but as yet slight of build, not as stocky as his father nor as long-backed as his uncle. Pale-skinned, with sensitive hands and long fingers, he looks delicate, almost feminine, and he favours dressing in the more fancy styles. But I am told he is a good horseman and already loves the chase. He has the royal hauteur and will be just as fastidious and demanding as his father. He has the will for kingship but whether he has the wit remains to be seen and a lot will depend on who gets his ear."

At that moment there were hurried voices downstairs and Ralph Strode burst in. "I've just come from Westminster. Guess what! The Commons have demanded that Richard be presented to them and be invested with the lands and title of Prince of Wales with his own household."

"This is brass bold!" exclaimed Chaucer. "While he should be invested with his father's title, this is surely a matter for the King not the Commons."

"And," went on Strode, "they have appointed a permanent council of twelve peers of the realm to be attached to the King."

"Taken together, this looks like a move to counter Gaunt," said Gower.

"Yes, and there is more," said Strode. "Rumour has it that Gaunt has designs on the throne: that he plans to have Richard poisoned – like, some say, he had Maude of Lancaster, the sister of his wife Blanche, poisoned so that he could consolidate the whole Lancaster estate."

"That is fantasy!" exclaimed Geoffrey. "I know for a fact she died of the plague."

"Yes, I agree," said Strode, "but there is also gossip in royal courts across the Channel, even including that Gaunt is plotting to declare Prince Richard illegitimate because of his mother's past liaisons."

Geoffrey Chaucer stood up, suddenly looking pale and grave.

"This is serious," he said. "These false tales are an insult to Gaunt but can be disproved. The demands of the Commons go deeper. They are using the occasion to wrest power away from the Crown and, with King Edward enfeebled, Gaunt is the main protagonist. They impute a disloyalty and are a slur on his honour and ethical code. I fear his reaction could be violent and vengeful. Remember he is a Plantagenet and they don't like to be crossed. His father would have hanged the burghers of Calais if Queen Philippa had not pleaded for mercy. It is in the blood. Gaunt is a good friend but a fierce enemy if slighted."

The friends were soon to recall Geoffrey's words.

Prince Richard, with the agreement of the King, was duly presented to Parliament and invested as Prince of Wales and the Council of Peers was ratified. Satisfied, Parliament dispersed. Gaunt moved immediately and decisively. Acting in the King's name, he repudiated what the Commons had done by dismissing the Council which they had tried to put around the King. He restored those who had been impeached and recalled the King's mistress to Court.

Then he acted against those he considered the moving spirits of the attack on the King's authority and on his own honour. Sir Peter de la Mare was arrested and imprisoned in Nottingham Castle. William Wykeham, Bishop of Winchester, lost his temporalities, which were granted to Prince Richard, and he was forbidden to come anywhere near the Court. To Gaunt, Wykeham's vociferous support for the Commons and the impeachment of Lord Latimer was the greater offence, for he had been elevated to his position and wealth as a great prelate by royal favour and now to use that position against the King amounted, in Gaunt's view, to treason. By so acting he posted a warning to others.

Six months after his brother's death he persuaded the King to call together all the feudatories, courtiers and leading Commoners. On Christmas Day 1376 they gathered at Westminster Palace in a splendid assembly. Before them all, John of Gaunt, Duke of Lancaster, presented Richard as heir to the throne and kingdom. He knelt down before the throne where his brother's son sat at the King's side, kissed his hand, swore allegiance and to accept him as his sovereign lord. By this public demonstration, John sought to consolidate the royal authority and to show the true mettle of his own fealty and loyalty.

Chaucer, who was present, caught the eye of Philippa, his wife, who was in attendance on Duchess Constance, raised his eyebrows and smiled. She nodded her approval in return.

But this rich tapestry only served as temporary cover for the mouldering walls of the royal citadel. The King's treasury was empty. Parliament had to be recalled and a vote of funds secured.

John of Gaunt had learnt a valuable lesson from the last Parliament. If the voice of the people must be heard, then care should be taken over who spoke for them. So, in the Parliament which convened at Westminster on 27th January 1377, both the Chancellor and the Speaker were the Duke of Lancaster's men. The Chancellor, Adam Houghton, was Bishop of St David's, a longstanding friend of both John and Duchess Blanche. Sir Thomas Hungerford, the new Speaker, was John's Chief Steward for Lancastrian lands north of the Trent. And many others on the Parliamentary benches representing both the Lords and Commons owed Gaunt allegiance as retainers or tenants.

At first everything seemed to be working well. The Commons voted a poll tax of fourpence and refused to respond to calls from a minority demanding the release of the previous Speaker, Sir Peter de la Mare. But Gaunt could not pack the bench of bishops who, led by the Bishop of London, refused to conduct any business until the ban on the Bishop of Winchester was lifted and he could be present. They petitioned the King and William of Wykeham was recalled. But this only served to fan a smouldering fire to life.

Chaucer was striding up Mincing Lane, bound for home after a long day at the Customs House, when he was hailed by Ralph Strode.

"Geoffrey! Blessings on you," he called. "Just the man I wanted to see. Have you heard about the Bishop of London's latest ploy?"

"Oh, what is that, Ralph? And blessings on you too, my friend," replied Chaucer and, seeing the archway into the Golden Fleece, drew Strode inside. "Come, we can talk better when our whistle is wetted with a pot of ale," he said genially.

"The Bishop has summoned John Wycliffe to the Court of Bishops at St Paul's to answer charges about his preachiness against the wealth and corruption of the Church."

"Ho!" said Chaucer as he took a sup of ale. "Wycliffe speaks but the truth. The Church and its ministers grow fat on the sale of indulgences and offerings of the poor. 'Tis well known. But you are the lawyer. It is surely not a matter that would stand scrutiny in court, is it?"

"Perhaps not," agreed Strode, "but Wycliffe has spoken dangerously against the very office of Bishop and this is popular with some country folk. He had also challenged the basis of the Communion against the bread and wine standing for Christ's passion and blood."

"Yes. I've heard that," said Chaucer, "and maybe his own passion gets the better of him in that. But why bring him to a religious account now when there are serious issues to face at Court and in the governance of the country?"

"Ah, well, there's the rub!" said Strode excitedly. "Don't you see, Geoffrey, the Lords and Commons are at the sway of Gaunt so Parliament does his bidding. But he can't rule the Convocation of Bishops where Courtney, the Bishop of London, dominates because Archbishop Sudbury is too meek and peaceful. Attacking Wycliffe now is a way of getting at Gaunt."

Chaucer chuckled. "Well, it will be a pretty scene at St Paul's, I'll warrant. Pity the Customs keep me here or I would bear witness!"

"I'll be there," said his friend. "And I'll bring you chapter and verse of it."

"Aye, but not *in* verse, I pray; that is my prerogative!" quipped Geoffrey.

Two days later, at about noon, Ralph Strode burst into the

Customs House all agog to tell Chaucer the outcome of the happenings at St Paul's. Once again Geoffrey calmed his friend, steered him to the stairs and towards the nearby Black Swan hostelry.

"Now, Ralph, let's have it: chapter, if not verse!" he grinned.

"Geoffrey, you should have been there. It was as good as a Punch and Judy show: the Bishop, high, mighty and superior, declaiming at Wycliffe and treating him like a common thief before he had said a word. Gaunt, stiff and imperious, flanked by the Earl Marshall of England, Lord Percy, demanding that the charges be properly read so that the four learned friars he had engaged could rebut them. The Bishop would not acknowledge the friars and that led to a shouting match with, at one stage, Gaunt threatening to drag the Bishop from the church by his hair!"

Chaucer's eyes gleamed as he imagined the drama. "So where was poor Wycliffe in all this? Was anything resolved?" he asked.

"No! It ended in utter confusion. Londoners fought with Londoners, their loyalties torn apart. Many agreed with Wycliffe but others were riled by the attack on their bishop and yet others boiled over at what they saw as an insolent assumption of authority by Lord Percy overriding the cherished autonomy of the City and the Lord Mayor."

"We live in fractious times, Ralph," said Chaucer reflectively. "An ailing King, a child to succeed him, fitful government, a corrupt church and an intemperate hand from the one man with the strength to guide us through. It is a recipe for high drama – tragedy even."

Later that evening, Chaucer was leaving the Customs House when he had to step aside as a band of men came by, arguing noisily together.

"I tell you, I know for sure that Percy has taken a bargeman who shouted out against him at St Paul's and locked him in the stocks at Marshalsea," he heard one shout. This excited others who agreed they should rush to the prison and release him. As they hurried away, Chaucer heard another claim that: "Gaunt and Percy are dining this night with Sir John d'Ypres," and their shouts of, "Let's root them out before they take over the City."

Chaucer paused, then climbed the stairway back up to the Customs where he had left Harry tidying up and sweeping the floor. He found a quill and parchment and penned a note to the Duke of Lancaster:

> *My Lord, a rough mob is bent on attacking the Marshalsea to release a prisoner and are seeking you and Lord Percy for they believe you are with Sir John. Their temper is hostile and they carry clubs. I bid you take care this night, but not at the Savoy.*
> *G. Chaucer*

"Harry," he called. "Would you take this note to my Lord of Lancaster who is at Ypres Inn, as fast as you can?"

"Yes, Master. I'll be glad to, and I know where it is," replied Harry, reaching for his cap.

"Hurry, it is urgent. But take care, Harry. There are rough crowds in parts of the City tonight and some are in an ugly mood."

Sir John d'Ypres was a Flemish merchant who had grown rich on the wool trade between England and France. Well connected in both countries, he regularly entertained with a lavish table since discourse, as much as a fair wind, promoted trade across the Channel. He and his guests, John of Gaunt and Henry Percy, had just started their meal with some fine whitebait fried with garlic and soused in a lemon sauce, when the steward entered and bent to his ear.

"Sir John, there is a lad here from the Customs House with an urgent message for the Duke."

Gaunt, his hearing ever sharp, looked up: "Customs House? What is this? I have no business there! And..." he paused, thinking, "surely Chaucer has no need..." and then decisively, "best see the lad!"

Harry Castle entered and bowed nervously, unsure who to approach until the Duke stretched out his arm: "Let me see the message."

Harry stepped forward, held forth the parchment and waited, his eyes fixed intently on the Duke's face as he read the message and passed it over to Percy. Then the Duke looked up at him: "Saw you any disturbances on your way here?" he asked, in turn looking straight into Harry's eyes.

"Yes, my Lord. Two bands of men rushed by me, making threats and waving sticks, and some with knives," he said.

"What threats? Did you hear?"

"Not that clearly, my Lord. There were that many shouting at once but I did hear 'the Savoy' said several times."

At that moment there was a loud banging on the door and the steward rushed in, hotly followed by a knight in Lancaster livery who kneeled immediately before the Duke and said: "My Lord! Forgive me, but there's mobs about being roused to attack you and Lord Percy. The Marshalsea's already been attacked and Lord Percy's house fired. Our men in your livery have been chased, and in Cheapside your coat of arms has been hung upside down. There's a rabble too by the Savoy."

Gaunt sprang up, furious: "Come, Percy, we must be away!"

Then turning swiftly to Harry, he asked: "Is there a barge at the Custom Quay we can use?"

"Yes, I am sure there is, sire."

"We'll make for there and go by the river to Kennington and Princess Joan. We'll be secure there and can marshal our forces as need be. Come! And, Sir John, our thanks and regrets at missing so promising a meal!"

Several days later, Chaucer was working at his desk in the Customs House, reconciling the records he kept of wool shipments with those submitted by the Collectors of the Customs. It was a task that taxed his patience for, though his records were clear and dated sequentially, the Collectors' were in different hands and not always consolidated in date order. His meticulous method was, however, beginning to be rewarded when a richly dressed figure appeared in the doorway.

Chaucer turned and exclaimed: "Why, John! This is an honour indeed – and a great pleasure to see you! How went the audience with the King?" for Chaucer knew, like most of London, that the King had agreed to receive a deputation from the City.

John Philipot, boyhood friend and now a prosperous fish merchant and Deputy Mayor of London, came forward and embraced Chaucer.

"Yes, and it is a pleasure to see you, Geoffrey!" beamed John. Then in reply to his question: "The King received us very graciously."

"Well, sit down," said Chaucer, drawing up a stool, "and share a bottle with me while we talk, for there's much to catch up on."

"Aye, much has changed since we were young, Geoffrey," mused Philipot. "The old certainties have slipped away. London is still the hub of the kingdom of course and much depended upon by the King with its commerce and wealth. But unlike your father's day, our markets on the Continent are shrinking. Our ships are attacked for want of a navy. Our armies have lost the winning habit and the King only shows flashes of his old bold confidence in government. Meanwhile doubt and jealousy abound."

"Yes, and gossip and rumour have set in, which a few hotheads used to create the recent riots," said Geoffrey.

"Yes, and on that score, Geoffrey, I do beg you to take care. Your warning to Gaunt was well done but there are those who may harbour a grudge," said Philipot.

"Thank you for that," said Geoffrey, "I am aware, and I have spoken with my assistant likewise. But, tell me, when you saw the King, were you able to heal this rift between the City and Gaunt?"

"Well enough, I believe. Although the King is clearly declining – he was propped up on pillows – he still retains that regal and persuasive charm!" said Philipot smiling. "We assured him that the City had in no way provoked the disorders or the attacks on Gaunt and Percy but we were rightly concerned to defend the rights of the City. He assured us that responsibility for the City remained fully in the hands of the Mayor and Aldermen and that the liberties and privileges of the City were assured. And he agreed to have the former

Speaker released from prison and a full pardon granted to the Bishop of Winchester."

"But Gaunt will not be pleased?" said Geoffrey.

"Maybe not, but we have agreed to a procession of the City aldermen to St Paul's to light a candle with the Duke's insignia to the Virgin as a penance for the harm done to the Duke."

"'Tis well done," said Geoffrey. "That should salve his pride."

"I believe it will. His actions may have been a trifle rash but we know that he was defending the authority and dignity of the throne rather than his own," said Philipot.

"But you say the King is ailing?" asked Geoffrey.

"Aye! He is really quite frail. Don't quote me, but I doubt he will see the year out."

In this, John Philipot proved correct. King Edward III died of a stroke at his palace at Sheen on Sunday, 21st June 1377.

He had reigned for fifty years, giving England peace at home and, for thirty years, glory abroad. In that period he maintained a firm and efficient government and a magnificent Court, the rival of any in Europe. He established at Windsor the select Order of Knights of the Garter as the epitome of loyalty and chivalry. But the country also suffered the ravages of the Black Death in 1348 and later recurrences which reduced the population by nearly one half. Whether or not this was the cause, energy and purpose began to drain away from the government and the Court. While his personal popularity never waned, he left a mixed and insecure legacy for his young successor.

Richard, aged 9, son of the Black Prince, was crowned King in Westminster Abbey on 16th July 1377 with elaborate and traditional ceremonial. All ranks in society were represented including the Mayor and citizens, with John of Gaunt, Duke of Lancaster, High Seneschal of England and senior uncle to the young King, leading the procession bearing the sword of state with his brother, Thomas of Woodstock, bearing the sceptre followed by the Primate and the

Bishops of London and Winchester. Richard was accepted by acclamation. He was invested with the tunic of St Edward, the sword and sceptre. The crown was placed on his head, the ring upon his finger and the Primate led him to the throne where he took the oath to do justice between man and man, to show mercy and to observe the laws of the land.

Three days later the work of government began with the appointment of a council of twelve to advise and guide the new King. John of Gaunt did not claim a place but, later, accepted an invitation to be one of the peers on a joint committee with the Commons. He was determined to keep his involvement to the minimum and mostly withdrew from public life so as to confound any who thought he wanted to take over the government and rule as regent for the child king.

Chapter Eight

JOHN OF GAUNT was sitting in bed at Hertford, the drapes thrown back while a shaft of sunshine flooded the room with specks of dust dancing in its beam. His 5-year-old son, Henry Beaufort, was standing at the foot of the bed frowning fiercely as he concentrated on using the abacus in answer to his father's questions.

"So," said John, "you've worked out that there are sixteen sheepskins in a bale of wool. So how many will there be in two bales?"

Young Henry looked up at his father with his mother's grey eyes, frowned and then said, "Is it thirty-two?" His father laughed. "Yes, it is, but why didn't you use your abacus?"

"Because I can see it in my head, my Lord: I know that two tens make twenty and two sixes are twelve and so I added them together."

"Well, that is very good but don't forget to check on the abacus what you see in your head."

"Is that what Uncle Geoffrey has to do at the Customs House?" he asked.

"Oh yes," replied his father. "He has to count all the bales as they are loaded onto all the ships sailing out of London and then work out how much duty has to be paid to King Richard."

Young Henry's eyes widened. "Well, I expect he has to use an abacus all the time."

"I am sure he does," laughed his father.

"I can count too," piped up 3-year-old Thomas. "Look," holding up his hand: "Five fingers," as he danced a little jig.

"And how many is it if you hold up both hands?" asked his father.

Thomas stood still thinking, with his finger on his mouth. "I don't know," he said.

"Yes, you do. Sing the song I taught you about the fish:

"One, two, three, four, five,
Once I caught a fish alive,
Six, seven, eight, nine, ten,
Then I let it go again."

"TEN!" shouted Thomas.

"Yes," said his father. "And why did we let the fish go?"

"Because it wasn't big enough to eat!" laughed Thomas.

"That's right – so that we could catch it another day when it had grown big enough: that's being a good fisherman.

"Now off you go to the schoolroom and see that you heed what Mistress Alice tells you, while I go to the nursery to see your mother and baby Joan."

"Yes, my Lord," said the boys as they bowed to their father and left the room.

As John entered the nursery, still wearing only his night shirt, Katherine smiled. She was reminded yet again of the strong magnetism of this man and the powerful presence he brought into a room. As she was sitting, breastfeeding the baby, she inclined her head and then looked into his face: "My Lord. You are in a gay mood?"

John flashed her a bright look. "The pleasures of the night are still upon me!" he chuckled and brushed her cheek with his hand. "I think I will hunt later in Hatfield Forest. There should be some fine bucks running. But, first, I had an idea while I was with the boys – and incidentally, young Henry is showing a bright intelligence – how would it be if we had the whole family gathered at the Savoy to celebrate my birthday? What do you think?"

Katherine stood, pulled her gown over her breasts, called for the nurse and handed baby Joan to her. When she had left the room, she turned to John, reached out and embraced him and then, with shining eyes, looked up into his face and said: "Why, John! What a lovely idea and especially as you were in France for your fortieth birthday last year! I am sure the family will be thrilled. But would you invite the King?"

"Oh no, I had not thought to invite him. I'd just rather have my children. It is some time since they were all together and I'm sure they would be pleased to see you and baby Joan, especially Philippa and Elizabeth."

"But what of Queen Constance and Katharine?" asked Katherine.

"Yes, of course, they are part of my family. They should come too," said John sternly.

Katherine took his arm, turned, placed her hands on his chest, looked earnestly into his eyes and said: "John, darling, you know that I abide by your every command, but could this really be so? The gossip about me is already hot. It will surely be said that your mistress thinks she is the equal of your Queen and this will be held against you."

John looked down, searching the worried grey eyes in which he always saw such love. He sighed and said: "You know I will not be cowed by gossipmongers or whining monks; but, yes, I think it best if I have a different celebration with Constance, but I will have Lady Blanche's children and yours all together with me at the Savoy." They kissed and then he wheeled round and left the room, calling to his groom to be ready for hunting.

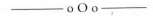

Gaunt's family gathered at the Savoy to celebrate his birthday in early May 1381: the children he had with Blanche, Duchess of Lancaster – Philippa, now aged 20, Elizabeth, 16, and Henry, his heir, aged 14; and the children, given the surname Beaufort, he had with Katherine Swynford – John aged 7, Henry, 5, Thomas, 3, and baby Joan aged 1. Also present was Thomas Swynford aged 13, Katherine's other son by Sir Hugh Swynford. It was an informal occasion which started with the three Beaufort boys playing a noisy and energetic game of blind man's bluff with Elizabeth, while her sister, Philippa, rocked baby Joan in her arms and gave her a finger to bite on to soothe her teething.

Meanwhile Henry of Lancaster and Thomas Swynford kept their dignity by standing in an appropriate male manner, talking together with their backs to the fire. Henry was tall for his age and much like his father. He had the same long straight back and the same clear blue eyes which, depending on his mood, could twinkle with pleasure or pierce with steely hauteur. Thomas Swynford had fair hair like his mother and an amiable temperament but was built like his father: short and stocky with strong broad shoulders.

Katherine and John sat watching the children while a meal was laid out on the table behind them. Katherine smiled at seeing Henry and her son Thomas talking together by the fireplace. She nodded towards them and said to John, "They seem as close now as when they were in the nursery. Do you remember?"

"How could I forget?" said John. 'That was when we first met. And, yes, they have a strong bond, I'm glad to say. Thomas will be the truest of knights to Henry, of that I am quite sure, and who knows how valuable that may be in the future?"

"And how grown up Philippa is," said Katherine, "so graceful and poised."

"Yes. It is time to think of a marriage match for her but, as yet, I see no worthy prospect, certainly not presently among the peers of this realm and none abroad either!" said John.

"Come," said Katherine, standing and offering her hand. "We should go to table and gather the children for your birthday treat."

Chaucer climbed from his horse, stiff and weary after the thirty-mile ride from Aachen. It had started to rain as they entered Cologne and the tired horses had stumbled on the wet cobbles in the narrow streets, adding to his discomfort. He stood and stretched, easing his back and legs. As he did so, he caught the eye of his travelling companion, Sir Edward Berkeley, who was smiling broadly.

"Too much desk work at the Customs House, Geoffrey?" he called.

"Aye, likely so," replied Chaucer. "But nothing that a hot toddy and a haunch of venison won't cure," he countered.

Sir Edward chuckled and slapped him on the back. Together they entered the timber-framed inn, leaving the servants to deal with the horses and baggage.

Chaucer had left London ten days earlier, travelling with Sir Edward, Roland, his esquire, two servants and two armed escorts. They had made a small cavalcade, including the two pack horses, as they travelled to Dover through the early summer countryside of Kent. Then after the Channel crossing to Calais, they had followed the regular merchant route, well provided with hostelries, through Bruges, Brussels and Maastricht to Aachen. Now, in Cologne, they could leave their horses and travel on by boat up the Rhine to Basle.

Chaucer had enjoyed the unhurried pace and gentle sway of his horse as they had moved through the generally flat landscape. It gave him opportunity to observe the countryside, the manners and customs of the people, the wildlife and to catch, on the wind, the scents of the herbs and flowers of the fields. And it gave him that precious commodity – Time: to think and reflect and to anticipate. He was looking forward to sailing up the Rhine with its mysterious castles and legends and, even, after Basle the climb over the Alps through the great St Bernard Pass. But most of all, he was eager to get to Milan and into the Visconti Library. The Viscontis, Lords of Milan, had been patrons of Plutarch and, he knew, had collected a vast range of works by Greek and Latin writers as well as Italians, including Dante and Boccaccio. He knew that this was not the purpose of the mission but for him it was the yeast in the dough that fed his spirit.

The next day, while Sir Edward negotiated a ship's passage up the Rhine to Basle, Chaucer made his way to the cathedral with its famous spire pointing high into the sky like a finger showing the pious the way to God. He entered through an iron-studded side door into the solemn vaulted cavern of the nave. As he walked forward, he could hear the echoes of soft footsteps and quiet voices. Then, as he approached the screen, a small choir began to sing the Mass to Our Lady written by Guillaume de Machaut. Chaucer was amazed. This was the selfsame Mass which he had heard being tried out before Machaut in Rheims Cathedral some seventeen years ago!

Chaucer sat and listened in wonder. The altar to the Virgin was set against the screen and the voices of the singers were reflected out into the nave by the wall of wood behind them. The pure tones seemed to hang in the air and gently ripple against the stonework like waves on the shore of a lake. He recognised the Kyrie sung to Machaut's polyphony in all nine sections, then the Gloria followed by the plainchant intonation of the Credo, the Sanctus and Agnus Dei. Chaucer sighed as the Mass ended with the short Ite, Missa Est, the sounds gradually dying away.

Chaucer sat on, feeling the effect of the music. He felt calm, almost cleansed, by its crystal purity. Looking round, he acknowledged the powerful spirituality of the great church. Was this because of the presence of God or the lingering echoes of praying worshippers? Whatever, he realised his response had not depended upon inter-pretation by a priest, bishop or pope even. Maybe Wycliffe and the Lollards were right in their radical views. The Church was corrupt and the mass of unlettered worshippers were intimidated. But was it right to deny the validity of the Eucharist itself?

Chaucer smiled to himself as he left the cathedral. He was no theologian. He would leave that to others. But he had enjoyed this interlude and was grateful for the experience and for the memory conjured up of his meeting with Machaut.

Two days into the voyage upstream, Chaucer was sitting on one of the forward hatches enjoying the spring sunshine and gazing across the fast-flowing river towards Heidelberg when Roland de Freitas, Sir Edward's esquire, approached.

"God's blessing on you, Master Chaucer," he said bowing. "If you please, may I sit with you a while?"

Chaucer smiled. Here was a merry youth, well versed in courtly manners, and bedecked in silk parti-coloured hose, long pointed shoes, embroidered tunic and studded hip girdle. His long shapely legs, narrow hips and straight bearing would no doubt serve him well at young King Richard's court.

"Yes, do, and welcome," replied Chaucer. "But tell me. How long have you been at Court?"

"Only since King Richard's coronation, sire," replied Roland. "Before that I was one of the pages at Kennington in Princess Joan's household."

Chaucer recalled his own youthful service in Countess Elizabeth's retinue.

"And I was there that Christmas when you read your poem 'The House of Fame'," continued Roland excitedly, his eyes shining. "It was wonderful. We talked a lot about it and for weeks afterwards we tried our own rhymings in English."

"Then maybe you would read me some of your writings?" asked Chaucer.

"Oh fie! But no, sire! I am no poet. But I can play and sing for you, if you will, for that is my accomplishment."

For the next hour as the river slid by, Chaucer was beguiled with a variety of French love songs and roundelays, sung sweetly and accompanied with practised ease on the cittern.

As they approached Basle, Chaucer was standing in the prow of the boat with Sir Edward Berkeley.

"Ah Geoffrey," he said, as he stretched his arms above his head and yawned. "It'll be good to have a horse between my legs again."

Geoffrey smiled. Sir Edward had been an impatient shipmate, forever striding the deck whereas he had found ease in the grey waters sliding by.

"What is the route from Basle?" he asked.

"We make for Lausanne by Lake Geneva and then climb up through the St Bernard Pass and down to Aorta. That will take about ten days, I reckon. Then it is a gentle ride down to Milan. We should be there in a fortnight."

"Have you met with Count Visconti before?" asked Geoffrey.

"No. I know Sir John Hawkwood but not Visconti. By all accounts he's not a man to cross. 'Tis said he murdered his own brother," replied Sir Edward.

"Aye," said Geoffrey. "And there's that mystery about how my former master, Prince Lionel, died after his marriage to Visconti's daughter."

"Oh ho!" chuckled Sir Edward, "to mention that will put the cat among the pigeons for sure." Then more soberly, "As you know, we will need to meet the Count formally and present our greetings and letters from King Richard. Then I suggest you go with his officials and start to sound them out about the loan King Richard wants while I tackle Sir John about help from his White Company of mercenaries for fighting the French when needed." At that, the boat bumped alongside the wharf in Basle and they were too caught up in the bustle of unloading for further talk.

Later as the cavalcade wound their way along the eastern shore of Lake Geneva, Chaucer reflected on their conversation. The procedure Sir Edward had outlined was familiar enough to Geoffrey: small groups talking in sombre rooms with serious faces, probing, testing the strength of purpose and real intent of the other side. Geoffrey had from the earliest days as a diplomatic envoy seen the irony of these wordy, overserious exchanges. It was a joust with words rather than with sword or lance – the search for a chink in the other's armour, the steely stare and straight purpose were akin to the tactics of the jousting field. And he had no doubt, on this occasion, that King Richard's needs would be met. The real question was 'at what price'? and that was where the parleying would need the deftness of the rapier rather than the lunge of the lance.

And so it proved. Geoffrey and his counterpart, an olive-skinned Italian with limpid brown eyes, had readily agreed a sum of 100,000 sovereigns. But there had been much haggling and agonised arm waving before the terms of the loan had been drafted. Geoffrey made sure that Sir Edward joined him for the final draft. Together they had obtained an acceptable annual interest rate of ten per cent over five years. Although this had yet to be approved and signed by the Count,

Geoffrey was now free to lose himself in the famous library.

For the next three weeks, Chaucer dwelt in the temple of the Visconti Library, worshipping at the altar of the great collections of writings stored there. He had his meals brought in – although they often remained uneaten. He had a truckle bed set up but rarely slept on it. Here were legends, myths, heroic tales of love and human suffering, as well as treatises on astrology, politics and philosophy. He read works in Latin, French, Italian; copied, translated, made notes and cross references from: Ovid and Virgil; Boethius and Tacitus; Benoit de Sainte Maure and Eustache Deschamps; Dante, Plutarch and Boccaccio.

He was especially enthralled by two works, both of which dealt with high ideals, loss, raw emotions and human suffering. Boethius wrote his *Consolation of Philosophy* when he was imprisoned by the Ostrogoth King Theodoric and put to death in AD 524 for being too outspoken in defending Roman liberties. Boccaccio, an Italian contemporary of Chaucer's, when suffering the infidelity and loss of his mistress, wrote 'Il Filostrato', based on the legend from the Trojan Wars of the lovers Troilus and Criseyde. Chaucer was thrilled by the intensity of this drama of Troy and the interplay of the heroic figures involved – Pandarus, Agamemnon, Priam, Helen, Achilles, Hector – and he avidly noted the ways that Ovid, Virgil and Dante portrayed these.

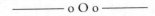

But, too soon, Sir Edward, who had been revelling and jousting in the company of Sir John Hawkwood, came to talk about the return journey to England.

"God's blessing on you, Geoffrey!" he said as he came into the library. "Hawkwood has offered to accompany us back to the Swiss border with some of his White Cavalry. It should be good sport. They are jovial company and we should get some hunting on the way. How does that suit you?"

Chaucer paused, searching for the right words, for it did not suit him at all. He was no hunter and nor did he relish riding with a band of carousing mercenaries. He had been looking forward to a quiet journey when he could study further the writings he had acquired and notes he had made.

"Sir Edward," he began tactfully. "As you know, two years ago I had negotiations on King Edward's behalf with the merchants in Genoa. Would it not be helpful if I kept the King's interests warm with them as a supplement to our mission here in case the promised support does not mature or that more is needed?"

Sir Edward looked intently at Chaucer. Surely he did not mean that Hawkwood would renege on his promise of armed support? But then, he reflected, these alliances were fickle affairs, especially in Italy and Hawkwood had other masters to serve. Maybe there was wisdom in this. Rubbing his chin, he said: "I take your point, Geoffrey. I think the King would welcome that but what route would you take back to England?"

"Oh, I fancy a Genoese captain bound for Plymouth or Portsmouth might see me as a fare bargain!" chuckled Chaucer, "and I would relish a sea voyage."

"Well, rather you than me, my friend! Give me a horse any day!" replied Sir Edward.

And so, after two days in Genoa, having agreed generous terms with a ship's master who had known his father, Chaucer prepared himself for the long voyage through the Straits of Gibraltar and across the Bay of Biscay. He then settled to the real task which he had promised himself: to translate Boethius' *Consolation of Philosophy* into English.

John of Gaunt, Duke of Lancaster, swept out from his audience with King Richard with his accustomed energy – tall, lean, bronzed, but greying – when he saw Chaucer standing with Sir Edward Berkeley.

"Why, Geoffrey! You are back then from the tainted embrace of the Visconti clan!" his eyes twinkling mischievously. "And you, Sir

Edward," with a slight bow.

"Yes, my Lord," said Sir Edward. "We are here to make report on our mission to King Richard."

"Quite so," said Gaunt, and turning to Chaucer: "And what of that famous Library? Did you see it?"

Chaucer's face lit up. He chuckled and said eagerly: "More than that, my Lord: I practically lived there and am replete with ancient tales of the Trojans and Rome and the works of Dante and Boccaccio!"

"I shall want to hear more," said Gaunt. "But now I must away north as I have an urgent commission from the King to make a settlement with the Scots over these persistent raids across the Borders and into Berwick. But you could call on Lady Katherine at the Savoy. She will be staying there for a few days and as always would welcome you with tales from your travels and news of her sister, your good wife."

After the Duke left, quiet settled on the room and soon Sir Edward and Chaucer were ushered into the King's presence.

When Chaucer arrived back at Aldgate, he was hot and sweating from his walk from Westminster in the early June sunshine. He took a long draught from the tankard of ale that Mostly Maggie welcomed him with. Upstairs he found his friends John Gower and Ralph Strode already well through similar pots. He greeted them warmly but they seemed to be more subdued than usual.

"What is the mood at Court?" asked Strode.

"Quiet, I would say," replied Chaucer. "King Richard was pleased with our report on the mission to Italy. We met John of Gaunt coming out of the King's chamber. He was in good humour. He had been commissioned by the King to travel north to parley with the Scots to stop the troubles on the Borders and their raids on Berwick."

"Mmmhhh! I fear there may soon be much bigger troubles here over this Poll Tax," said Strode. "There is such resentment among the common people. Yesterday at Brentwood an angry crowd refused the collector's demands for payment and there would have been bloodshed had he not retreated back to London."

"And this is not an isolated case," put in Gower. "There is seething unrest too in Kent where I have heard demands for the end of the bondage of villeinage, feudal duties and church tithes."

"But forgive me," said Chaucer. "I have been away in Italy. Surely these conditions are not new. Why is such issue being taken now?"

Strode and Gower looked at each other, uncertain as to who should speak first and then Gower, the poet, came out with an apt simile: "It is like a kettle on the hob, Geoffrey. It takes time for the fire to build and the water to boil and then it explodes with a blast of steam."

"Yes!" cried Ralph Strode, for once pleased with this imagery. "And this kettle has been boiling up for thirty or more years! Remember the years of the Black Death. As many as one third of the population died and in some places whole villages were left empty and the fields left untilled. This meant that labour was in short supply and many of the peasants saw the opportunity to bargain for higher wages or improve their position by acquiring land for themselves."

"Yes," broke in Gower, "and that is why the government, quite rightly, passed the Statute of Labourers in 1351 to peg wages at their pre-Black Death levels."

"But over time that has only added fuel to the fire," said Strode shortly, warming to his lawyer's style of argument. "Labour is scarce in many parts, especially after the second outbreak of the plague in 1367. And landlords have bigger incomes because of the higher price of wheat. Peasants know this. Yet their wages are held down. They have rents and other dues to pay and manorial services to carry out. Defaulters are regularly kept in check by being brought before the manorial courts. This is at the heart of the trouble."

"Did you say 'heart' or 'heat'?" quipped Chaucer, seeking to calm his friend. "But there have been poll taxes before; why is this such an issue now?"

"Previous poll taxes like those of 1377 and 1379 were graduated according to status and ability to pay; this one is not," explained

Gower. "It is levied at the very high rate of one shilling per person, as opposed to fourpence in 1379, and everyone is counted including women, youths and dependants."

"So," said Strode with a laugh, "not surprisingly, many taxpayers are concealing the existence of unmarried females, widows, aunts, sisters and so on. Apparently, nearly half a million taxpayers have 'disappeared' from the registers since 1379! And this is why the tax collectors are now being sent to ferret out the missing persons, which has led in some places to fights between neighbours because one has informed on another."

"My worry is that this could lead to violence," said Gower. "There are some very rough elements among the poorer peasantry. They are used to working with tools like billhooks, scythes and mattocks, and they are likely to pick these up and use them if they are roused." And then standing as he prepared to leave: "I pray to God that I am wrong!"

"Amen to that," replied Chaucer.

"And you take care, Geoffrey," said Strode as he also prepared to leave. "Aldgate is the main route from Essex into London."

When his friends had gone Chaucer sat quietly reflecting on what they had said. He felt uneasy with a sense of foreboding.

This was increased when next day at the Customs House he heard that three villagers had been killed by an angry mob outside Brentwood. They had been set upon and beheaded because they had given the names of tax avoiders to the collectors. Chaucer broke off from making the latest entry in the Customs Book, sat down and pondered. The thought had been growing on him during the night that his foreboding was because of his concern for the safety of Katherine Swynford at the Savoy. Among the common people, John of Gaunt was thought to be the root of this evil because of his domination of the young King. He flaunted his position at the most opulent palace in London and he openly favoured his mistress. They would be likely to vent their anger on the Savoy and on her if they found her there.

He rose and went down to the quayside where a Portuguese barque was moored, discharging its cargo of wine. The Captain, Jose Marinda, was well known to him and greeted him with a broad smile and open arms. "Geoffrey, amigo!" he called, but his humour faded when he saw Chaucer's serious face. He led him to his cabin below, filled two ample glasses of wine and looked expectantly into Geoffrey's face.

Chaucer described the situation, including the violent deaths in Essex that morning, the danger that his sister-in-law was in, and asked if Jose could help to get her away from the Savoy by boat using the river. Jose's eyes had opened wide at the description of the killings and the thought of that happening to her.

"Holy Mother!" he cried. "Of course we must rescue her!" And jumping up, he cried: "We can go now! It is best we row there in the ship's boat. Come!"

On the journey upriver, Chaucer explained that he had not talked to Katherine about this; that she was sure to have a knight of the Lancastrian retinue with her and she would decide with him if and where she wanted to go.

"That is no problem," said Jose. "I am at her service – provided it is navigable for my ship!"

After tying up at the Savoy landing stage, Chaucer and the Captain were quickly taken to Katherine who was talking with Sir Andrew Lutterel.

"Geoffrey!" she exclaimed, moving towards him with a bright smile which faded when she saw his troubled face. "What is it?"

Chaucer moved forward and kissed her hand. "Katherine, have you had news of the riot and killings at Brentwood today?"

"Yes," she replied "Indeed Sir Andrew and I were discussing this when you arrived."

Sir Andrew stepped forward and with a slight bow said: "I was just pressing the seriousness of this on Lady Katherine and my view, as the Duke's liege man entrusted with her safety, that she should leave the Savoy immediately. She agrees, but we were just weighing the odds of where to go and how."

"This is why I came," said Chaucer. "The river is surely the best route. And this is why I have brought a ship's captain with me – Jose Marinda. His barque is lying at the Customs House and he wishes to help."

Jose stepped forward and bowed. "My Lady. My ship and I are at your command!"

"He regularly plies between London and Calais or Flanders," put in Chaucer. "Maybe you could go on to Hainault—"

"No, never!" interrupted Katherine sharply. "I will not leave the country – nor be far from my children, although to join them at Kenilworth just now may not be possible."

Then turning to Sir Andrew, she said: "I have a house at Wisbech on the east coast with tenants who are loyal to the Duke and to me. Do you think that would be a safe sanctuary?"

Sir Andrew smiled. He knew the tenants, Amos Snell and his wife, who had recently retired from the Duke's service at Lincoln. "I would say that would be a good solution – provided the Captain here is prepared to navigate into the waters of the Wash."

Marinda stepped forward. "My Lady! I have not been to this Wisbech but, no problem, I will get out my charts and we will find it, for sure! But you will need some warm clothes. It can be cold out at sea."

"And, I suggest," added Chaucer, "outer garments of plain fustian so as not to draw attention…? And I will take my leave, as there will not be room enough for us all in the rowing boat."

With that, the party broke up to make their preparations and Chaucer, after embracing Katherine and Jose and nodding to Sir Andrew, took his leave to walk back to the Customs House.

———— o O o ————

As Chaucer made his way down the Strand after leaving the Savoy, the streets were empty and he sensed an eerie sort of calm. But as he neared the Vintry he began to hear a commotion of raucous laughter, shouting and bellowing coming from a jostling mob of twenty or thirty men outside St Martin's Church. Then as he drew nearer, he heard screams of terror and saw a woman being dragged from the church by her hair and two men being marched and shoved forward with their arms tied behind their backs. Chaucer guessed by their clothes that they were Flemings.

They were being marched and dragged towards a horse trough beyond the church and he thought they were in for a ducking. But then he saw beside the trough a stone mounting block which was running red with fresh blood and beyond that a pile of severed heads and lifeless bodies. He hurried on, not wishing to see or be part of what was now to happen. But he heard the swish and striking of an axe and the huge roar of triumph from the excited mob. He winced and continued on his way.

Chaucer knew the Vintry well from his childhood and that Flemings were resented by some people for their foreign ways, their seemingly aloof, abrupt manner and capacity for hard bargaining. Their houses had occasionally been stoned by groups of youths trying to prove their manhood. But this carnage was beyond his knowing. It was clear that the genuine anger roused by the injustice of the Poll Tax was infecting other elements who had their own grievances or scores to settle.

Before going home he climbed the steps to the Customs House.

"Why, Harry, you should be away home by now," he said with a smile as he walked in.

"I have a bag for you, Master," replied Harry. "Captain Marinda called me down to the quayside just before he sailed and asked me to give it to you. 'For safekeeping for Lady K'," was his message," as he handed over a heavy leather bag.

"Did you see him leave?" asked Chaucer.

"Yes, he had his foresail up and was pulling away as I left," Harry replied.

"No other news?" he asked.

"No, except that there has been a flurry of activity at the Tower where it is rumoured that the King is expected there this night."

"Thank you, Harry. You had best get home – but take care and God's blessing on your father and mother."

When Harry had gone, Chaucer contemplated Katherine's bag. He could not risk taking it to Aldgate tonight so he locked it in a cupboard under his desk. Having done that, he secured the front door and went to the Black Swan where he knew he could learn more of the happenings at the Tower.

"Why, Master Geoffrey, welcome!" called the landlord as he pushed a tankard of ale towards him.

"And this is most welcome too!" replied Geoffrey raising the drink. Then, after wiping his mouth with the back of his hand and leaning on the counter, he said: "Troubled times, William."

"Yes, and I fear it might get worse before it gets better. The King went by boat down to Rotherhithe today to meet with a horde of rebels from Kent but they were so hostile he did not risk a landing. So he has called for another meeting at noon tomorrow at Mile End to hear their demands and treat with them. You know, Geoffrey, this is a monstrous thing for the young King to have to face."

"Indeed! But he has Privy Councillors and such to advise him. Are they with him?" asked Chaucer.

"Yes, several as far as I know. By all accounts there's a fair number at the Tower: the Chancellor, Archbishop Sudbury and the Treasurer, Sir Robert Hales, with the Earls of Warwick, Salisbury and Oxford, the Mayor, William Walworth and Sir Robert Knolles among them."

"Good! He's not alone then," said Geoffrey, proffering his empty tankard for a refill. "For there are loose gangs causing dreadful mayhem. Just now, I witnessed a gang pulling some Flemings out of St Martin's in the Vintry and, would you believe – beheading them! It will take a miracle to cool this hot broth!"

"I fear so," said William. And then, knowing how Chaucer liked to bandy with words added: "Maybe there'll be a cold wind tomorrow to take the heat out of it!"

"Amen!" said Chaucer with an appreciative smile. "But the King will need a cool head too!"

Early next day, Friday, 14th June, Chaucer was woken by a crowd of men banging on the closed gate beneath him. As soon as the bolts were drawn, they were joined by others from within the City. Amidst the clamour of shouting and counter-shouting, Chaucer deduced that the majority argued for going to Mile End to meet the King 'to get our rights and justice from him' while others wanted to stay in the City 'to ferret out the traitors'. Gaunt, Sudbury and Hales were named as well as cries of 'the Savoy' and 'Newgate Prison'.

Eventually the commotion subsided, with the majority leaving for Mile End and the others running into the City in gangs waving their makeshift weapons. Chaucer decided to go to the Customs House to make sure it was secure, including any cargo that had been discharged. He was on the quayside when he heard a series of loud explosions coming from upriver in the direction of Westminster and saw a plume of black smoke rising from that quarter. His first thought was that the palace itself at Westminster had been attacked but as he climbed up to the Customs House he knew that it was nearer. Then he could see that the Savoy was in flames as minor explosions rent the otherwise clear June sky. His worst fears had been realised: his rescue of Katherine justified.

Too restless and perturbed to stay longer, he left the Customs House and joined William White in a crowded tap room at the Black Swan. The bar was buzzing with loud, excited talk. To his surprise, this was not about the blaze at the Savoy but even more tragic happenings at the Tower. Apparently an excited horde of rebels had overpowered the guards, broken into the Tower, dragged out the Archbishop, Hales, the Treasurer, and two others, beheaded them and hoist their heads on spikes on the bridge!

"I tell you I saw it," shouted a tall figure at the centre of the group by the bar. "It took seven blows before Sudbury's head fell off. Hales was easier with only two chops." Someone shouted, "He must have had a skinny neck!" which caused some guffaws.

"And they did for that sneak of a tax collector, John Legge," put in another eager voice. "And Gaunt's doctor, that friar, William Appleton," put in another.

"Aye," resumed the tall man. "Some of them had rushed up from sacking the Savoy, bent on finding Gaunt. Frustrated at not finding him, I reckon poor Appleton paid the price for his master's absence."

Chaucer turned away, his face grim and pale and said quietly to William: "Do we know what happened at Mile End?"

"No, not yet," replied the landlord. "I saw the King's party ride out early on but they are not back yet, nor any news."

"If the King has made peace with the rebels, these beheadings may undo that," mused Chaucer, in a quiet voice. "But I must get home. I am expecting Strode, who may know more as he keeps a sharp ear to the ground."

"Take care then," said William, as Chaucer made his way to the door.

Chaucer had been at home above Aldgate for a while before he heard the sound of horses walking through the archway. He looked down from his window and saw the Earl of Salisbury riding alongside the young King Richard with the Earl of Warwick and Sir Richard Knolles behind him. Chaucer sighed. So, the King had returned safely: well and good.

While he had been alone waiting, he had been pondering on the troubles and particularly the seeming preference of the rebels for beheading their victims rather than using a knife or dagger to stab the chest or back. He had no answer. Maybe the preference for the neck arose from their day-to-day methods of killing domestic animals? And beheading was a quick and certain slaughter – or usually was – he added to himself, remembering the time it had taken to despatch Archbishop Sudbury.

Soon there was knocking at the door and he hurried downstairs to welcome Ralph Strode.

"Ralph! Welcome, come in. Leave your hat and cloak here and join me upstairs. I have a bottle of Burgundy ready and waiting."

"Thank you kindly, Geoffrey. Yes, that would be welcome," as he stretched his back and legs which were stiff from riding, before sitting down and lifting a glass of the red wine.

"I decided to go with the King's party to this meeting at Mile End. There was no objection as I am a lawyer. And I am glad I did, Geoffrey," he said. "There was a huge assembly of peasants, three or more thousand I would say, most of them carrying some sort of weapon. They fell quiet when the King rode forward alone to them and said: 'I am Richard, your King. I have summoned you here to hear your grievances,' which brought forth a loud cheer, and then a tall, saturnine-looking man stepped forward, bowed and addressed the King:

"'My liege Lord. We are honoured that you have come to meet us. I am Jack Straw and I have been elected by my fellows to present you with our petition against the intolerable servitude and heavy oppressions we endure which is:

1. That all traitors like the Chancellor, the Treasurer, John of Gaunt be handed over to us;
2. That villeinage be abolished and labour services be by free contract without wage restraint;
3. That we have the right to rent land at fourpence an acre.'

"Richard moved his horse forward three paces and addressed the crowd: 'You shall have the heads only of traitors that have been so judged by law. I am prepared to confirm and grant that you should be free and charters of manumission will be drawn up.'

"At this," Strode continued, "there was an enormous cheer. Clearly many in the crowd thought they had won the day. Jack Straw was mobbed while others joined into smaller groups and began to hurry back into the City, shouting the names of traitors – I fear they may be thinking the King agreed there were traitors and that they should deal with them."

"Thank you for that, Ralph. I much admire your effort in going to Mile End," said Geoffrey. "But while the King was meeting the rebels another horde forced their way into the Tower, dragged out Sudbury, Hales and Gaunt's doctor William Appleton, beheaded them summarily and spiked their heads on the bridge. And another group burnt the Savoy down."

"Oh no!" shouted Strode. "The King showed his royal lineage with calm composure and some sympathy for the peasants but his concessions will not stem the revolt, I fear, especially after this savagery."

Next morning Chaucer rose early. There were still noisy elements of the rebels moving through Aldgate into the City, so he decided to go to the Customs House as a safeguard. Harry was already there with news that the King had sent a message to the rebels to meet him at Smithfield at noon. He also reported that a ship from Calais had arrived on the tide and was moored in midstream, waiting to discharge its cargo. Chaucer sent Harry to the quayside to explain the unrest and violence to the captain and to advise him to stay moored away from the quay for the time being.

By noon there was no movement through Aldgate. The streets outside were empty. An eerie calm had settled over London. Then around three o'clock in the afternoon there were sounds of people moving from the City and out towards Essex through Aldgate: at first in twos and threes; then in a swarm. And, Chaucer noticed, the rowdy, roistering cockiness of the past two days had gone. Clearly something dramatic had happened at Smithfield. It was not until the evening, when he was joined for an evening meal by his friends John Gower and Ralph Strode, that he learned the full story.

Maggie had roasted a fat pheasant with parsnips, carrots and thick onion gravy spiced with mint and pepperwort and a suet pudding with apples and bramble jelly to follow. As usual, Chaucer, blessed with a vintner's nose inherited from his father, provided some fine red wines: a Rioja from Spain and a vintage Burgundy. As soon as their glasses were full and they had settled down to their meal, Chaucer looked eagerly at his friends: "I am agog to hear your news."

"To be brief, Geoffrey," said Strode in his courtroom style, "It started like a repeat of yesterday's meeting at Mile End. There were at least as many rebels facing the King and their leader, Wat Tyler, started with the same demands: abolition of villeinage and feudal services, rights to rent land, punishment for traitors. Then, it was clear he was enjoying being the centre of attention. He became bolder and more familiar, addressing the King as 'Brother', demanding that all men should be equal with no more lordship save that of the King, that the Church should be disendowed and all bishops, save one, abolished."

"That last would have come from John Ball," put in Gower. "He has been fuming against corruption in the Church and the opulent lifestyle of bishops. His supporters in Kent want him to lead a reformed church as the single Bishop!"

"Quite so!" said Strode, continuing his account. "At that point, an esquire from the King's entourage shouted out and denounced Tyler as the most notorious thief in Kent. Tyler snarled and rounded towards him, flashing a dagger. The Mayor moved forward to intervene. Tyler flashed his dagger at him but missed and the Mayor struck out with his sword, injuring him on the shoulder. Tyler staggered back, clasping his shoulder which was bleeding badly, before collapsing, at which one of the King's knights ran him through with his sword.

"There was a roar of anguish from the crowd and a movement forward, some raising bows and fixing arrows, when the King spurred his horse forward and shouted: 'Sirs, will you shoot your King? I am your leader. Follow me,' and he drew them away towards Clerkenwell Fields."

"So that is it!" said Chaucer. "That was bold action by the young Richard: shades of his father, the Black Prince! And with their leader gone, I suppose they lost the fire in their bellies?"

"Just so," said Strode. "There was no further bloodshed. Mayor Walworth called up some troops from the City who shepherded the peasants away to return to their homes."

"Well, much thanks to you both," said Chaucer, replenishing their glasses. "Let us deal with this pudding before it cools!"

After that, they withdrew to the more ample chairs of the parlour.

"And do you think that will be the end of the revolt?" asked Chaucer.

"Yes, I do," replied Strode. "I hope the Poll Tax is annulled and that there will not be harsh reprisals by the government, although there is bound to be some rounding up of the ringleaders. What do you think, John?"

"I agree. Most of the peasantry are simple, hardworking folk who if they feel treated fairly repay that with loyalty. Most of the local lords of manors in the shires know that and would, I am sure, not want to upset that balance in the local community by a witch-hunt."

"So, are you saying that, after all this, the peasantry have gained nothing?" asked Chaucer.

"No," replied John Gower. "I think the Poll Tax will be withdrawn and the imposition of local taxes and their manner of collection will also change. And gradually, if only because of the shortage of labour, freely negotiated labour contracts will replace the feudal obligations. It works well enough on my manor and with a number of my neighbours."

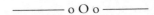

And so it proved. The Poll Tax was cancelled. While some lords insisted on exacting every duty from their villeins and tenants, using the manorial courts to inflict fines and punishments, most local squires were more understanding and sought to restore the practical give and take of working life in their communities. Although some nineteen leaders of the rebels in Essex and others in Kent were rounded up, tried before the courts and hanged, many were pardoned and there was no witch-hunt.

But there was no ease for John of Gaunt. Two days after returning from Scotland and after attending on the King, Gaunt, his face drawn and his eyes hooded, stood and contemplated the ruins of the Savoy. Built by his grandfather, Henry, Duke of Lancaster, and inherited by him through his marriage to his cousin Blanche, his face softened as he remembered the festivities here at their wedding and those other occasions when the palace resounded with the entertainment of kings, princes and ambassadors, including his father and mother, King Edward III and Queen Philippa, and King John, King of France.

And then his face set again as he recalled the words of the poet John Gower, Chaucer's friend: 'The only security of princes lies in the affection of their subjects'. He could not believe that these ruins before him were caused by anger and jealousy at his position. The bonds between Lords and their retainers and Commons were too strong, based on rightful positions, bonds of allegiance, trust, support and duties deriving from a mutual chivalrous code. This devastation was not caused by his dishonouring this code. No, there was a greater force at work, a greater power: it was an act of God.

He thought of the last nights he had spent here and of the sweet loving with Katherine. And therein he saw the cause. This was God's wrath at his wantonness and betrayal of Constance, his Queen. He saw now that he must renew his vows to her and prosecute with full vigour her claim to the throne of Castile. And he must forswear life with Katherine and her body. He knew she had now returned safely to Kettlethorpe. He would see her, make provision for her support and that of their children and go with her to Lincoln where, together, in the cathedral, they could confess and make atonement.

Chapter Nine

CHAUCER WOKE EARLY on a day in late May 1384. The weather promised well: a clear sky, an early heat haze over the City, a tempering breeze off the river. Thanks be for that, thought Chaucer as he walked down to the Customs House, for a busy day was also promised. Wool from the spring sheep-shearing in the Cotswolds was now arriving for shipment to the wool staple in Calais. Bought by wool merchants from the farmers in centres like North Leach and Broadway, it had been baled and brought by packhorse to the Staplers Mart at Leadenhall. Weighed and certified for quality, the bales were now ready for shipment. It remained for Chaucer as Controller of Customs to record their loading and apportion the customs duty owing to the King.

When Chaucer reached the Customs House a familiar scene awaited him. Two ships were already tied up and being loaded at the wharf while two others, having arrived on the evening tide, were moored in midstream. He checked the slate board behind him and saw that Harry had already chalked up the ships at the wharf: The *Jesu*, with John Lollington as master, and the *Mary*, with William Sordyvale as master. He smiled at the quick competence of his young assistant and, looking down, saw the familiar figure of John Lollington standing on the wharf directing the work of the deckhands. He went down to greet him.

"Master Chaucer, God's blessing on you!" called John on seeing Chaucer hurrying along the wharf towards him. "Truly it is good to see you!"

"And you, my friend!" replied Chaucer as he looked into the mariner's familiar creased leathery face and shining blue eyes. "And the seaway twixt Calais, is it clear?" he asked, knowing the trouble with pirates in the Channel.

"Aye, well enough," replied John. "'Tis best to keep company. So we will sail with the *Mary* here and I have a staunch crew adept with bows and shot! But come on board and share a dram in my cabin!"

Meanwhile Harry Castle, while recording the bales loaded on the *Mary*, was listening to Thomas Henman's description of his life as a wool stapler's prentice.

"Basically, I record the loading of every bale of my master's shipment, how it is marked and where it is stowed, that is fore or aft the mast, and whether it is under or over others' stowage."

"So do you then travel to Calais with the ship?" asked Harry.

"Oh, I have been," said Thomas, enjoying his status with his eager young audience, "but not this time. My brother is there. I will send to him a note with Master Lollington of the amount and stowage of our bales so that he can check and report on their arrival."

Harry would have liked to know more, particularly about life in Calais, but the ship's crew were battening down the hatches and he had to attend to the other ship.

Later, back at the Customs House, Chaucer watched as the *Jesu* moved out under a foresail into midstream, followed by the *Mary*. He had sent them off with warm and sincerely felt words for a safe passage. Now their replacements were moving in to tie up at the wharf.

"Master Chaucer," called Harry, as he marked up their names. "Have we seen this *Thomas* before?"

"Only once, last year, I think," replied Chaucer. "She's out of Newhithe on the Medway. But the master, Robert Ewen, is new to me. But the *Christopher* is a regular and the master, Harry Wilkins, was a great favourite with your father, God bless his soul!"

Chaucer looked over at Harry and his face softened. Since Tom Castle's death he had a fatherly concern for his son.

"Harry," he said. "I saw you having a good chinwag with Thomas Henman, the stapler's assistant. What was that about?"

"I've watched him and some of his colleagues a few times," said Harry. "I was asking him about his job, which doesn't seem overly difficult to me, and they get to travel in the ships and see places like Calais."

Chaucer noticed the excitement in the young man's eyes as he spoke and decided now was as good a time as any to talk about the future.

"Harry, you've helped me wondrously well. You figure well and keep true records. Maybe it is time to think of using those skills elsewhere?"

"Oh no! Master Chaucer, I didn't mean that! Truly I didn't!" protested Harry.

"I know that," said Chaucer smiling. "But I have been thinking that I should have a change too. I need more time for my reading and writing. Maybe it won't be long before I give up as Controller of Customs and move out of my lodgings over the Aldgate? If you wish, I will talk with Thomas Betson, a Merchant of the Staple, and ask him if he, or any of his colleagues, would take you on as a prentice."

Harry had been looking intently into Chaucer's face as he was speaking.

"It is a calling I would fancy, Master Geoffrey, if you truly could let me go."

Chaucer smiled. "Let me see what I can do then. And now we must attend to these two ships at the wharf."

The journey from Newcastle had meant two days' hard riding for John of Gaunt and his entourage with a change of horses every forty or fifty miles. But now, as they rode over the moat and through the keep at Kenilworth Castle, his mood lightened. Kenilworth was his favourite castle, especially since the destruction of the Savoy and because it brought back memories of happy times with Blanche, his first wife, when they had planned together the building of the great hall, the pools and double-moated pleasance.

Then, as he dismounted and passed the reins of his horse to a groom, he saw his Constable of the Castle, Sir Roger Curson, hurrying towards him. A quick instinct warned John that he was bringing important news.

"My Lord! Welcome!" said Sir Roger, bowing before John. "We have just heard the news of a battle in Portugal. King John has defeated the Castilian army that were threatening to invade his kingdom!"

Gaunt's face lit up with joy: "Oh! Thanks be to God! This is an auspicious day! Come, have a toast prepared so that we can all bless the occasion."

Soon the great hall was filled with excited chatter as the news was digested. Would the government now respond to the overtures from Portugal for an alliance to be sealed between the two countries? What did this mean for Gaunt's claim to the throne of Castile by right of his wife Constanza? Would Parliament now vote supplies for John of Gaunt to lead an army to Castile to take the throne by force?

The Duke was also discussing the import of this news with his circle of close retainers. Lord Neville of Raby was certain that the way was now clear for an invasion of Castile. Michael de la Pole was more cautious. "But Parliament has twice refused to vote supplies for this," he protested.

Sir William Ashton, Gaunt's Chancellor, was more measured as he weighed the diplomatic and political issues.

"There is a lot to be gained from an alliance with Portugal," he said. "Our ships continue to be harassed in the Channel by pirates and Castilian vessels. The Portuguese navy would be a big deterrent. The issue of sending an army is less clear cut. Raising taxes to finance it would not be popular." He paused and looked at the Duke: "The King seems besotted with Robert de Vere and would, I guess, follow his opinion." Then, looking again at Gaunt: "If your Grace will permit, I think de Vere would be pleased to use this as an opportunity to have you out of the country."

"No more glad than I!" said Gaunt. "Look at the fiasco of the invasion of Scotland we have just come from. We all mustered our feudal levies to support the King, and an impressive force it was, with upwards of five thousand men-at-arms and nine thousand archers. And what happens? De Vere argues against the advice on tactics of seasoned soldiers like Sir Robert Knolles, and we retreat to Newcastle!"

"I thought you were admirably restrained, my Lord," said Ashton tactfully.

"Yes!" said Gaunt, and then, with the hint of a smile, "I heartily support your analysis if only so that I will be relieved of that odious young upstart!"

And so it proved. A Treaty of Friendship and Alliance with Portugal was made and Parliament agreed to support the sending of an army under John of Gaunt's leadership to wrest the Crown of Castile from the usurper Juan.

John Gower had invited Chaucer to spend the day with him at his manor house in Blackheath near Greenwich. They were sitting outside in the shade of a large apple tree.

"You are in a gay mood, Geoffrey!" said Gower. "What provokes this?"

Chaucer smiled. "Yes! The tale of the siege of Troy by the Greeks and the double sorrow of Troilus and Criseyde has really gripped me."

He leaned forward towards his friend. "Despite being shut in their city, here are the Trojans celebrating the Feast of Palladion. Dressed in their finery in holiday mood, they mingle around the Temple: princes, their ladies, knights and squires as well as serving wenches and among them Troilus, son of the King, with his band of followers. While they laughed and flirted with the ladies in the crowd, he kept aloof, impervious to their smiles and charms, content in his freedom. And then, like a bolt from the blue, he saw Criseyde. And – well, let me read to you what I have written about this:

> *"And suddenly he felt himself astounded,*
> *Gazing more keenly at her in surprise*
> *'Merciful God! O where' he said, confounded,*
> *'Have you been hiding, lovely to my eyes?'*
> *He felt his heart begin to spread and rise.*
> *And he sighed softly, lest his friends should hear.*

"Now she was not among the least in stature.
But all her limbs so answerable were
To womanhood, there never was a creature
Less mannish in appearance standing there;
And when she moved, she did so with an air
Of ease and purity, so one could guess
Honour and rank in her and nobleness.

"Never had he seen so beautiful a sight.
And as he looked at her his pulses thickened;
Such passion, such desire, began to race
That at the bottom of his heart there quickened
The deeply printed image of her face.

"And from then on love robbed him of his sleep
And made an enemy of his food; his sorrow
Increased and multiplied, he could not keep
His countenance and colour, eve or morrow,
Had anyone noticed it; he sought to borrow
The names of other illnesses, to cover
His hot fire, lest it showed him as a lover.

"And she was quite unaware of the turmoil she had caused in him!"
said Chaucer. "But fortunately:

"Bewailing in his chamber thus alone,
To him there came a friend called Pandarus;
He slid in unperceived and heard him groan,
And seeing his distress, addressed him thus:
'Good gracious! What's the reason for this fuss?
Merciful God whatever can it mean?
Is it the Greeks have made you look so lean?'

"'What mischief brings you here, or has selected
This moment to intrude upon my care?
But if you think me ill because of fear,
You may take back your scorn; for I am one
Whom other cares oppress and hold me here,
Greater than anything the Greeks have done.'

"Pandarus, almost melting with compassion,
Kept saying, 'O alas! What can it be?
Dear friend, are love and friendship out of fashion?
Come, let me have a part of your despair,
And even if I cannot comfort you
One of the rights of friendship is to share
Not only in pleasure but in sorrow too.'

"This sorrowful Troilus began to sigh
And said 'God grant it may be for the best
To tell you everything...
Lest you think I do not trust a friend
Here is how it stands, now listen and attend:
Love so grievously assails me that my heart is sailing
Straight into death...'

"'What could be more unnatural or dafter
Than hiding this, you fool?' said Pandarus
'Perhaps the very one you're pining after
Is placed where my advice could profit us.'
'A wonder that would be!' said Troilus
'In your own love-affairs you seldom shine,
So how the devil can you help mine?'

"'Now listen Troilus' said Pandar 'Yes
I may have lost my way when I went rutting,
But my mistakes should teach you all the rules –
The wise I say may take advice from fools.
Look up I say and tell me who she is
At once, that I may go about your need:
Come, do I know her? Can't you tell me this?'

"A vein in Troilus began to bleed
For he was hit and reddened up in shame
As if some fiend were taking him to Hell,
And said 'The fountain of my woe, my well
Of grief, my sweetest foe, is called Criseyde.'
He trembled at the word and almost died.

"When Pandar heard the name that he had given,
Lord, he was glad and said 'My dearest friend,
I wish you joy, by Jupiter in Heaven.
I am ready and shall always be,
To go to work for you in this affair
For both of you. I have a hope in me
We shall be happy – all three of us.'"

Chaucer turned to Gower, who had been listening closely: "I have not read it all but that is as yet as far as I have gone."

"And splendid it is!" beamed Gower. "I like well the worldly character of Pandarus – much better than the limp young cousin Boccaccio portrayed in his version 'Il Filostrato'. I shall look forward to hearing more."

"And so you shall. Much thanks," said Chaucer. "Now may I ask a different favour of you?

"I recently quit-claimed my father's house in Thames Street in favour of the tenant, John Ashwell. I am thinking of moving from Aldgate to have more time for my writing: but where to? What is your advice?"

"I have found this a peaceful haven here in Blackheath, well suited to my own writings," said Gower. "I would think Greenwich would suit your needs. There are some ample town houses with spacious solars, and it is on the river, which would make an easy journey across to the Customs House and up to Westminster. I will, if you wish, make some enquiries, for, to quote your Pandarus, 'One of the rights of friendship is to share'!"

Chaucer chuckled. "My thanks and blessings on you, John!"

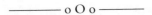

On the 30th June 1386, ten Portuguese galleys and six smaller craft sailed into Portsmouth harbour, where they joined a fleet of thirty or more English ships which had arrived from around the coasts of England over the past two weeks, requisitioned by royal summons, with another twenty lying off in Southampton Water. John of Gaunt, who stood watching from the harbour ramparts, slapped his thigh with pent-up energy. "At last!" he cried, "now we can embark and sail for Castile!"

Sir Thomas Percy, his admiral, who was standing with him, smiled and said, "Indeed and so we shall, my Lord! When we have embarked the nigh on ten thousand men that are enlisted!"

At that point, a squire, who had been using an eyeglass, approached.

"My Lord, a boat is being rowed ashore," he said. "It looks like their admiral standing in the stern."

"We must go down to greet him," said Gaunt and hurried away, followed by Percy. At the quayside, John of Gaunt, as putative King of Castile, stepped forward to greet the Portuguese admiral, Don Alfonso Furtado.

"Señor! You are most welcome."

"Your Majesty, the pleasure is all mine," he said with a bow and, bending forward, he took and kissed John's hand. "I bring greetings from my royal master, Dom John. We are here at his command and at your service."

John of Gaunt bowed. "Let me present my admiral, Sir Thomas

Percy, who will direct the English fleet in concert with you."

"Sir Thomas," said Don Furtado, bowing, "I shall look forward to sailing in your company."

"It is my honour," replied Sir Thomas. "Shall we go up to the castle where, maybe, we can begin to discuss our sailing plans?"

"And I will be pleased if you and your captains and retinue will join me and Queen Constance for a banquet in the great hall tonight to celebrate your safe arrival and to bless our joint enterprise," said Gaunt.

"We will be enchanted," said Furtado with a smile.

That evening, the great hall of the castle resounded with the lively talk of the assembled company: the ships' captains from both the Portuguese and English fleets; the leaders of the army of 3,000 archers, 2,000 lances and 4,000 pikemen and foot soldiers mustered for the invasion of Castile. On arrival, all had been presented to King John and Queen Constance of Castile and their entourage, which included Sir John Holland, Constable, Sir Thomas Percy, Admiral, leaders of the English force, and Alfonso Furtado, Admiral of the Portuguese fleet, and the Bishops of Hereford and Llandaff who represented the papal sanction to the enterprise. But the most especial places in the royal party beside the King and Queen were reserved for the members of their family and household who were going with them to Portugal: Katharine, their 14-year-old daughter; Philippa, John's 24-year-old eldest daughter by his first wife Blanche of Lancaster; her sister Elizabeth, now married to Sir John Holland; and Philippa Chaucer, lady-in-waiting. Henry, Earl of Derby, John of Gaunt's eldest son and heir, was also present although he was to stay in England to look after the Lancastrian estate.

And a fine regal party they made, resplendent in richly embroidered, colourful silks and satins. Both the King and Queen were dressed in the Spanish style houppelande, a long voluminous garment, starting with a high ruffed neck down to a tight jewelled waist belt from which fell a full skirt of rich material which trailed the ground. Queen Constanza wore a simple coronet set off by her shining black hair and the rich luminous sheen of her purple silk gown. John wore a black houppelande with a white fur neck ruff and the coats of arms of Castile and England richly embroidered on his chest. The full skirt was slit on both sides from the waist showing yellow silk hose and black soft leather shoes with pointed toes. The wrists of the wide sleeves were trimmed with white fur matching his ruff.

Princess Katharine was dressed in a close-fitting pale green cotehardie, trimmed with white fur, with a jewelled hip girdle round her slim waist and a full skirt in dark green velvet. The more mature Philippa of Lancaster wore a tightly fitting cream-coloured cotehardie, silver buttoned from a low neckline to the waist with a simple leather girdle on the hips from which flowed a full skirt in light blue satin silk. Over her shoulders was draped, in the style of Queen Anne, a black velvet ankle-length mantle lined with matching blue satin. Her younger brother, Henry, Earl of Derby, wore a short dark blue cotehardie with wide 'bagpipe' sleeves, a jewelled waist belt, dark blue hose and black slippers with long pointed toes.

Together they exuded a truly regal presence, magnificent in their jewels and richly adorned costumes – an indelible and intended statement of the legitimate royal court of Castile.

A week later, on Sunday, 7th July, the Earl of Derby stood on the ramparts and watched as the fleet hoisted sail and, before a fresh wind, sailed out into the Channel, bound for Castile.

At about the time that Gaunt was sailing from Portsmouth, Chaucer arrived at John Gower's house to find John's fiftieth birthday being celebrated by a lively company. The guests were well known to Chaucer for most were Knights of the King's Chamber whom he had met over the years at Court and on royal business. He was drawn into the company immediately by Sir Richard Sturry, a frequent associate and his senior when they had been captured outside Rheims and with whom he had completed a diplomatic mission to France in 1377.

"Geoffrey! It *is* good to see you," handing him a tankard of ale. "So you have at last joined us in Kent? At Greenwich, I hear?"

"Yes, indeed. And the house promises well although I have not yet moved in," replied Geoffrey.

"But you have a deputy now at the Customs?"

"Yes, and although he is learning quickly the painstaking rules of the Exchequer, he will need more time before I can be released."

"Make it soon, Geoffrey. We need men of your calibre and experience in Kent!"

Chaucer laughed: "Hold your horses, Richard. I'm not in residence yet and I need time for my writing."

This pricked the ears of Sir John Clanvowe, a fellow poet, who joined them.

"Geoffrey, I hear you are writing the saga of Troilus and Criseyde and the siege of Troy. How goes it?"

"Well enough, thank you, John. I have written three parts but have two more yet to draft," replied Chaucer.

They had also been joined by Sir Lewis Clifford, who was well acquainted with writers in Europe and had given Chaucer a work by the French poet Deschamps, praising Chaucer as a great English writer.

"So has the love-sick prince won over his lady yet?" asked the bluff Clifford with a twinkle in his eyes. "Come on, Geoffrey... tell us how he did it!"

Others had gathered round now and Geoffrey knew there was no escape from this audience – most of whom, and especially Clifford, were well versed in the arts of lovemaking!

Geoffrey fetched his manuscript and settled himself on a high stool, while the others grouped themselves round him in a semi-circle.

"You all know the story, I am sure, of how during the siege of Troy, Troilus is smitten with love for the beautiful widow Criseyde, whose father, Calkas, had defected to the Greeks. Troilus pines for Criseyde from afar until her uncle, Pandarus, connives to get them together and then:

"This Troilus, by sudden bliss surprised
Put all into God's hand, as one who meant
Nothing but well, and, suddenly advised
By impulse, took her in his arms and
     Bent her to him…
Criseyde, on feeling herself taken thus,
    In the enfolding arms of Troilus
Lay trembling, like an aspen leaf she shook.

"And then this Troilus began to strain
Her in his arms and whispered, 'Sweetest, say,
Are you not caught? We are alone, we twain,
Now yield yourself' and soon she answered him:
    'Had I not yielded long ago, my dear,
    My sweetest heart, I should not now be here.'

"Criseyde unloosed from care or thought of flight,
    Having so great a case to trust him,
    Made much of him with welcoming delight,
And as the honeysuckle twists her slim
    And scented tendrils over bole and limb
    Of a tall tree, so, free of all alarms,
They wound and bound each other in their arms.

"Her delicate arms, her back so straight and soft,
Her slender flanks, flesh-soft and smooth and white
He then began to stroke, and blessed as oft
Her snowy throat, her breasts so round and slight,
    And in this heaven taking is delight,
    A thousand, thousand times he kissed her too,
    For rapture scarcely knowing what to do.

> *"Of all their ecstasies and joys, the least*
> *Was more than I can convey:*
> *But you, if you have tasted, judge the feast*
> *Of their delight, the sweetness of their play;*
> *I can say little but at least I say…*
> *They learnt the honour and excellence of love!"*

Chaucer smiled and put his papers down, amidst a chorus of approval, laughter and some ribald comments. Sir Lewis Clifford came forward, slapped Chaucer on his back and said: "Thank you, Geoffrey! You certainly know how to tune into a fine woman!"

"It takes one to know one, Lewis!" quipped John Gower as Chaucer smiled, and the company began to disperse.

Late in the afternoon of 25th July 1386, the English and Portuguese fleets were approaching Corunna on the north-west coast of Galicia. John of Gaunt was standing at the masthead of his flagship with his wife, Constance. She turned to him, tears on her cheeks, and said: "Oh John! Forgive my tears. This is such a sweet moment for me! It is fifteen years since I last saw my homeland! And it is seventeen years since my father Pedro the First was coldly murdered by his cousin, Enrique!"

John put an arm round her shoulders and drew her to him.

"I know; and it is against his son Juan that we must now claim back the throne. With God's blessing, you will soon take your rightful place as Queen of Castile."

And then as he withdrew his arm he added: "We will anchor off the harbour tonight, but I will send Sir Thomas Percy ashore this evening with an armed guard to prepare the way for our landing tomorrow. I am confident you will be warmly welcomed!"

Later that evening, Sir Thomas Percy, having returned from his reconnaissance ashore, reported to John of Gaunt.

"Coruna is quiet and submissive, my Lord. I met with the Capitan,

Ferdinand Andrada, the Constable, and some clergy who assured me of their allegiance to you and Queen Constance. To prove it, they handed me these keys to the city," and he gave a set of large keys to the Duke, whose eyes lit up as he smiled.

"Good! Sir Thomas, thank you! That is much as we had expected… but gratifying, nonetheless!"

And then he turned to the commander of his army, Sir John Holland. "John, as soon as you can get your men disembarked and marshalled, we will move on to the capital of Galicia, Santiago, where I expect a similar welcome – but leave a small garrison in Coruña – to guard the back door, as it were!"

"My Lord," replied Holland, with a smile and slight bow. "With your leave, I will meet with my captains and issue the orders immediately."

As he withdrew, Gaunt turned, smiling and with his hand extended, to Alfonso Furtado, the Portuguese admiral, who had been listening: "Señor! Blessings on you and our bounteous thanks to you for our safe passage," as he pumped his hand vigorously.

"Your Highness! The pleasure to serve with you is all mine. And when you are ready to release your English ships, I will escort them home. That is the word I have from my Lord, King John, in Lisbon!"

"That is most gracious! But come now: you must stay and dine with Queen Constance and me. She will wish to thank you herself and you will see how brimming with delight she is at being in her homeland again!"

Two days later, King John rode on a fine black stallion into Santiago, with his Queen, Constanza, wearing a golden crown given to her by Richard the Second, their daughter Katharine and John's eldest daughter, Philippa of Lancaster, following in an ornamented coach. They were met by a procession of clergy who conducted them to the shrine of St James, patron saint of Spain. Then, nobles from Galicia and Castile came into the monastery to kiss the hand of Queen Constanza and do homage to John as their rightful King.

Leaving his Queen to continue receiving homage from a press of city dwellers and hidalgos from the surrounding countryside, John withdrew to a side chamber, where he dictated letters announcing his arrival to his opponent, the usurper Don Juan, and to his ally, King John of Portugal. Both letters produced early responses.

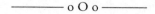

By August, John had advanced his army from Santiago south-eastwards to Orense on the River Minho. There he was met by envoys from Don Juan with a reply to his letter. Led by the Prior of Guardelupe, they were received with due formality and courtesy by John and his advisers in his council chamber. The Prior then propounded, using lengthy legal arguments, that Juan's succession was true and right and urged Gaunt not to proceed with the invasion of the kingdom in an improper cause.

Next day this was refuted by Gaunt's lawyers with counter arguments supporting the right of Constance's succession as the direct heir of her murdered father Pedro I.

It was then, during a break in the formal proceedings, that the Prior asked for a private audience with the Duke. When they were alone in a side chamber, the Prior bowed formally and said: "My master, Don Juan, wishes to avoid the devastation of our country and the loss of lives that would ensue if you proceed with this invasion. He proposes that if his son and heir, Enrique, were to marry Queen Constance's and your daughter, Katharine of Lancaster, that would settle the dynastic issue between us and ensure peace in the kingdom."

If the Duke of Lancaster was taken aback by this he did not show it: he was too well versed in the art of diplomatic negotiation. Instead, he raised his eyes and looked steadily at the Prior: "That is gracious of Don Juan and well presented by you. This will of course be given our serious consideration – by me, the Queen and our advisers. Let us sleep on it and we will talk again in the morning."

The Prior bowed, his hands clasped together, and said: "Praise be to God," and then withdrew.

John sat alone for a few minutes turning this over in his mind and then, with his usual briskness, called for his steward to summon Sir Thomas Percy to his presence.

"Thomas!" he said as Percy entered. "Here's a different throw of the dice! The Prior has just conveyed that he has secret instructions to propose a marriage between Don Juan's son, Enrique, and my daughter Katharine as a way to settle the dynastic issue and avoid an invasion! What do you make of that?"

Percy paused before answering and then, reading nothing from the Duke's face, said: "It is worthy of consideration, my Lord, and has some merit, but how much of this is a play for time? Don Juan last year suffered a heavy defeat at the hands of the Portuguese. His army needs time to recover before he can fight again. How could you be certain he would hold to this arrangement?"

"Yes, I agree," said John. And then, pacing the room, he weighed his thoughts aloud: "There is also our relationship with the King of Portugal to be considered. King Richard has signed the Treaty of Alliance which is important to English interests as a counter to the French. King John magnificently repelled an invasion of his kingdom by Juan. He is keen for us, I am sure, to finish his work and take over Castile – maybe with the help of his army. I cannot deal with this proposal from Juan without conferring with him."

"Indeed, my Lord," agreed Sir Thomas, bowing and, unspoken, because it trespassed on intimate territory, he added to himself, "... and with Constanza."

"We will temporise," decided John, "neither rejecting nor accepting this offer but seek clarification of Juan's intent," and then added, "I will entrust you with this task, Thomas; you know my thoughts. Go with the Prior and his colleagues back to Madrid and see what you can ferret out."

"That I will most gladly do, my Lord," replied Percy.

After Sir Thomas had withdrawn, John again sat alone quietly thinking. Constanza had not attended the talks with Don Juan's envoys but he had kept her informed. Should he now tell of this secret offer or await the return of Sir Thomas? He feared she would be outraged by the offer but he could not shield her from that pain. She had to know of it and delay would not help. So he went to her, asked her to dismiss her ladies, including Philippa Chaucer, and sat beside her.

"Constanza, the Prior asked for a private meeting with me today at which he revealed a secret proposal from Juan: 'to resolve', as he put it, 'the dynastic issue between us'."

Constanza stiffened and said haughtily: "And what *is* this proposal?"

"Simply put, Constanza: that Katharine should marry his son Enrique so that they eventually succeed him on the throne."

Constanza jumped up, threw her arms in the air and raged: "What impudence! Never! My daughter defiled by the bastard's issue. And my rights swept away! NO!"

"Constanza, I agree and my firm intent is to take back the Crown by force of arms. But – it is always as well to find out your opponent's true position and this gives us an opportunity to do that. Sir Thomas Percy suspects that Juan is just playing for time while he reassembles his defeated army. So I am sending him back with the Prior to meet with Juan and find out his true intent."

"Oh! If that is all, my prayers will go with him," replied Constanza, only partly mollified.

No sooner had the Spanish envoys departed, accompanied by Sir Thomas Percy and four of his knights, than a delegation arrived from the Portuguese court. They were warmly welcomed, for Lorenco Fogaca and his colleague Vasco de Mello were both well known to John of Gaunt from when they had often met in London during negotiations over the Treaty of Alliance.

As soon as the initial salutations were over, Fogaca bowed formally before John and said: "My Lord, my master sends you a warm welcome and desires that we should arrange for you to meet him as soon as possible. We suggest that it would be appropriate for this to be on the northern frontier between our two kingdoms and, if it pleases you, we suggest a suitable place would be at Ponte do Mouro on the River Minho."

John looked towards his Constable, Sir John Holland, and his colleagues who were standing nearby and, seeing their nods of approval, immediately agreed.

So it was that at noon on 1st November 1386 at Ponte do Mouro, John of Gaunt, 'King of Castile', met Dom Jo'ao, King of Portugal, for the first time. Surrounded by their retinues – English, Castilian and Galician knights on the one hand – and Portuguese knights, with the crimson cross of St George, emblem of the Knights of Avis, and the white robes of the Cistercian Order, on the other. Silence reigned as the two monarchs greeted each other and then, as they embraced, clapping and hurrahs broke out, which continued as the two Kings walked, between the ranks of a guard of honour formed by their retinues, into the royal pavilion where refreshments were waiting.

The two Kings moved to a side table which had been especially prepared for them. John of Gaunt, long-backed, lean, brown and weather-beaten, stood nearly a head taller than Dom Jo'ao, who was in contrast black-haired, sallow in complexion but broad, muscular and deep-chested with a strong physique.

When they were seated, Dom Jo'ao leaned forward and said earnestly: "We were so pleased to have made this Treaty of Alliance with England. You will please convey this to King Richard?"

"Yes, indeed I will," replied Gaunt, smiling, "for the pleasure, I assure you, is mutual: as are the benefits – to both England and Portugal, but also to Castile."

"Ah yes!" said Dom Jo'ao, his eyes sparkling. And then leaning forward again, he said with a stern look and in a serious tone: "We honour your right to the throne of Castile and we will fight along-side you to reclaim it."

John of Gaunt stood, extended his arm and the two Kings shook hands warmly.

"Thank you! And now, as comrades in arms, I suggest we get our generals to confer as to how best to achieve that!" said Gaunt.

Then, when they were sitting again, he said in a quieter voice: "Dom Jo'ao, there is another way to consolidate this friendship between our two countries and that would be by a dynastic alliance." He paused to see the effect of this and, seeing the warmth in Dom Jo'ao's face, continued, "I have two unmarried daughters with me: Philippa, my firstborn by Blanche, who was the daughter of my uncle Henry, Duke of Lancaster; and Katharine, my daughter by Constance, rightful Queen of Castile. I would be honoured if you were to choose one of them to be your wife and so bond our ties with a family alliance."

"My dear sire! It is I who am honoured!" exclaimed Dom Jo'ao. And then more pensively: "I am aware that, if I am to secure the stability of the throne of Portugal, I need to provide for the succession. There is an impediment at the moment in that, as a Cistercian monk and Master of Avis, I am in holy orders. But no doubt, on appeal, His Holiness the Pope in Rome will release me. But, may I ask: what are the ages of your daughters?"

"Philippa is twenty-six and Katharine is fourteen," replied Gaunt.

"Then I am sure I would favour Philippa, for I am twenty-seven!" said Dom Jo'ao brightly. "Although," he added more seriously, "strengthening the alliance with England is also a strong factor; whereas I am doubtful that the possibility of an eventual union of Portugal and Castile through the Crown would be welcomed by my people."

"I should add," said Gaunt, "that I have received overtures from Don Juan for my daughter Katharine to marry his son Enrique – so, he says, settling the dynastic problem and avoiding the suffering and devastation that would ensue from our invasion! I have not accepted his proposal."

"I think you are right in that," said Jo'ao. "Although, it might be something you could propose when we have defeated his army! Meanwhile, please, would you and Queen Constance join me here, tomorrow, with your two daughters? And hopefully Philippa and I will suit each other…?"

"Delighted!" said John and, remembering his own betrothal to Blanche, added, "I will see that Philippa is well prepared!"

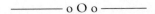

After his meeting with Dom Jo'ao, Gaunt returned to the Benedictine Monastery at Cellanova where he and Constance had temporarily set up their Court. He immediately withdrew with her to their private chamber. She sat quietly composed, as he recounted for her his meeting with Dom Jo'ao.

"He fully supports your right to the throne of Castile and will put his army into the field with us. The leaders of our two armies are working out the details now."

He paused and sat down beside her. "And, my dear, he wishes to meet you. He is arranging a banquet for tomorrow evening in your honour and we are to take Katharine and Philippa with us."

"Ah!" Constance exclaimed, well aware of the significance of this: "So what is the prospect for a marriage?"

John paused, cautious after her recent outburst on this subject.

"Good, I would say. The King knows that he needs to produce an heir to secure the succession and that his country needs that. His interest in our daughters is clear, and let us hope he favours one of them! But he has first to be released from his monastic vows."

"Mmmhh! The two girls should be prepared for this. I will talk with Katharine."

"Yes, I agree. And I will see Philippa," added John.

Over the next fortnight, the alliance between Lancaster and Portugal was swiftly consolidated. On 11th November, Gaunt signed the Treaty of Ponte do Mouro which provided for:

1. A joint offensive against the usurper Juan;
2. Dom Jo'ao to lead an army of 5,000 to help Lancaster from 1st January for eight months at his own cost;
3. Lancaster to cede to Portugal a line of towns on the border between Portugal and Castile on the successful conquest of Castile;
4. Jo'ao to marry Philippa to unite England and Portugal in a blood alliance.

As soon as this was concluded, the King of Portugal left for Lisbon to prepare his army for the invasion. Philippa, accompanied by Philippa Chaucer, now her housekeeper, was entrusted to the care of the Archbishop of Bragas and lodged in the Franciscan Abbey at Oporto to prepare for her marriage. But then progress stalled for three months because of delay in the Vatican in clearing the way for the marriage. It was not until early February 1387 that Pope Boniface IX finally issued the Bull releasing Jo'ao from his priestly vows and blessing his union with Philippa.

At last, on 14th February 1387, John of Gaunt, Duke of Lancaster, 'King of Castile', led his daughter Philippa down the long high-vaulted nave of Oporto Cathedral to the altar rail where the groom, Jo'ao, King of Portugal, awaited her. They moved slowly, acknowledging, as they went, the bows and smiles of the richly clothed ranks of nobles, clergy and gentry and their ladies: on the left from England and Galicia and Castile; on the right from Portugal.

Philippa, at her insistence, wore the dress that her mother, Blanche, had worn at her own wedding: an ivory gown of silk satin embroidered with pearls, a close-fitting bodice and a mantle in dark green velvet, edged in red silk with the Lancastrian emblem, a large red rose, crocheted in the centre. She was attended by four bridesmaids: her two sisters, Elizabeth, Lady Holland, and Katharine, daughter of Queen Constance; and two ladies-in-waiting, one of whom was Philippa Chaucer.

————— o O o —————

Chaucer was sitting at his desk in his new home in Greenwich when he heard the familiar voice of John Gower calling: "Ho, Geoffrey!" as he entered by the front door.

Geoffrey turned to greet him with a smile which fell from his face when he saw Gower's expression and asked: "What is it, John?"

"'Tis Ralph Strode, Geoffrey. He is dead… two nights ago… in his sleep, I am told," replied John.

"Oh!" cried Chaucer, speechless for once, and he murmured, "how cruel fate can be!"

"Yes," said Gower. "May the Lord have mercy on his soul," crossing himself.

"Indeed," said Geoffrey, also crossing himself, and then: "Forgive me, John. My mind was toiling with the death of Troilus when you came in."

"So, you have finished the saga?" asked John eagerly.

"Not quite," replied Geoffrey. "Let me tell you where I am, and then perhaps your comments will help me resolve the ending."

"You will recall," he said, "that the Trojan parliament decided that Criseyde be sent to the Greeks, who were besieging Troy, in exchange for the Trojan warrior, Antenor, who had been captured. Despite her promise to Troilus that she would return within ten days, after having been escorted to the Greek lines by their warrior, Diomede, there was no sign of her. And so I have continued:

> *"In spite of all, they say, a man will finally at last*
> *Perceive the truth; this happened and quite fast*
> *To Troilus; she was — he came to see —*
> *Less kindly-natured than she ought to be*
> *And in the end he knew beyond all doubt*
> *That all was lost that he had been about.*

> *"Standing one day in melancholy mood,*
> *With his suspicions clouded in a frown*
> *Thinking of her he heard a multitude*
> *Of Trojans clamouring about the town,*

Bearing, as was their fashion, up and down
A fine piece of coat armour (says my story)
Before Deiphebus, to show his glory.

"This coat, as says my author, Lollius,
Deiphebus had rent from Diomede,
That very day, and when this Troilus
Beheld it there, he gave it sudden heed:
The length – the breadth – the pattern in the bead
And all the worked embroidery in gold –
And suddenly he felt his heart turn cold.

"There on the collar, could he not perceive
The brooch he'd given her when they had to sever
Yes on the very day she took her leave,
In memory of his grief and him for ever?
Had she not pledged her faith that she would never
Part with that brooch?

"'Was there no other brooch you had in keeping
To fee some newer lover with?' said he,
'Except the brooch I gave you, wet with weeping,
For you to wear in memory of me?'

"And then 'O God Almighty, send me grace
That I may meet again with Diomede.
For truly, if I have the fighting space
And power, I shall make him bleed.'

"In vain however; Fortune had not planned
That either perish at the other's hand.

"The wrath of Troilus from that day
Was cruel and the Grecians bought it dear,
For there were thousands that he made away,

Who in his time had never any peer
Except his brother Hector, so I hear
But O Alas, except that God so willed,
He met with fierce Achilles and was killed.

"And having fallen to Achilles' spear,
His light soul rose and rapturously went
Towards the concavity of the eighth sphere,
Leaving conversely every element,
And as he passed, he saw with wonderment
The wandering stars and heard their harmony,
Whose sound is full of heavenly melody.

"As he looked down, there came before his eyes
This little spot of earth, that with the sea
Lies all embraced, and found he could despise
This wretched world and hold it vanity,
Measured against the full felicity
That is in Heaven above; and at last,
To where he had been slain his look he cast.

"Lo, such an end had Troilus for love!
Lo, such an end his valour, prowess!
Lo, such an end his royal state above,
Such an end his lust, such an end his nobleness!
And such an end this false world's brittleness!
And thus began his loving of Criseyde
As I have told you, and thus he died."

Putting down his manuscript, Chaucer looked to his friend and said: "John, that is my ending so far. Yet I am loth to leave it there for there is more to this tale than a sad love affair."

"Yes," replied Gower. "I have thought more than once as you have shared your writing with me. that it raises deep questions about the influence of ancient gods, of Destiny and Fortune – of predestination; and of how our actions are shaped by human choice or God's will."

"That is it exactly," put in Chaucer. "Thank you, John. And it is just what troubled Boethius in his jail. Clearly I need to reconcile these questions with our own faith in Christ." And then he turned to Gower: "I am grieved at the loss of Ralph. We will miss him sorely."

Later, when Gower had departed, Chaucer went back to his desk and completed his tale of Troilus and Criseyde with the following lines:

> 'Oh all you fresh young people, he or she,
> In whom love grows and ripens year by year.
> Come home, come home from worldly vanity!
> Cast the heart's countenance in love and fear
> Upwards to God, who in his image here has made you.
>
> And give your love to Him who, for pure love,
> Upon a cross first died that He might pay
> Our debt, and rose, and sits in Heaven above;
> He will be false to no one that will lay
> His heart wholly on him, I dare say.
> Since He is best to love and the most meek,
> What need is there a feigning love to seek.
>
> Behold these old accursed pagan rites!
> Behold how much their gods are worth to you!
> Behold these wretched worldly appetites!
> Behold your labour's end and guerdon due
> From Jove, Apollo and Mars, that rascal crew!
> Behold the form in which the ancients speak
> Their poetry, if you should care to seek.
>
> O moral Gower, I dedicate this book
> To you, and you, philosophical Strode
> In your benignity and zeal to look,

To warrant, and, where need is, to make good;
And to that truthfast Christ who died on rood,
With all my heart for mercy ever I pray,
And to the Lord right thus I speak and say:

"Thou One and Two and Three and Never-ending,
That reignest ever in Three and Two and One,
Incomprehensible, all comprehending,
From visible foes, and the invisible one,
Defend us all! And Jesu, Mary's son,
Make us in mercy worthy to be thine,
For love of her, mother and maid benign!"'

The invasion of Castile by the English and Portuguese allies began in March 1387. By Easter they had advanced into the heart of Leon to Benaventre, which was defended in force under the leadership of a noble of Leon, Alvar Peres de Osorio. Then gradually a stalemate set in. The Castilians, following tactics learnt from the French, cleared the countryside before the invaders, garrisoned the strong towns and abandoned the weak. Frustrated, Lancaster's forces captured several nearby smaller towns – Matilla, Roales, Valderas, Villa Lobos – but then the English invaders, weakened by fatigue and starvation, were decimated by disease – first dysentery and then the plague.

Weakened as a fighting force, and himself with dysentery, Lancaster withdrew his army towards Portugal to regroup and consider his options, including whether to call for fresh troops from England. When the Duke had crossed the border at Almeida, he was overtaken by envoys from Don Juan who again offered the proposal made at Orense.

Lancaster immediately sought Dom Jo'ao's views.

"As you know, I have been pressing for you to get fresh forces from England. But I think this renewed offer is a worthy solution: *if* you can trust Don Juan and if you and Constance are prepared to forego your own claims to the throne of Castile."

"Yes, I agree this has merit," replied Lancaster, "and apart from avoiding further fighting, in the long term it may provide a happier and unifying solution for the Castilian people."

"And Constance?" prompted Dom Jo'ao.

Lancaster smiled indulgently, for he was already fond of his new son-in-law. "She expected a quick solution. I think now she is wearying of the delays, discomfort and uncertainty and will accept."

In this Gaunt proved correct, but he now had to be certain that this would happen and that the details secured a favourable settlement.

It was not until the spring of 1388 that the Treaty between Juan, King of Castile, and the Duke and Duchess of Lancaster was concluded. By its terms:

1. John and Constance renounced their claim to the throne of Castile;
2. Katharine of Lancaster was to marry Enrique, son of Juan I. But as Enrique was only ten it was agreed that Juan's second son, Don Fernando, would remain unmarried until the union had been consummated and that should Enrique die before that, he would take his brother's place and wed Katharine;
3. The Duke and Duchess of Lancaster were to be paid an annuity of 40,000 gold francs and John of Gaunt was to be reimbursed the cost of his campaign over three years.

In September 1388, Katharine of Lancaster was married by the Archbishop of Seville to Enrique, the heir to the throne in the Church of St Antolin in Palencia. So although John of Gaunt's claim to be the rightful King of Castile was given up, he had ensured that his daughter would be Queen of Castile.

Chapter Ten

As CHAUCER APPROACHED the wharf at Greenwich, he was hailed by John Croyser, the boatman he hired for his regular journeys to Westminster.

"Morning, Master Geoffrey!" he called. "'Twill be a bit choppy this morning in this wind!"

"And blessings on you, John!" replied Chaucer. "An occasional splash won't hurt."

John steadied his skiff as Chaucer stepped aboard and then, pushing off with his right oar to point the boat out into the river, he began rowing upstream.

"Is it Westminster Pier again today?" he asked.

"Yes please," replied Chaucer. "I've another meeting with Henry Yevele, the architect, to settle his needs to start building a new roof for Westminster Hall."

"Sounds like there's a long job in hand there," said Croyser.

"Indeed there is!" replied Geoffrey with a wry smile.

Then they fell silent as the oarsman rowed steadily with a practised rhythm, and Chaucer listened to the swish of the oars and the slapping of the waves on the sides of the clinkered boat as they moved upstream.

Chaucer began to ponder on his new and unexpected role. He had been appointed Clerk of the King's Works in June 1389, two years after he had finally left the Customs House. His new role meant managing the finance and provisioning of the upkeep and improvements to the fabric of the royal castles and manors around London, including: the Tower, the Palace and Hall of Westminster; and the palaces at Sheen, Kennington, Eltham and Byfleet. This included the ordering of building supplies, materials and equipment, the recruitment of skilled and unskilled workers and the payment of wages.

He had soon learned that this was no sinecure, especially since the young 20-year-old King Richard was insisting on a programme of improvements and extensions in keeping with his ambitions to be a leader of style and taste in Europe. Fortunately there were two able and experienced deputies to help him: William Chetwynde and Hugh Hayward.

He had had a number of meetings with them both and liked them. Chetwynde, in his early fifties, was the older of the two: short, bald, strong with a deep chest, ruddy cheeked and with a bluff humour. This contrasted with Hugh Hayward who was tall, lean, angular, observant and not much given to words. They had worked together for the past six years under the two previous Clerks and already Chaucer knew the value of their experience in building works and that he could trust them and their judgement.

But he also knew that ledger work – keeping accounts, records and inventories – was not their strong point. Since his appointment he had visited all of the royal properties with one or other of them. He had been surprised to find so many and varied a range of items left behind at most sites from previous works. These included: winches, lathes, windlasses (one with a broken rod), three broken wheels, a considerable amount of timber – beams, posts, planks and scaffolding – and, at Westminster, seven stone statues of kings!

From his experience at the Customs House he was well versed in the ways of the Exchequer and the detailed reckoning they carried out each Michaelmas of all the goods passing through the port and the customs dues owing to the King. He could only assume that 'King's Works' did not warrant such close scrutiny. Nonetheless he had insisted that records be kept of all equipment and stores and of breakages, losses and surplus stock.

Chaucer came out of his reverie as they approached Westminster.

"Here we are then, Master Geoffrey," called John as he shipped his oars and the boat glided alongside the pier.

"Many thanks, John," replied Chaucer. "I expect to be finished by evensong at six o'clock, if you could fetch me then?"

"That I will and gladly," replied John.

With that Chaucer made his way past the Abbey to Westminster Hall.

As he approached he could see the familiar figure of Henry Yevele standing talking with his two assistants. He was a tall, shapely man with broad shoulders, large hands and muscular arms, as befitted a renowned master mason. When he saw Chaucer he stepped forward, his hand outstretched in greeting, his face crinkled in a broad smile.

"Why, Geoffrey! You adorn the day!" he called, shaking Geoffrey's hand in a fierce grip.

"And it is a joy to see you, Henry!" beamed Chaucer.

Then, never one to be idle, Yevele explained that he had given Chaucer's two assistants designs of the beams he proposed to use to support the new roof.

"But, look," he said, restless as ever and walking towards the Hall. "It would be best if we stepped inside where I can show you what I mean."

The group followed. Once inside and after their eyes had accustomed to the gloom, he continued.

"You see," said Yevele, pointing down the length of the Hall, "the problem with the old roof was caused by the difficulty of spanning the whole width of the Hall from one outer wall to the other without intermediary columns which obstruct the floor space. I am proposing to put in a series of beams projecting inwards from stone corbels in the walls and to cantilever the roof timbers from these beams, thereby in effect reducing the width of the Hall. It will, of course, require really strong timbers for the beams and studs, but William and Hugh here say that won't be a problem."

"Indeed, Master Geoffrey," put in Chetwynde. "We have already identified with the forester a source in the Royal Forest in Hampshire where there is a tract of one hundred acres of mature and straight-standing oaks. Thirty acres of this were felled last year and the trees have been trimmed and are seasoned and suited for this job."

"But has royal approval been granted?" asked Chaucer.

"No, begging your pardon, Master Geoffrey," replied Chetwynde. "Your approval and approach to Court are needed for that."

"I have to go to the Exchequer from here so I will at the same time have this request submitted to the King. But I will also require details of the numbers of craftsmen and other workers needed so that I can register them and indent for their wages."

The required lists were soon compiled, including details of the master craftsmen Yevele proposed to use and when the first works would begin. That done, Chaucer turned to the architect and said: "This is a magnificent project, Henry! I rejoice in being involved. I look forward to seeing it take shape. Meanwhile…" he added mischievously, "I will go and do my best to woo the Exchequer!"

After the marriage of their daughter, Katharine, to Juan, heir to the throne of Castile, Duchess Constance remained in Castile, not only to support and watch over her daughter but also to enjoy the regard and attention she received from an increasing number of Castilian nobles, and the happiness she felt at being with her own people in her own country. John, however, went, with the support of King Richard, to Acquitaine where there was a need to strengthen the English hold on the province against French encroachments and inducements to encourage local nobles to renew their allegiance to the French Crown.

But King Richard had been having his own difficulties while his uncle was in Castile. In 1388 he had been forced to curb his extravagance and indulgence of his favourites by the appointment of a Council of Regency which would, in effect, govern the country in his place, led by his younger uncle, Thomas, the Duke of Gloucester. A counter-attack by his young favourite, Robert de Vere, whom he had made Duke of Ireland, was defeated by John of Gaunt's son, Henry, Earl of Derby, and de Vere fled to the Continent. Worse than that, five of Richard's supporters were condemned as guilty of treason and hanged, including the King's tutor and friend, Sir Simon Burley.

Then in May 1389, King Richard, now 22 years of age, declared his intention of ruling himself, dismissed the Council of Regency, reinstated his personal rule and recalled the Duke of Lancaster.

So it was, that on 19th November 1389, John of Gaunt landed at Plymouth and then rode northwards towards Reading where there was to be a meeting of the King's Council. Approaching the town, he was met by the King himself and welcomed profusely, since Richard had learned through the hatred and violence of the past year how much he needed the support of his senior uncle, especially to counter the volatile and ruthless Duke of Gloucester.

Chaucer had admitted to Gower that he was enjoying his time as Clerk of the King's Works. He was particularly fascinated by the variety of craftsmen he met: their dedication to their craft and, often, the sublime result of their skill. He was on his way by horseback to the royal manor at Sheen with monies drawn from the Exchequer to pay off the workmen who were just completing the restoration of the private chapel. This included a superbly carved Madonna with silken-smooth buttocks, back and shoulders and a newborn child cradled against her full, round breasts. Over the last weeks Chaucer had watched this beautiful work of art emerge from a solid block of Barnack stone as the master mason, Simon Brewster, deftly chipped away.

Once inside the chapel he greeted Simon: "So, Simon, you are finished?" he called.

"Aye, Master Geoffrey, reckon that's it!" he said, rubbing his hands together.

"Well, it is truly wonderful," replied Geoffrey. "And I am sure the King will be well pleased. You must feel proud doing such work, Simon."

"Pleasure rather than pride is my feeling," replied Simon. "The Lord gave us skills and I reckon we owe it as our duty to use them. That's how I see it," he said. "But then, you don't often get such a fine opportunity as this, do you?" he said with a grin.

Just before Christmas 1391, Chaucer left Westminster on a cold wintry day under a heavy sky threatening snow. He wore over his woollen smock a heavy outer coat with a fur collar and a velvet hat to combat the cold. He was on his way to inspect the works at the King's small manor at Byfleet and to pay the foreman, carpenters and labourers their wages for the past fortnight, with an extra Christmas bonus from King Richard. That morning he had drawn £12. 13s. 4d. from the Exchequer to cover this and payment for timber and other materials. He also carried with him a small cask of wine as his own tribute to the men.

He was jogging along a track beside a spinney when three men sprang out of the trees and barred his way. Two were holding staves and billhooks while the other was brandishing a sword which he twirled above his head. Then, moving forward, he pointed it directly at Chaucer.

"Whoa! My friend," he shouted with an evil snarl. "Let's be having you off that horse, shall we? And then you can open those bags for me."

Chaucer looked steadily into his face and, remembering the challenge outside Rheims when Sir Richard Sturry had cautioned discretion as the better part of valour, he quietly dismounted and loosened the clasps on his saddle bags.

"Now you stand away!" roared the ruffian, waving his sword and delving into the bags.

"My! Rich pickings here, boys," holding aloft the purse which he had found in the first bag. "And, look you, a cask to quench our thirst!"

Then he turned to Chaucer, bowed extravagantly and said in a mocking tone: "Thank you, my Lord. Your generosity will be well rewarded, I am sure!… but in heaven!"

Then he laughed, jumped astride the horse, shouted, "Come on, lads," and they all disappeared into the trees.

Chaucer stood and pondered his predicament. He had passed the Fox and Hounds alehouse about five miles back at Hampton, so he set off at a brisk pace to walk there, for it was cold with light flutters of sleet blowing in the wind. The landlord, Bill Watkins, would, he knew, welcome him and provide another horse if he had one in the stable. Then he would have to go back to Westminster and report the loss. But at least he could sup some ale in front of a warm fire before he left!

Back at Westminster, the Exchequer Clerk was as cool as the weather and faintly scornful when Chaucer reported his loss. Although he was told he would be able to draw the expenses again, it was made clear that Chaucer may have to repay the lost amount himself. He left the building in sombre mood. This was not helped when he met John of Gaunt, who was just leaving the Palace.

"Geoffrey!" he called across the yard. "Is it true, what I have heard, that you have been robbed? Were you hurt?"

"Only my pride, my Lord," said Chaucer, and then with a rueful smile he added: "…and… likely my purse!"

"Was it much that they got away with?" asked Gaunt.

"A goodly sum of money, my Lord – £12. 13s. 4d. – to pay off the workmen at Byfleet before Christmas, including a generous bonus from the King. But they also took my horse, which my feet are sore about! Although the innkeeper at Hampton set me up with another steed, may the Lord bless him!"

"Geoffrey, you must in future travel with an escort. I will instruct Sir Richard Dudley in my retinue here to arrange that, whenever you let him know about your journey."

"My grateful thanks, my Lord," said Chaucer with a small bow.

"There are too many of these gangs roaming the countryside," continued the Duke. "I have just returned from Cheshire and Yorkshire where armed robbery like this is rife. They are mostly soldiers, idle for want of war.

"But, come, Geoffrey, 'tis Christmas: no time to be glum. The family are gathering at Ely Place for the festival. Join us – and maybe we shall hear some of your latest verse?"

"My Lord, I am honoured, and I will gladly join you," replied Chaucer.

When John of Gaunt had returned from Spain he leased Ely Place from John Fordham, the Bishop of Ely, to serve as his London house in place of the Savoy Palace which still lay a blackened ruin beside the Thames. It was an imposing palace in Holborn, between Leather Lane and Charterhouse Street, with large rooms, a private chapel, extensive gardens and an impressive stone gatehouse which fronted the street. While not as sumptuous as the Savoy it provided John and his family with a dignified ambience suited to his status – and, moreover, it was close to Westminster and the Court.

When Chaucer arrived there at noon on Christmas Eve 1391, he was shown into a comfortable sitting room with two tall windows which, in summer, opened onto a spacious terrace bordered by box hedges with lawns beyond. But on this cold December day, it was the welcome warmth of the stone-mantled log fire which drew Chaucer. As he was warming his hands, the door opened and, with a rustle of her skirts, Lady Katherine Swynford entered with arms outstretched in greeting.

"Geoffrey!" she cried, a tear running down her cheek. "It has been too long a time. And I have never really thanked you for getting me away from the Savoy."

They embraced in a long hug. As they drew away, Chaucer said: "No matter, my dear, you were safe. And do you remember this?" he asked as he pulled forward a stout leather bag. Katherine, wide-eyed as she stared at the bag, put her hands to her mouth.

"Geoffrey," she said, hesitating. "Is it? Can it be the bag I left with you at the Customs House?"

"Yes, my dear, it is, just so," replied Chaucer.

"In all the turmoil of that time, I had forgotten it," said Katherine.

"And I," said Geoffrey, "until recently when my successor called me to the Customs House to open a locked cupboard, and there it was covered in dust with some old ledgers!"

"We must give it to the Duke," said Katherine firmly. "The things in it belong to him."

Chaucer looked kindly at his sister-in-law and smiled. For a moment he had seen the same anxious face as when she had left the Savoy ten years ago.

There was no time for further talk. Soon the house was vibrating with energy and laughter as members of the family arrived for the Christmas Festival and greeted each other. Katherine's sons, John and Thomas Beaufort, and Thomas Swynford, as regular jousting companions, boisterously punched each other's uplifted hands in greeting but then knelt in turn to kiss their mother's hand and the cheek of their smiling young sister, Joan. Chaucer at first stood smiling indulgently at this scene but was soon drawn in by Thomas Swynford and his other nephews who embraced him warmly. Then quiet reigned again as the party went to check that their luggage had been delivered to their rooms and to see that their horses had been rubbed down and were well stabled.

Left alone, Katherine led Geoffrey back to the sitting room and their places by the fire. As they sat down, Katherine hesitated and then looked at Geoffrey and said, "It is a signal honour for my sister Philippa to be lady-in-waiting to the Queen of Portugal, but you must miss her?"

Geoffrey looked at Katherine, paused, and then said pensively in a quiet voice: "Yes, I do. I miss the *thought* of her presence. As you know, for the last ten or so years we have rarely been under the same roof – because of my travels abroad on the King's business and her position as joint head of Queen Constanza's household.

"But she has always been there – in my mind – as a reference, or Pole Star – for as you know, she could stamp her foot if she thought my behaviour unseemly, especially at Court or if I was too easygoing and unambitious. So, it is an abstract rather than a physical thing."

"And what of your writing, Geoffrey? I know the Duke is hoping you will recite for us… But, hark, that is he!… Maybe I can persuade him in here so that we can present him with the bag from the Customs House?" she said, as she hurried out and then returned with John of Gaunt.

"Geoffrey!" he exclaimed, "I am so glad you are here!"

"And I, my Lord," replied Chaucer with a brief bow.

"Now! What is this conspiracy you two have been up to?" asked Gaunt, smiling.

Chaucer smiled back. "'Tis no conspiracy, my Lord – but a lapse in memory... and I hope forgivable!" And then in a more serious tone: "When at that dreadful time of the Peasant's Revolt Katherine had to get away from the Savoy, she left with me this bag for safe-keeping at the Customs House, where it lay forgotten until now."

Katherine took the bag from Geoffrey and continued: "We had to leave the Savoy in a hurry. I did not know what to take with me... nothing to attract a robber's eye... so in my desperation I filled this bag with some of your valuables and left it with Geoffrey. So, John, my dearest Lord, it belongs to you!" handing the bag to him.

John of Gaunt had been attending carefully to what they said, at first with an amused smile but then with a stern face and a flash of steel in his blue eyes as he saw the scene at the Savoy. This faded as he took the bag from Katherine, undid the buckles and drew out: the coronet of pure gold which he had then been accustomed to wear on royal occasions; a hip belt inlaid with emeralds, rubies and sapphires with silver buckle; and, then, a pair of silver goblets which made him gasp at the memory of them. They had been presented to him by Blanche on their wedding day. His face softened as they brought back the memory of using them to toast each other, arms entwined, on their wedding night.

He turned to Katherine, pulled her into a tight embrace and whispered into her hair: "My dear, dear love. To think of saving these for me under such awful duress: I am truly humbled by your unself-ish devotion."

Later he found further evidence as he emptied the bag and took out golden rings, amulets, silver buckles, head and neckpieces, garters – all studded with precious stones. Then he found a padded red silk cloth with the three wheels of St Katherine's emblem embroidered in gold thread: the only keepsake Katherine had put aside for herself.

Next morning the house was quiet, for Gaunt and his sons

even on this Christmas Day had gone hunting in Hatfield Forest. Remembering that Katherine had said the Duke was looking forward to hearing him recite some of his recent writings, Chaucer spent the morning looking over what he had written as the Prologue to his *Canterbury Tales* and then wrote descriptions of three more of the pilgrims: an Oxford Cleric, a Doctor and a Wife from Bath. Around noon, Katherine called him to join her and her daughter, Joan, in a toast to Christmas with mulled claret and some finger snacks.

As they sat round the leaping yellow flames and crackling of the logs from the newly laid fire, Katherine asked him again about his writings and what had he thought to present to them that evening? Chaucer smiled and paused. Most of the family were familiar with his work from recitals at Court or at social gatherings in great houses: courtly romances like the 'Romance of the Rose', 'The Book of the Duchess' and 'Anelida and Arcite' or heroic tales like 'Troilus and Criseyde'. The work he had now embarked upon was different in concept and texture. So, he welcomed the opportunity to explain.

"When I was travelling on the King's business to France and Italy and other countries, I often encountered on the road out of London groups of pilgrims on their way to the shrine of St Thomas a Becket at Canterbury. I remember stopping one evening at the Black Swan in Canterbury and watching, as I ate my evening meal, a group of newly arrived pilgrims. I was struck by the ease and familiarity between them but also how well they mirrored the range of ranks and occupations in our society – except the very high and low – the lords and courtiers and the serfs and poor. This has given me the context for my new work: a series of tales told by such a group of pilgrims as they travelled from Southwark to Canterbury – beginning with a description of each pilgrim in a prologue to the tales."

"That is fascinating," said Katherine. "And do you have a favourite tale to tell us tonight?"

"No, my dear. I am still working on the Prologue with a description of each pilgrim. The tales each tell will come later and be like the folk tales that are commonly told here and on the Continent, whenever groups are gathered together," replied Geoffrey.

They were interrupted by the arrival of Henry, Earl of Derby, Gaunt's son and heir, with his wife, Mary de Bohun, who was pregnant with their first child. Soon Katherine drew Mary away to rest and settle in her sleeping quarters, leaving Henry and Chaucer together before the fire.

Chaucer was impressed at how much Henry had grown and developed since he had known him as a callow boy at Hertford Castle. Now he was tall, lean, bronzed, lithe and muscular with the hauteur and royal bearing of a true Plantagenet. He exuded confidence and enthusiasm as he regaled Geoffrey with tales of his tournaments in France and fighting as a Crusader in the Levant against Turkish infidels.

Then Chaucer decided to use this private moment to share a personal sadness.

"Forgive me, my Lord," he said. "May I say how much I admired the way in which you stood out before the King against the cruel execution of Sir Richard Burley? He was a colleague and friend of mine: I thank you for that."

As Henry looked at him, Chaucer saw for a moment that same flash of steel in his blue eyes that so resembled his father.

"Yes! A great and unwarranted tragedy," said Henry, "and thank you for your words. But, Geoffrey, do not talk of that time with my father, for he berates me for being one of the Appellants: he fears King Richard's vengeful nature."

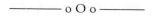

Darkness had fallen by four o'clock, and by five o'clock the whole family was gathered in the hall where a sumptuous dinner was served: with turkey, pheasant, salmon, trout, venison, beef and sweetmeats to choose from, followed by plum pudding laced with brandy, fruit pies, fresh apples and pears, oranges and peaches – all accompanied by fine wines from France, Spain and Italy. The social chatter from the diners was accompanied by the playing of a variety of roundelays and songs by the Duke's minstrels from the small gallery above.

Then when the food and finger bowls had been cleared, the company gathered to sit at the other end of the hall in readiness for hearing Geoffrey's presentation. As he took his place before them he said: "My Lords and Ladies, it is my pleasure to stand before you and if you are pleased with my offering, then I shall be doubly pleased! This is a new work inspired by seeing groups of pilgrims on their way from London to Canterbury and noticing the joy they had in telling tales to amuse each other on their journey. This is how I have described some of these pilgrims:

> "There was a Knight, a most distinguished man,
> Who from the day on which he first began,
> To ride abroad had followed chivalry,
> Truth, honour, generousness and courtesy.
> He had done nobly in his sovereign's war
> And ridden into battle, no man more,
> As well in Christian as in heathen places
> And ever honoured for his noble graces.

> "He was of sovereign value in all eyes.
> And though so much distinguished, he was wise
> And in his bearing modest as a maid.
> He never yet a boorish thing had said
> In all his life to any, come what might;
> He was a true, a perfect gentle knight.

> "There was a Yeoman with him at his side,
> No other servant; so he chose to ride.
> This Yeoman wore a coat and hood of green,
> And peacock feathered arrows, bright and keen
> And neatly sheathed, hung at his belt the while –
> For he could dress his gear in yeoman style,
> His arrows never drooped their feathers low –
> And in his hand he bore a mighty bow.

"His head was like a nut, his face was brown.
He knew the whole of woodcraft up and down.
A saucy brace was on his arm to ward
It from the bow-string and a shield and sword
Hung at one side, and at the other well-equipped.
A medal of St Christopher he wore
Of shining silver on his breast, and bore
A hunting horn, well slung and burnished clean.
That dangled from a baldric of bright green.
He was a proper forester, I guess.

"There was a Friar, a wanton one and merry,
A Limiter, a very festive fellow.
Highly beloved and intimate was he
With County folk within his boundary,
And city dames of honour and possessions,
For he was qualified to hear confessions,
Or so he said, with more than priestly scope;
He had a special licence from the Pope,
He was an easy man in penance giving
Where he could hope to make a decent living.
And certainly his voice was gay and sturdy
For he sang well and played the hurdy-gurdy
At sing-songs he was champion of the hour.

"His neck was whiter than a lily-flower
But strong enough to butt a bruiser down.
He knew the taverns well in every town
And every innkeeper and barmaid too
Better than lepers, beggars and that crew,
For in so eminent a man as he
It was not fitting with the dignity
Of his position, dealing with a scum
Of wretched lepers: nothing good can come
Of commerce with such slum-and-gutter dwellers,

But only with the rich and victual sellers."

Chaucer paused because he could see that this caused some stir and amusement. Then he heard Tom Swynford say: "Oh! I know that fellow! I have seen him in taverns near here, making up to the women and offering confessions – for a fee!" which caused a ripple of laughter. And then Chaucer went on:

> *"The Miller was a chap of sixteen stone*
> *A great stout fellow big in brawn and bone.*
> *He did well out of them, for he could go*
> *And win the ram at any wrestling show.*
> *Broad, knotty and short shouldered, he would boast*
> *He could heave any door off hinge and post.*
> *His mighty mouth was like a furnace door.*
> *A wrangler and buffoon, he had a store*
> *Of tavern stories, filthy in the main,*
> *He was a master-hand at stealing grain,*
> *He felt it with his thumb and thus he knew*
> *Its quality and took three times his due –*
> *A thumb of gold, by God, to gauge an oat!*

> *"A worthy Woman from beside Bath city*
> *Was with us, somewhat deaf, which was a pity.*
> *In making cloth she showed so great a bent*
> *She bettered those of Ypres and Ghent*
> *A worthy woman all her life, what's more*
> *She'd had five husbands, all at the church door,*
> *Apart from other company in youth –*
> *No need just now to speak of that, forsooth.*

> *"She had gap-teeth, set widely, truth to say.*
> *Easy on an ambling horse she sat*
> *Well wimpled up, and on her head a hat*
> *As broad as is a buckler or a shield;*

She had a flowing mantle that concealed
Large hips, her heels spurred sharply under that.
In company she liked to laugh and chat
And knew the remedies for love's mischances,
An art in which she knew the oldest dances."

This caused another ripple of amusement among the company, to which Chaucer bowed and then said, "Thank you. More anon, when I can charge my pen again!"

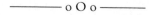

Immediately after Christmas, John of Gaunt was called to an audience with the King at Westminster. As soon as he arrived, he was shown into the royal presence where he bowed before Richard, who was sitting on a raised dais in a brocaded chair.

"Ah, my dear Uncle! Come, join me," said Richard, gesturing to a chair alongside the dais. "As you know, Parliament has supported my wish that we should make peace with France. I want you to lead the negotiations. I will write to King Charles who, I believe, wants this as much as I do; so, God willing, a treaty will not be long in the making."

"My liege Lord! I am honoured and I will be pleased to carry this forward for, as you know, it is near my heart too," said John.

"Yes, I know," replied Richard, smiling. "I am blessed by that," and then added with a dark frown, "unlike our uncle Gloucester."

Gaunt, noting the waspish tone, stood back, bowed and said: "Indeed, my Lord," and then bowing, said, "I will leave for France without delay," and withdrew.

John left the Palace, lost in thought. The task he had been given was not as easy as the King supposed. The current truce with France expired in less than a year. The negotiation of a Treaty of Peace and Friendship required that issues that had merely been shelved under a series of truces would need to be brought into the open and resolved. These included the English possession of the enclaves at Calais, Brest and Cherbourg, as well as the big issue of the status of English rule in Acquitaine. It could take many months, if not a year or two, to resolve these.

As he rode back from Westminster to Ely Place, he began to consider who it would be best to take with him to help with the negotiations. He immediately thought of Sir Henry Percy, who had been invaluable in Spain. And then he recalled how much he had learnt when his father had taken him to Edinburgh. His son Henry, Earl of Derby, was older, experienced in soldiering but not in the arts of diplomacy. He would ask both to meet with him in Holborn next day.

Sir Henry Percy arrived early the next day at Ely Place in response to the Duke's summons. After explaining the King's commission, Gaunt said: "You've a wise head, Henry, as you showed in Spain. I want you to join me in leading these negotiations with the French."

"Thank you, my Lord. That I will gladly do!" replied Percy.

"And I am thinking of taking my son Henry with us. He needs to know about the nuances of diplomacy."

"I am sure that is a wise move, my Lord. He is renowned as a fighter and jouster but fencing with words at this level is quite a different art!" replied Henry.

They broke off as they heard the Duke's eldest son arriving. As usual, he filled the room with energy as he joined them, and Percy smiled at the likeness, not only between father and son, but also with his namesake, his maternal grandfather, the former Duke of Lancaster. After Gaunt had explained and his son had expressed his eagerness to join them, they moved to sit round a table to prepare for their mission.

John outlined his doubts that a peace treaty could be agreed as quickly as the King seemed to think, particularly because of the disputed territorial possessions. Percy joined in: "I agree. But Cherbourg and Brest are only held on short-term leases. Giving them up may be a useful bargaining counter, especially as their annual upkeep costs the royal purse one thousand pounds a year. But Parliament would never agree to giving up Calais, and there's Acquitaine—"

"Yes, well. Let us leave that for now," interrupted Gaunt, showing a touch of impatience, perhaps because as the King's lieutenant in Acquitaine he knew he had not yet pacified the Province. "The King has written to King Charles so we should plan to travel to France to meet him as soon as he replies. Henry, will you arrange shipping to Calais and a body of knights and esquires from the Lancaster retinue to accompany us?"

"Indeed, my Lord," replied his son.

Lancaster and his entourage arrived in Amiens in mid-February 1394 where they were lavishly welcomed and accommodated by Charles, the French King. His enthusiasm for the meeting was obvious. After a lavish meal he proposed a toast to the assembled delegates: "With God's blessing and with a Treaty of Peace and Friendship between us," he declared, "together we can settle the schism over the Papacy, unify the Church and lead a united Europe against the Muslim infidels. I am so happy to share in this with King Richard: *Vive l'Angleterre! Vive la France!*" The assembled company shouted back the toast to the two countries and drained their drinks with a flourish.

After further festivities, the King withdrew with his court to Paris and the delegates began their discussions, at first in plenary session and then in specialist groups to consider the finer details.

A week later, Percy and Henry, Earl of Derby, were pacing around the terrace of the chateau where the peace talks were being held, enjoying a welcome break from the discussions and a breath of fresh air.

"Sir Henry, how is it that the real issues seem to be lost in a cloud of legal language?" asked the young Earl.

"Ha!" laughed Sir Henry. "Some might call it a lawyers' smoke screen! You see: when you are agreeing a Treaty or an Act of Parliament, in the end you need to seal it with a binding legal document. And then, if you are not careful, the lawyers turn it into language that only they fully understand! And they get doubly paid: once for the drafting and again for the interpretation!" he added light-heartedly.

At that point, they were approached by a liveried page: "*Excusez moi*, there is a messenger to see you, if you follow me, *si'l vous plait.*"

He took them into the entrance hall where they recognised Sir Giles Rawsthorne from the Duke's retinue.

"Sir Giles! What brings you here?" said Sir Henry and then, seeing his strained face, said "What is it, Giles?"

Sir Giles stepped forward, bowed and said: "I am sorry to say, I bring sad tidings. And maybe it is better that I tell you than the Duke himself. The Duchess Constance died last week at Leicester Castle of a sudden fever."

Percy and Henry stared wide-eyed at each other. "But she was with a hunting party before Christmas at Much Hadham…" said Henry, and then added: "Sir Henry, I suggest it would be better if my father had this news direct from Sir Giles, rather than from us."

Sir Henry looked at the young Earl and nodded, appreciating that he was thereby giving his father space to digest this news privately.

Three days later, Gaunt, after sending a message to the French King, and instructing Percy to negotiate an extension of the truce, left for England together with his son Henry, Earl of Derby.

———— o O o ————

Two days later, Gaunt and his son Henry stood side by side on the deck of the ship taking them from Calais to Dover. It provided them with the first quiet and intimate interlude together since the news of Duchess Constance's death. John had obviously been thinking about what awaited them when they arrived in England and what arrangements were needed for her funeral.

"As Duchess Constance died at Leicester, she is no doubt lying in state either at the Hospital or in the Collegiate Church of St Mary which have been under our patronage since they were founded by the first Duke of Lancaster. I think it best that we make arrangements for her to be buried there," he said quietly to Henry. "But…" he continued, "the funeral and interment must be appropriate to her status as rightful Queen of Castile and, latterly, their Queen Mother, and to her position for twenty-two years as Duchess of Lancaster."

"Yes, my Lord," said Henry quietly, for he sensed that his father was still engaged with his own thoughts.

"Although ours was a marriage born of political expediency, she was a truly sincere, forbearing and regal person and she shall be honoured so, at her burial and thereafter."

After a while of leaning on the ship's rail and watching the waves of the slight swell glide by, he continued in a quiet tone: "And I must give thoughts to the future."

Then after another long pause, his face brightened and he turned to Henry, his son, put a hand on his arm, and asked: "How would it be if I were to marry Dame Katherine? Could you accept that?"

"Oh yes! With great joy, my Lord!" replied Henry. "She has been a mother figure to me since you brought her to our nursery. And she still is. Maybe you are not always aware of how much she quietly counsels me… and on occasions, chides me! And she has supported Mary through the births of all our children. Indeed she is there now helping with the delivery of our seventh child! And," he added, "I know that Philippa loves her too… and Elizabeth, in her own independent way!"

His father smiled. "Well, thank you… 'tis as I thought… but, mind you, I shall need to seek dispensation from the Pope and the consent of King Richard as my feudal Lord."

On arrival at Dover, John and Henry were welcomed by two knights and two esquires from the Lancaster retinue ready to escort them on the ride to London. They stopped for a change of horses at Canterbury where John and Henry went to the shrine of St Thomas a Becket, lit candles and prayed for Constance's soul. That evening they dined at Ely Place with their retainers and set off early next morning for Kenilworth Castle where they parted: John to go to Leicester, where Duchess Constance having departed this life was lying, and Henry to his manor at Peterborough where his wife was bringing into life a new baby.

John, having spent a week at Leicester, including daily offerings and prayers beside the bier on which Constance lay by the altar in the Church of St Mary, moved to Kenilworth Castle. It was there that he received news of the birth of another son to Mary in a letter from Dame Katherine.

> *My dearest Lord,* she wrote, *I was shocked and grieved to learn of the sudden passing of Duchess Constance and I sorrow for you at your loss. I have kept her in my prayers and will do so, to help ease her spirit's journey.*
>
> *I am glad to have been here with Mary for the birth of her son. It was not an easy time for her and she is still weak. But with Lord Henry's loving support and with God's will, she will, I am sure, soon recover.*
>
> *I pray you are well, my Lord. God's blessing on you.*
> *Katherine.*

John bowed his head, rose and went to the casement overlooking the inner courtyard where he stood quietly smiling, recalling Katherine's face and grey eyes.

Then there was a knock at the door and his valet entered, bowed and said: "Begging your pardon, my Lord, but Sir Richard Sturry is here from Westminster seeking urgent audience with you."

"I have already informed the King about the state of negotiations in France, so what can this mean…? Well, show him in," he said.

As Sir Richard entered, John moved forward to greet his friend but stopped as he saw Sturry's set face and stiff, formal bow.

"My Lord, I am sorry to intrude, especially at this time," he said, "and to be bearing such sad news, but I have to inform you that Queen Anne died suddenly two nights ago of the plague at the royal manor at Sheen."

"But…" faltered Gaunt, "…and King Richard?"

"I am told he is very distressed and refusing food or to see anyone.

The Chancellor believes he would respond if you were to go to see him and has asked me to escort you, my Lord, if you so wish."

"Yes, of course I will come," replied Gaunt, and then added almost to himself, "theirs was a true and deep love: the hurt will run as deeply."

Late the following morning, Gaunt was lost in thought as he was leaving the Palace of Westminster, having just seen King Richard again. The King was, he felt, now beginning to attend to the business of government and had called for the Duke of Gloucester to join him to continue the preparations for his campaign in Ireland, but there seemed to be an underlying resentment at the loss of his Queen. It was then that he was hailed by Geoffrey Chaucer who had just come out from the Exchequer.

"Good morning, my Lord," he called, and then in a sombre tone said, "we are indeed suffering sad times. Your sudden loss of Duchess Constance is now capped by Queen Anne's death. And…" he faltered, "…I have had news from Portugal that my Philippa has also died."

"Oh no, Geoffrey! But when… and how was that?" Gaunt said, breaking off from his own sombre thoughts.

"Some four weeks ago from the flux and fever, I am told. I received the news yesterday from my friend Jose Marinda, the Portuguese captain, who also brought a letter from Queen Philippa… and," he added, "…a letter addressed to Dame Katherine which I will bring to you at Ely Place this night, if that is convenient? But now I must go as I am summoned to see King Richard."

"Yes, of course, you must not delay. We will be able to talk tonight. Come as soon as you can… and God's blessing on you, Geoffrey."

"And on you, my Lord," replied Chaucer, bowing as he turned away and walked quickly towards the Palace.

That evening, Gaunt and Chaucer dined alone at Ely Place. They had already exchanged their mutual sorrows at the loss of their wives when Chaucer said: "My Lord, I would welcome your advice. After I left you, my audience with the King was… well… disturbing. I was shown into the throne room where, to my surprise, he was sitting wearing his crown. At first he seemed not to see me. Then he began walking round the room and shouting out against the loss of his Queen and her support, describing it as a devilish plot and how could he carry out the divine cause entrusted to him without her… Then he returned to sit quietly on his throne until he raised his eyes and saw me, at which I bowed again and said: 'Your Clerk of Works at your service, sire.'

"'Yes!' he shouted. 'You!' pointing his finger. 'You shall rid me of this demon! Go and demolish that part of the palace at Sheen where she died: all of it!'"

Chaucer turned to Gaunt and said: "My Lord… I need your advice. My appointment as Clerk of Works finishes next month. Do you think the King really wants that done?"

John had been listening intently to all that Chaucer said. "Yes, I am sure he does. Anne's death has hurt him. This is his way of taking revenge on the forces that took her away from him. Richard does not forget and neither does he forgive. So, yes, he does mean it and you should carry out his orders and continue in office until the work is done – or he will turn against you."

"I understand," said Chaucer quietly. "It is akin to the wrath of the ancient gods when their will was thwarted!"

"Indeed," said Gaunt. "And it is because of this that I fear he may yet seek his revenge against those he thinks plotted against him ten years ago, including my brother Gloucester and my son Henry."

Next day, Chaucer met with William Chetwynde and Hugh Hayward, his two assistants, who were both astounded at the King's direct order to demolish part of the palace that they and their workmen had worked so diligently on. But Chaucer explained that this was a task they could not avoid, and together they marshalled a body of workmen to carry out the demolition of that part of

Sheen Palace where Queen Anne had died. And Gaunt returned to Leicester to complete the arrangements for the funeral of his late wife, Duchess Constance.

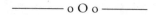

Constance's burial was planned to take place before the high altar in the Church of St Mary in the Newarke at Leicester on 5th July 1394. At noon on the day before, John of Gaunt, satisfied that all the arrangements had been made, was about to leave the church when one of the chaplains hurried towards him and said: "My Lord, forgive my intrusion, but two heralds have just arrived and are seeking urgent audience with you."

John paused, gripped by a sudden sense of foreboding, before nodding and going with the chaplain towards the door. His sense told him that another disaster awaited him, but what…? Then he saw the two heralds and recognised that they wore the Hereford livery of his son, Henry. "Oh dear God, what can this mean?" he said to himself. Then the senior herald bowed before him and held out a package sealed with his son's insignia.

"My Lord, I am to give you this from Earl Henry and to await your reply, if you so please." Then he and his colleague stepped back to await John's response.

John turned away, broke open the sealed package and drew out a short letter from his son:

> *Father,* he read, *Mary died yesterday. She gave us a beautiful little girl but after the birth developed a fever that took her away from us. Dame Katherine was with her and we are praying together for God's blessing to receive her soul.*
> *Henry*

John of Gaunt crumpled the letter in his fist and stood, head bowed, staring unsightedly at the ground. Then he breathed deeply and turned to the two heralds and said gruffly: "I will ride with you back to Peterborough," and called for his horse to be saddled and brought to him.

John of Gaunt, accompanied by the two heralds, set a fast pace on the journey through Uppingham and Wansford to the manor at Milton outside Peterborough. On his arrival, he dismounted, threw the reins to a waiting stable boy and walked quickly into the hall where he was met by his son Henry. As Gaunt advanced he threw his arms open and they embraced in a tight hug. Then the Duke drew back and looked directly into his son's face.

"This is such an undeserved tragedy," he said.

"Yes," sighed Henry. "Mary had the sweetest of natures: generous, kind, always sympathetic to the needs of others and…" he paused, "dearly loving to me."

John stepped back and laid his whip and the gauntlets he did not realise he was still carrying onto a side table. The door swung open and Katherine Swynford entered and went immediately to him into his outstretched arms. They held each other in a long embrace and then she looked into his face and said: "Oh John! I am so grieved…" as tears ran down her cheeks.

John drew her to him and as they held each other he could feel the spasms of her sobbing. Then with his arm around her shoulders they went together to where Henry was standing.

"I shall have to arrange her funeral," he said quietly.

"Yes, I was thinking about that on the way here," said his father. "As all is now prepared for the funeral of Duchess Constance at the Collegiate Church of St Mary in the Newarke at Leicester, if you so wish, we could arrange for Mary also to be buried there… while the family and others are gathered? But," he quickly added, looking into the drawn face of his son, "at a separate ceremony on, say, the following day."

Henry considered this and then said: "I am sure Mary would be pleased by that. Yes, my Lord, if it can be done."

"Then so be it," said Gaunt. "I will ride back to Leicester today and make the arrangements. But first I must speak with Dame Katherine."

As Henry bowed and withdrew, Gaunt drew Queen Philippa's letter from his tunic and said: "Katherine, my dearest, this letter has come for you from Portugal," passing it to her. Then, having broken the seal and scanned the contents, she cried: "Oh John, no... not my sister too!" With a stricken look she went into John's arms and sobbed as she pressed herself into his chest.

"We will be able to pray for her soul and honour her, especially in her services to royalty, when we get to Leicester," said John quietly, as she raised her head to look into his face.

"Yes. Yes, we will. And does Geoffrey know?" asked Katherine.

"Yes, my dear. And he will be there to pray with us," replied John.

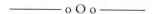

On 5th July 1394 the last rites for Constance, Duchess of Lancaster, were performed at midday at Leicester in the Collegiate Church of St Mary in the Newarke led by the Dean of the Foundation, William Chuseldine. He processed down the aisle to the high altar with John of Gaunt, Duke of Lancaster, at his side, led by six canons and followed by six priests chanting the Miserere. In the body of the church they passed between nearly all of the 100 poor inmates of the Foundation Hospital who shuffled to kneel or bow and cross themselves as the procession passed.

Then as they moved slowly between the choir stalls where there were members of her family and representatives of the royal courts of Castile and England, the priests chanted the responsory Sub Viente:

> *"Come to her assistance, ye Saints.*
> *Come to meet her, Angels of the Lord."*

As the Duke and Dean approached the bier beside the high altar, John of Gaunt stepped forward and placed a small gold cross between Constance's hands which were folded on her chest. The Dean then intoned the Prayer of Absolution:

"Oh God, we humbly present our prayers to Thee for the soul of thy servant, beseeching Thee to command Thy Holy Angels to receive it and bear it into Paradise. Through Christ Our Lord. Amen"

A priest stepped forward and sprinkled holy water over the grave as the body of Duchess Constance was lowered into the vault prepared for her beside the high altar as priests intoned the Libera me Domine.

The Dean then turned to address the assembled congregation:

"It is also meet and proper that on this day we pray for the soul of Philippa Chaucer, nee Roet, who died in Lisbon a month ago while serving devotedly as lady-in-waiting and head of the household of Queen Philippa of Portugal and who, for twelve years with similar devotion, served Duchess Constance.

O Lord, we beseech you to bless her soul and receive her into your bounteous care."

After the interment of Duchess Constance, the family and guests walked from the church through the cloistered precinct to Dean Chuseldine's house where they were served with light refreshments by women helpers from the hospital. While John of Gaunt was engaged in receiving the condolences of the Castilian nobles and their praise and admiration for Constance, the mother of their young Queen Katharine, Chaucer was talking with his late wife's sister, Dame Katherine.

"I was very moved by the Dean's tribute to Philippa, and I thank you and the Duke for that," said Geoffrey. "That would have made her very proud."

"Yes, I was too, although, as ever, she would have played down her role. And, it was John's doing so maybe you can thank him directly," replied Katherine.

Then they were approached by the tall figure of Sir Andrew Lutterel and a bronzed Jose Marinda, the Portuguese captain, who came forward, bowed before Katherine, took and kissed her hand

and said: "My Lady, it is the greatest pleasure and honour to see you again. Let me tell you the great sadness that my Queen feels at the loss of your sister…" and turning to Chaucer, "…and of course, my old friend… of your wife, who so lovingly served and was treasured by my Queen."

"And let me please add my condolences to you both," said Sir Andrew, bowing.

"Well!" said Katherine. "This *is* a surprise – seeing you two together again – my rescuers from that dreadful time when the peasants burned the Savoy! Oh, I am so grateful to you for coming!"

The next day at noon, the mourners from the royal courts having departed, the family and friends gathered again in the Church of St Mary for the burial of Mary de Bohun, wife of the Earl of Derby. The quieter and more intimate service of committal beside the choir was again carried out by the Dean, William Chuseldine, supported by the canons and priests.

Three weeks later they were all gathered together again at Westminster for the burial of King Richard's young Queen, Anne of Bohemia. The Abbey was filled with the lords and ladies of England, knights from the Court and Members of Parliament from the cities and shires together with nobility from Germany, Bohemia, France, Flanders, Spain and Portugal, all joining together in the solemn act of devotion and prayers for the soul of the departed Queen, to be blessed and conveyed by angels into the mercy of God in heaven.

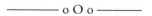

With the demolition of the wing at Sheen nearly complete, Chaucer was able to be released from the Clerkship of the King's Works. He now spent his time mainly at his house in Greenwich, reading and writing, mostly on his *Canterbury Tales*. He had completed the Prologue with its list and description of all twenty-five in the band of pilgrims who assembled at the Tabard Inn for the journey to Canterbury and was now reviewing what he had written before going to see John Gower, who had moved from his manor house near Greenwich to a house in the precincts of Southwark Cathedral. On arrival, he was warmly welcomed by his friend and they were soon settled, each with a pot of ale in the small garden at the back of the house.

"So," said Gower with a grin, "no more knocking down the works you have been building, then?"

Chaucer replied with a rueful smile, "No, and I must say that was a thankless task: and it hurt the workmen even more than me. But I am glad to be released – not only from the whims of the King, but also from the endless journeying and accounting."

"But now how goes the journey to Canterbury?" asked Gower, playfully.

"Oh ho!" said Chaucer, his face brightening, "all my pilgrims are now assembled at the Tabard Inn and I have completed my description of each of them as a Prologue to the journey. Here, I have made a fair copy for you," reaching into his bag and handing it to Gower. "I shall look forward, as ever, to hearing your comments and discussing it with you!" he added with a smile.

"Geoffrey!" exclaimed Gower, "generous as ever; and what joy I shall have in the reading! But can I not prevail on you to recite one or two of the descriptions... to whet my appetite?"

"Well," replied Geoffrey. "They are a varied bunch – culled from life around us – and some not all that wholesome in looks, morals or manners! For example:

> *"There was a Summoner with us at that Inn,*
> *His face on fire, like a cherubin,*
> *For he had carbuncles. His eyes were narrow,*
> *He was as hot and lecherous as a sparrow.*
> *Black scabby brows he had, and a thin beard.*
> *Children were afraid when he appeared.*
> *No quicksilver, lead ointment, tartar creams,*
> *No brimstone, no boracic, so it seems,*
> *Could make a salve that had the power to bite,*
> *Clean up or cure his whelks of knobby white*

Or purge the pimples sitting on his cheeks.
Garlic he loved and onions too and leeks,
And drinking strong red wine till all was hazy.

"He was a noble varlet and a kind one,
You'd meet none better if you went to find one.
Why, he'd allow – just for a quart of wine –
Any good lad to keep a concubine
A Twelvemonth and dispense him altogether!
And he had finches of his own to feather!"

"If that's a taster, I shall enjoy this meal!" exclaimed Gower. "Thank you, Geoffrey! But how will you continue now that you have finished the Prologue?"

"My plan is that as the pilgrims ride along on their way to Canterbury, each will in turn entertain the others by telling a tale of their own making… much as is done in a tap-room bar in a tavern or when groups gather round a campfire. Where they come from and where they have been will throw up some lively tales, I reckon!"

"I've no doubt your pen will see to that, Geoffrey! I shall look forward to their tales!"

———— o O o ————

After the royal funeral and burial of Queen Anne in the Abbey, John of Gaunt travelled with Dame Katherine to one of his favourite castles at Pontefract. The day after their arrival they were relaxing together, walking in the formal hedged garden, enjoying the warm summer sun.

"Katherine, my dear," said John. "Do you remember when you first came to the nursery at Hertford? I can still recall how I first saw you there: sitting on the floor in a pool of sunlight, showing Elizabeth how to do needlework, your hair shining gold in the light and your grey eyes looking anxiously up at me."

"Oh, my Lord, yes! I remember I was so abashed at your sudden arrival and I felt I had disgraced myself!"

"Not so, my love. In fact your clear grey eyes had quite abashed *me*! And," he said as he moved in front of her and put his hands on her shoulders, "'tis still so much so that I want us to marry!"

Katherine gasped, put her hand to her mouth and cried: "But, John…" and gasped again.

"But me no buts, my dear! You know that our love is too strong to be denied."

"Yes! Yes, it is," she replied with shining eyes as she looked up at him. "I only thought what would the courtiers and their wives say?"

"Well, yes of course, there will be talk, and I will have to get a dispensation from the Pope – and the King's agreement as my feudal Lord."

And so it was, with the blessing of both King and Pope, that John and Katherine were married in a simple ceremony conducted by the ageing Bishop Buckingham in Lincoln Cathedral on 14th January 1396. And Katherine, mother of four of his children, became Duchess of Lancaster.

———— o O o ————

While John of Gaunt had been seeking a dispensation from the Pope to allow his marriage to Katherine, King Richard also began to think of marrying again, for he had, as yet, no offspring as heir to his throne. Early in 1395, he instructed his Council to begin a search for a new bride. Having already achieved alliances with Portugal and Castile through the marriages of Gaunt's daughters, the Council's first choice was Yolande, daughter of King John of Aragon, which would further strengthen the English position in Iberia in relation to France.

But the French King, Charles, alarmed by this, made a personal appeal to Richard to abandon the plan, and, in the interests of peace between France and England, he offered Richard the hand of his 6-year-old daughter, Isabella. This was accepted and after lengthy negotiations over the terms of the marriage, including the size of the dowry, preparations were begun for the marriage to take place in Calais in November 1396.

A great encampment was prepared at Ardres to accommodate the large numbers of French and English courtiers, princes, princesses and ambassadors from the courts of Europe. It was here where the two Kings met for the first time on 26th October 1396. Richard was dressed in a long scarlet gown bearing on his chest the emblem of the white hart. Charles wore a shorter gown of darker red with a diagonal band of black sable trimmed with silver in respect of the memory of the late Queen Anne. The pair advanced to a central point, shook hands, embraced and kissed while their retainers knelt and clapped their approval. Then fine French wines and sweetmeats were served while the two Kings withdrew to the privacy of the French marquee.

Then on 30th October, at the same venue, King Charles led Isabella, his young daughter, out from his marquee, advanced towards Richard and formally presented her to him. Richard bowed and thanked Charles for his precious gift. The Duchesses of Lancaster and Gloucester moved forward and took Isabella into their care to prepare her for marriage to Richard. This was solemnised on 4th November in the Church of St Nicholas in Calais by Thomas Arundel, the Archbishop of Canterbury.

Chapter Eleven

KING RICHARD WAS sitting at his desk in his privy chamber going through a sheaf of state documents which needed his signature. His confidence was high since his return from Ireland. He had led an army of over 7,000 men and had taken great heart from the enthusiastic support of his nobles and troops, particularly his band of Cheshire archers. He had faced down the boastful Art MacMurrough, the self-styled King of Leinster, who was made to swear fealty and to withdraw from Leinster. Most of the remaining Irish nobility had followed suit when summoned to Dublin, and he had left the Earl of March to settle with those in Ulster. Now, he was intent on strengthening his royal authority in England.

Among the documents awaiting his attention was a list of owners of sizeable manors in the shires of Middle England which he had ordered to be prepared before he left for Ireland. When he saw this he told his squire to summon Sir John Russell and Sir Edward Dallingridge to his presence. As they entered, dropping to one knee and then bowing deeply, he called out: "Ah!" holding out the document, "how sure are you that these holders of manors will honour a pledge to me? Are they not already in the pay of local lords?"

"From our enquiries, we think not, Your Majesty," replied Sir Edward. "The influence of the premier lords is not strong in the shires of Stafford, Nottingham and Northampton."

"No… but in Warwickshire?" the King interjected.

"The five named there, Your Majesty, are known for their opposition to the Earl of Warwick," replied Sir John Russell.

"Be that as it may, I do not want to stir the already suspicious Earl, so leave them out," said the King. "As for the others: so be it! Issue letters patent summoning them to me here in Westminster where they will swear their allegiance to me in person and be rewarded with an annual retainer of sixty marks for the knights and twenty-five to the esquires."

As the two knights bowed and were about to withdraw, Richard asked: "How many now is it that we have retained in the shires?"

The two knights glanced at each other and then Sir John bowed and replied: "Including those on the list you have just approved, Your Majesty… that makes a total of fifty-nine knights and fifty esquires."

"Good! But I need more: men, as you know, who are socially and politically influential, especially in the northern and western counties and the Welsh Marches, so that I shall have support for my royal needs in their local communities. And I need that to be in place before the next Parliament," ordered the King.

"It shall be done, Your Majesty," replied the two knights as they bowed, took three steps backwards, bowed again and withdrew.

Katherine, Duchess of Lancaster, was sitting with the young Queen Isabel, at a table by a bay window on the river side of the Palace of Westminster. Since the Coronation and with the King away in Ireland, Katherine had often spent time with the young Queen – to keep her company, to answer her questions about England and Court procedures – but also because she enjoyed the vitality and French hauteur of the Queen and her natural impishness. It reminded her of the happy days she had spent over twenty years ago with the Duke's children in the nursery at Hertford.

Now she watched as Isabel, her face wrinkled in concentration, applied herself to the needlework they had been working on, which was a spray of white lilies wrapped round with sharply pointed leaves. With Lady Katherine's help she had already completed the delicate task of the floral heads of the lilies. Now, the light from a hazy morning sun helped Isabel to work her needle carefully through the warp and weft of the stiff linen material as she developed the leaves in a rich dark green silken thread. She had been humming a tune from a roundelay, when she stopped, needle in mid-air, and addressed

Katherine: "My Lady! You said you would get your brother, Master Chaucer, to come to see me and tell me about his tales! When... Oh!" she broke off as a lady-in-waiting came in and announced that Geoffrey Chaucer had arrived.

"Oh," shouted Isabel, clapping her hands, "bring him in!"

Chaucer hurried across the room and, with a smile and a nod to Katherine, bowed before Isabel and said: "My Lady. *C'est mon plaisir!*"

Isabel gave a tinkling little laugh, clapped her hands and said: "I love tales!"

Katherine smiled and pointed to a chair for Chaucer to sit down. As he did so he said: "I am still writing the *Tales*, my Lady, but I can describe for you some of the pilgrims."

"Oh! Yes please!" said Isabel eagerly. "I expect they were great lords and beautiful ladies in silks and satins and some handsome squires singing love songs?"

"Well, no, my Lady! These are more ordinary folk who you would meet in the towns and villages of England – just like you would in France. There were five craftsmen from a town – a haberdasher, a dyer, carpenter, weaver and a carpet maker – all dressed in the livery of their guild, and three in holy orders: a nun, a monk and a friar. The Nun was full of grace and was all sentiment and tender heart (she would weep if she saw a mouse caught in a trap!). But the Monk was more of a horseman and hunter than a priest, while the Friar was a wanton and merry man who would absolve sinners for a gift if they would grease his palm!"

At this, Isabel looked up at Katherine with a frown and asked, "What does that mean?"

"It means they would have to give him money," replied the Duchess.

"Oh! But that surely is wrong!" exclaimed Isabel, holding her hand to her mouth.

"Well, yes, it is," replied Katherine. "And maybe that is why this friar was seeking forgiveness by going on a pilgrimage to the Holy Shrine of Thomas a Becket at Canterbury?"

"Well, when he gets there he should give back all that money!" said Isabel.

Katherine and Chaucer smiled before he continued: "There were also two brothers of a different sort among the pilgrims. One was a Parson, poor in goods but rich in holy thought and work. He gave to poor parishioners from church offerings and his own property. There never was a better priest, and his brother, a plowman, was as honest a worker, good and true. He went steadily about his work – to thrash corn, dig or to manure – and he would help the poor for the love of Christ.

"But I have something else to show you," said Chaucer, drawing out a smooth round metal object which fitted neatly into his hand. "I expect that even Lady Katherine does not know what this is!" as he held it out in the palm of his hand to show it to her.

Katherine peered at the instrument and, with a laugh, exclaimed: "No, indeed I don't!" But then she said: "But I recall having seen the captain of the ship when I sailed to Wisbech holding something like it up towards the sun."

"Very likely, for this is called an astrolabe and it is used to read the skies in the daytime and at night."

The young Queen laughed out loud. "Oh, Master Chaucer! You are teasing us! There is no writing in the sky… and anyway it is too dark at night to see anything."

"There *is* a form of writing in the sky if you look carefully, even at night," replied Chaucer. "You see, the sun and the moon and the stars all move round the Earth and if we note carefully where the sun or the moon are in the sky it will tell us a lot of things: like what time of day it is, what month it is and whether it is winter, spring, summer or autumn.

"Many fine astrologists from Arabia, Africa, Greece and Rome have studied this, even Franciscan friars like John Somer and Nicholas of Lynne in our country, and they have drawn up calendars to help us in our readings of the sky."

"But how does this astrolabe help?" asked Katherine.

"You see all these lines on the back," he said as he held out the astrolabe for Isabel and Katherine to see, "those are used to track the paths of the sun and moon and stars…"

"Why, they look like a spider's web!" cried Isabel, with a laugh.

Chaucer smiled because he had often thought the same. "Yes, they do! And sometimes we call spiders 'loppe', " he said.

Then Katherine, seeing that the little Queen's interest was waning, said: "Well, next time you come, Geoffrey, maybe we can hear more of your stories?"

"Oh, yes please!" cried Isabel, clapping her hands.

"Of course," said Chaucer. "It will be an honour."

Two weeks later the Duke and Duchess of Lancaster were travelling from Ely Place in Holborn along the Strand to the Palace of Westminster. They were in a small town coach pulled by a single horse and escorted by two mounted retainers.

"John, dearest," said Katherine, "I am still puzzled that King Richard wants to see us both together. Is he expecting royal visitors from one of the European courts and wants us to entertain them?"

"Not that I know of," replied John. "Maybe he wants to thank you for your devotion to the young Queen?"

"Surely not, for he has already done that – more than once and fulsomely!" she said.

"Well, you know Richard," replied John. "He is full of surprises and sudden whims! But we shall soon know," he added as the coach drew up at the Whitehall Gate.

A footman helped Katherine from the coach and then escorted her and the Duke to the King's privy chamber. Richard was seated at his desk when their arrival was announced. Discarding formality, he immediately came forward, took Katherine's hands in his and kissed her on both cheeks before leading her to a couch by the window.

Then, turning to the Duke, he waved him forward and cried: "Come! Welcome, my truest Lord and Uncle!"

With his arms outstretched, he wrapped John of Gaunt in a tight hug, kissed him on both cheeks and then led him to a chair opposite Katherine before seating himself beside her.

If Gaunt was taken aback by this rare affection he did not show it – except that there was a warmth in his eyes as he looked at Richard and saw the likeness to his brother, the Black Prince – the shining black hair and flashing blue eyes, alive with the excitement of his own thoughts.

"My dears," said Richard, leaning forward. "We have now received the full written text of the Pope's blessing on your marriage and confirmation of the legitimate status of your children."

Katherine smiled and glanced nervously at John. They both knew that, as their sovereign lord, Richard's formal approval was needed. Her worry was swept aside as Richard grasped her hand and that of John and said: , "And I bless their place in our royal family and, so that this shall be known and observed, I will call all the family to join us here next week in celebration."

As Katherine leaned forward and kissed Richard's hand tears ran from her brimming eyes. John bent over the King's hand, brushed it with his lips and looked intently into his face and said, simply, "My Lord. Thank you."

Chaucer had asked his usual boatman, John Croyser, to take him upriver from Greenwich to Westminster and as he walked from the pier to Westminster Hall he wondered again what was the meaning of the royal summons he had received 'to attend a gathering of King Richard's Royal Family'. True, he had a connection through his sister-in-law, Katherine, who was now Duchess of Lancaster and therefore aunt to the King, but this hardly warranted his own inclusion. Maybe, he mused, he was included because of his poetry and that some 'entertainment' would be needed. Well, he had brought with him some of his writing about the Canterbury pilgrims – just in case.

As he entered Westminster Hall he was surprised by the size and splendour of the 'family gathering': the King's three uncles, the Dukes of Lancaster, Gloucester and York and their Duchesses; their offspring – Henry, Earl of Derby, Edward, Earl of Rutland; the King's half-brother, John Holland, Earl of Huntingdon, and his wife, John of Gaunt's daughter, Elizabeth; Thomas Mowbray, Earl of Nottingham, a descendant of Edward I. To Chaucer, these were mostly remote figures with whom he had little acquaintance – except Henry of Derby. But then he saw that all the Beauforts were present too – Katherine's children by John of Gaunt – John, Henry, Thomas and Joan with her husband, Ralf, Lord Neville – and even her son Sir Thomas Swynford by her first marriage.

So! thought Chaucer: maybe his connection with Katherine as her brother-in-law was sufficient for his presence… and a recitation would not be called for!

And then a royal herald entered and announced the arrival of the King. Two trumpeters preceded him with a shrill fanfare. King Richard, crowned and richly attired in a black tunic with silver and diamond embroidery including his emblem, the white hart, walked slowly, accompanied by his young Queen Isabel, to a small dais on which were placed two thrones ornately worked in gold leaf. Having mounted the dais, he turned and nodded his head to the assembled company who bowed and curtsied before him. Chaucer, standing to one side, joined in and noticed, out of the corner of his eye, how slight and perhaps grudging was the bow of the Duke of Gloucester.

The King rose. Tall and slim, his height enhanced by his crown and the richly embroidered black cape draped over his shoulders, he looked into the eyes of the faces before him.

"My dear family: Welcome. This is an occasion to celebrate our shared regality and the duty entrusted to us by the Almighty in the governance of our country. Together we are making our country the envy of Europe – and this magnificent Hall is witness to that. I am fascinated by the web of veins through which our royal blood flows. And I am especially blessed by the support and wise counsel of my three royal uncles" – bowing to each in turn – "the Dukes of Lancaster, Gloucester and York.

"And now, with the Pope's blessing, I welcome into their proper place within the family my Beaufort cousins – John, Henry, Thomas and Joan," turning towards them. "And to confirm their place in the bosom of my royal family, I now appoint John Beaufort as Earl of Somerset and Henry Beaufort as Bishop of Lincoln in succession to our valued friend and servant John Buckingham, the present Bishop, on his retirement."

At this, there were murmurs of approval and some clapping from the assembled family. Then, at the King's beckoning, John Beaufort went forward, knelt before King Richard who formally dubbed him 'Earl of Somerset'. Following him, the young Henry Beaufort, his hands clasped together before him as in prayer, bowed deeply before the King who responded with a similar blessing with his hands.

Richard then called for drinks to be served and four pages came into the Hall bearing trays with wine in silver goblets which they served to the royal family.

John reached for his goblet from the proffered tray and was joined by his brother, Thomas, Duke of Gloucester. "Well then, John! You've got your bastards into the family but not with right of inheritance, eh?" said Gloucester.

Gaunt's eyes momentarily flashed with blue steel at the term 'bastards' but, refusing to rise to the bait, he smiled and said: "No, Thomas! As you know, an Act of Parliament would be needed, and I have no intention of pursuing that."

"Be it so: you are probably right. 'Inheritance' is a sore spot for Richard with his lack of issue – and none likely with an eight-year-old Queen! He covers his inadequacy with all this pomp and display and crown wearing. We never had to address our father as 'Your Majesty!'" he grumbled.

Meanwhile, Katherine was talking with John's daughter, Elizabeth.

"You've had the good news from Lisbon, haven't you?" she asked.

"Oh yes! Philippa has had a daughter – *at last!* – and they are going to call her Isabel," said Elizabeth excitedly. "That is five children she has now: what a nursery!"

"Yes! Reminds me of old times at Hertford," said Katherine.

Elizabeth put her hand on Katherine's arm and said: "I know I was naughty at times" (at which Katherine threw back her head and laughed loudly) "but we were happy and…" she paused, and lowering her voice, said, "I've never said this before, but I always wished when my mother died that my father would marry you… and I am so pleased that now he has!" as she embraced Katherine.

Standing to one side, Chaucer had heard Katherine's laughter and seen Elizabeth's embrace. He smiled with pleasure as he returned to his conversation with her son Henry, who was staring up at the vaulted roof.

"I have never seen anything like this roofwork. It is magnificent; but why so many heavy beams?" asked Henry.

"Well," said Geoffrey, smiling. "It is really a simple solution to a difficult problem. You see, the outside walls are too far apart for a normal roof span. For that you would have had to build interior walls and so spoil the space in the Hall. Instead, Yevele projected what are called hammer beams out from the wall and cantilevered the roof timbers up from that. But it does mean there are more solid timbers than for a traditional roof."

"It is indeed a wonder to behold," said Henry. Then, turning his eyes away from the roof, he looked at Chaucer with a smile and said: "You must have enjoyed working with Yevele and seeing this being built."

"Indeed I did!" beamed Geoffrey. "And you have a fine cathedral at Lincoln to cherish!"

"Yes! And a great deal to learn! I am humbled by the prospect but with God's guidance and my faith in Him, my doubts and incapacity will be overcome."

On their return to Ely Place, John of Gaunt joined Katherine in their sitting room. She was standing by the window, looking out into the garden, when he came in. She turned and went to him with her arms outstretched. "Oh John… I am so overjoyed, I can hardly speak." Then as the tears ran down her cheeks, she looked up at him and said simply: "Thank you, my dearest, for I know how you worked your will with the Pope and Richard."

John looked down into her grey eyes. "It is but meet and proper, my dearest, and Richard is fully seized of the support he will get from our family."

Katherine smiled and said, "Yes… but—"

"What is it, my love?" asked John.

"It is not my place to say, John, but…" then she burst out, "why, oh why does Richard spend so much time alone – sitting on his throne, richly dressed and wearing his crown? I have seen him there often when I visit Isabel."

"Yes, I have seen that too." Then John took Katherine by the hand and said: "Come… let us sit closer to the hearth and the warmth of the fire."

When they had settled, he said quietly, "Richard is very like his father, the Black Prince: able, arrogant, wilful, entirely sure of his royal rights and destiny and, as such, demanding of obedience. He was a brilliant army commander and strategist… but, when thwarted he could be vengeful and cruel. Richard is not a soldier. His interests are in what he would call 'higher' things: beauty, art, fine buildings, sculpture, jewels and, of course, clothes. He thinks this show of 'magnificence' expresses his closeness to God and his divine right to rule."

"But he seems so lonely," said Katherine.

"Yes, he is. Since his right to rule is divinely inspired, he believes this raises him above his people and sets him apart. His father, the Black Prince, kept a lavish court in Acquitaine where, as his heir, the young Prince Richard was duly feted. But the court was filled with lords and knights who were battle-hardened, loyal comrades in arms. Richard had no such companions to call on when he came to the throne at the age of ten. He began to attract round him, not soldiers, but young men and favour them at Court with honours… such as Robert de Vere, whom he made Duke of Ireland. That was the root of the problem in 1387 when a group of lords, led by my brother Gloucester, appealed against this and forced Richard to accept a Ruling Council. De Vere was banished and others executed, including Richard's tutor, Simon Burley."

"Yes, I remember that," said Katherine. "And then, of course, Queen Anne died."

"Those twin hurts: losing close companions and having his sovereignty overruled, I think made Richard withdraw into himself. Anne's death compounded that. This broodiness – sitting alone on his throne – started then. And while he relies more on his uncles and younger family members – as we have seen today – I still worry that he nurses a deep resentment."

Geoffrey Chaucer had been to the Treasury to draw his pension and, having taken a skiff across the river, was walking away from Westminster to Southwark. It was a bright but cool morning in May with a brisk wind blowing upriver which quickened Geoffrey's steps. He was on his way to visit his friend John Gower in his new lodgings at the Priory of St Mary Overie. Geoffrey had been surprised at first by his friend's move from the leafy, almost pastoral Greenwich to the busy area off the south bank of the Thames. But he knew his friend's sight was failing and he needed a caring environment. He had found this at the Hospice of the Priory where he had not only the spiritual comfort of the monks but also personal care from the sisters.

Their joy at seeing each other was palpable as Geoffrey was shown into John's lodging. "Why, Geoffrey! It is a true blessing to see you!" cried John as they embraced and smiled into each other's faces.

"Indeed it is," responded Chaucer, smiling broadly. "And the lack of country air has not paled your cheeks, I see!"

"No! Far from it," chuckled Gower. "I walk most days up to the river and the fresh breezes are a welcome tonic. But how are you? And have your pilgrims reached Canterbury yet?" he asked.

"Oh yes, at last!" replied Chaucer, as he took the proffered seat. "I have brought a copy of the Prologue for you to read and see what a mixed bunch my pilgrims are."

"Geoffrey, what a pleasure I have in store! Thank you, my friend!"

John replied.

"But what now?"

"Well, as I have explained before, my intent is that each of the pilgrims in turn keeps the company entertained as they ride on their journey to Canterbury by telling a tale out of their own experience – much like soldiers or wandering minstrels do when they are journeying or gathered round a campfire. I have started with the Knight and his story of Arcita and Palamon, two princes from Thebes captured by Theseus and held captive in Athens, who both loved Emily, sister of the Queen. It is a noble tale of love and grief, courage and despair, death and fulfilment."

"I shall look forward to hearing more," said John. Then, frowning, he asked: "But how are affairs at Court?"

"Uneasy, I would say," replied Geoffrey. "King Richard seems to be promoting himself as a peacemaker in Europe – seeking to heal the split in the Church and against war with France – and acting, at times, imperiously – like an emperor."

"Yes, I have heard that," said Gower. "And, of course, in so doing he alienates lords like his uncle Gloucester, who is furious about Brest being handed back to the French."

"Fortunately, Gaunt still seems to have a calming influence with both – and in affairs of state and in the Council. But he is not as vigorous as he was since he suffered that bout of fever in Castile."

Gaunt's worries about Richard and Chaucer's sense of unease – far from groundless – were soon to be fulfilled.

On 10th July 1397 King Richard, without warning, acted against the three senior lords who had forced him in 1386 to accept a council to rule while he was under age. He invited all three – the Earl of Warwick, the Duke of Gloucester and the Earl of Arundel – to a banquet in Lombard Street, London. Only Warwick was able to attend and at the end of the banquet he was arrested and sent to the Tower. Richard then gave orders for the arrest of the other two.

The King, accompanied by his half-brother Holland, his cousin Rutland, Nottingham and a force of armed men, rode out through the night to Gloucester's castle at Pleshy in Essex. There, in the early hours of the morning of 11th July, Richard personally arrested Gloucester and ordered that he be held in custody at Calais. A ship was lying ready in the Thames and the Earl of Nottingham was appointed to convey the prisoner into custody at Calais. Soon after, the Earl of Arundel, on the advice of his brother, the Archbishop of Canterbury, surrendered and was taken to the Tower. To allay any mood of alarm, on 15th July Richard ordered all sheriffs to proclaim that the lords had been arrested for 'distortions, oppressions, grievances and other offences against the King's majesty unconnected with their roles in 1386/7', details of which would be reported to Parliament. Writs were issued for Parliament to meet at Westminster on 17th September 1397.

On that day, as the Members began to convene in Westminster Hall, Sir Thomas Percy and Sir John Bushy stood watching.

"There are only a few familiar faces that I can see," said Percy. "Do you think the experienced Members have been put off by these arrests and are nervous of the King's intentions?"

"Maybe," replied Bushy. "But it is more likely that the King's patronage is paying dividends. I am told that over a hundred of the new Members are retained by the King or by the lords who are supporting him, like Nottingham, Rutland and Huntingdon."

"But that is at least half the total Members!" exclaimed Percy, with raised eyebrows.

"Indeed," said Bushy. "I must leave you... The King has taken his throne and as the Lords and the Commons are assembled, I should start proceedings."

Bushy bowed to his friend and moved forward to the Speaker's Chair. He called the House to order and asked the Chancellor, Bishop Stafford of Exeter, to give the blessing and preach the opening sermon.

Taking as his theme Ezekiel 37, '*There shall be one King over them all*', the Bishop proceeded to emphasise what this meant: "To be powerful enough to govern, the King must be in full possession of his regalities and it is the duty of the Estates to report on any encroachment and on appropriate punishment."

After further elaboration the Bishop concluded his sermon and the House was adjourned until the next day.

Opening the proceedings the next day, Speaker Bushy began: "In the light of the Bishop's sermon and the legitimate rights of the King, we should first review the establishment of the Ruling Council in 1386," and he called for the details to be produced. The document establishing that Council was then read out and the Speaker continued: "You have heard the details. I now ask you to consider whether this curtailment of the King's sovereignty was a legitimate act and whether it was extorted by force?"

Uproar ensued among the members of the Commons, with cries of 'Treason', 'Traitors' and 'hang them'. When the hubbub abated, the Speaker called the House to order and, on acclamation, the establishment of the Council was repealed. Then the pardons granted to Gloucester, Warwick and Arundel in 1388 were also repealed and all three were charged with treason.

The first to be tried before the House, with John of Gaunt, Duke of Lancaster, presiding as High Steward, was the Duke of Arundel.

"Your pardon is revoked, traitor," he told him.

"Truly you lie!" replied the Earl. "Never was I a traitor!"

"Why in that case did you seek a pardon?" asked Lancaster.

"To silence the tongues of mine enemies of which you are one!" retorted the Earl.

"Answer the charge," interjected the King.

"I see it all now," the Earl said. "You who accuse me, you are all liars. I claim the benefit of the pardon you granted when you were of full age."

"I granted it provided it were not to my prejudice," replied the King.

"The pardon was worthless," added Lancaster. "You are adjudged as guilty of treason. Take him to the Tower."

Then, later that day in the paved square outside the Tower of

London, the Earl of Arundel, one of the senior lords who had deprived the young King Richard in 1386 of his temporalities, knelt at the block and was beheaded.

The Earl of Warwick and the Duke of Gloucester were also charged and found guilty of treason. Warwick confessed his guilt and pleaded with Richard who commuted the death sentence to banishment for life to the Isle of Man.

The Duke of Gloucester was also found guilty of treason, but the Captain of Calais had to report that the Duke had died in Calais ten days before Parliament was convened.

Before Parliament was dissolved on 30th September 'at the request of the Commons' two complementary statutes were passed:

1. The male issue of the three lords were declared incapable of sitting in Parliament or Council;
2. All future peers were required to swear to maintain the Acts of this Parliament.

Chapter Twelve

O N 30TH SEPTEMBER 1397, at the invitation of King Richard, the high and mighty of the royal court and English nobility began to assemble with their ladies at Westminster Hall in London. The King's summons was not specific but all attending knew that this was another celebration of the King's majesty and power. Richard had recently demonstrated this by the way in which he had seized and redistributed the lands and titles of the three treasonable lords the previous day. His cousins and close favourites at Court had been the main beneficiaries: Gaunt's son Henry, the Earl of Derby, was made Duke of Hereford; his cousin Edward, the Duke of York's son, was appointed Duke of Aumerle; while Thomas Mowbray, Earl of Nottingham, became Duke of Norfolk. Staunch supporters and officers at Court, like Sir William Bagot, Sir Henry Green and Sir John Bushy, were rewarded with lands, manors, estates and lesser titles.

As the Hall filled, goblets of wine were served by royal pages and the huge timbers of the new roof resounded with excited chatter. King Richard, in a short black tunic, emblazoned on the left breast with the royal arms, counterbalanced on the right with his personal emblem, the white hart, moved among his guests receiving their bows and curtseys with a nod or smile and words of welcome.

It was a rich and resplendent gathering. Fine jewels – rubies, sapphires, diamonds – flashed, set off by gold and silver trimmings to the brightly coloured and embroidered silks, satins and velvets of the clothes. The younger ladies wore a close-fitting sleeved tunic, called a cotehardie, with a low neckline, buttoned down the middle to a jewelled girdle round the hips, from which a full skirt flowed to floor level. The more senior ladies like the Duchesses of Lancaster and York preferred the newer and fuller style of the houppelande – a fashion introduced from Germany and Spain – which had a high, close-fitting collar, tight bodice and sleeves to the elbow that then flared out with wide draping edges or daggers down to knee-length. The waist was pulled in with a jewel-encrusted leather belt, from which a full skirt of velvet fell in rich folds to sweep the floor.

But the newest and brightest fashions were worn by the younger male courtiers. The hose now was seamless from toes to over the hips, close-fitting into the fork between the legs over which a codpiece, or small bag, was attached to cover the front fork. Most now favoured hose in a plain colour – such as grey, or a pale blue – to set off their brightly coloured cotehardie tunics, many of which were highly patterned or with bright light and dark contrasting colours set off in a trellis design. The hose was worn without shoes – a slim sole being inserted into the foot – and with exaggerated pointed toe pieces reaching out from the foot for ten or more inches. These young males were the peacocks of the Court and caused a stir with many admiring looks as they strutted among the guests with their long, slim legs and firm, round buttocks.

And then, when the serving of wine had finished and the pages had collected the goblets, a trumpet fanfare rang out and a herald called for attention to Bishop Stafford of Exeter, who was standing on a low dais alongside a draped screen.

"Your Majesty," called Stafford, bowing deeply, "with God's blessing, you asked me to present to your distinguished guests this magnificent altarpiece which you commissioned for your private devotions: a truly magnificent diptych!" as he pulled away the drapes to gasps and exclamations. "If Your Majesty will allow, I suggest the company gathers round and I will interpret its meaning.

"Here you see the two outer panels, where the decoration is entirely secular. On this one there is the King's emblem of a white hart lying on some branches of rosemary."

"Oh! Isn't that hart just beautiful," exclaimed the Duchess of York.

"And," continued the Bishop with a frown, "on the other outer half, there is the King's personal emblem – the royal arms of England and France impaled with those of Edward the Confessor."

"Now… if you will follow me… we will see the two inner

panels." The guests moved and formed a semi-circle around him.

"Here, on the left-hand panel, you see King Richard kneeling and offering his orb and banner, the symbols of his kingdom, to the Virgin Mary in the opposite panel, as her dowry. He is supported by his three patron saints: Edmund, John the Baptist and Edward the Confessor."

The Bishop paused as the guests moved round the panel: "Oh! Just look at the rich patterns of the King's cloak," one exclaimed, while another said, "Yes, and the bright colours!"

"And now," continued the Bishop, "on the opposite panel you see the Virgin Mary, carrying the Christ child, having received the orb, she is returning the banner of England to Richard to enable him to rule under her protection and with her blessing."

The guests stood quietly absorbing the meaning of this. And then the Duke of Aumerle remarked: "And, see, the crowd of angels surrounding the Virgin, all have the badge of the white hart on their left breast."

The Bishop ended by thanking the King for the privilege of sharing his remarkable private treasure and said: "We should pledge ourselves to support him in his God-given mission," which was answered by murmured 'Amens'.

As the King's uncles, the Dukes of Lancaster and York, walked together across Palace Yard towards their carriages, John of Gaunt said to his brother: "You can't help but admire Richard! He may not be the valiant fighter his father was but he has a great sense of what is beautiful and artistic, like the diptych we have just seen."

"And in the work he has commissioned at the cathedral at Canterbury," said York, "and indeed the new roof here at the Hall. These will be treasured long after we have gone!"

"Yes," murmured Gaunt. "But at times he spoils it with self-promotion… like all the angels wearing his white hart emblem. Did you notice that?"

"Yes," said York with a smile. "It made me think of his gangs of Cheshire archers!"

"And they are no angels!" laughed Gaunt as they made their way to their own carriages.

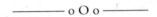

Geoffrey Chaucer, deep in thought, was hurrying from Westminster towards Southwark. He had just heard about some astonishing events that had happened at the Court and he felt an urgent need to discuss these with his friend John Gower. As he approached the precinct of the Priory of St Mary Overie where John had his rooms, he saw his friend sitting at his desk near the window and caught his attention by knocking on the casement.

"John!" he said as he was ushered inside. "I have just heard that the King has ordered a trial by battle between the Dukes of Hereford and Norfolk!"

"What!" exclaimed Gower. "Why?"

"Apparently, Hereford and Norfolk happened to meet while out riding near Brentford just before Christmas. Norfolk told Hereford that there had been a plot to kill him and his father, the Duke of Lancaster, in September after the last Parliament and even now there was a conspiracy to destroy the Lancastrian inheritance and the close family, including Aumerle, Dorset, Exeter and themselves. Moreover, he said that he and Hereford were about to be 'undone' by the King for their part as Appellants in the events of 1386/7."

"This is incredible," said Gower, wide-eyed in disbelief. "They were both pardoned by the King."

Chaucer smiled at his friend's concern and then said gently, "So were Gloucester, Warwick and Arundel."

"Yes," said Gower, "but this does not explain why the two are to go against one another in battle."

"Apparently, the King heard about what was said at Brentford and brought the two Dukes before him to settle the issues between them. Instead this added fuel to a smouldering fire. Hereford accused

Norfolk himself of plotting against Lancaster and ordering the murder at Calais of the Duke of Gloucester. Richard ordered them to desist and be reconciled but this was refused. Hence, Richard decided that under the rules of the Court of Chivalry the dispute should be settled by trial by combat."

"Oh Geoffrey!" exclaimed Gower, shaking his head, "I can make no sense of this. But you have always had a keen eye as a spectator and see more of the game than the rest of us."

"Ha!" laughed Chaucer. "My father always called me a 'watcher' rather than a 'doer' and Philippa used to get quite impatient with me!"

"But what *is this really about?*" insisted Gower, as he refilled their tankards.

"Ah, thank you," acknowledged Chaucer as he took a draught and wiped the froth from his lips with the back of his hand.

"Underneath all the pageantry and display at Richard's court," he continued, "there is a lot of pushing and shoving going on among the King's cousins and courtiers – like jockeys at the start of a race! This is provoked by jealousy at the huge wealth of the Lancaster inheritance and uncertainty over the succession – Richard not having produced a direct heir. If Lancaster and his heir Henry, Duke of Hereford, can be got rid of, there could be rich pickings in terms of redistributed lands and titles.

"And apart from all this, there is the King. He is a big spender and unpopular because of his demands for subsidies and forced loans. He veers between certainty in his divine right to rule and uncertainty in his aloneness – hence the comforting protection of his Cheshire archers. And he is a Plantagenet and capable of acts of irrational revenge – like when he had the manor at Sheen destroyed because that is where his first wife died. I suspect that he may see this quarrel between Hereford and Norfolk as an opportunity to get rid of one, if not two, of the remaining Appellants who acted against him in 1386."

"Ah! I see! Well, thank you for that," said Gower thoughtfully, "… but surely one of them would survive the combat?"

"Yes!" replied Chaucer. "And that most likely would be Henry, heir to the Duke of Lancaster, because he is a renowned fighter!"

"Well, and then what…?" added Gower.

"Indeed," smiled Chaucer.

A month later, Chaucer was again on one of his regular visits to Gower at Southwark.

"Geoffrey," began Gower, when they had settled comfortably into armchairs by the hearth and in the warmth of a leaping log fire. "I have just been reading again the copy you kindly gave me of the Prologue to your *Canterbury Tales*. Geoffrey, what a delightfully colourful and mixed bunch of characters you have got together! Wherever did you find them?"

A slow smile spread across Geoffrey's face and his eyes twinkled in the firelight.

"By watching, of course! And how better to defeat the tedium of padding along the road between London and Canterbury – or Dover – than to study and engage with your fellow travellers!"

"Yes, of course! Silly of me to ask!" chuckled Gower. "But, even so, Geoffrey, I find it hard to see some of your pilgrims riding and conversing together. For example, the exquisite Nun 'full of courtly grace… singing through her nose and intoning daintily in French' would surely find it hard to ride alongside the Miller with his 'mighty mouth and filthy tavern stories'? Nor would the goodly Parson 'rich in holy thought and work' be able to sit comfortably alongside the Pardoner with his sale of holy relics and 'tuning his honey tongue to win silver from the crowd'."

"No," agreed Chaucer. "As with any group, like would tend to go with like."

"Even so," put in Gower, "some of your 'pilgrims' seem unlikely penitents!"

"Yes!" laughed Chaucer. "But that is life: sinners beg forgiveness and are shrived often only to resume their old ways! The sort of people I have met on my travels are a mixed bag. I have heard some rare tales – some joyful and colourful, others crude and foul. Just like the countryside, you find beautiful flowers blooming alongside coarse and stinking weeds."

"True!" concluded Gower, nodding. "But have you further news of the trial by battle?"

"I hear that preparations for the contest are being made at Gosford outside Coventry where there is a large open green, spacious enough for tents to be put up at each end for the contestants and, in between, for seating to be erected for spectators. And the contest is attracting a lot of interest! Numerous dukes and nobles and knights from across Europe are excited about it and are planning to attend. And of course the two contestants are making their own preparations: especially in terms of their armour and equipment. Hereford, it is said, is having his armour and equipment specially made in Milan, while Norfolk has gone to Bohemia for his."

Gower sighed audibly at this description. "Oh Geoffrey!" he said. "What a mess. I thought we in England were more civilised than this: why otherwise do we have courts of law?"

Chaucer raised his eyebrows and smiled in sympathy at his friend's outburst.

"Apparently, chivalrous trials like this still happen in Europe," he said quietly.

"Well, it saddens me," said Gower and then shrugged, "but… what will be, will be, I suppose!"

"Indeed," said Chaucer. "And I will be able to tell you what happens, for I am bidden to accompany Duchess Katherine, which I will do, for her sake… and to support the Duke. God forbid that his son Henry is killed… for I fear that that would also kill the father, such is his frail state."

The sun was just rising in a hazy dawn on 16th September 1398 when John White ducked under the flap of his tent out into the cool morning air, yawned and stretched himself. "Arrh!" he cried as he dipped his face into a wooden pail of cold water and rubbed the water round his neck and pate.

"Come out, you lubbers!" he called to his two sons, Alan and Thomas. "We've work to do!"

John and his sons had been camping out on Gosford Green outside Coventry for the last four weeks, charged with the task of preparing the Green for the trial by battle ordered by the King between the Dukes of Hereford and Norfolk. Although John and his boys were experienced in preparing arenas for jousts and royal tournaments, they had never before prepared a venue for a fight to the death such as this. With the King presiding, and with an audience of nobles, foreign visitors and local people, John knew that his preparations must be faultless. So, with his sons, he began a final tour of inspection.

They went first to the western end of the Green where the Duke of Hereford's retinue were installed. Already, there was a bustle of lively activity as blacksmiths, armourers and grooms carried out their final checks and adjustments. While Alan and Thomas stopped to talk with a saddler, John sought out the Duke's Herald, Sir William Fortescue, a seasoned soldier who had been with John of Gaunt in Spain.

"Good morning, Sir William!" he called. "Is all in order?"

"As well as can be," came the answer. "Our needs are well met, thank you, John! What we need now is a positive outcome!"

"Amen to that!" said John.

Then, with a short bow, he withdrew, collected his sons and walked off to check on the opposing camp at the other end of the Green. As they approached the enclosure they were met with the familiar sounds of men making their final preparations in support of their lord. And they could see grooms walking two huge tournament horses beyond the tented enclosure. The Duke of Norfolk's Herald, Sir James Holt, assured John that his preparations were well made and nothing more was needed.

Satisfied, John sent his sons to make a close inspection of the grass sward between the two camps to see that the jousting track was clear of stones, debris or potholes which could unsettle the stride of a horse in its charge. He then went to inspect the area of his greatest concern – the rows of seating that he had set up for spectators alongside the tilting track.

He knew from experience how excitement in a crowd could lead to falls and injuries from breakages in the wooden structure. He tested again the solidity of the benches and their supports. Satisfied, he then went to the royal enclosure and made an even closer inspection of the seats, armrests, cushions, steps and aisles. While he was doing this, he was hailed by the King's Constable and Marshal, Sir Richard Drury, who was responsible to the King for the tournament arrangements: "Good morn to you, Master White. Your work looks as good as the morning!"

"Why, thank you, Sir Richard," replied John with a slight bow.

"I see the commons are beginning to arrive. You can expect the lords and ladies to follow shortly. The contestants are summoned to be here for nine o'clock and the King, who stayed the night nearby with Sir John Bagot at Baginton, is expected shortly after that. And then…" as he looked upwards, "it is in the hands of the Almighty?"

There was a low murmur of voices from the crowd that had gathered and a general air of pent-up tension rather than excitement. Then, just before nine o'clock, there were some louder cries as the Duke of Hereford rode into the arena, flanked by six mounted attendants. The King's Constable, Sir Richard Drury, moved forward and addressed the Duke: "In the name of His Royal Majesty, King Richard, state your name and business!"

"I am Henry, Duke of Hereford, and I come to do my duty against the false traitor, Thomas, Duke of Norfolk. I swear by Almighty God to uphold my claim." Then, having crossed himself, he turned to the left, spurred his horse and rode to his pavilion at the far end of the Green.

The shrill notes of a trumpet fanfare rang out and the King entered, accompanied by his retinue and a company of Cheshire archers who moved down to the edge of the grass sward in front of the royal pavilion. The King took his place alongside his uncle, the Duke of Lancaster, and the Duchess, whom he acknowledged with a smile and brief nod.

Immediately, the Duke of Norfolk rode into the arena and bowed his head before the King, where, challenged by the Constable, he also gave his name and business and took the same oath as his opponent.

Then, standing on his stirrups, he cried, "God speed the right!" and cantered off towards his pavilion.

At their respective pavilions the two contestants were helped into their armour – breastplates and steel cladding on their shoulders, arms, thighs, shins and feet – and handed their helmets to their household knights to assist them in putting them on before pulling on their meshed gloves. While this was taking place, specially appointed Knights of the King's Household measured the lances of the two Dukes and grooms walked their great tournament horses, who nodded and snorted their impatience, until the contestants signalled their readiness to mount. Then, assisted by their household knights using a specially erected tripod and ropes and pulley with a hook attached to the back of the armour, they were hoisted onto their horses.

Hereford and Norfolk, now fully armoured and holding their lances upright, settled their horses by first walking and then trotting them around their tented compound before pulling up to face each other across the long expanse of the Green. They signalled their readiness. They lowered their lances and visors and started to move forward, preparing to break into a full gallop.

Then, suddenly, King Richard jumped up and cried: "HOLD!"

There were audible gasps of astonishment from all sections of spectators, with many wide-eyed as they sought to understand what this meant. Standing next to the King, John of Gaunt, Duke of Lancaster, felt the hand of his wife, Katherine, gripping his arm, before he turned to Richard. Then as the contestants reined in their horses and returned to their pavilions, the Brittany Herald climbed the dais in the King's enclosure and called for silence. Sir John Bushy came forward and in clear tones announced the King's decision.

"Hear me, hear me!" he called. "His Royal Majesty, King Richard, by the Grace of God, has halted the trial by battle, so as to avoid the spilling of blood and to ensure peace throughout our land. Instead, to prevent further discord, he has ruled that the two antagonists shall be exiled: the Duke of Hereford for ten years and the Duke of Norfolk for life. They will now be brought here to swear their allegiance and obedience before His Majesty."

As soon as these words had sunk in, there was a babble of voices among the crowd with neighbour next to neighbour seeking to extract not only the 'whys and wherefores' but also the 'rights, wrongs and what nexts?' of this news. Similarly, John of Gaunt turned towards Richard and said with a bow: "My liege Lord, I praise your wisdom and thank you for your forbearance. Your commands will be obeyed. But I ask you to consider whether, with the Dukes separated, a reduction in the term of exile for my son Henry would just as well achieve the peace you demand?"

King Richard looked directly at his uncle and, seeing the drawn and ageing face, saw also the meaning behind his request. He smiled. "Yes," he said. "Perhaps ten years is too long and six would do just as well!"

His uncle bowed his thanks but persisted. "And even in exile, the Lancastrian inheritance, lands, titles and assets – will be assured?"

"Surely so!" exclaimed Richard, with a smile but cool eyes: "Do not worry! You know that I have already pledged this."

The two Dukes, recalled from their pavilions, appeared before King Richard. The terms of their banishment were read out to them by Sir John Bushy and they were required to kneel in homage to King Richard, their liege Lord, and swear to abide by the terms of their exile.

"And I require that you quit our shores within five days," added Richard.

Richard's instinctive insight into the state of his uncle's health proved true. After the aborted trial at Coventry, he had gone to Berwick at the request of the King to negotiate an extension of the truce along the Borders with the Scots. He was well respected and trusted by the Scots but the due processes of negotiation had to be honoured, including the social niceties, before the expected extension of the truce for a further two years was agreed. Finally he was able to take his leave and ride south to Leicester Castle where he and Katherine had agreed to spend Christmas.

He was tired and drawn when he arrived at the castle. Katherine, seeing this, cosseted him and looked for a way to have a quiet observance of the Holy Festival. Sitting with him by the fireside the day after his return, she said: "John, dearest! Why don't we take Holy Christmas Mass here at home with Father Aubrey, rather than go with all the congregation and ceremony at the Church of St Mary?"

John looked up into her anxious grey eyes, smiled, and said: "That is the best idea I *haven't* had in ages!" bursting into laughter.

Overjoyed by his reaction, Katherine got up, embraced him fondly and said: "I will so arrange it."

"I confess," said John more soberly, "with Henry in exile in Paris, I have little appetite for social discourse. We know that he is safe and welcome at the French court and well provided for at the Hotel de Clisson. But, I have a gnawing doubt nagging at me."

"You mean," asked Katherine, "that he is not really safe with the French?"

"There is always a risk of shifting sands on foreign shores," replied John.

"But it is not that. At the bottom of it: *I don't trust Richard!* Exiling Henry and Norfolk was a blatant act of revenge for their part against his rule in 1386 and the exile of de Vere and killing of his friends, like Burley. He has promised me, and avowed publicly, that the Lancastrian inheritance is secure but… I am not sure…"

"But, my dearest," he then smiled and took Katherine's hand, "your inheritance is secure because it is entailed clearly in your name and entirely separate from the estate of Lancaster! So come!... Let us enjoy our Christmas together."

So it was that John and Katherine spent Christmas of 1398 quietly together – trying to put aside a year of grief and sadness, with the banishment of Henry and the death – probably murder – of John's younger brother, the Duke of Gloucester. They exchanged presents: a fine silver brooch set with a large ruby for Katherine and a gold cup for John, then dined quietly and retired early. On Boxing Day they attended a small reception given by the Dean of the Collegiate Church, William Chuseldine, attended by four canons and three sisters from the Hospital Foundation, at which John presented the Dean with an altar cloth, finely wrought in gold and silver thread.

On the Eve of the New Year, Katherine's son Sir Thomas Swynford arrived, on his way from Kettlethorpe to rejoin Duke Henry in Paris, and stayed two nights. This was a delight for both Katherine and John. Katherine was eager to hear news of Kettlethorpe since Thomas, on reaching his majority, had formally inherited the manor from his father.

"The restoration of the Hall is nearly finished under the supervision of John Palmer, whom I have recruited as my steward and manager," he told Katherine. "He is already proving good value."

"If he is the son of Amos Palmer, you have done well," she said.

"What about that drainage problem and the waterway link between Lincoln and Boston? Is there any progress on that?" asked the Duke.

"That is still a sore issue, my Lord!" Thomas replied with a smile. "There are too many landowners with a finger in that pie – or should I say 'foot in the water'!" he added, laughing.

"Yes," acknowledged John, smiling. "And no doubt counting their pennies!"

And then John sighed and looked intently at Thomas: "So tell me straightly: you know Henry as well as anyone – you were brought up together. How do you think he is managing his exile?"

Thomas paused and looked at his mother. Katherine smiled and nodded encouragement for him to speak up.

"On the surface, my Lord, he is doing well. Socially, he is popular with King Charles and the French court and regularly wined and dined. But he is not satisfied with that. As you know, he is a very active person, full of energy and at the moment that is bottled up. He has talked of going on a crusade but I doubt he means it. I think he is waiting and watching."

John smiled, leaned forward and patted Thomas' knee.

"Thank you for that!" he said smiling. "Keep by him, Thomas, and hone his patience. He will need that and he will need you. And I will write a letter for you to give him."

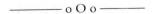

Ten days after Katherine's son had left, John began to suffer from a recurrence of the bloody flux, a severe attack of which he had survived at the end of his campaign in Castile. This started with stomach pains and mild diarrhoea. Katherine was distraught. She sat by his bed, mopped his brow and encouraged him to drink plenty of water.

But the symptoms grew worse and he developed painful cramps with blood and mucus on his stools.

Katherine called on William Chuseldine, the Dean, for help and soon an apothecary and two nursing sisters from the Foundation Hospital were tending to John while Father Aubrey calmed Katherine's anxiety. John rallied under their care and, sitting up, began to take some solid food again. Katherine sighed with relief when he smiled at her and then lay back on his pillow and went to sleep.

For two days John seemed to be recovering. Then the severe stomach gripes began again and the fever developed into bouts of delirium. Father Aubrey knelt at the foot of the bed, hands telling his beads while he recited prayers beseeching the Lord's comfort. Katherine stayed at John's side saying her own prayers. Then they were joined by John and Katherine's son, Henry, Bishop of Lincoln, who had ridden from Oxford to Leicester when he heard of the gravity of his father's sickness.

Kneeling by the great Duke's bedside, they prayed together. Suddenly, John sat bolt upright, his eyes wide open and staring upwards with a bright intensity, his face wreathed in a wonderful smile. Then, as suddenly, he fell back onto his pillow, lifeless.

Father Aubrey leaned forward, closed the lids of the staring eyes and prayed for the Almighty to receive the soul of John of Gaunt, Duke of Lancaster, Seneschal of England, third son of King Edward and Queen Philippa, brother of the Black Prince, uncle to King Richard, father of the Queens of Portugal and Castile, and beloved lord and husband of Katherine, Duchess of Lancaster.

It was the 3rd February 1399, one month short of John of Gaunt's 59th birthday.

John's body was carried by clerks of the Foundation to rest in state beside the altar of the Collegiate Church of St Mary in Newarke while arrangements were made for transportation to St Paul's in London. Candles were lit and incense burned while two clerks kept a continual vigil with prayers for the safe passage of his soul into the care of the Almighty.

Katherine and her son Henry, having made their own devotions beside the altar and spent time quietly offering their own prayers, left to return to the castle for the night.

As they walked, Katherine slipped her hand through her son's arm.

"Henry," she said. "I am not familiar with death… and what a sudden and final end it can be – at least on this earth. Yet, I found John's departure somehow… beautiful… his sitting up staring with a radiant, happy face. Is that usually how it is?"

"No," replied Henry. "It is rare. I believe it is a sign of angels coming to guide and protect a favoured soul on its journey to heaven. And so also, it is a recognition of the completion of a life lived with the Holy Spirit, in accord with God's will."

Katherine walked on, quietly thinking about what her bishop son had said, and then said: "I remember John telling me once how he was present at the death of Sir Ralph Runes, the knight to whom as a boy he was apprenticed by his father, King Edward, who sat up smiling like that before he died." And then she asked: "So, you say it is rare. Is it only lords and great knights who have lived a true life that get this angelic welcome?"

Henry smiled and squeezed his mother's hand.

"No. Although rare, it is as likely among the poorer and humble people. Recently I was present at the death of a simple plowman, who had lived a good life caring for his neighbours and sharing what he reaped from his labours. He was welcomed to heaven in the same way."

"Oh!" exclaimed Katherine. "He sounds just like one of Chaucer's pilgrims! I will let you have a copy of Geoffrey's description of all his pilgrims and you can tell me which ones you think might be conveyed to heaven like this!"

"Oh! Yes please! I shall look forward to that," smiled Henry.

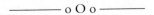

John's body arrived for burial at St Paul's Cathedral on 15th March 1399, having, according to his wishes, remained uninterred for forty days as an expression of humility and penitence. The next day, Passion Sunday, he was laid to rest in the presence of the King and all the nobility, beside his first Duchess, Blanche, in the sepulchre built next to the high altar by Henry Yevele. Katherine was chief mourner and was wearing widow's garb of a long flowing black gown with a barbe, pleated above the chin, a wimple, falling nun-like over her shoulders, and a gold ducal coronet above the wimple. She was escorted by her son, Bishop of Lincoln, and Robert Braybrooke, Bishop of London, and accompanied by her grandson the 11-year-old Henry of Monmouth representing his exiled father, Henry – now Duke of Lancaster.

After the coffin was laid in the sepulchre, Katherine went forward, kissed John's forehead and placed on his chest a gold locket and chain, a long-ago present she had given him as an expression of her enduring love.

Twenty-five large candles were lit and grouped around the coffin: ten for the Ten Commandments; five for the Five Wounds of Christ, and three for the Holy Trinity.

Three days after the burial of John of Gaunt, King Richard banished his son Henry for life and ordered the seizure of the whole Lancastrian inheritance.

Chapter Thirteen

A DAY LATER, JOHN of Gaunt's son Henry, now Duke of Lancaster, was sitting reading some Duchy papers at the Hotel de Clisson in Paris when Sir Thomas Swynford burst into the room.

"Apologies, my Lord!" he said, somewhat breathlessly, "but a Lancaster herald has just arrived post haste from London with urgent despatches for you."

Henry frowned, picking up the tension in Swynford's manner, and then said: "Well, show him in."

Sir Giles Roper entered, bringing a distinct whiff of sweat and horseflesh into the room.

"My Lord," he said, as he bowed, and then moving forward, continued: "I was charged yesterday by Sir Richard Sturry to bring these urgent messages to you," as he held out a satchel bearing the Lancaster coat of arms and the red rose emblem.

As Henry took the satchel he looked directly at the knight and said: "Yesterday? Then you must have had a quick crossing of the Channel and have ridden all night to get here!"

"Those were my orders, my Lord," replied Sir Giles.

Henry smiled: "You have done well; thank you!" And then turning to Thomas Swynford, he added, "See that Sir Giles is well accommodated while I see what all this means."

When Swynford returned, Duke Henry was standing staring out of a window, clutching the despatch from Sturry in his hand. Swynford hesitated. Then Henry turned, thrust the papers towards him, his face drawn, his blue eyes flashing like steel, and said: "SO! My father was right! This is Richard's revenge – the devious, vengeful, twisted, self-promoting liar! He has banished me for life and seized the Lancastrian inheritance – lock, stock and barrel!" as he strode round the room in anger. "We will see about that!"

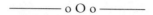

Over the following days, Henry had meetings with his supporters including fifteen Lancastrian retainers who had followed him into exile and, later, with two other exiles who, on hearing the news, joined him from Germany – the Arundels, Thomas the ex-Archbishop and his nephew, the Earl of Arundel. As Henry's initial anger cooled, his intent to reclaim his inheritance hardened. But, when and where to return to England and then, how to get Richard's agreement were key issues, as were questions of what support and what opposition to his cause would there be?

To his surprise, King Richard himself helped to resolve some of these issues. First he angered his father-in-law, King Charles of France, by making a separate agreement with the Pope in Rome over the appointment of bishops, when Charles had been working to resolve the papal schism. Secondly, Richard summarily dismissed Lady Courcy, his wife's governess, and some of her staff, for alleged extravagance and indiscretion, without consulting Isabel, his Queen. Thus, Richard's own actions made it unlikely that King Charles would intervene to stop Henry from returning to England.

Then, in May 1399 Richard decided to lead an army to Ireland to reinforce his rule and settle issues of obedience to the Crown.

While Richard's absence offered a golden opportunity to strike, Henry still had to decide where would make the best landing place. The south coast was nearer. There were pockets of Lancastrian holdings, including a castle at Pevensey, and likely support from the Arundels. But the north was a traditional stronghold of Lancastrian influence, including across Yorkshire with castles at Pickering, Knaresborough and Pontefract.

Keeping his options open, he arranged for secret contact to be made with supporters in both areas and for negotiations with ships' masters.

There remained the crucial issue of purpose. He was clear that he wanted to reclaim his rightful inheritance – lands, manors, castles and the feudal dues which went with them. But there was also the question of his role and place in society and the government of the country. His father, John of Gaunt, had been Seneschal of England and the senior figure at Court and in Parliament, after the King.

As Thomas Swynford argued, Gaunt consistently honoured his oath of allegiance to the King and his feudal duties in the interests of England as a nation. If Henry returned he could surely claim and fulfil that role. He decided that that should be his objective. He certainly did not want to divide the nation in a bloody civil war. He sincerely believed he could help Richard in the government of the country. So he must try to persuade Richard to that end – if only he could lift the veil of divine right!

Henry, the exiled Duke of Lancaster, began his return to England at the end of June 1399. He had assembled an armed force of sixty experienced fighting men from among his retainers and other supporters and had made secret arrangements with ships' masters to carry them to England from French ports – Boulogne and Dunkirk. Two ships left Boulogne on the evening tide of 23rd June, carrying a small force led by John Pelham, one of his retainers. Their mission was to act as a decoy and land on the south coast near Hastings. Then they were to secure the Duchy castle at Pevensey, which they did the next morning. The ruse worked, for the Duke of York, the Keeper of England in the absence of Richard in Ireland, ordered sheriffs in the south of England to muster forces to repel an invasion.

The same day, 24th June, Henry's main force left on the morning tide from Boulogne and Dunkirk, bound northwards, keeping close to the coasts of France and Flanders so as to be out of sight from the English shore. There was a rolling sea whipped up by a brisk south-westerly wind. They made good time as they sailed up the coastline alongside the North Sea.

Duke Henry joined the ship's master, Aubrey Percival, at the wheel.

"Good morning again, Captain!" he called. "Do you think we got away without much notice?" he asked, his words almost being snatched away by the wind.

"Arrgh!" grunted Percival. And then, taking a well-worn clay pipe from his mouth, he grinned broadly, showing the gaps in his brown-stained teeth and added: "I've never yet left a port without someone noticing! But there was no stir and, as I had put it about that we were bound for Antwerp, and I see no followers, I reckon we are cleanly away!"

"Splendid! Well done and thank you!" said the Duke with a smile. "And we have a fair wind behind us, although some of my men are not comfortable with it!"

"Ay! Landlubbers!" cackled the Captain. "But I expect this south-westerly will ease after midday and turn a degree or two to the south, which will help us as we bear away from the coast and out into the North Sea."

Duke Henry nodded and then asked: "Do you still expect it will take three days' sailing to reach the North Yorkshire coast?"

"Yes! That's a fair reckoning. No need to change my mind as yet! But old Neptune may have a trick up his sleeve! We'll know better when we get abaft the Humber and that will be tomorrow eventide."

Sure enough, at five o'clock in the evening the next day, the small fleet were sailing some way out to sea off Withernsea just north of the Humber Estuary, backed by a steady south-by-east wind. As Henry joined the Captain again he said: "Well done, Master Percival! True to your word, here we are by the Humber! I think that calls for a toast!" as he handed the Captain a flagon of ale.

"Ah! Thank ye kindly, my Lord!" he said as he raised it towards the Duke and supped down a long draught. Then, wiping his hand across his mouth, he said: "The winds have been kindly, sir, and still are. The weather looks to stay fair. So we should have a smooth passage round the shoulder of Yorkshire."

"Are you are still intending to land at Ravenscar?" asked the Duke.

"Yes!" Percival replied. "That's what we agreed, since you said it would well suit your purpose in getting to Pickering. But we must see what the morning brings. Sometimes as the tide turns in the early morning, the breeze picks up and you get a choppy sea and, since there's not much of a jetty at Ravenscar, your men might get an early morning bath!"

Next morning as the sun rose, the wind having dropped, the sea was calm and the coast was shrouded in the mist of a sea fret. The Captain edged his ships closer to the shore and the outline of Robin Hood's Bay came into view.

He turned to Duke Henry with a glint in his eye: "This suits us well, my Lord. The tide is running in with a fairly flat sea and, with this mist, we can get in practically unseen!"

"Splendid!" replied Henry.

"I will lead the way," said Percival. "That will help the other ships' captains, since not all have been in these waters before. And," turning towards the Duke with a broad smile, he said, "we will be done by midday!"

The Duke put his hand on the Captain's shoulder and replied with a smile: "I congratulate you, Aubrey! A job well done!… But mine is just about to begin!"

As Duke Henry swung his legs over the side of the ship and jumped down to the quayside at Ravenscar, he saw the Constable of Pickering Castle, Sir Geoffrey Fanthorpe, coming towards him, smiling broadly.

"My Lord! Welcome! It *is* a relief and a joy to see you! God's blessing on you!" as he bowed and held out his hand.

"Likewise!" replied Henry. "We've had a fair passage but I'm glad to have dry land under me – and Yorkshire soil, too!"

"I've brought some horses with me but, as your message said, not enough for all your men, so as not to attract too much attention, although the folk here knew your father, God rest his soul, and are fiercely loyal. I've some foresters with me too, under our head gamekeeper, John Plant, who is over there with Sir Thomas Swynford. They know the moors and woodlands like the backs of their hands. They'll guide your men across to Pickering and should be at the castle well before sundown."

"Thank you, Geoffrey, your plans are well made!" said Henry.

And then, as he mounted his horse and waved to Swynford and Grant, he cried: "Let us be on our way then – to Pickering!"

Henry only stayed two nights at Pickering before moving on with his band of retainers to other Duchy castles: first at Knaresborough and then to the great stronghold at Pontefract. He had been pleased by the warmth of his reception at the castles but not surprised – after all he had chosen this route for his return into England because of the strong Lancastrian ties and tradition. The real test for his cause, he mused, would come when he moved further south and particularly when he was in territory owned by lords and courtiers who were close to King Richard.

He was interrupted by his squire. "My Lord, a herald has arrived with a message and is asking to see you. The Keeper of the Castle has sent me to ask if you wish him to receive the message on your behalf?"

"Do you know the herald?" asked the Duke.

"No, my Lord. I was not told – but I think he wore Percy livery."

"Really! Well done!" said the Duke. "Tell the Keeper I will see the herald and ask him to join me." As the squire bowed and turned to go, he added, "And ask Sir Thomas Swynford to join me too."

"Well, well!" he said out loud to himself after the squire had left. "Is this a breakthrough?"

And indeed it was. The message was from the Duke of Northumberland asking if he and his son, 'Hotspur' Percy, could meet with Henry at one of their mansions, High Melton Hall, near Doncaster the next day. He passed it to the Keeper and then to Swynford before turning to the herald.

"Will you tell the Duke that I will be pleased to meet him tomorrow at… say, noon as he suggests."

"Yes, my Lord, I will," replied the herald and, bowing, he withdrew.

"This promises well, my Lord," said Swynford when the herald had withdrawn.

"They would be facing you with arms rather than parleying if they were against you."

"Exactly!" said Henry, slapping his thigh.

"Melton Hall is about fifteen miles from here, my Lord," put in the Keeper. "I suggest, if I may, that I accompany you with an armed escort. We can keep in the background but be ready should you need us."

"That is well said!" replied the Duke and, turning to Swynford, said: "And I want you to accompany me with three of the senior knights who were with us in Paris."

Next day, Henry arrived at High Melton just before midday with Swynford and the three knights wearing the Lancastrian arms. Immediately stable boys came to hold their horses and Hotspur, the Duke's son, came out smiling in welcome, bowed before Duke Henry and said: "My Lord, this is a great pleasure! Allow me to escort you inside where my father is waiting."

But as Henry and Hotspur made their way to the front door, the Duke of Northumberland, the head of the Percy dynasty, came out to greet them.

"Henry! It is good to see you back in England," he said. "Come, let us go in, there is much to talk about."

Inside the manor, as they gathered round a beautifully grained and polished oak table and having been served with goblets of wine, Northumberland, looking directly at the Duke of Lancaster, said: "Henry, we never agreed with your exile after that sham display of trial by battle… although the King was within his feudal rights. But then to exile you for life and seize your inheritance three days after your father was buried was a capricious, vengeful and sordid misuse of his regality. This threatens our own and others' feudal rights as lords and landholders. Who is to say that we will not be turned upon?

We are therefore glad you have returned, and we will support you in claiming back your inheritance."

"My Lord, you do me a great honour. I am much bolstered by your words and support," replied Henry. "My purpose is to get Richard's agreement and then to take my rightful place in the country, at Court and in Parliament."

Northumberland laughed, smacked his hands together and retorted: "Well now, *I am bolstered* by what *you* say!" And then, leaning forward in a sober tone, said quietly, "Richard, we know, is vengeful and swollen with the conceit of his divine right to rule. But he is increasingly like that Greek who fell in love with himself… Hotspur, what was his name…?" snapping his fingers.

"Oh! You mean Narcissus!" exclaimed his son with a smile.

"That's it," said the Duke and then turning to Henry, "Richard is so aware of himself that he demands attention through rituals and ceremonies where he is the centre of attention. I think he feeds off the fawning of others and so he has surrounded himself with self-seekers and has bought support through a system of bonds, oaths and rewards.

"In a way this expedition to Ireland is a good example. There is no real threat to the Crown. His presence is not essential. He could have sent March or Aumerle to settle with the unruly elements which are endemic in Ireland. But it puffs his ego to parade with his Cheshire archers."

Then he paused and said, looking directly at Lancaster: "Forgive me, my Lord. These thoughts have been pent up for want of outlets."

Duke Henry had been listening intently.

"My Lord," he said quietly, "I have been kept aware of some of this, but you have opened my eyes to other aspects. Thank you. Nonetheless, my intent is to negotiate with Richard and to follow in the tradition set by my father in loyal support of the throne and his government. What you describe makes that more difficult, but I must try. And I shall succeed better with your support and counsel!"

———— o O o ————

Chaucer was on the move again. He had been impressed by John Gower's move to Southwark and the quiet support he received from the Sisters and Fraternity of the religious foundation of the Priory of St Mary Overie. With Gower's sight beginning to fail, Chaucer knew that one or other of the sisters would often sit and read to him from a text that John was working on. And John of Gaunt's unexpected death had also shocked him into a sense of his own mortality. Gaunt, his contemporary and friend, despite their difference in rank, was gone. And so was the glue in the framework of the Plantagenet house. Fiercely loyal son to Edward III, calming brother to the Black Prince and wise counsellor to his nephew Richard II, Gaunt's influence was gone.

Geoffrey knew too that his own capacities were slowing down with a shift in the balance of his bodily humours from phlegmatic towards choleric. He was becoming irked by the regular journey he needed to make from Greenwich to the Treasury at Westminster to collect his pension and annuities. While he greatly valued his visits to his friend Gower at Southwark, these too wearied him physically. Perhaps, he had reasoned, he should take a leaf out of Gower's book? So it was that he was able to negotiate a tenancy (rent-free with the help of the King) within the precincts of Westminster Abbey! The house overlooked the garden of the Lady Chapel and provided Chaucer with just the kind of peaceful and secluded space he needed.

Clearing his house in Greenwich and choosing what to take with him and what to leave might have been beyond his capacity were it not for the good sense and help of his faithful clerk and copyist, James Glover, and his friend and boatman, John Croyser. James, who had worked with Chaucer for seven years and knew his squirrel-like ways, had a clear sense of what manuscripts must be kept and which – often unfinished or scribbled-over early drafts – could be scrapped. Books, some having been brought back from Italy, were Chaucer's most treasured possessions and James knew that they were not open for discussion! At the same time, the practical common sense of John Croyser was invaluable – both in packing up in Greenwich, loading onto the boat and in unpacking and deciding where and how to arrange things in the house at Westminster.

Geoffrey was clear in his own mind that the room looking out into the garden would provide him with the quiet peace he needed for his writing. And the adjoining room would provide a suitable social space for meeting with his friends and guests. Beyond that he was happy to be guided by his two helpers. He recalled the house at Aldgate where he, Gower and Ralph Strode (God bless his soul) had discoursed endlessly, including during the Peasants' Revolt. And he thought wistfully of how Mostly Maggie had looked after them. That reminded him that he would need to find a housekeeper. He decided that he would talk about that with the Abbot on the morrow to see if he knew of a suitable person.

He was about to bid farewell to his two helpers as they prepared to leave for the wharf to sail back to Greenwich, when he heard a familiar voice asking the way to the "Chaucer House?" Outside… there was John Gower!

"John!" he cried, going towards his friend. "What a great surprise… and pleasure!"

"I have been all knotted up with curiosity since you told me of your move and couldn't wait any longer!" beamed Gower. "But I would have been lost if Sister Mary here had not insisted on coming with me."

Geoffrey turned as a nun with round face, high cheekbones and bright blue eyes came forward towards him, smiling broadly.

"Master Chaucer!" she said, holding out her hand. "This is for me a great honour."

As Chaucer took her hand, he bowed and said "*Enchante!*" which brought a peal of laughter from Sister Mary who then said, her eyes twinkling: "But I do not have the French – not even that from 'Stratford-atte-Bowe'!"

At which Chaucer burst into laughter. "I see I am undone!" he said and then, "but, come let me show you the house."

After a brief tour of the house, Geoffrey seated them in his new parlour and, having found a bottle of red wine, together they raised their goblets to him in his new house.

"May the Lord's blessing be upon you… and your writings!" said Sister Mary.

"Thank you," said Geoffrey, smiling and looking quizzically at Sister Mary.

"As you have guessed, Geoffrey," said Gower, "Sister Mary has been reading the copy you gave me of your pilgrims gathering to go to Canterbury."

"Yes," put in Mary, "and it is such a pleasure and refreshing to be able to read in our own language, English rather than Latin!"

"Amen to that," added Gower, smiling. And turning to the Sister, "He's even converted me to writing in English!"

"But," continued Sister Mary, "while I smiled much at your description of Madam Eglantyne, the Nun Prioress, I did feel she was over-refined, or, as you put it, '*straining to counterfeit a courtly grace*'.

Chaucer laughed and slapped his thigh. "You see, John," he said, "I knew I was found out!" And then more soberly, turning to Sister Mary, said: "You are right; but then nearly all my pilgrims are larger than life caricatures."

"Well, thank you, Geoffrey," said Gower rising. "The day is dying and we must be on our way!"

As they moved out of the house, Gower said quietly to Geoffrey: "What do you make of this news of Gaunt's son Henry coming back from exile?"

Chaucer looked over at Sister Mary and said quietly: "I hope it will be for the good. I will visit you soon and we can discuss it more fully then."

"Yes, of course," smiled Gower. "And make it soon, my friend – before you become too comfortable here in this house and garden!"

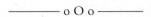

On 19th July 1399, three days after their meeting at High Melton Hall, the Dukes of Lancaster and Northumberland learned that Richard had sent the Earl of Salisbury to North Wales to rally an army against them and to secure his citadel at Chester. To counter this, the Dukes decided to move south, initially to Coventry. The Duke of Lancaster, since his landing at Ravenscar and journey south to Pontefract, had been joined by several bands of eager supporters so that, with Northumberland's men, they were able to muster a force of over 1,000 armed men. On their way south they received further intelligence that the Duke of York, as Keeper, had ordered the muster of forces around Gloucester and Bristol in support of the King. On 27th July, Lancaster caught up with York at the village of Berkeley.

Henry, arm aloft, signalled to his troops to stand off as he rode slowly forward together with Northumberland. York responded similarly and, while their forces stood facing each other, they exchanged greetings.

"My Lord of York!" cried Lancaster. "We are well met! For I bear neither you nor King Richard any ill will."

His uncle smiled briefly. "I too am pleased, Henry, by our meeting. Rather this way than by force of arms. Let us repair to the parish church over there where we can talk more easily."

Once inside the well-kept late Norman church, with its lingering smell of incense, Henry went over to his uncle and embraced him.

"My Lord, it is a great relief to see you. It would grieve me sorely if we had to lead our men into combat against each other."

York smiled and said quietly, "I think that unlikely. The men I have mustered have no stomach for a fight. Over half of those I recruited have already left and most of the rest would follow, I warrant." And then after a pause, looking directly at Henry, he asked: "But what are your plans?"

"We intend to move up to Chester and secure it since that is Richard's citadel. Then we will seek a meeting with Richard to negotiate an acceptance of my return and my place in the governance of our country."

"You are not intent then on taking the throne from Richard for yourself?" asked York.

"No. As you know, my father, John of Gaunt, taught me the meaning of fealty – as much by his actions as his words. He truly strove to honour his sworn bond, not only to Richard but also to his father, Edward III, and his brother, the Black Prince. It is my wish and intent similarly to help Richard in governing the country."

His uncle's drawn face relaxed. He smiled and said, "I am relieved to hear it and you can count on my support." Then he paused and added: "It will be difficult, Henry. Richard sees advice as criticism and accepting help as acknowledgement of his own weakness."

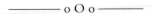

After his meeting with his uncle, Henry headed northwards to Chester, via Hereford and Ludlow. He reached Shrewsbury on 5th August where he was asked to receive a delegation led by Sir Robert Leigh, the Sheriff of Chester. Intrigued, Henry received the Sheriff and his colleagues in the town hall.

Sir Robert bowed to Duke Henry and said: "My Lord, the burghers and Council of Chester are proud of our city, with its fine buildings and history dating back to Roman times. We do not want to see it sacked in battle between you and King Richard. Mindful of this, I am deputed to offer you entry and possession of the city so that it will not be despoiled and to seek your assurance and protection."

Duke Henry bowed before the Sheriff and said: "Sir Robert, you and your colleagues have nothing to fear from me. I gladly accept your offer and give my pledge to protect and honour the city."

Four days later, on 9th August 1399, Henry and his close colleagues made a ceremonial entry into Chester to the acclamation of the citizens. Thus, the inner citadel of Richard's kingdom fell to Henry without a fight. This would prove to be a fateful omen for Richard.

King Richard had landed in North Wales towards the end of July. He then made his way northwards up the coast to link up with Salisbury at Conway, arriving there late on the 8th August. As he rode into the castle yard, ever sensitive, he felt an atmosphere of gloom. He had already been hurt by the lukewarm support he had received on landing and on his journey north. What now? he wondered.

As he dismounted, he saw the Earl of Salisbury come out from an inner door and hurry towards him.

"Your Majesty!" he cried, bowing deeply before Richard and then kissing his hand before standing in front of him. "My Lord," he said, "I am so pleased and relieved to see you."

Richard squinted his eyes a moment and then said, "Relieved?! That sounds portentous… but let us go in where we can talk."

Richard was accompanied into the large drawing room of the castle by his senior courtiers: the Dukes of Exeter and Surrey, the Earl of Gloucester and the Bishops of Carlisle, Lincoln and St David's.

The Earl of Salisbury began: "Your Majesty! I regret that I have not been able to muster the forces we expected. Even royal tenants have found excuses, like getting the harvest in, or have left after a day or two, and numbers have dwindled."

"They will not be so fickle when they lose their land!" snapped the King.

"But there is more, Your Majesty," said the Duke of Exeter. "Yesterday we received intelligence that the Duke of York had met with Lancaster near Bristol, made terms with him and pledged him his support."

"The traitor!" burst out Richard, pacing round the room. "The true royal blood flows from my father, the Black Prince, in my veins, not in this weakling… nor in this traitorous son of Gaunt!" he shouted.

But then, seeing the faces round him, he stopped and said quietly: "Your demeanour tells me there is more?"

"Yes, Your Majesty," said Salisbury. "A herald arrived this morning with the worst news: Lancaster has taken Chester!"

Richard stumbled backwards, visibly shaken, and covered his face with his hands as tears ran down his cheeks.

After a while, the Earl of Salisbury suggested that they should sit down and discuss what now should be done and how best to support the King. The Duke of Exeter took the lead. "Your Majesty," he began, "We do not yet know precisely what Lancaster wants, except, we hear, to return and reclaim his inheritance. But if you grant him that, is that all? Will he not want a finger in the pie of government?"

"Without any doubt!" broke in the Bishop of Carlisle. "Like father, like son: the young Lancaster is a chip off the Gaunt block. He would find ways to direct you not only in government but in taxation and finance, including the spending of the Royal Household."

King Richard looked up with a mournful face and said tersely: "My privy purse is not up for discussion."

"Of course, that is so, Your Majesty," continued Exeter. "But I say again, do we not need to know exactly and fully what Lancaster wants? What are his hopes and intentions?" And after a pause, as he tried to read Richard's face, "Your Majesty, I humbly suggest that you appoint a delegation to meet with Lancaster to find out his true intention."

Richard made no reply until it became clear from further discussion that this view had the general support of those round the table. Then he stood up, still looking drawn and mournful, and said: "So be it. Exeter, you go to meet Lancaster… and take your nephew Surrey with you."

But before Exeter had made his preparations to leave, a herald arrived at the castle with a request that the King receive the Duke of Northumberland as a spokesman for Lancaster.

The King was sitting in a high-backed chair, wearing a coronet, when the Duke of Northumberland entered. He bowed before Richard and said: "Your Majesty. I come with goodwill greetings from the Duke of Lancaster and to express his earnest wish to achieve a peaceful settlement with you. To achieve this he asks that his inheritance be restored to him; that Parliament, over which he would preside as hereditary seneschal, is summoned; and that those counsellors found to have carried out treasonous acts be put on trial."

King Richard had sat pale-faced and still while he listened to Northumberland.

He paused and then nodded and said: "I will need time to consider this… but…" He paused again and then said: "Do you swear on the Host that Lancaster intends no deceit and that the royal powers and dominion will remain vested in me?"

Northumberland bowed to the King and said: "I hereby so swear that the Duke intends no deceit."

Richard spent the next two days considering his position. He was depressed. Crewe was lost. His army and followers had dispersed. Supplies were short. Lancaster had attracted support from the outset after his landing in Yorkshire. Privately he raged to his friends: "I swear that Northumberland will be put to a bitter death for this outrage… Doubt not, there will be no Parliament on this… I will muster men from all over Wales."

But despite his vengeful rantings, he knew he had no alternative but to accept Lancaster's terms.

As soon as Lancaster knew that Richard had accepted his terms, he summoned a Parliament to assemble at Westminster at the end of September. Then, having met with Richard at Chester, together they began the journey to London. Henry was beginning to doubt that his offer to work with Richard in the governance of the country was feasible. Shorn of his supporters, Richard was a depressed and moody figure and Henry sensed a deep underlying resentment.

Lancaster called for Thomas Swynford to join him.

"Thomas," he said. "I am having doubts about working with Richard. I don't trust him."

"I have wondered similarly, my Lord… and so has Northumberland," said Swynford.

Henry nodded. "I want you to ride ahead to London. Go to the Bishop of London and ask him to convene a group of lawyers, doctors, learned monks and bishops to research the governance of

England and precedents for setting aside King Richard and choosing me in his place."

"Yes, my Lord," replied Swynford. "I will leave as soon my horse is saddled."

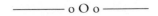

"Well, Geoffrey! Westminster must have been buzzing round your ears this last fortnight!" said Gower with a broad smile.

Chaucer laughed. "Yes, my friend," he replied. "I have come to the tranquillity of your corner of Southwark, for a rest… and to sup your good ale!"

"Well, there is plenty of that! But tell me," said Gower, "did you get any sense of opposition in Parliament to Richard's dethronement?"

"Not really. I heard that Thomas Merks, the Bishop of Carlisle, tried to say that Richard should not be condemned unheard, but he was ignored and there was general agreement to that and to his replacement by Lancaster," replied Chaucer.

"And the coronation yesterday of Lancaster as King Henry the Fourth was a relatively quiet affair without any of the rituals and flamboyance that Richard loved."

As Gower leaned over and refilled their tankards he sighed and said: "Well, Geoffrey, this is all a blessed relief. Richard's direction of government was becoming more and more dictatorial and unreliable, and the fawning fools he had round him could neither see it nor do anything about it. And for Lancaster to have achieved this without any real opposition or bloodshed… well… it is a miracle!"

"Yes," said Chaucer. "Henry has started well in Gaunt's style by sparing the sword. But he will need to watch the likes of Salisbury, Gloucester, Exeter, Aumerle and March who resent his claiming the throne through the male line."

"Yes," agreed Gower, "and isn't there a potential for Richard to be a source of treachery?"

"There is, of course," replied Geoffrey. "And on that score, I hear privately that there are plans to move him to Pontefract."

"Oh?" exclaimed Gower. "You've been there, haven't you? Is it secure enough?"

"Yes. I spent two, I may say, 'uncomfortable' nights there!" said Geoffrey, remembering with a rueful smile. "I would say it is probably the most impregnable of the great Lancastrian strongholds... and just the place to keep Richard... and..." he added with a smile: "to keep mischief away from Richard!

"But enough of that," he added brightly. "I have brought a tale for you to share with Sister Mary! You remember that each of my pilgrims will tell a tale to keep the company amused on their journey. I hope this might interest the Sister for it is the tale told by the Nun's Priest."

"Oh Geoffrey! How apt!" said John. "We will enjoy it together, I am sure. Thank you!"

"I shall look forward to hearing your comments," said Geoffrey, "for the tale is in the form of a fable. A proud cockerel called Chanticleer is tricked and caught by a cunning fox but escapes by serving a trick on the fox to the delight of his favourite hen and wife, Pertelote!"

Gower laughed. "I shall be intrigued to know what Sister Mary will make of that!"

"And so will I, my friend!" said Chaucer. "For she might expect a more pious tale!" And then, standing up, he said, "But thank you, I must be away, John. I will see you presently."

In fact, Geoffrey was not able to see his friend again until near Christmas time. The weather had turned against him, first with heavy fog and then rain which turned to snow and frost as cold air swept in. In some places the banks of the Thames had frozen up, stopping much of the river traffic.

Fortunately John's rooms were warm and cosy with a roaring log fire. But, mindful also of the need to warm the inner man, Gower had served up some fine whisky!

"God's blessing on you, Geoffrey!" he called as he raised his drink.

"And on you, my friend," replied Geoffrey before raising his glass, sniffing in the fumes of the fiery liquid and taking a draught.

"Ah!" he exclaimed. "That, John… is most welcome!"

As they settled into their chairs before the fire Gower said: "Sister Mary was much amused by your Nun's Priest's tale and I expect will join us later. But, for now, have I heard correctly that Richard has been taken to Pontefract Castle, as you forecast?"

"Oh yes!" replied Chaucer. "That was some six weeks ago. And I fancy, from what I hear, that he is liking it even less than when I stayed there – although I hasten to assure you – I was a proper guest, not locked in a dungeon cell!"

They both laughed, and Gower added, "And so I should hope – a senior and distinguished government servant!"

As Chaucer looked into the fire, the smile left his face. "Richard is alone. The guards have strict orders not to engage with him," he said. "This is a fiercely proud man who enjoyed being the centre of attention and fed off the dutiful and admiring reactions of those round him. Solitary confinement must be destroying him!"

"You paint a bleak picture," responded Gower. "Can he survive this, do you think?"

"I don't know," replied Chaucer. "He has a fierce will. The answer will lie in whether that can override his languor. At the moment, I gather, he is very despondent and barely eating."

But Richard continued in this condition, refusing the poor food put in his cell and starving until his death in mid-February. After a requiem mass at St Paul's attended by King Henry, the nobility and London citizens, he was buried at the Dominican Friary at King's Langley.

Chapter Fourteen

GEOFFREY CHAUCER WAS in his study reviewing some writings he had done the previous day when his young housekeeper, Rupert Draper, a novice appointed by the Abbot to help him, knocked on the door and came into the room.

"Master Geoffrey, sir," he said. "There is a messenger from Court asking to see you."

Chaucer looked up in surprise. It was rare for anyone from the Palace to come seeking him. "Well, thank you, Rupert. I will come and see what it is about."

Outside, a young squire wearing the Lancastrian insignia was waiting. He bowed to Geoffrey and said: "Master Chaucer, God's blessing on you, sire! I bring greetings from her Ladyship, Katherine, Dowager Duchess of Lancaster. She commands me to say that she has a personal matter that she would like to discuss with you. I am to enquire whether it would be convenient for her to come to see you."

Chaucer smiled at the youngster's earnest manner. He was sure Katherine had not framed her message so formally. Chaucer bowed in response and replied in kind.

"Please tell her Grace, the Duchess, that, as it is her wish to come here, I will be honoured to receive her at her convenience and I will await her arrival with joyous expectation!"

Katherine arrived next morning, travelling in a small gig escorted by two Lancaster retainers. As soon as he heard them arriving, Chaucer hurried out to greet her.

Although still dressed in black she no longer wore the customary widow's wimple and veil.

"Katherine, my dearest!" he exclaimed, going forward to meet and embrace her. "This is such a pleasure and more so for being unexpected!"

Katherine responded with a laugh and broad smile, her grey eyes twinkling.

"Geoffrey, dearest brother!" she cried. "It has been too long."

"Well, come inside," he said. "I am all agog for your news!"

Once settled comfortably in Chaucer's drawing room and with no need for polite talk between them, Katherine explained her visit.

"Geoffrey," she began in a serious manner. "I am sure you know that, Richard having died, Isabel, his young Queen, has to be returned to France into the care of her father, King Charles."

"Yes, I assumed that would be so," said Geoffrey.

"As you know," continued Katherine, "since she first came to England I have tried to support the young Queen and we get on well together."

Geoffrey smiled and said: "You are too modest, my dear! She dotes on you as a mother figure."

"Well, be that as it may," said Katherine. "King Henry wishes me to travel with her to Dover… and…" looking directly at Chaucer, she said, "Geoffrey, Isabel loves you too! Will you come with us to Dover?"

"Ho! Ho!" cried Geoffrey. "Me, a squire to two royal ladies! What an honour!" And then seeing Katherine's anxious face, he leaned forward, took her hand and said: "Of course, my dear! I am greatly honoured… but she will want more tales on the journey so I shall have to think of something suitable to amuse her!"

Geoffrey had many times, on royal business, travelled the road to and from Dover – but only on horseback and often alone. Now he was travelling in a royal carriage pulled by four matching black horses with an escort of six royal Lancastrian knights, followed by three further carriages carrying court attendants, baggage and stores. Along the way, in villages and at crossroads, the locals stopped to stare and wonder or wave a greeting when they recognised the royal insignia.

After they had settled to the rhythm of the horses' hooves and the swaying of the coach, Queen Isabel, who was sitting beside Lady Katherine and had not seen Chaucer for nearly twelve months, leaned towards him and said: "Master Geoffrey. Isn't this the way your pilgrims travelled to Canterbury?"

Chaucer smiled and nodded.

"Oh!" exclaimed Isabel, "this makes your tales so real." And then, looking at him with a feminine archness, she said, "I hope you have another tale or two to tell me on the way?"

Chaucer smiled, put his hand to the side of his nose and winked, which made Isabel giggle. "Ah, Your Majesty, how could I have known your wishes! Except that a little bird whispered it to me last evening!" looking sideways at Katherine with a smile. "Yes, indeed, I do have a tale to tell you. This one was told to the rest of the pilgrims by the Nun's Priest as they made their way along this road to Canterbury."

"Oohh! Let me hear it," said Isabel. She curled herself into her seat and snuggled against Katherine as Chaucer began to tell the tale:

> *"Once, long ago, there dwelt a poor old widow*
> *In a small cottage by a little meadow.*
> *Since the sad day when she was last a wife*
> *She had led a very patient single life.*
> *She had a yard, enclosed about*
> *In which she kept a cock called Chanticleer.*
>
> *"His voice was jollier than the organ blowing*
> *In Church on Sundays: he was great at crowing.*
> *His comb was redder than fine coral*
> *And battlemented like a castle wall*
> *His bill was black and shone as bright as jet*
> *Like azure were his legs and they were set*
> *On azure toes with nails of lily white*
> *Like burnished gold his feathers, flaming bright.*
>
> *"This gentle cock was master in some measure*
> *Of seven hens, all there to do his pleasure.*
> *She with the loveliest dyes upon her throat*

Was known as Lady Pertelote.
She held the heart of Chanticleer.

"But there was also a coal-tipped fox of sly iniquity
Who that very night burst quickly
Into the yard where Chanticleer
Was wont with his ladies to repair.
Still in a bed of cabbages he lay
Until the middle of the day
Watching the cock and waiting for his cue.

"As Chanticleer happened to cast his eye
Towards the cabbage at a butterfly
He saw the fox lying low…"

"Oh!" gasped Queen Isabel, who had been listening intently and holding her hand to her mouth. "I hope Chanticleer flew away!" she cried.

Chaucer smiled and said: "Well, he was about to. But the fox was very cunning. He called to the cock in a sweet voice:

"'Dear Sir. Truly I came to do no other thing
Than just to lie and listen to you sing.
You have as merry a voice as God has given
To any angel in the courts of Heaven.'

"At this Chanticleer began to beat a wing
As one incapable of smelling treason
So wholly had this flattery ravished reason
He stood high upon his toes
He stretched his neck, his eyes began to close
His beak to open; with his eyes shut tight
He began to sing with all his might."

"Oooh!" cried Isabel, reaching out to hold Katherine's hand. "Why doesn't he fly away?"

And just as she feared:

> *"Sir Russell Fox leapt in to the attack*
> *Grabbing his gorge he flung him over his back*
> *And bore him to the woods, the brute…*
> *And for the moment there was no pursuit."*

"Ooohh!" cried Isabel again. "Is there nobody who can save him?"

"Well, maybe so," said Chaucer with a twinkle in his eye. "But not perhaps as we think…

> *"The blessed widow and her daughters too*
> *Heard all these hens in clamour and halloo*
> *And rushing to the door at all this shrieking*
> *Saw the fox towards the covert streaking,*
> *And on his shoulder, Chanticleer stretched flat*
> *'Look look' they cried 'Oh mercy, look at that!'*

> *"'Ha! Ha! the fox!' and after him they ran*
> *And stick in hand ran many a serving man,*
> *Ran cow and calf and ran the very hogs*
> *In the terror of the barking dogs.*
> *Up flew the geese over the trees,*
> *Out of the hive came forth a swarm of bees."*

"But surely," exclaimed Isabel. "How could cows and pigs and bees and geese do anything to save poor Chanticleer?"

"No, not on their own," said Chaucer. Then looking seriously at Isabel, he said softly, "Maybe, the stir they made was heard in heaven…?

> *"See how Dame Fortune quickly changes side*
> *And robs her enemy of hope and pride!*

> *"This cock that lay upon the fox's back*
> *In all his dread contrived to give a quack*
> *And said 'Sir Fox, if I were you as God's*
> *My witness, I would round upon these clods*
> *And shout: "Turn back you saucy bumpkins all.*
> *Now that I have in safety reached the wood*
> *Do what you like, the cock is mine for good."'*

> *"The fox replying, 'Faith it shall be done!'*
> *As he opened his mouth and spoke, the nimble bird*
> *Breaking away upon the uttered word*
> *Flew high into the tree-tops…"*

Isabel clapped her hands! "Oh! Master Geoffrey, that was a good tale. He was saved! Thank you!"

"Well," smiled Geoffrey, looking at Katherine, "as you might expect, since this tale was told by a priest, it had a moral:

> *"Lo, such it is not to be on your guard*
> *Against the flatterers of the world or yard*
> *And if you think my story is absurd…*
> *A foolish trifle of a beast and bird*
> *A fable of a fox, a cock, a hen,*
> *Take hold… upon the moral, gentle men."*

On arrival at Dover, Katherine and Chaucer had little more time with Isabel for a group of senior courtiers from France awaited the young Queen's arrival. Katherine was fulsomely honoured as the Dower Duchess of Lancaster and stepmother to Henry, King of England. Amidst all the greetings and bustle of unloading and loading, Chaucer stood watching and smiling indulgently.

Before they had left their coach, he had given Isabel a full copy of the tale of Chanticleer, Pertelote and the Fox. She had thanked him and given him a simple silver cross, kissed and hugged him and told him he was her favourite Englishman.

Now, as Katherine and Chaucer stood on the quayside waving, the French frigate, sails filling, pulled away, taking Isabel back to France.

Back in their carriage on their return journey to London, Katherine wiped away some tears. "Oh Geoffrey," she said, "I so feel for the poor dear girl. She is just a piece on her father's royal chessboard. She will be used, again, to seal an alliance with an ally of France."

"Yes, that is the way of things," said Chaucer. "But maybe it will turn out to be a love match as has happened between Philippa and King John of Portugal."

Katherine smiled. "Dear Geoffrey. You ever were the optimist! Let us hope for her sake that that will be so!"

On a pleasantly warm day in September 1400, Chaucer walked over to Southwark to see John Gower. The two friends had not met for over a month and, as usual, had plenty to talk about. Settling Chaucer down outside in a comfortable chair with a pot of ale, Gower was keen to know about the journey to Dover and particularly how was the young Queen, Isabel.

Chaucer's eyes twinkled. "Oh, she is a joy to be with," said Chaucer. "Full of life, with a mischievous sense of humour. On the way I told her the tale of Chanticleer and the Fox. She really lived the cock's plight when he was captured and was jumping with joy when he escaped!"

"Wonderful!" said Gower. "But what happens to her now, do you think?"

"You do well to ask," replied Chaucer. "Katherine expressed her own concern that King Charles would marry her off again to secure an alliance with France – such is the way of things. But I think she is already showing enough spirit, womanly pride and – I sense, guile – to manage her future."

"Amen to that," said Gower soberly. "Women are so often nothing but pawns in male hands… especially royal and aristocratic ones. Look at Sister Mary. There is a fine, intelligent, gentle, caring woman born of a noble family. Yet, as a younger sister, she was put in a nunnery so that her family could avoid paying her dowry were she to marry." He sighed and looking straightly at his friend, said quietly: "But, how are you, Geoffrey? You seem somewhat burdened."

Chaucer smiled a little wanly. "I have realised, John, that I will not be able to complete my *Canterbury Tales* as I had intended."

"But why is that, my friend?" asked John.

"My intent was that each of the pilgrims should tell two tales on the outward journey to Canterbury and two on the way back to London – that would be over one hundred tales in all! As I came to complete the first set, with 'The Parson's Tale', I realised that the original intention was too much. So the *Tales* will now end with what the Parson tells his fellow travellers… and that is not about courtly love, or knightly daring, or roistering tavern tales, but a monologue in prose on the Seven Deadly Sins."

"Ooh!" exclaimed Gower. "Doesn't that sit somewhat oddly with the other tales?"

Chaucer looked at his friend and nodded soberly. "Yes," he said. "It does… because, on reflection, it seems that some of the tales are too bawdy or immoral and that is what is weighing me down." Then with a smile, he raised his tankard and said: "But your good ale will, I am sure, restore my humour!"

"Let us drink to that!" said Gower, raising his own tankard. "But," continued Gower, "if you will take the word of your old friend, I see your band of pilgrims as an artful portrait of our society: high and low, young and old, male and female, lay and clerical, learned and ignorant, rogue and righteous. And so, of course, the tales they tell from their experience or imagination range from the rude and crude to the refined and sublime. Leave them be, my friend, is my advice. They provide a rich tapestry of our times."

But at home over the next week, Chaucer still wrestled with his problem. Despite Gower's warm words, he was still troubled with the thought that some of his writings could be ranked as lewd and immoral. Since the death of John of Gaunt, who was the same age, he had begun to think about his own mortality and legacy. He had also been rereading his translation of Boethius' *Consolation of Philosophy* – a man, imprisoned and eventually executed after years of loyal service to his emperor, who spent his time in gaol analysing the meaning of life and death and divinity. Chaucer, in thinking about his own position was continually impressed by the clarity of Boethian thinking:

> *Happiness is the natural state of humanity, but (when) man pursues it in some other guise – fame or wealth – ultimately cannot acquire it.*
>
> *If we are in touch with the soul side of our personality, we may not commit evil...*
>
> *Human souls are of necessity more free when they continue in the contemplation of God...*
>
> *Man's freedom of will remains inviolate and God embraces any changes in its constancy... as a spectator from on high His vision dispenses reward to the good and punishment to the bad... Avoid vice, therefore, and cultivate virtue.*
>
> *A great necessity is laid upon you, if you will be honest with yourself, to be good since you live in the sight of a judge who sees all things.*

Having mused over his thoughts and readings, Geoffrey Chaucer decided to resolve his misgivings by adding a postscript to his *Canterbury Tales*.

CHAUCER'S RETRACTIONS
The maker of this Book here takes his leave.

Now I beg all those that listen to this little treatise or read it, if there be anything in it that pleases them, they thank Our Lord Jesus Christ for it.

And if there be anything that displeases them, I beg them also to impute it to the fault of my want of ability and not to my will... For our Book says: 'All that is written is written for our doctrine'... and that is my intention.

Wherefore I beseech you meekly... to pray for me, that Christ have mercy on me and forgive my sins: and especially for my translations and editings of worldly vanities, which I revoke in my retractions, as are:

The Book of Troilus
The Book of Fame
The Book of the Nineteen Ladies
The Book of the Duchess
The Book of St Valentine's Day of the Parliament of Fowls
The Tales of Canterbury – those that tend towards sin
The Book of the Lion...

And many other books, if they were in my memory; and many a song and many a lecherous lay... that Christ in his great mercy forgive me the sin.

But the translation of Boethius, *De Consolatione*, and other books of saints' legends, of homilies, morality and devotion, for them I thank Our Lord Jesus Christ and His blissful Mother and all the Saints of heaven.

So that I may be one of those that at the Day of Judgement shall be saved.

Two days later, early on the morning of 25th October 1400, Rupert Draper, the novice appointed by the Dean to help as Chaucer's houseboy, walked from Westminster Abbey across the garden of the Lady Chapel towards Chaucer's house. Entering by the back door into the kitchen, he called: "Master Geoffrey! It is Rupert! God's blessing on you this fine morning!"

He tidied some platters that he would need for serving breakfast. Then, having had no response from Chaucer, called again. "Master Geoffrey, sir!"

Still hearing no answer, he frowned and climbed the stair to the bedroom where Chaucer slept. He knocked on the door, entered hesitantly and saw Chaucer lying still on the bed, his right arm flung out to one side, his eyes open and staring upwards. Rupert gasped and put his hand to his mouth. "Ooohh!" he cried and then rushed downstairs and out of the house to find one of the monks.

On the opposite side of the garden he saw Father Jacob talking with a colleague. He rushed towards them and blurted out: "Oh Father! Help me please. I cannot raise Master Chaucer from his bed. I do fear that," he paused and then said, "he looks oddly…"

Father Jacob laid a calming hand on the boy's arm and turned to his colleague, Father James: "Would you go with the boy to find the apothecary or hospitaller? I will go to see if I can rouse Master Geoffrey."

Later, the hospitaller confirmed what they all feared: Geoffrey Chaucer was dead.

At noon, the monks assembled in the Abbey before the altar where the Abbot waited to address them.

"Brethren," he called. "We come together to pray for the soul of our dearly beloved friend and resident, Geoffrey Chaucer."

As he held his hands in front of him, the gathering of monks bowed their heads, clasped their hands likewise and joined him in prayer.

"Christ Our Lord and Saviour, we beseech you to receive the soul of our brother, Geoffrey Chaucer, and to convey him to our Almighty Father. And we pray that, purged of his sins, he will be received with God's bountiful mercy into heaven. Amen."

Two of the monks then lit candles which were placed on the holy altar: one for the Holy Spirit, placed to the left; one for Jesus Christ, placed to the right; and in the centre one for God Almighty. Standing alone, beneath these, a fourth candle represented the supplicant Chaucer praying for his place in heaven.

By the evening, arrangements had been made for the body of Chaucer to be conveyed into the Abbey and placed beside the altar, alongside the flickering candles, where it would rest for three days before being interred in a quiet corner of the Abbey.

Just before noon on 28th October 1400, Katherine, Dowager Duchess of Lancaster, stood between John Gower and her son, Sir Thomas Swynford, with a small congregation of mourners, by the open coffin of Geoffrey Chaucer before the Abbot of Westminster and the Bishop of London.

"In the name of our Saviour, Jesus Christ," the Abbot began. "We are gathered together to inter the body of our dearly beloved friend and muse, Geoffrey Chaucer, into the ground under this quiet corner of our Abbey and to commit his soul to the mercy and glory of Almighty God in heaven."

"Amen," responded the mourners with bowed heads, as the Abbot finished by making the sign of the Cross.

Duchess Katherine moved forward to the bier, kissed the cold cheeks of her dear brother-in-law and placed on his chest the small cross of fine silver which had been given to him by Queen Isabel. Four monks then moved forward and lowered the coffin into the grave as a choir intoned the Twenty Third Psalm. The Abbot and the Bishop then led Katherine and the mourners from the Abbey to his Hall where wine and refreshments awaited them.

Katherine had been surprised by the number of people who had made their way to the Abbey for Geoffrey's funeral and further surprised to realise how few of them she recognised. She commented on this to John Gower who was standing with her.

"Yes," he said, "I had much the same thought, although I have noticed some from Geoffrey's days at Aldgate and the Customs House… Ah!" he broke off: "Isn't that the Portuguese captain who helped to rescue you from the Savoy?"

Jose Marinda came forward to Katherine with a wide white-toothed smile flashing in his suntanned face.

"My Lady Katherine!" he said as he bowed before her and took her hand. "This is a sad meeting but I am so pleased and honoured to be able to come to pray for Geoffrey and to offer you my condolence and support."

Katherine smiled and nodded. "Jose," she said, looking into his eyes, "as ever, I am warmed by your presence… as, I am sure, in spirit, is Geoffrey! But now, forgive me, I feel I must meet with the other mourners."

"Of course, and God's blessing on you!" said Marinda as he bowed again, kissed her hand and withdrew.

Katherine then moved among her fellow mourners with a quiet grace, acknowledging their sadness and prayers for Geoffrey's soul, and receiving the warmth and affection they felt for him in his life. These included: Harry Castle, his young assistant at the Customs House and now a trader in wool at Calais with John Lollington, master of the ship *Jesu*; William White, landlord of the Black Swan near the Tower; Amos Snell, archer who served with John of Gaunt in France; Henry Yevele, master mason; William Chetwynde, forester and deputy to Chaucer as Clerk of Works; and Simon Browser, mason who carved the Madonna at the royal palace at Sheen.

Katherine then saw a smiling John Gower approaching with a little, white-haired but well-rounded old lady.

"Katherine, my dear, here is someone you must meet: one of Geoffrey's most loved friends, his housekeeper at Aldgate: Margaret Martin!"

"Oh yes! I remember him and my sister speaking of you," replied Katherine, smiling broadly.

"But please, ma'am, I was always 'Mostly Maggie' to him! Because when he first asked my name I said I was called 'Margaret' but mostly Maggie! That so amused him, he kept with it – such a lovely man he was!" wiping a tear from her eye.

"And bless you for looking after him and for making the effort to come today," said Katherine.

"Oh well," said Mostly Maggie. "When I heard, I couldn't not come, and Master Geoffrey's boatman friend, John Croyser, brought me."

"Well, thank you, Mostly Maggie!" said Katherine, leaning forward to hug the old lady and kiss her cheek.

As Maggie moved away, Katherine said to John Gower: "Oh John! All these people coming here to honour and bless Geoffrey! What an expression of love!"

"Yes!" said John. "And doesn't it show what a capacity Geoffrey had for knowing and understanding his fellow human beings? Indeed, I can almost see many of Geoffrey's pilgrims in this band of mourners."

"Amen!" said Katherine, and laying her hand on John's arm, kissed his cheek and said: "And you, John: Geoffrey's close companion and friend. Thank you!"

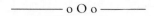

Two weeks after the funeral, John Gower returned to the Abbey to Chaucer's grave to find the gravestone covered with fresh green leaves: *parsley, sage, rosemary and thyme.* What an augury: that Chaucer's words and language would be spread, across England as if by the wind, like the seeds and scents of these herbs from hedgerows and gardens.

SOURCES

Although the book is a fictional interpretation, the context and quotations are drawn from the following:

Armitage Smith, Sydney, *John of Gaunt Duke of Lancaster* (Constable, 1904)

Benson, L. D. (ed.), *The Riverside Chaucer* (OUP, 1987)

Boethius, *The Consolation of Philosophy* (Folio Society, 1998)

Brewer, Derek, *The World of Chaucer* (Boydell and Brewer, 1978)

Coghill, Nevill, *The Canterbury Tales* (Penguin Books, 1977)

Coghill, Nevill, *Troilus and Criseyde* (Penguin Books, 1971)

Landsberg, Sylvia, *The Medieval Garden* (British Museum Press, 1996)

Power, Eileen, *Medieval People* (1924; Folio Society edition, 1999)

Saul, Nigel, *Richard II* (Yale University Press, 1997)

Weir, Alison, *Katherine Swynford* (Jonathan Cape, 2007)

Wilkins, Nigel, *Music in the Age of Chaucer* (Brewer, 1979)

Yarwood, Doreen, *English Costume* (Batsford, 1961)

The Works of Chaucer (Globe, 1932)